I0782267

THE KINGS OF DUSK & DAWN

THE HEIR TO MOONDUST: BOOK 4

LOU WILHAM

Midnight Tide
PUBLISHING

PRAISE FOR THE HEIR TO MOONDUST SERIES

"Lou has done it again! The adventures in this book are even more high stakes and they kept me turning pages. Lou wove everything together beautifully and kept things mysterious enough to leave you hanging and begging for more."

   - **Whitney L. Spradling**, Author of *The Obsidian Sword*

"The Heir to Moondust Series pulls you deep into a magical land filled with shifters and curses. Book Two, The Prince of Daybreak, raises the stakes with a journey that will have you questioning every alliance and prejudice, and eager to find out what Wilham has planned for the series next."

   - **H. R. Truelove**, Author of the *Alter Series*

Copyright © 2023 by Lou Wilham

All rights reserved.

No part of this book may be reproduced in any form or by any electronic or mechanical means, including information storage and retrieval systems, without written permission from the author, except for the use of brief quotations in a book review.

❀ Created with Vellum

To my biggest fan, Mika.
Embrace your dreams.
Let your imagination run wild.
Tell your story, whatever form it takes.

THE KINGS OF DUSK & DAWN

THE HEIR TO MOONDUST: BOOK FOUR

LOU WILHAM

PROLOGUE

The tricky thing about stories is this, they all have to end somewhere. For some it's "and they lived happily ever after" for others it's simply "the end" more still have no ending at all, they just stop.

This story will end thusly. . .

A die cast.

A fate wound up.

A curse unbound.

And many wishes granted.

It began many years ago with a king who wished for a child, a prince who wished for an impossible love, and a goddess who granted both those wishes and one of her own. A silent, secret wish that she shared with no others, not even those closest to her. A wish that she kept close to herself, hidden away.

Cricket was the answer to all of those wishes. But he had desires of his own. A life he wanted to lead. A love he wanted to marry. And a family he wanted to protect.

It will come as no surprise to you, dear reader, that none of those things came easily. Life is like that, after all, it makes a mess of things, and very often people must take the long way around to get what they desire most.

For Cricket that long way around involved the betrayal of his uncle, the death of his father, exile, war, a child, and the finding of his soulmate.

For Takayoshi it involved a journey of self-discovery in as much as a journey of finding answers to save the man he loved, and finding the family he never knew he wanted.

Both men had one more challenge to face before they could find happiness. One more war to win. . .

And the goddess of the moon, Selene, could only do so much to aide them, to her continued frustration.

"I heard there is war coming to Lunette," Jaxith said where he stood by Selene looking through the window of the palace of the gods that gave them the best view of Cricket— her son. It was tucked away, hidden from the other gods lest they discover her transgressions. Not that they did not already know, she was sure, but there was little proof of it yet. And even if there weren't, Selene wished to hoard this away to herself. Keep Cricket safe from their eyes as best she could. Her son. Her light.

"You've heard correctly," Selene replied impassively, not taking her eyes off the glass. War was inevitable. The mortals of Cytheria had seen to that. Estia with zir deception, and quick hands. And Craven with his ruthlessness that seemed to know no bounds. If it were up to Selene she'd have removed the blight that was the king of Cytheria ages ago, but that would be meddling in such an obvious way that the other gods would turn against her. They would punish her. Just as they had punished *him*.

"I heard there will be losses." Jaxith's voice pulled her from her thoughts, but only for a moment.

Selene took a breath, pinching her eyes shut, and wondered who Jaxith had been speaking with. It was not uncommon for the gods to know the future, or at least glimpses of it. But the mortals who joined them once their time on the land had passed were never supposed to receive that information. Lest they do something intolerably stupid like try to interfere. Not that Selene could judge Jaxith for this. She too wanted to use what powers she had to see to it that what was to come would go easier for Cricket and his family. To protect her son's heart and his body. But as the other gods stayed out of mortal affairs so too must she. Even if that was her son down there.

"On both sides, I imagine. That is what happens during a war." She knew what he was speaking of. She'd heard the same rumors. Whispers in the halls of the gods. Gossip. But that didn't make it untrue. They said in hushed tones that the sun would fall. They said behind their hands, leaning in close so that no one could read their lips that Helios had forsaken his kin. They said in darkened corners that the moon would break. They said that the curse of Venus would be the end of them both once and for all.

"This will destroy him." Jaxith's hands twisted together, worry lingering in the lines of his face. He had grown younger since coming to them and reuniting with his wife. Taking on the appearance of the man his wife had married. But Selene could see the years now, the ones he had given to protect and raise her son—*their* son.

"It will not." She needed for that to be true so badly it ached within her. How strange, a goddess knowing pain just the same as any mortal. Motherhood really had made her soft.

"How can you be so sure?" Jaxith turned to face her, his brows raised high. There was hope in his eyes. Fragile and so, so mortal. Selene forgot sometimes that Jaxith was mortal. He was the father to a god, after all. But it was visible there now in the wrinkle between his brows. He was just a man standing before a god, begging for her to spare their child.

Mortal.

And so was their son, even if he had come from the powers of a goddess. The land saw to that. Stripped him of his immortality the way it would any other being. It was why the gods no longer walked on the land. Why they had cloistered themselves away in their realm separate from their descendants, and instead used their influence to move them around like pieces on a go board.

But Fate would have her way. She always did. Even the gods could not go against her, though Selene had tried on more than one occasion. And what was to come was set in stone, there was no denying that, though Selene had tried.

Jaxith shifted uncomfortably beside her indicating she had been silent for too long, and she sighed.

"Because he is yours, and he is mine," she said simply. "And I have given him everything he needs, and you have taught him all you know. He will prevail. He will not break."

"I pray that you're right." Jaxith returned to where he had been watching Cricket play with his daughter in the palace gardens. His smile was bright, brighter than it had been in some years. At ease. He did not know what was coming. And she could not warn him.

"I pray that too," Selene agreed, her voice soft.

If she was not. . . Well. She was a goddess. She did have one or two more tricks up her sleeve. And if there was a price to be paid for what she did, so be it.

BOOK I
THE ROT

CHAPTER 1

"You cannot just *elope*!" Ignacia's exasperated tone echoed off the walls of his father's office—not his because he still felt every day as if he were playing pretend at being king. He hoped no one was nearby to hear his captain of the guard shouting at her king like this, that would damage even a pretend king's reputation. They probably weren't. He couldn't imagine Ignacia would make that kind of mistake. She must have Claudia nearby keeping people away from this section of the castle. Ignacia's hands twitched at her sides like she wanted to grab Cricket—her dear friend, her brother in many ways—and shake some sense into him.

Joke's on her, that likely wouldn't help.

"And why not?" Cricket asked, not looking up from his work to fix her with an expression of mild annoyance. Because what point was there? It had never stopped Ignacia from berating him before, it seemed very often that was simply the role of an elder sister. It hadn't stopped her from barging in about ten minutes ago.

"Because."

Cricket waited a beat, his scales scratching against the inside of his sleeve, making him itch, and when she didn't sound like she was going to continue any further he said, "I beg to differ. I think you'll find, Iggy, that since I'm king I can do whatever I please."

He knew that wasn't true. If the last few months had taught Cricket anything, it was that he couldn't just do as he pleased simply because he was in charge. It was the exact opposite, actually. Everything he did now had to be thought through carefully. He had to consider all of the implications, and the impacts. His people depended on him to make good decisions. And when he made the wrong ones, bad things happened. Lives were lost. Homes were burned. Families were separated.

The consequences of him not executing his uncle still echoed through the many empty buildings in the capital. Cricket hadn't spent much time in the city since returning home, but the time he had spent there had him realizing how badly Sunil had treated his people. A quarter of the population wasn't even remaining. They had either left for safety, or died so Sunil could raise them for use in his undead army against Cricket. How Sunil meant to rule an empty kingdom, Cricket didn't know. But every time he thought about the loss, his heart sank a little further in his chest.

Lunette's army too had been decimated by Sunil's actions.

And all of this was laid at Cricket's feet. Every choice he made seemed to carry double the weight now. He had to be careful. Even when it came to wedding plans.

"Yes," Takayoshi agreed when the silence stretched on too long and it looked like maybe Ignacia was going to start shouting again. He'd been quiet the entire time Ignacia was in the room, sitting back and taking in everything around him, as was his way. "Cricket is king. He can do what he likes."

Cricket fought tooth and nail against the smile that

threatened to overtake his face at Takayoshi's words. It was a trying thing, not grinning broadly at the man he loved. Not showing to the world just how soft he was for this one person. But Cricket managed somehow.

Kings were not meant to be soft. He had learned *that* as well from his brush with his uncle. His softness had nearly cost him everything. His kingdom. His daughter. His family. The man he loved. If he was soft then others could take from him everything that he cared for. He could no longer afford to be *soft*.

"That's all the more reason he can't," Ignacia hissed, her eyes darting to the closed door of his father's office as if she had just now realized that someone might be listening. They had done their best to ferret out Sunil's spies, but there was no way to tell if they had gotten them all, and Cricket wasn't willing to punish people on suspicion alone. There needed to be proof. Another example of his softness that was likely to get him into trouble, he recognized. But he would not cow to the pressure to become a tyrant like Sunil had been, like some other rulers were.

"There is an expectation," Ignacia said.

"Expectation," Cricket repeated in a murmur, and tightened his hold on his pen reflexively. He hated that word, hated the weight that came with it, settling heavy and suffocating on his shoulders. He missed the days when he was free. Just a silly little prince who could run out in the middle of his lessons to buy the last of the season's strawberries with his best friend. *Years.* That had been years ago. Before he'd met Takayoshi. Before he'd found his daughter. Before he'd lost a sister, a father, a friend. Before he was king.

"Cricky," Ignacia's tone softened, and when he looked up he found her eyes had fixed him with a gentleness that made him feel small again. Gods, it had been so many years since he'd felt small like this. Like someone else was caring for him. Kings didn't get that. Not even from their elder sisters. "I know this isn't what you want to hear—"

"But it's the truth," he said, cutting her off and shaking his head. He knew she was right. He'd known since this argument began. That he was just railing against the truth of it, the honesty. Plus it was kind of fun to get under Ignacia's skin a little. He hadn't allowed himself that in a while. A fact that Ignacia and Takayoshi both seemed to realize if the expressions on their faces were anything to go by. But Ignacia's sudden softness, the seriousness of her tone, cut through the playful mood.

Even still—

"There is no time now for a proper ceremony," Takayoshi answered, as if he'd read Cricket's thoughts. He couldn't. Not when they weren't in their phoenix and dragon forms. But Takayoshi knew Cricket, down to his marrow. Cricket wondered how long Takayoshi had, sometimes. Wondered when it was that he'd given himself away so wholly to another. That first day as he flopped down across from Takayoshi and nearly spilled his tea? Or had the understanding come later? He didn't ask. He didn't really want the answer.

"There isn't," Ignacia agreed. "You'll just have to wait until after we've finished cleaning up the mess Sunil left behind."

Wait. More waiting. It had already been a month since the final battle with Cricket's uncle, and they were going to put this off even further? Acid churned in Cricket's stomach, making it burn.

"Yoshi's curse. . . " The words scraped Cricket's throat raw. He hated the curse. That vile, foul thing. The thing that might one day take him from Takayoshi and his family. And all because of what? Because of a petty jealousy that was centuries old. A grudge that the caster had long since forgotten herself, if he were to guess. It wasn't that he was afraid to die. He never had been. It was the pain of the people he would leave behind that had him fighting to live now more than ever.

It was also the vagueness of it. The amorphic cloud that hung over all their heads. That one day Takayoshi's love would kill Cricket in some as yet unseen way. Sickness. Or war. Or— Well, maybe all the events of the past few years had been just that, the curse trying to kill Cricket. It had failed so far, but how much longer could he outrun it?

"We have to join the sun and the—"

"We should perhaps speak with your mother before the ceremony, as well. To get her blessing." Takayoshi had begun doing that more and more these days, cutting people off when he had something to say. Growing impatient with waiting his turn. Maybe he always had been. Maybe it was just that before Cricket—before he'd decided to leave Helios and tame a dragon—Takayoshi was too polite to do so. Still holding fast to his uncle's rules. Rules that he had abandoned when he gave up trying to win his uncle's approval and followed Cricket down the mountain.

"My mother." Cricket sighed, leaning back in the chair to run his hands through his hair. His fingers caught briefly on the antlers at his temples. They were still not quite as long as they had been before he'd found his pearl, but their presence combined with the scales itching under his clothing were a constant reminder that just as soon as Cricket had found his pearl, he'd lost it again. Some guardian of the people he was turning out to be.

"Yes," Takayoshi insisted, seeming to understand that Cricket was reluctant to speak to the lady Selene. There was sympathy in his expression too, his eyes softened around the corners. Which was deeply unsettling, although maybe not as unsettling as finding out that his mother was the goddess of the moon.

Cricket hadn't wondered who his mother was since he was about five, and just a few weeks ago Takayoshi had given him the answer. A goddess. Who'd have thought? Not Cricket. They hadn't tried to contact Selene since he'd learned, and Takayoshi hadn't pushed him to. Cricket wondered if it was because Takayoshi saw the anxiety lingering in every movement when they spoke of her. The way his muscles seemed to twitch, and he struggled to meet anyone's eyes.

What if she didn't like him? What if the reason she hadn't reached out to him all these years was because she didn't approve of what he'd become? What if he was left for his father in that forest because he was a mistake? The gods were fickle, and Cricket wouldn't put it past one of them to create a child and later regret the choice.

"He's right." Ignacia kept her words gentle, as if she too saw the thought flitting across Cricket's mind. He was painfully transparent as of late, he supposed. Or maybe it was just them. Two of the three people in his life who knew him the best. Thankfully, Anstice wasn't there to stick her nose into things too. "Selene should be consulted on this union. Not that if she doesn't approve you'll listen, but it'd be a slight to not recognize her parentage and thus her place in this all together."

Cricket twitched a little at the blow the word *slight* landed. No one wanted to slight the gods. There would be consequences. Consequences he and his kingdom couldn't afford to pay at this stage in the rebuilding process, or ever really. "All right. We'll speak to my mother, and ask for her approval. Now can we stop talking about my impending marriage for about two minutes so we can discuss the more serious matter of the refugees?"

Ignacia nodded her agreement and settled into the chair on the other side of Cricket's desk next to Takayoshi. "We've managed to find homes for all of those displaced during Sunil's attacks. Unfortunately because of the number of people killed when he attacked the city directly, there was plenty of room for those from the nearby towns and villages."

Cricket's heart clenched in his chest. It wounded him deeply to know so many of his people had suffered while he was away in Helios hiding from Sunil. But there was nothing that could be done for it now.

"We'll still need to rebuild their homes," he said unfurling a map from a drawer. Each town Sunil decimated in his bid to become king sat a black dot, a blight, on the land. Cricket's kingdom was wounded, but not broken, he had to remind himself of that frequently. Sunil had not irreversibly ruined anything. "And see to their dead. I don't want any of those Sunil used in his attacks to be left unattended."

"I've already got a team working on that. Claudia is just looking for someone who can go with them and perform the rights required to lay them to rest. Many of the priestesses who could were utilized by Sunil to raise the dead in his war." Ignacia's face twisted as if she'd swallowed something foul. "Those who didn't do so willingly were tortured within an inch of their lives."

"I know you don't want to." Cricket's fingers tapped against the surface of his desk through the map, and he chewed on the inside of his cheek. They didn't need to be fighting amongst themselves at this particular moment, but someone needed to say this. Even if Ignacia were going to be angry with him for the suggestion. "But reach out to Anstice. She always kept meticulous records of those in any kind of power. She'll know who we can trust with this and who we can't."

The scowl on Ignacia's face told him exactly how she felt about that particular suggestion. But if Cricket had to force this issue, he would. He couldn't have infighting in his family, even if Anstice was no longer a part of the kingdom of Lunette. He needed those closest to him, especially the Celestials—those with the power to shift into mythical creatures and wield great magic—to be a team. And the only way he could think to force his sisters to make up, was to make them speak to one another. It had always worked in the past. . .

"Is that an order, Your Highness?" Ignacia asked, her tone flat.

"Yes. It is." He tilted his chin back and met Ignacia's green eyes, daring her to go against him.

She stared back for a moment, unblinking, and he recognized it as the intimidation tactic she'd used on him all his life. It worked sometimes still. When she was trying to bully him into doing something he knew was good for him, like speaking to his mother, like having a grand ceremony for his wedding. It wouldn't work now.

Ignacia blinked first. She ducked her head in respect, but he would swear he heard a smile in her voice when she said, "Yes, Your Highness." Then, without further argument, she dismissed herself with a soft, "Claudia and I will get in contact right away."

The door closed quietly behind her, leaving behind the heaviness of what lay between Cricket and Takayoshi in its wake.

Cricket swallowed with an audible click in the ensuing silence, Takayohi's golden gaze burned into him like a brand. "I suppose you ought to show me the best way to reach my mother?"

Takayoshi's lips twitched almost imperceptibly. "We will begin when the moon is at its zenith, that is the best time to speak with the goddess."

"All right." Cricket let out a long slow breath that did nothing to quell the anxiety rolling through his belly making him queasy with it. "All right."

Takayoshi rose from his chair, and leaned over the table to brush a kiss to Cricket's temple, so tender and quick it was hardly there at all. "You will be fine, my prince. She loves you."

Cricket nodded, but didn't say anything. He could argue that point until he was blue in the face, but he supposed Takayoshi would know better than him, after all, he'd actually spoken to Selene. "Right. Okay. In the meantime, should we start looking at things for the wedding?"

"If you would like." Takayoshi settled back into his chair, and pulled it in closer to the desk so they could work. Then he lifted his head to fix Cricket with the most genuine smile he thought he'd ever seen on Takayoshi's face before. "I believe Becka would like to help."

Cricket laughed a little, shaking his head. "Was she standing out there when Iggy left?"

"I believe so."

"Then by all means, let our daughter in." Cricket leaned back in his chair, his hands settling on his stomach. "I'm sure she'll have something to say about what I should and should not wear to our wedding."

"I believe she also wants to be involved in choosing the flowers."

"Of course she does."

The door to the office opened and in stepped Becka, her long black hair tied up in a braid down her back, a smile split across her lips. "You'll have to include sunflowers of course."

"Oh of course," Cricket crowed. "In honor of our little sunflower."

"Not so little anymore." Becka pouted, dropping into the chair beside Takayoshi.

"No," Cricket said with a wistfulness that left him aching. "Not so little anymore."

Then he leaned back and he let Becka's excitement, and Takayoshi's gentle guidance wash over him.

CHAPTER 2

"Are you sure this will work?"

Takayoshi would be offended by Cricket's question if it were not accompanied by the shifting of his weight from one foot to the other. It was honestly a little frightening how well Takayoshi could read Cricket these days. When they had been in Helios, Cricket seemed so guarded, so distant, and now Takayoshi wondered how he had missed all of the signs that Cricket felt the same way he did. The affection, and love was there clearly on his face any time he smiled at Takayoshi.

Perhaps it was simply that Takayoshi had been in denial. That he was so sure that no one, least of all his own soulmate, could love him in that way that he had convinced himself Cricket was merely indifferent to him. How foolish he had been. Not just in that, but also in the time he wasted away from Cricket searching for a "cure" to his condition when there was none to be found. Still, had Takayoshi not gone on that journey, he never would have discovered Cricket's mother was the Lady Selene. That would have been a pity.

"It will work," Takayoshi confirmed, his fingers working

over the characters that he knew by heart now. He had not been in contact with Selene that often, but it did not take Takayoshi long to memorize things. Especially things that were this important. He sincerely hoped Selene answered this time and did not make him seem a liar. Not only because she should allow him to save some face in front of the man he loved, but also because Cricket might begin to think that his mother did not care for him. That simply would not do.

Cricket shifted again, the floorboard creaking beneath him. Takayoshi would have preferred to do this in the gardens where the rain could wash the marks away, but Cricket had insisted on doing it in Cricket's private chambers. A room Takayoshi had not been in, because it seemed wholly improper. They were to be married, yes, but that did not mean Takayoshi should know what the inside of Cricket's private rooms looked like until that day. Call him old fashioned if you will.

Which meant of course that he couldn't help but notice the unmade bed through the door into the bedroom, dark blue sheets thrown about. Or the overflowing papers on the desk near the window. Or the book that lay forgotten on the table beside the chaise that they'd moved out of the front of the fireplace . It all felt very Cricket, right down to the plush rug that was now rolled up in the corner.

"What is it?" Takayoshi asked, abandoning his work, and rising to his feet to cross the room to where Cricket sat in a chair at his desk. He took Cricket's hands in his, giving them an affectionate squeeze, and bent to press a kiss to Cricket's lips before pressing on. "What is really wrong?"

Cricket sighed—annoyed, perhaps, that Takayoshi had seen through him once again—and a little rush of happiness flooded Takayoshi's veins at that knowledge. He knew Cricket. Knew him well enough to read his tells when he was anxious, and for it to be annoying to the man himself. How novel.

"Tell me," he prompted again, knowing that sometimes Cricket needed an extra push to get his words out. A funny little thing for someone who usually tended to be so verbose. Not that Takayoshi minded it at all. It was a privilege to see Cricket when he was feeling weak and unsure. Vulnerable. Something he did not show to many. "Let me help you."

"What if she doesn't like me?" Cricket asked in a voice so small it nearly broke Takayoshi's heart.

He wanted to tell Cricket that that was impossible. That everyone who met Cricket loved him on sight, himself included. That there was not a soul alive who could help but look at Cricket's light and not be warmed by it. But he knew all of those words would be lies, and empty platitudes. For there was the matter of Sunil. Someone who had helped to raise Cricket. Who had seen him when he was small and chubby cheeked, and hated him still. It baffled Takayoshi, but he supposed there was no accounting for taste and greed.

Instead of saying those things, he knelt before Cricket, looking up into his face where Cricket had tried to hide behind his still unbearably short hair. Cricket's pale blue eyes flickered around Takayoshi's face as if he were searching for a lie. He would find none. Takayoshi did not lie, and even if he did, he would not lie about this. He would not lie to Cricket.

"Your mother," Takayoshi began, taking Cricket's hands again and rubbing his thumbs along the thin skin at Cricket's wrists, "loves you very much."

Cricket opened his mouth to protest, but Takayoshi did not give him room for that. He continued without pause.

"She has done so much to prove that love to you. She sent you to King Jaxith who was good to you, and ensured you were happy all your life. She tied me to you so that I could protect you, and care for you. She gave you power to protect her people and defeat her enemies, and then allowed that power to grow enough that it could not be contained by a single person. The dragon, and phoenix are proof of her love, Cricket. She may not have spoken to you. She may not have touched your life directly. But she has helped you in a thousand other ways that we do not yet understand. Please," Takayoshi begged softly, "do not let what Sunil did to you color your world. You are better than that. Stronger than that."

"Am I?" But it was asked like a joke.

"I think you know very well that you are." Takayoshi smiled gently, and lifted Cricket's hands toward his face so he could brush kisses along his knuckles. "Now. Come. The sooner we receive your mother's blessing, the sooner we can be married."

"Are you that eager to bind yourself to me?" Cricket's voice had gone light, and teasing, a smile twitching at the corners of his lips, barely restrained. Takayoshi's heart leapt in his chest. How he loved to see Cricket like this. Full of joy, and laughter. How he would give anything to ensure Cricket never had to know suffering. But he knew that was impossible. Suffering was a part of living. Suffering made the joy sweeter.

"I think you know that I am." Takayoshi pushed up from where he had rested his weight back on his heels so that he could meet Cricket's searching lips halfway. A long lingering kiss. Heat buzzed along Takayoshi's nerves, setting every fiber of himself alight so much so he was amazed his phoenix fire did not catch on something. No. He would trade this for nothing. All of the suffering and the hardships, he would not trade, because it had led them here, brought them this. It was worth it in the end. And once Lunette was rebuilt, once they were married, he would make it so Cricket never had cause to be unhappy again.

Cricket pulled away from the kiss to laugh, his eyes bright, and sparkling and so, so blue. Blue. It still took Takayoshi's breath away to see Cricket this way, surrounded by a world awash in color. He still shone brighter than everything else, even if Takayoshi could make out the deep blue of the walls now.

"Better?" Takayoshi asked gently as he rose.

"Better." Cricket agreed, and allowed Takayoshi to pull him to his feet. He took a deep inhale, and squeezed Takayoshi's hand before saying, "All right. Let's contact my mother."

Takayoshi led Cricket to the circle. The dagger scraped against the sheath as he pulled it out, the blade glinting in the low light.

"Should we kneel?" Cricket fidgeted a little more at Takayoshi's side, and Takayoshi turned to face him. To give Cricket his full attention in the hopes that it might bring him some peace. Cricket smiled, and that was enough.

"I do not think that is necessary." Takayoshi rolled up his sleeve, mindful of the blood he would be spilling, and cut a small wound into his forearm. It was the fourth in a neat row of scars. Proof on his skin of all the times he had bled for Cricket. To bind him. To help him. To save him. To love him. And Takayoshi knew he would do it as many times as it took.

The blood dripped onto the chalk circle, and the characters lit up near blinding, making Takayoshi see spots after. He blinked, his eyes watering against the light, but did not allow himself to close his eyes. He had to remain looking at Cricket, to ensure he was happy, to ensure he was not hurt by anything Selene had to say.

"Lady Selene," Takayoshi said when silence remained, a held breath between them. "We seek your blessing for our coming marriage."

"Well it's about time," Selene said, a laugh in her voice.

Cricket laughed too, a short, sharp bark. Half surprise, half disbelief. "Is that a yes?"

"Of course it's a yes, silly child." Selene chuckled, and Takayoshi could imagine her shaking her head exactly the way Cricket was doing. Her hair falling into her face to hide her eyes the way Cricket was. It was amazing how similar they were when they had not even spoken till now. "But, my darling," she said, her tone suddenly serious, "how are you?"

Takayoshi reached for Cricket, gathered him into his arms, and pulled him to his chest to lend him support when it seemed that Cricket's knees might buckle under him. He pressed his face in close, his lips against Cricket's temple, to offer the comfort and reassurance he knew Cricket needed. It was a lot to meet one's parent for the first time. Even more to feel the weight of their caring heavy on one's chest. Takayoshi had never experienced it, but he could imagine how it must be. So he held on.

"I am better than I was," Cricket said after a long moment of hiding his face in the fabric of Takayoshi's tunic, breathing in the warm air there. "I think. . ." Takayoshi heard Cricket swallow, the motion an audible click. Then he whispered, as if perhaps this ought to not be allowed for all the grief he had known, "I think I might be happy, mother."

"Good," Selene said, and it sounded like she breathed the word. Like it was an exhalation of her own worry. "That's very good."

"So we have your blessing then?" Cricket asked again, as if perhaps he could not believe it. As if he needed to be sure that this too would not be torn from his grasp. It would not be, not so long as Takayoshi had anything to say about it.

"Of course you do." Selene huffed a laugh that was all exasperation. "As if I could deny you anything. But. . ." she paused here, seemed to take a moment to gather herself, and when her voice returned it was as stormy as the sea they had named after her. "You had better wait until you find your pearl again, my dear. There is. . ." Takayoshi may have been imagining it, the way her voice lowered as if she were concerned about being overheard. He may have been reading too much into things. But he did not think he was. "There is a war coming your way, and you both need to be ready."

A war. Another war. How much more could the battered kingdom of Lunette take before it crumbled under the forces that stood against it? Takayoshi did not wish to find out.

"Who?" Takayoshi asked, tightening his hold on Cricket, needing the weight of him in his arms as much as Cricket seemed to need the support. Cricket was there, safe and whole, for the moment. And whatever came their way next, they could face together, he was sure of it.

"Cytheria." Selene sounded as if perhaps she were frowning, her tone gone grave. "Craven seeks to take over Lunette in its weakened state. He means to rule all of the lands he can. Lunette will be just the beginning."

"He'll move to Helios when he's through here," Cricket said as if he could read Craven's movements as one might a map. Maybe he could. He had learned a fair bit about battle tactics in the last war, and he was consistently borrowing books to learn more. Takayoshi was proud of him and the ruler he was becoming. He would be a great king.

"He will not get that far."

"He won't," Cricket agreed, his fingers tight in Takayoshi's tunic. "We will stop him."

Selene made a soft sound of acknowledgement. "I will do everything I can to help you, but I'm afraid it's not much. The gods can't be seen to be playing favorites."

"Of course not." Cricket sounded very much like he wanted to roll his eyes, but had decided that might be disrespectful so he resisted.

"Can we ask for one favor?" Takayoshi said, sure that

Selene would deny them, and if she did they would simply fight through this as they always had before. "Is there a way to slow down Venus' curse? We plan to marry—"

"I'll do what I can." Selene sounded like she was smiling now, and Takayoshi wondered if that was because she had a secret she was not telling, but he decided it best not to ask. Let the goddess keep her secrets. So long as she helped him keep Cricket safe, she could lie as much as she liked. "But I have been here too long. Someone might take notice, and we're not meant to be communicating with the mortals. So I must bid you farewell."

"Goodbye, Mother." Cricket leaned more heavily against Takayoshi.

"We will speak again soon, Cricket."

Then the light faded, and the connection closed. Cricket's knees buckled under him again. Humming gently to try to calm his rapid breathing, Takayoshi led Cricket back to the chair, and guided him to sit. When he knelt in front of Cricket again, his chest was heaving.

"Look at me," Takayoshi prompted, and forced Cricket to tilt his chin down to meet his eyes. "In." He inhaled deeply to show Cricket what he meant. Then exhaled the word "out" a moment later. "Good," he murmured softly when Cricket had completed one deep cycle. "Again."

"There's. . . There's. . . Another. . . A war." Cricket gasped.

"We will speak of that in a moment. In." Takayoshi inhaled, held it, then murmured, "Out."

Cricket and he took several more cycles of deep breaths until he was calmed down enough to breathe without Takayoshi's gentle reminders.

"I will reach out to my sister," Takayoshi volunteered as he rose. "Perhaps she can send some back up forces. Are there any other allies we could speak to?"

"I don't know." Cricket sighed, scrubbing at his face. "Craven may have already struck deals with them."

Takayoshi nodded. "Then it would be best to keep this close to the vest, and only deal with those we are sure of."

"I think so. But I'll meet with Claudia and Iggy right away. We need a plan in place."

"We will have one," Takayoshi assured, brushing a piece of hair back from Cricket's face. "We can do this. Together."

CHAPTER 3

Together, Takayoshi said.

They would face everything that came for them from here on out together. It was a stressor as much as it was a relief. So much could go wrong. So much could end badly. But at least Cricket wouldn't have to be alone?

Still, when it was time to head outside of the gates of the palace, and the capital, Claudia said, "You don't have to come with us to do this, Your Highness."

She didn't know him well enough to know that he did, in fact, have to. She didn't know that he felt responsible for what Sunil had done in the name of stealing his crown from him. Maybe it wasn't his fault that his own uncle had turned against him in such a way. But it *was* his fault that he'd fled to Helios in a bid to protect himself and his daughter. It *was* his fault that he had left his kingdom virtually unprotected when he should have stayed and fought.

What was done, was done, Cricket knew that well enough. That didn't mean he didn't have regrets. It didn't mean that he didn't feel it was his responsibility now to assess the damage left behind by their battle.

"For your own safety," Claudia tried to argue, her tone unsure. She would make a good advisor, one day. She was knowledgeable, and kind. But the fact of the matter stood, she didn't know Cricket well enough yet. She didn't know that mentioning his safety wasn't going to stop him. If anything, it would only encourage him.

"He will be all right, Claudia," Takayoshi said. He was ever present these days, always at Cricket's side. The calming presence Cricket desperately needed as he faced down the uncertainty of what was to come. As his mother's words rang in his ears. *War is coming to Lunette. Craven means to take your kingdom.*

"I just. . ." Claudia shifted on her horse, her head turning to look at the streets of the capital. They had repaired what they could of the city Cricket had grown up in, but so much of it was beyond that. So much of it had to be leveled and rebuilt. None of it would ever be the same, and that knowledge sat a dull ache in Cricket's chest. Right alongside the place where his pearl had once been. "We should have brought more guards."

"We have plenty." Takayoshi shook his head. Not that any of the guards could do quite what Cricket and his little family could. But maybe Claudia was uneasy because she wasn't a Celestial. She didn't wield the power to transform at will into a mythical being who could take a sword to the gut and keep fighting. That was fair, Cricket supposed. But. . . Well if Claudia and Ignacia kept going the way they were going, it wouldn't be long before she was an official member of the family. Cricket wondered what would happen then. Would the magic trickle down as it had with all the others? Or would it remain just those closest to him? He supposed they'd see. "And Leo has already gone beyond the wall to scout. He saw no dangers outside the usual."

"I know. I know." But it didn't seem to ease any of Claudia's worries. "It's just with what. . ." She paused, pressing her lips together hard enough to make them go pale. "With what she said, we should likely be more careful."

"There has been no word on Craven's movements yet," Cricket offered, and turned to wave at a little old woman leaning from her window to hang out her laundry. She smiled back, delight turning her eyes to crescents. "Besides, it's good if the people see me doing something about our problems. I can't just hide away in the castle and hope this all goes away. I have to show that I'm trying to right the wrongs my family committed."

"That wasn't your fault," Claudia argued. Passion gleamed in her eyes, she hadn't said as much but Takayohis assured Cricket that it bothered her still that he blamed himself for everything that had happened, and Cricket appreciated it. But even if she saw that there was no blame to be cast his way, that didn't mean all of his people felt the same. Especially those who had lost their homes, and their families. "That was—"

"Regardless," Cricket cut her off, and turned his head finally to meet her gaze. "I am going to do all that I can to fix what my family has broken. That means going beyond the wall and investigating why it's the only bit of land that hasn't grown grass since the spring."

"Yes, Your Highness." Claudia ducked her head, seeming to realize that the discussion was over, and she should let it lie. If it had been Anstice, she wouldn't have let it go. Cricket's younger sister, the one raised to be his advisor, would have bullied and wheedled him until he did what she wanted him to. In fact, they wouldn't have left the castle without enough guards to qualify as a whole parade for the capital, and there would have been no talking her out of it—even if Cricket didn't currently have enough for that. Claudia, it seemed, didn't feel comfortable enough in her position to do that.

That might be for the best.

"There is Leo," Takayoshi said, nudging his horse a little further ahead to meet the man waiting for them just outside of the city limits. Leo leaned heavily against a cane, his face hidden by a dark hood even in the summer heat. Cricket hadn't gotten the full story on him yet, but he knew that Leo was someone important, someone recognizable. And that he was on the run from Cytheria. Another way this war with Craven could potentially get personal.

"I see you made it here in one piece," Leo said, tilting his head back so they could see his smile in the shadow of his hood.

Claudia scoffed, but Takayoshi smiled gently, the corners of his mouth turned up just so. If Cricket were a lesser man, he might be jealous of that little smile. There was a bond between Takayoshi, Leo, and Claudia that he didn't fully know the depths of, and couldn't hope to interfere with. Born of blood and sweat. Born of danger and shared trauma. Thankfully, Cricket was not a lesser man.

"I've seen no sign of Cytheria's forces," Leo continued conversationally as they all dismounted and walked out into the field of dead grass and blood-stained earth. So much of it was black from the blood of the fallen that Sunil had raised to fight his war for him. Still, Cricket could see the places where his own forces, his family, had bled for his kingdom. It turned his stomach, what little breakfast he'd managed to eat going sour. "But just because I can't see them, doesn't mean they haven't been there."

"Very comforting." Claudia sighed, running a hand through her hair.

"We won't be out here long." Cricket padded softly against the ground, worried he might disturb whatever spirits left over from those he himself had slain. So many lost. And for what? A plot of dead land.

Crouching among the dried earth, Cricket looked out across the field. It was brown as far as the eye could see. Not even dried up bits of grass remained. Just dirt, and blood, and scorch marks from the battle that raged. Was this his fault too? Was this because he'd set fire to too much of it and it couldn't bounce back? Or was it because of what Sunil had done? Raised the dead, and drained the soil? There was no real way to be sure of causation, but one thing he did know as he pressed his hand to the earth and felt for the magic in the soil. . .

"There is no magic left behind. No life." The words scraped sharp like blades in his throat, leaving behind a rawness that Cricket couldn't help but associate with the dungeons Sunil had locked him in not more than a few months ago. Panic set in a moment later. Squeezing his chest in a vice. Making it a struggle to expand his lungs. His vision swam, the world going liquid and wobbly. Weakness settled into his knees, but he hardly knew he was going down until he felt the pressure of someone's fingers on his elbow. Firm, unyielding.

"My king," Takayoshi said, but the words reaching Cricket were muffled and indistinct, like they were coming through glass.

Gods. How long would he suffer from these attacks? How much more weakness would he have to struggle through before he was normal again? Would he ever *be* normal again? Maybe not. Maybe this was a thing he would live with all of his life until he died. The shadow of what Sunil had done to him hanging over him every hour of the day.

"I need you to breathe with me, Cricket."

Cricket. Takayoshi never called him that. Not unless it

was serious. Not unless he was upset in some way. What had Cricket done to upset him? He hadn't meant to. . .

"Cricket." Takayoshi had raised his voice, almost yelling, and then there was a pressure on Cricket's shoulders. A squeeze so tight it pinched. The sharp pain brought him back to himself though. Placed him firmly back in his own body. "Good. That is good. Now. Breathe with me," Takayoshi instructed and took a deep inhale to show Cricket what he wanted him to do.

Although it was a struggle, Cricket did it. He filled his lungs with air, almost surprised to find it fresh and clean, not filled with the stench of the dungeons. Where was he again? Oh yes. He was out in the field beyond the capital. There with Takayoshi, and the others to investigate the dead patch of land just outside the city.

Sunil was dead.

Lunette was rebuilding.

Becka was safe.

He was safe.

"That is better," Takayoshi encouraged softly. He didn't lean in to press his forehead to Cricket's as he might have done if they were alone, but he also didn't go far, and didn't remove his hands from Cricket's shoulders. The continued pressure burned like a brand through Cricket's tunic. But it was a nice burn. A grounding burn. He needed that.

Once he'd recovered himself, Takayoshi helped him to his feet. He continued to hold onto Cricket, large hands gripping his shoulders until he was sure Cricket could stand under his own power again. Then Takayoshi released him, and took a careful half step away.

"What do you mean there is no magic left behind?" Claudia asked. She and the others had averted their eyes while Cricket panicked, and he wasn't really sure how to feel about that. Were they giving him his privacy? Or were they embarrassed for him? There was no need for them to be embarrassed on his account, he was plenty embarrassed himself. What sort of king had a panic attack simply investigating a plot of land?

"I mean." Cricket bent to press his hand into the dirt again. His magic reached out, refreshing but warm, like the lake at peak summertime, but where normally there was an echo, an answering call, now there was nothing. An emptiness that left behind a hollow feeling in his veins Cricket didn't think he'd ever be able to put to words. It ached like old joints in the snow. "There's no magic left. Yoshi, feel it and tell me what you think."

Takayoshi squatted beside Cricket, a posture that Cricket recognized he'd probably never used before, it did look rather undignified, and Takayoshi was nothing if not dignified. But he settled beside Cricket just the same, and pressed his hand to the dirt.

After a moment of gentle prodding, Takayoshi hummed, the sound disconcerted. "It reminds me very much of when we encountered the hungry spirits in the forest. It is as if the land has been sapped of magic."

"Either it was sapped by Sunil's tactics." Cricket agreed, vindicated by Takayoshi's assessment. "Or he's done something else to it."

"What else could he have done to it?" Leo frowned. He looked like maybe he wanted to reach down and see for himself, but thus far the only one of them who could reach out to the magic of their world and have it react the way Cricket could was Takayoshi. Not even any of the other Celestials had managed it. Cricket wondered what that meant, but he didn't really have the energy to devote to it.

"It could have been siphoned off for use in some other spell." Claudia started pacing, her fingers tapping against her face where she held her cheek. "Did he lay a trap maybe?

Leave something behind to ensure that even if you took the kingdom you wouldn't keep it for long?"

"It's possible." But Cricket hoped not. There was too much else to worry about now, he didn't have the extra resources to devote to more of Sunil's malicious tomfoolery.

"We will check," Takayoshi volunteered. "Leo and I will take care of it. His Highness should focus on preparing for. . ." Takayoshi's words drifted off, unable or unwilling to say the word war, Cricket wasn't sure. But he was grateful for it nonetheless. There were too many ears here. And if Craven was coming, he didn't want them to lose the element of surprise.

"In the meantime, we ought to try growing something here," Cricket said, straightening up, and brushing his hands on his trousers leaving behind a dirty smear. "It might not work, but I'd rather try it and be proven correct then not and miss an easier solution. Claudia, are there any plants in particular that could replenish the magic and nutrients in soil?"

"I'm not sure off the top of my head. But you know I love a good research project." Claudia bounced on her heels a little.

"Good. Then we've all got our marching orders." Cricket nodded, a settled-ness sinking into his bones. It was good to have a plan. It was good to know where things were going, and to be moving forward finally. Anything was better than standing still. "Let's head home."

CHAPTER 4

"I know you're worried," Leo said as he bumped the door to Takayoshi's study closed with his hip.

The study itself was on the smaller side, certainly smaller than Takayoshi's study back in Helios, and had once belonged to Cricket, so it was quite a mess when he had inherited it. Was still quite a mess, in fact, because although Takayoshi found it difficult to work in a space that was disorderly, he found it even more difficult to get rid of anything that had a trace of Cricket on it. It was as if the room breathed with the life of the man he loved, and any cleaning up might spoil that. So Takayoshi worked around the mess. Which included moving a stack of papers from the corner of the desk to the chair, leaving no place for Leo to sit once he had picked his way across the room.

"I know you're worried," Leo repeated when he was standing close enough to Takayoshi that Takayoshi could no longer avoid his gaze.

"So you have said." Takayoshi looked down at the map spread across the surface of his desk to avoid Leo's annoyed expression. It was hard to tell from a map alone where

Craven would strike from, but Takayoshi had dedicated some of his time to the idea over the last couple of days since learning that a war was coming. They needed to be prepared, and the best way to do that was to predict which direction their enemy would be coming from, and shore up their defenses there. Not that that was in any way a guarantee, but it was better than simply waiting for Craven to attack, and reacting after the fact. "What, pray tell, is it that I am worried about?"

Leo glanced down at the stack of papers in the chair as if he were considering moving them, but when Takayoshi did not offer to do so himself, he turned his gaze back to Takayoshi. It was rude not to offer him a seat, especially as his leg was likely bothering him, but Takayoshi had learned during their lengthy acquaintance that Leo did not care for being seen as weak. And Takayoshi making a special effort to offer him a place to sit would definitely be taken as an indication that Takayoshi saw him as such. Then Leo would lash out, and it would become a whole thing that Takayoshi honestly just did not have the time nor the energy for.

"Why don't *you* tell *me*?" Leo asked when the silence had stretched to a breaking point.

There were two ways of dealing with Leo's not so gentle prodding. Takayoshi could give in to his demands for answers, and tell him everything. Or he could play at being obtuse, and hope that Leo would simply grow bored of the conversation and go away.

Takayoshi chose the latter. "There is quite a bit to be worried about, as you well know. A war is coming. The land outside the city has yet to take seed. And, of course, my upcoming nuptials are requiring a fair bit more planning than I originally estimated. Take your pick."

Leo, it seemed was wise to this tactic, and was not taking the bait. "Yes, yes. All of those things of course." He flapped his wrist, and moved to sit on the edge of Takayoshi's desk, making himself quite comfortable it seemed. "But there's something else, isn't there?"

Takayoshi's eye twitched a little at the rudeness of the act of sitting on someone's workspace. It was a clear show of disrespect toward Takayoshi and what he was trying to do. Unfortunately, Takayoshi also realized it was a ploy to get him irritated enough to talk. A ploy, which annoyingly enough, worked.

Damn Leo.

"Cricket's pearl is still missing." Takayoshi sighed, leaning back in his chair so that he could finally meet Leo's gaze, although not far back enough as to be considered slouching. "As is Estia. There is some small chance that Estia got zir hands on it during the battle, and returned to Cytherea to deliver it to Craven."

Leo nodded, taking this concern seriously, and not brushing it away out of hand as many others in Takayoshi's life prior to Cricket might have done. His sister and uncle, in particular were very difficult to speak to when he was in a place where his anxiety became this high. They meant well, but they both seemed to think that he was overreacting about most things, getting himself worked up over nothing. Which, granted, sometimes he was. But saying so did not make the thing seem smaller.

"That might be what happened," Leo acknowledged after a moment. "But if it were, would we not see some change in Cricket? The idea behind taking the pearl is that it can be used to control the dragon, right?"

"Correct." Once he had the pearl in hand again, Takayoshi was going to lock it away in a place where no one could set eyes on it again, much less use it against Cricket to hurt him or his people. Although, he wondered if perhaps Cricket would need to wear it, to keep the effects of being a dragon at bay. Experimentation would need to be conducted. But first, they had to find the blasted thing, and return it to its rightful owner.

"While I grant that you do know His Highness better, it seems to me that nothing much has changed with Cricket," Leo continued, his tone annoyingly reasonable. But it was calming Takayoshi little by little. Applying logic to the problem in a way that Takayoshi had been unable to do himself until that moment. "So, either Estia didn't steal the pearl, and it's simply lost somewhere else, or ze didn't deliver it to Craven."

"Yet," Takayoshi added.

"Yet," Leo allowed. "Which means we still have some time."

Some, but not much, Takayoshi wanted to say. All he could hope was that if Estia did have the pearl then zir conscience would get the better of zir, and they would not give it to Craven. He knew there was more to it than that with Estia and Craven, but he could not help but hope.

"Not enough time, very likely." Takayoshi rubbed at his forehead in an attempt to alleviate the oncoming headache. It did nothing. Although the talk with Leo had helped with his anxiety a little. Not enough, just like they did not have enough time, but a little.

"Has the search for the pearl yielded no results?" Leo asked hopefully, but the expression of deadpan annoyance Takyoshi sent him must have been enough to tell Leo that the question was a silly one. "Of course not."

"It has been months. If the pearl were lost somewhere in the capital, it would have turned up by now." Not that Takayoshi had not hoped for the same thing, he had. It had been a foolish hope to think that perhaps Cricket had merely misplaced it, or it had fallen from his pocket somewhere during the battle. There had been so much going on at the time that anything was possible. But they had tried multiple scrying spells and come up short. If the pearl were in the capital, they would have found it. Thus, it was not here. "I plan to try another scrying spell with Cricket this evening. We will cast a wider net, if it is not in Lunette then we will know what kingdom it is in."

Leo shifted uncomfortably, and if it were anyone else Takayoshi might have thought it was because Leo's leg was bothering him. But he had learned enough about Leo over the years to know that the other man had a very high threshold for pain. That he had been injured, and bloody, his leg near unusable, and he had still gotten back up to defend those who needed it. He was a marvel, in Takayoshi's book.

"I know that you want to believe the best of Estia," Takayoshi said when it seemed that Leo was not going to broach the topic himself. Takayoshi resisted the urge to remind Leo that they were friends, that he was a safe place for Leo to voice his concerns and the things that bothered him. Sentimentality never really worked with Leo. Claudia was more the type who needed such reassurances. Between Leo and Takayoshi there was an understanding instead. That speaking was hard. And feeling was harder. "I understand that you want them to be innocent of this, because you care deeply for them as I care for Cricket."

Leo inhaled sharply, his brown eyes taking on a wild, trapped expression. But he did not run away, did not try to escape as some might. They had not spoken of this, not at length, what Leo felt for Estia. But Takayoshi understood it, even without words. Knew that Estia had been to Leo as Cricket was to Takayoshi. That Estia had been Leo's North Star for much of his life. That Leo had given up everything to keep Estia safe, and ultimately had failed. It was a painful reminder for Takayoshi how things could have turned out for Cricket if events had shifted just slightly, if the brush Sunil had used to paint Cricket a villain had perhaps not been quite so heavy handed.

"They are my friend too." It was important to acknowledge this, even if it made Takayoshi ache. Not as badly as Leo, of course, but in his own unique way. For Takayoshi had not had friends before Cricket, and in his journey to save his prince he had found three. One of which had betrayed him in the end. "And believe me when I say that if ze were to seek my forgiveness for what ze has done, I would give it to zir."

"Why?" Leo asked, the word choked as if his throat were tight with emotion. Takayoshi could understand that too.

"Because ze is my friend, and sometimes we must forgive our friends for the mistakes they have made in the past." Takayoshi paused, thinking for a moment on his words, measuring them out carefully like ingredients for bread. "But ze must be sincere in zir asking of forgiveness. And ze must not betray us again."

Leo nodded, his hand falling to grip tightly at the edge of Takayoshi's desk. Then he laughed, lightly, the sound a startled rasp. "You've grown up a lot since I first met you, Yoshi."

Takayoshi ducked his head to hide the pleased smile that twitched at his lips, and they sat there in contented silence for a long moment. Just being in one another's company, knowing what had passed between them as friends, and all that they still had to face. It was a comfort Takayoshi had not allowed himself often, but he appreciated it now that he had people like Leo in his life. How things had changed over the years since Cricket had flopped down at his table, and nearly spilled his tea.

"Do you think ze will?" Leo asked, breaking the silence. He was not looking at Takayoshi anymore, his head turned so he could stare out the window beside Takayoshi's desk that overlooked the gardens. The bunnies were racing about the small yard, enjoying the early summer sunshine, and

Takayoshi enjoyed the view more than he would be able to express, having spent so many years surrounded by snow.

"Do I think ze will what?" Takayoshi prompted, although he thought perhaps he knew the answer.

"Ask for our forgiveness. Try to be a better person. Mend the friendships ze has broken."

"Bent. Not broken," Takayoshi corrected, feeling it was important to be specific, especially in matters such as these. "And if Craven allows it, I think Estia will do everything ze can to come back to us. I think ze only left because of Craven, and his hold over Cytherea. Without that. . ."

Leo nodded slowly, understanding settling around them. "Then I suppose we ought to win this war."

"I suppose we ought," Takayoshi agreed.

CHAPTER 5

Cricket was beginning to think maybe they just shouldn't have induction ceremonies for royal advisors anymore. There were several reasons for this, not the least of which because these types of ceremonies were boring and grew steadily more boring every time they had to hold one as the master of ceremonies aged. The man had to have been the one who crowned Cricket's father's father there wasn't a single doubt in Cricket's mind.

And then there was the matter that there were no swords involved in this particular ceremony at all. At least with his coronation, Cricket had received a fresh new blade. Claudia was receiving nothing of the sort. Just reciting the vows the master of ceremonies spoke—he was practically staring through her, reciting the words as if he didn't even have to think—in a tone so flat and slow that it would have put even the widest awake to sleep.

Honestly, how was Claudia even still upright? Cricket was nodding off and he had to be in the most uncomfortable chair they could find in the whole of Lunette. And yet, Claudia stood unblinking, reciting the vows with enough passion that it almost invigorated the crowd. Almost.

But the real reason they should stop having these ceremonies was. . .

The doors to the hall burst open, smacking loud against the walls to either side. Cricket swore he heard someone snort loudly as if they'd been roused from sleep just as the young knight made their way up the aisle toward the raised dais.

Well, the real reason they should stop having these ceremonies was their propensity to be interrupted by the announcement of some kind of emergency.

The soldier in question looked far less frazzled than the messenger who had interrupted Anstice's induction ceremony some years ago, at almost exactly the same moment, but no less upset. Cricket's heart slammed against his chest, but he did not allow that to show on his face. Out of the corner of his eye Takayoshi shifted slightly, as if perhaps he might move in front of Cricket to protect him, and Ignacia took a step forward.

"Forgive me, Your Highness," the knight said, their voice steady and echoing in the ensuing silence of the hall. "But there is an urgent matter I must discuss with you. Leo sent me with news from the Hermes mountains."

The master of ceremonies let out a long-suffering sigh—the most animated he'd been in what felt like hours—and said, "I suppose I ought to hurry this along then?"

"Yes, I think that would be best." Cricket waved to Takayoshi, and the man at his side moved in closer, bending down a little to listen. "Take them into my study, and wait. Ignacia, Claudia and I will be with you shortly."

To his credit, Takayoshi didn't even raise a brow, much less ask why the head of the guard wasn't put in charge of this task. Ignacia made a sound like she might argue, but it was soft enough that only Cricket could hear it, and once Takayoshi and the knight were gone she didn't try again. She'd never say so out loud, but Cricket knew it was important to her to be here for this, important to Claudia too. They hadn't made anything official, and did their best to hide their relationship, but it was obvious to Cricket who had grown up with Ignacia how she felt about Claudia. How she leaned into Claudia's space sometimes like a flower seeking the sun. How when Claudia was in the room Ignacia could hardly look anywhere else.

It would be cute if it weren't so infuriating how subtle they tried to be about it, while at the same time failing miserably. He'd have to have a discussion with Ignacia about that at some point, see the reason behind it. Maybe they were afraid of what people would say if it was found out that the head of the guard and the advisor were together. But nothing about Cricket's court was traditional, and he certainly wasn't about to get in the way of their happiness.

"Please, continue." Cricket motioned to the Master of Ceremonies which only seemed to make the man more annoyed, but he sped through the rest of the ceremony at breakneck speed. Even faster than when it had been Anstice's induction. Cricket wondered if maybe it was out of annoyance at being interrupted twice in nearly the exact same way, or if he too felt that there was something amiss that Cricket couldn't put off for longer than a few minutes.

Shame really. Cricket didn't think he had the fortitude for another complication, more bad news. He would rather this ceremony have taken another hour or two, if just to prolong the inevitable. But that was the thing about the inevitable, it was inevitable. Cricket was going to have to face what was coming for him and his people regardless of him wanting to or not. Because he was king, and he couldn't shirk his responsibilities.

Once everything was said, and done, Claudia rose from her knees, and turned to meet Cricket's gaze with a steely expression behind her spectacles. An expression that Cricket would wager hadn't been there before Claudia had joined Takayoshi on his quest all those years ago.

He shook his head a little to himself, before giving Claudia a firm nod and rising from the throne to lead the way off the dais, out of the hall, and down the corridor to his study. Those around him had known so much pain in the last few years, seen so much fighting, so much war. It didn't seem fair that by being connected to him they would know only strife, and he wished things were different. Wished he could offer them peace, and happiness, but it seemed their enemies were not going to give them that.

Enemies. When had he become a man who had enemies?

In his youth Cricket had always thought he'd be the kind of king who would only have friends, and allies. He'd thought he'd be the kind of man who would draw people to him, and keep them smiling. That Lunette would prosper under his rule just as it had under the rule of his father. He'd been so very wrong, foolish to make such assumptions.

Lunette was not built for war, it hadn't known war in many generations, but now with a Celestial on the throne, it seemed it would know nothing but. If he thought stepping down, and allowing someone else to rule would save them, perhaps he would. But Cricket knew better.

Greed had festered and spread throughout their country in silence for the last several years, maybe longer. Those who had known prosperity during times of peace had grown to want more of it, to not be satisfied by what was in front of them. And those who had been content had grown complacent.

War was inevitable.

If not against Cricket and his kingdom, then against

someone else. It just so happened that Cricket with his otherness, was the most convenient target.

"He refused to rest," Takayoshi reported the moment the doors to Cricket's father's study opened. There was a thin layer of annoyance to his tone, his brows drawn together just slightly enough that no one else but perhaps Cricket and Claudia would notice the difference in Takayoshi's features, but it was there just the same. Cricket wondered how many times Takayoshi had tried to get the knight to rest but the man was set to pacing from one end of the room to the other, his chest beginning to heave from an ensuing panic.

"Youta," Cricket called, poking his head out of the door to the maid on her way past. "Could you please have some tea brought?"

"Yes, Your Highness." She dipped into a quick bow then continued on her way. Cricket didn't bother to ask how she'd been exactly where he needed her to be at that moment. She always seemed to manage that somehow, and he'd learned long ago it was better not to ask women to reveal their secrets.

He shut the door behind himself and turned to the small collection of people in the room, and motioned to the chairs. "Everyone, please sit."

With the king's order heavy in the air, and everyone else sitting, the knight could hardly do anything else, so he settled into one of the chairs. But even then, he didn't stop moving, his heel jittered against the floor, knee bouncing up and down. It was a wonder he hadn't shouted his message the moment Cricket entered the room with how agitated he was.

"Now," Cricket said calmly, because even as his heart raced in his chest, and his fingertips grew cold with anxiety, it would not do to let anyone see their king that way. He had to remain the picture of collected, especially in times of crisis. "Tell me what has happened."

"There is a village in the mountains of Hermes, right where the border between Cytherea, Lunette, and Hermes intersects," the knight said, shifting in his seat, uncomfortable now that the attention was on him. Cricket wasn't sure why he was telling Cricket this, he knew about the village. He'd rebuilt it after all. It was under his protection.

"We know of it. That's where our daughter is from." Takayoshi's annoyance only grew at the knight's words. As if he felt the knight were wasting their time. He likely was, but Cricket couldn't quite get past how Takayoshi had called Becka *their* daughter. She was, of course, but it was still something he had yet to get used to. He and Takayoshi were a pair, engaged to be married, a team. And Cricket didn't think he'd ever get tired of being reminded of that.

He bit back a smile. "Yes, as Takayoshi says, we're aware of that village. Please continue."

"Craven has taken the village."

Cricket's heart lodged itself into his throat, and he choked, his eyes watering a little. How many times would he fail to protect that village? How many times would he prove to everyone that he was not worthy of the position of king? He didn't know. But surely this was one time too many.

"I see," Cricket croaked past the thumping of his heart in this throat. It hurt to speak, but he didn't have any other choice. He was the king, and he needed to resolve this problem. "Has Leo sent any other information?"

"He has not been able to get close enough to see how large Craven's forces are yet. He asks that His Highness send reinforcements."

"I see," Cricket said again, fear dancing down his spine. He sounded like an imbecile, didn't he? He was sure that he did.

Thankfully, a soft knock pulled him from his thoughts.

"Come in," Cricket called, hoping his voice sounded at least somewhat normal.

Youta joined them with the tray laden in cups and hot water. Her movements careful, and practiced. Cricket didn't think he'd ever been so grateful to see her in his life.

"Youta, will you see this knight to the barracks? We have much to discuss." It would be a relief to have the knight out of the room. To be able to show himself for the scared young man that he was.

"Of course, Your Highness." Youta dipped her head in respect, and when she raised it again Cricket could tell that she had seen right through him. Because of course she had. Youta had been a member of the castle's staff since he was young enough to request his sandwiches without crust. She'd indulged him. She'd looked after him. And in the years since Sunil had tried to take over the kingdom the first time, she'd become indispensable to the running of his house.

Once the knight was gone, Cricket slumped, the fight leaving him so quickly it was hard to even remain in his chair.

"We don't have the resources to send an army to meet him," Ignacia said after a moment. "It would leave the capital entirely unprotected."

"Which is likely what he wants," Claudia added.

"Technically," Cricket sighed, brushing his hand through his shoulder length hair. He wished it would hurry up and finish growing out so that he would have a braid to fiddle with nervously when he felt like this. "That land doesn't belong to any of us. It's under my protection, yes, but that was never really sanctioned by the other kingdoms."

"So this isn't *technically* an act of war." Ignacia scowled.

"No. And were we to treat it as such, in the eyes of the other kingdoms it would be *us* declaring war on *Craven*, not the other way around." Cricket had to give it to Craven, he'd thought this through. He'd hit Cricket exactly where it would hurt, and exactly where he could do nothing about it. It was infuriating.

"So what do we do?" Claudia pushed her glasses back up her face even though they hadn't really moved. "Leave him there to do whatever it is he's up to?"

"No." Takayoshi shook his head. "I will go to meet with Leo, and we will do our best to assess the situation. If there is something more going on than Craven simply occupying the space to be a nuisance, we will find out, and we will report back. We will also assess how large Craven's forces are so we are prepared when the reach Lunette."

"That's a good compromise." Ignacia nodded, but she didn't look happy about having to doll out a compliment to Takayoshi. Cricket resisted the urge to roll his eyes at her antics. Now wasn't the time for bickering and infighting.

"Yoshi," Claudia said, her voice suddenly frightened in a way Cricket decided immediately he didn't care for. "That's where that plant was."

"I slayed the plant." Takayoshi sat up straighter, his face smoothing out to show none of what he was feeling. "But I will be careful."

Claudia and Ignacia agreed, and a moment later they left Takayoshi and Cricket alone in the study, their tea untouched.

"When do you leave?" Cricket asked, knowing already what the answer would be. Because what other choice was there? They needed answers, and they needed them now.

"At first light."

"You had better say goodbye to Becka before you go."

"Yes, my king." Takayoshi rose from his chair, and Cricket thought he might be smiling, but Takayoshi did not give him the chance to see before he too left Cricket to his worries.

CHAPTER 6

"You can't leave," Becka said, her dark brown eyes narrowed, her arms crossed over her chest. There was no pout in her voice, no pleading, this was an order. An order from a seven-year-old. Takayoshi swallowed back a smile.

"I am afraid that I must. Someone needs to help Leo, and we do not have the knights to spare for such a task." Their lack of adequate forces to even send on this simple mission did not sit well with Takayoshi. There was little doubt in his mind that they would soon have to request aid from one of their allies. Likely Helios, but he would wait to contact his sister until he had spoken to Cricket, and they had a better idea of what Craven's retinue looked like.

"Send someone else."

"Becka," Cricket warned, his tone soft and chiding. "Don't make this harder than it has to be. Yoshi will be back as soon as he can, but the longer it takes you to say goodbye, the longer it will take him to get back."

Takayoshi did not think that logic made sense, but he

could see why Cricket was using it, and so he nodded his agreement. "I will be back very soon."

"Before I know it?" Becka asked, her arms uncrossing, her shoulders slumping a little in defeat.

"If that is possible, yes." Takayoshi nodded solemnly. "Now. May I please have a hug before I leave?"

"Oh very well." Becka huffed, a gesture so like Cricket that Takayoshi's chest ached with it, and he pulled her into a tight hug, pressing a kiss to her hair.

EACH STEP UP the mountain took Takayoshi further and further from where he wanted most to be. His king was in the valley. His daughter was in the valley. His family, his friends, his people, they were all down below—behind him— in Lunette. And if he wanted them to stay safe there, if he wanted to protect them, he must go into the mountains and meet Craven and his men.

Perhaps that was oversimplifying things, and maybe being a touch dramatic. But Takayoshi had been by himself for a few days by this point, and he had not been on his own in this way in quite some time, so he had to amuse himself somehow. And even if it were a touch dramatic, that did not make it any less true. He had, indeed, left everyone he cared for—apart from Leo who waited up ahead—behind him, in more ways than one.

There had not been time in the weeks since the battle with Sunil to really sit with the decision Takayoshi had made to leave behind Helios, his uncle, and his sister. To leave behind the kingdom he was meant to rule in favor of another.

It was strange, perhaps, from the outside looking in. To

watch the young man who had abdicated his throne at a young age marry into another, but it felt right to Takayoshi in a way he would never be able to put into words.

Yes, Helios had born and bred him. Turned him into the white knight he was. But it had never been home. Not in the way Cricket's castle was.

Perhaps part of that was because when he was very young his uncle had sent him to the summit of the mountain to be trained by the monks there. Or maybe it was because his uncle had always set strict rules for them growing up, and it was only when Takayoshi met Cricket that he had seen how wrong those rules were.

There were at least a dozen different reasons he could choose from, and none of them would be wrong per se. But none of them would be right either.

The right answer was that Lunette was where Cricket was, and wherever Cricket was, was home.

Rose whinnied beneath him, her mottled brown mane fluttering in the breeze. He would have sooner brought Lily on such an excursion, but since the fire in Becka's village she had been unable to make long treks.

The horse's slower pace drew Takayoshi out of his thoughts and when he followed her line of sight he saw the small encampment a few feet into the woods off the path.

After dismounting, Takayoshi found the fire burned down to embers, and no sign of Leo, his horse, or the small contingent of knights he had left Lunette with about a week prior.

Takayoshi took a moment to survey the surrounding wood, leaving Rose tied to a tree near the cold fire left over from Leo and his men. The forest was quiet, no sound of insects or birds, eerily similar to when he had confronted the vicious spirits some years ago. His gaze flicked from one spot to the next, searching for any sign of where Leo might have gone, and found—

Cold steel pressed to his throat. The sword sharp enough to cut with even the barest amount of pressure and angled in such a way that whoever held it was off to his right. Takayoshi glanced at them from the corner of his eye, but even without the blurry shape of a dark blue clad figure, Takayoshi knew who the sword belonged to.

"You've gotten sloppy sitting beside His Highness," Leo rasped warningly, but Takayoshi was sure if he could get a good look at Leo's face the man would be smiling.

"I knew you were there." Takayoshi took a step back, careful of the sharp blade, then turned to face Leo.

Leo clicked his tongue, and lowered the sword. "Of course you did." Although he did not sound as if he quite believed it. "Are you the reinforcements he sent?"

"For the time being." Takayoshi could tell from Leo's tone that he did not like this development, and Takyoshi had to be honest, he did not either. But the fact remained that their hands were tied for the moment. "There is some concern that if we were to attack Craven when he was occupying a place which is not technically under Lunette rule, it would be considered an act of war."

"Isn't him taking a village Cricket just finished rebuilding also an act of war?" Leo nodded to a trail that led further up the mountain. It was narrow, and not as well trod as the one Takayoshi had brought Rose up, a foot path more than anything else. Then the two started in that direction, one behind the other.

"Has he taken it by force?" Not that it would matter, there was no way to prove that. Cricket would say one thing, and Craven would say another, and in the end, it would be Cricket who was seen as the antagonizer. Which was not a thing he could afford with the rumblings left behind by Sunil's lies.

"He's not holding anyone hostage if that's what you

mean." But Leo sounded grumpy about it. Likely because he knew just as well as Takayoshi did that such a thing could be seen as proof that Craven had taken the village as a personal attack on Cricket and thereby extension Lunette. But Craven was not that foolish. Unfortunately. It would be convenient if their enemies were a little less cunning. Takayoshi mourned the loss of Sunil's blatant attacks.

"Then he has not taken it. He is simply staying there, as far as the other kingdoms are concerned." Takayoshi ran his thumb over the hilt of his sword, reassuring himself that it was there should he need it. "Have you heard anything from Hermes?"

"Not yet. I did send a messenger their way, just to make them aware of the situation, but I don't think anything will come of it."

"Likely not." Takayoshi did not think they could count on any of the other kingdoms in this, apart from Helios. And with Helios his sister would only send them aid on account of Takayoshi being engaged to the king of Lunette. None of the other kingdoms had an obligation to them in that way. Nor were they likely to pick sides in a fight such as this. Not that Takayoshi could blame them. There was no way to tell who would win. Lunette's forces were decimated from the civil war with Sunil, and while they had the Celestials on their side, Cytherea had always focused more on their military than the other kingdoms.

"I could reach out to Claudia's family. They're all—"

"No." Takayoshi shook his head, with a sigh. "We will not draw more people into this than we have to. If Claudia wishes to ask for their help, then she will. If they wish to offer, we will accept. But I will not reach out to them on behalf of Cricket. It could be seen as a betrayal against the crown of Hermes if they were to help us, regardless of the fact that Claudia is the advisor to Lunette."

Leo did not argue, but Takayoshi could tell from his pointed silence that he did not agree, and that something else was bothering him.

They walked on in silence for a time, the path slowly becoming steeper as it seemed to curve around the backside of the village to come at it from the forest at its back instead of the main road.

With a sigh, Takayoshi waited for Leo to tell him what was wrong, but he did not. He had become so accustomed to his other friends, and Cricket, to being able to wait them out, that he had forgotten how taciturn Leo could be when he was of a mind. "Are you going to tell me what is bothering you, or am I going to have to find out for myself?"

Leo's shoulders seemed to grow stiffer. Takayoshi knew they were alike in the way they did not like discussing certain things, but he also knew that sometimes it was necessary. Cricket had taught him that. "Estia is with them."

"As a general?"

"As a hostage."

Takayoshi's stomach dropped. "I am sorry."

Leo said nothing else.

It made sense. Well, it made sense in the context of Leo's upset, it did not make sense in the context of Estia acting as a hostage to Craven. As far as Takayoshi knew, Estia had betrayed them all to pass information to Craven. Meaning they were working together. Or, at least, they had been some years ago when Estia left Takayoshi and his friends stranded on an island with no way to return to the mainland apart from building themselves a boat. Takayoshi could not help but wonder, what had changed?

Takayoshi thought to ask how Estia was. But he had the answer to that question in the set of Leo's shoulders. Not well. Maybe that meant Estia had not given Craven everything ze learned in the archive. Or maybe it meant that it had simply not been enough. Takayoshi did not know enough of Craven's character to be able to tell. And as they came upon the village, he supposed he would have his answers soon enough.

"This is as close as you or I can get without drawing attention," Leo said, pulling them both to a stop some feet away from the edge of the tree line to the north of the village. They were above the village by some meters, but not enough to really see anything. "I've got a couple of men stationed inside, but they can't check in very often. Craven has men awake at all hours of the day, wandering the streets."

"Keeping guard."

"He knows we're here."

Takayoshi frowned, then nodded. "He did not pick this village by accident. He knew eventually Cricket would send men to check in, and that when he did, they would find Craven occupying it." It was annoyingly smart.

"How many know Cricket rebuilt this place?"

"He made a royal proclamation about it before we returned to Lunette. It is no secret." Because Takayoshi's beautiful, wonderful, sweet husband-to-be could also be terribly sentimental. Of course he did not think that anyone would use that knowledge against him. Why should he assume that? It was only by some miracle that Sunil had not burned it to the ground again just to spite his nephew.

Takayoshi shook himself, and settled back on his heels. "Are there any breaks in the guard rotation? I would like to get a closer look at what we are dealing with myself."

"None." Leo scrubbed at his face. "I just told you, he keeps men on the streets at all hours of the day and night. If there were any openings, I'd have gone in there and slit that man's throat myself. But there hasn't—"

The words died in Leo's throat as a figure was dragged into the small square at the heart of the village. Guards flanked them, and although Takayoshi had never seen Estia in color—did not know that they had a head of turquoise colored hair—he could tell who it was by the way Leo jolted at his side.

"No," Leo whispered, and Takayoshi had just enough time to grab him by the waist to keep him from running out into the open as Estia was thrown onto the ground.

There was blood on zir face. Crimson, and garish where zir turquoise hair clung to it, was dyed a frightening shade of mauve .

Takayoshi's stomach turned, he did not think he would ever get used to the color of blood on skin, not so long as he lived. It had been easier to deal with when the world was a wash of grays. But now that everything was so vibrant, so alive, seeing that life drain from a person would forever make him uncomfortable.

He held tighter to Leo even as he struggled.

"Come out, come out, wherever you are, Lionel," Craven called, his voice a soft, leading sing-song tone, his face stretched into a rictus of a smile.

Takayoshi did not know how Craven had found out that Leo was Lionel, nor how Craven knew that Leo was there, but he did not care either. All he cared about at that moment was keeping Leo from doing something foolish.

"No?" Craven tilted his head, as if listening to something in the distance. "There, you see? He's not coming, Estia. He's here, and he's going to let me do this. So you may as well give me everything."

Leo strained harder against Takayoshi's hold as Craven raised a whip, but Takayoshi held fast, his arms wrapping tight around Leo's waist to pull him into his chest. To hold him close the way he might a child. He knew all too well what it was to stand back and watch the person he loved most be abused by someone they had once thought of as family.

The whip landed like a crack, but Estia did not cry out, ze just made a muffled sound like a whimper, and buried zir face into zir arms where no one could see while shaking zir head. Whatever it was Craven wanted, it did not seem that Estia was going to give it to him.

Craven tsked, and raised the whip again. "What was the point in coming back if you weren't going to give me everything?"

Another crack. Another muffled whine.

It went on and on, and eventually Leo stopped struggling against Takayoshi's hold. Estia fell limp, not even the muffled cries leaving zi anymore, zir back coated in thick crimson. light failed as the sun began to dip below the horizon. dragged Estia back inside.

"We have to get zir out," Leo said, his voice rasping and rough, like he had been screaming when Estia could not for the last several minutes. "I don't care what ze's done. I don't care what punishment ze'll face from Cricket. It has to be better than this. Please. Please. Yoshi. We have to get Estia out."

Takayoshi wished that he could deny Leo this. He wished that he could be colder, and harder, closer to the ruler his uncle had always wanted him to be. But he was soft, and in spite of what Estia had done, he cared for zir too.

"We will," he promised. "Tonight."

Because Estia might not survive much longer, he did not add. It would only make Leo more frantic.

"Gather the others."

CHAPTER 7

"And still nothing?" Cricket asked for what felt like the hundredth time. It wasn't that he hadn't understood what Claudia was telling him, it was that he hadn't understood how that was at all possible. They were doing everything right. At least, as far as he knew. Cricket wasn't a farmer, but by all logic what they had tried should be working.

And Claudia *had* brought in a farmer to help them.

The farmer sat on the other side of Cricket's desk now, looking about as bewildered as Cricket felt. Cricket didn't care for that particular emotion, never much had. He liked a good puzzle, for sure, but not one that he couldn't seem to solve, and this one was proving unsolvable.

"It seemed like we had made some progress for a couple of days," the farmer—Adler, he'd introduced himself as—said. "There were some sprouts, and I thought perhaps we had found a way to replenish the vital nutrients and the magic in the soil."

Yes, Cricket remembered those few scant hours of hope. They'd burned hot and fast through him. Had been the only thing to really help as he saw Takayoshi off, and the loss of him settled like a hollow place deep in Cricket's sternum. The thought that perhaps it would be the last time invaded Cricket's mind, making a home for itself there, burying deep. Cricket had tried in vain over the last couple of days to shake it loose. To focus on other things, like any sensible person would do. The trouble with that was that Cricket had never really been the sensible sort. And so the missing stayed with him, and the reminder that anything could happen while they were apart made itself known at the most inopportune times.

Like now, when Cricket was meant to be focusing on their problem of the dead land outside his father's capital. How much easier life would be if Cricket could close the gates to his father's kingdom, and to his heart, and keep all others out, while keeping those inside safe.

He was better than that, but not much.

"And what happened to the sprouts?" Cricket asked, again, not really wanting the answer. Because the longer they talked about this the more he realized what a failure he was.

What was done was done, he supposed. Nothing for it now.

"They withered shortly thereafter, Your Highness." Adler shifted as if uncomfortable in his chair, as if afraid to give the king bad news. It creaked beneath his weight, and Cricket resisted the urge to sigh. Sighing would only make Adler feel worse. He didn't want Adler to feel like Cricket was upset with him. Because it wasn't the farmer's fault. Cricket was upset with the situation.

"*How* did they wither?" Cricket pressed. The *how* was important, he reasoned. It would tell him what happened to the plants, and what way they could go about fixing this.

Adler shifted again, his eyes flicking about the room, unsettled, and unsure. It would seem Sunil's rumors of his volatile and violent nature persisted. How much of his life would he spend trying to undo the damage his own family had wrought? Years? Decades? Would he go to his grave with this hanging over him still?

"You can tell His Highness," Claudia prodded gently. "He will not be angry with you. We are just trying to better understand the problem to find a solution."

Perhaps this meeting would have been better taken out in the gardens, or somewhere a little less formal. Maybe then Adler would have felt more comfortable.

Cricket was drowning on dry land as far as all of this was concerned. Jaxith died without imparting to Cricket everything he'd need to be king, or at least it seemed that way much of the time. His father's focus had been on ensuring that Cricket was good, and kind, and just. There had never been any discussions on what to do should someone betray him. On how to act when his own people feared him, and the nobles that surrounded him thought him weak enough that they could take Lunette from him with little trouble. Jaxith had ruled during a time of peace. When discord and greed were a thought for another day.

That other day had come, and Cricket found himself wholly unprepared for it. Maybe Sunil had been right, maybe Cricket was too soft for this.

"They shriveled," Adler said. "It was as if they had gone without sun and water. They browned, then dried completely."

"And the seeds?"

"When we dug them up, they were blackened as if burned by the sun." Adler reached into his pocket and pulled a couple of black seed pods out to set on Cricket's desk for him to inspect. "We didn't dig them all up, but these few. . ."

"Yes. I see what you mean." Cricket picked one up to hold it to the light. It had been cracked open to allow the seedling to grow, but the shell itself had gone black as if thrown into a fire, and when he shook it, it made a dull, hollow jingling. Proving that whatever had been inside of it was dry as well.

"There's more, Your Highness," Adler hedged, the chair creaking beneath him again. Cricket really wished he'd sit still.

"More?" Cricket asked. He set the seed gently on his desk, as if it were something precious and sacred, instead of the dried husk that it was. "What do you mean more?"

"You really need to see it for yourself, Your Highness."

"Very well." Cricket rose from his chair. "Show me."

THE FIELD where Cricket fought Sunil not but a few scant weeks ago still reeked of blood in Cricket's mind. Even as he breathed fresh air, the foul stench of death and dying clogged his nose making it a struggle to take a deep inhale. No one else seemed to be having a problem, even Claudia and Ignacia who had been a part of that battle. So Cricket did his best to breathe normally, to appear that nothing was wrong.

How much longer would that battle haunt him? It didn't matter. He lifted his chin, he'd push through it as he'd pushed through so many other things in his life. He may not be the king Lunette needed, but he was the one they had, and he would ensure he protected them to the best of his ability.

Cricket followed Adler past the little rows of soil that had been tilled and infused with magic to get something to grow, past the place where Cricket had confessed his love to Takayoshi, and up the hill a ways.

"Adler, where are we—"

Confusion quickly turned to horror as he realized that the ground he was standing on was as brown, and dead as that of the field below. And more still, the tree at the top of the hill, the one Takayoshi had helped him up into all those years ago, its leaves were brown and withered. They littered the ground like autumn in the middle of spring.

"How—" Cricket cleared his throat, trying to keep the words from catching in it again, but they were stubborn and they stuck like glue to the insides of him, threatening to suffocate him. Stars, he couldn't breathe. And this was no time for a panic attack, not when Takayoshi wasn't there to talk him out of it. Not when there were so many eyes on him in this small contingent of people. Not when anyone could see. He clenched his jaw, and forced the next words out even if they left his tongue raw. "How far does the rot go?"

"It spreads a little farther each day, Your Highness." Adler's voice was quiet, clearly still afraid of what reaction he might garner from his king for what he had to say.

And yes, Cricket was angry. He was furious. Outraged. His temper flared inside of him, going first hot, then cold as it burned through his veins. A chill settled in the air around him that he hoped no one else noticed. But even if they didn't, they could hardly miss the way his breath puffed a little when he next spoke.

"And this was not brought to me sooner, *why?*"

"We needed to be sure," Claudia offered, stepping forward as if to put herself between Cricket and Adler. Like Cricket would strike out at Adler in some kind of rage. He wouldn't. But Claudia didn't know him well enough to know that yet. "But, Your Highness. . ." She hesitated, but unlike Adler, she met his gaze. "Look."

Cricket turned to see what she was pointing at, and his breath caught in his chest anew. He staggered on his feet, nearly losing his balance but for his training with a sword.

The rot spread around the capital in a circle. Leaving only the capital untouched, and green. As if it had begun there, and branched out from the center of the city, from the palace itself.

Before Cricket could stop himself, he thought, *Oh. This is my fault.* And even if it were untrue, logically he knew it had to be, the thought took root. It planted itself there like a seedling and grew until even his fingers tingled with the knowledge that his kingdom was failing, and it was all his doing.

And still, he knew without a shadow of a doubt, he would fix this. He wasn't sure how yet, but he would.

"Causation?" he asked, hoping that Claudia would have some answer, something to squash that seedling before its vines choked every part of him.

"As yet, unclear." Claudia's tone had gone distant, and scholarly as if she were a doctor or a healer describing some new treatment. Cricket wanted to appreciate her professionalism, but he couldn't. Although he had not seen it firsthand, Takayoshi told him enough of how Claudia reacted to a new discovery or puzzle to know this was not it. Claudia should be excited, and pacing. She should be spouting wild theories, and throwing off the wall ideas at him. The same way Cricket would solve any problem. But. . .

But they were both stuck. Weighed down by the enormity of this. Even as they both were resolved to find a solution.

"The fact that it's spreading does make one thing clear," Claudia said, and although the words themselves would have normally meant good news, her tone told him it was anything but.

Cricket made a questioning sound in the back of his throat, half choked. He didn't want the answer to that sound, not really. But he'd take it on the chin, as he did so many other things.

"The magic is actively being leached from the ground. This is not just a problem left over from the battle with Sunil.

This is something that is currently being done to the land now."

"Okay." Cricket inhaled deeply and regretted it immediately as the stench of rot and death clung to the inside of his nose, making a home for itself there. It would haunt his hours and live in his nightmares. He didn't have time for that now, though. "Okay. So if it's been sapped from the soil, then it must be going somewhere, right?"

Claudia and Adler nodded their agreement.

"So we need to find where it's going, and stop whatever it is that's using the magic of our land as fuel." It sounded easy when broken down that way, simple, really. Just find the thing that was sucking the land dry like a leech and put a stop to it. But Cricket knew enough of magic these days to know that there was no way it would be that straightforward.

Still, he took another deep breath, and straightened up, lifting his chin. "Adler, thank you for your help in this. You are free to return home, or stay in the capital if you so choose." Cricket dipped his head out of respect, and only twitched a little when Adler fell into a deep bow before turning to Claudia. "Claudia, you and I are going to come up with some method to track the flow of magic in the land. I don't think a talisman will do it, but an array maybe?"

Claudia hummed in thought, but a spark had been lit in her eyes behind her glasses like she was excited by the prospect of finally getting to put her mind to work. "It'd have to be quite large. I'm talking around the entire capital."

"Then we have our work cut out for us." Cricket tilted his head, and felt the corners of his mouth twitch up in a smile. Stars, it had been so long since his face had done that, it was almost foreign feeling now. "Let's begin at once."

CHAPTER 8

This was not the best plan Takayoshi had ever come up with. But it was the only one that seemed to have a reasonable chance of actually working with what they had on hand, and the time constraints he was put under.

Ideally, he would have waited for reinforcements to come from Cricket. He would have learned more about the ins and outs of Craven's men and the little village where he was currently residing. He would have had contingencies for his contingencies.

Leo's desperation allowed for none of these things. Takayoshi had to throw something together in a matter of hours, and be ready for the rescue mission by the time the moon was on her descent.

"If anything goes wrong—" Takayoshi said.

"I know, I know. Run like my life depends on it." Leo huffed.

Leo was probably not going to do as he was instructed. He rarely did. But Takayoshi hoped that he would at least take into account that if Leo were to be caught, then that would be another rescue mission Takayoshi had to stage, and they did not have time to be fooling around up here on the mountain when they needed to get back to Cricket and tell him all they had found.

"And I will get Estia out," Takayoshi finished and shook his head. "Leo." He reached over to give his shoulder a firm squeeze, drawing Leo's gaze to meet his own. "You can trust me with this. I will ensure Estia is safe."

"I do trust you. It's just . . ."

Takayoshi understood perhaps better than any one of their other friends might how Leo felt in this exact moment. He had struggled many times to trust Cricket's safety to others. To believe that someone else would take the same risks he did to protect the thing most precious to him. It was why coming up the mountain to seek out Craven's forces when there was a war brewing had been so difficult for him. Why every step that he put between himself and Cricket had sunk into his bones making him heavy as lead with guilt and betrayal. But he also understood that sometimes the best way to protect the person one loved was to leave them behind for a short time. It was not ideal, but it was the truth.

"I will get zir out," he vowed, and Leo nodded, finally appeased.

They used the trees as cover for as long as they could, creeping ever closer to the village until they reached the tree line that was the closest. Even then, there was some feet of open field between the trees and the nearest building. And with the moon near full, the space was too well lit for either of them to make their way across unnoticed.

Just before they parted ways, Takayoshi grabbed Leo's forearm and gave it a firm squeeze. "Do not get caught."

"I don't plan to." Leo winked, and disappeared into the

forest around them while Takayoshi settled in to wait for his signal.

It did not take long for chaos to ensue. Leo, it seemed, was good at stirring things up when he had a mind to, which was amusing because as far as Takayoshi had known him, Leo had been the type to remain in the shadows. To hide away beyond notice and allow others to shine. They had that in common. But hearing the shouts from the village and watching as Leo ran about each pass gathering more and more people chasing him, Takayoshi saw how Leo could be an agent of mischief the likes of which even Cricket would approve of.

A delighted laugh ran through the dark night, proving even further that Leo was enjoying the commotion he was causing.

One more pass and Leo whistled loudly, the signal, before running for the trees on the opposite side of the village.

Takayoshi knew it would not be enough to draw all of Craven's men. They would not be foolish enough to not realize that Leo was some kind of distraction. But he hoped that Leo would have drawn enough attention to make his entrance into the village, at the very least, go unnoticed.

That part seemed to be going to plan, Takayoshi was relieved to find, as he crossed the distance from the tree line to the village with none the wiser. But Takayoshi did not believe his luck would hold out, so he took his time, cowering in the shadows of the village, hoping that no one would notice the white clad figure skulking around in the dark.

It was a gamble to move slower. It put him less at risk of being caught, but increased the likelihood that those following Leo would catch up to him. All Takayoshi could hope was that Leo had the endurance to keep them at bay, and that his leg did not cause him too much pain after the fact.

Finding the place where they were keeping Estia was surprisingly simple. It was one of the larger homes in the village, likely built by the owners themselves as it did not match the others that Cricket had built some time ago. The people who owned it were a little more well off than the others, but not too much so, probably the mayor or governor.

It was also the only home with lights still lit on the inside. While all the other homes slept, this one's windows glowed faintly from some deep interior room.

Takayoshi held his breath for a moment, and listened. The world was quiet around him, even the sounds of those pursuing Leo had faded off into the distance, but he was trained for this, good at listening to the noises that others would miss.

Boot steps on wood. A floorboard creaking beneath someone's weight. There was at least one person still on guard, left behind by the others to ensure Estia did not escape on zir own. Although how they thought ze would do that after the beating ze had endured, Takayoshi was uncertain.

Was it Craven, or one of his soldiers?

Craven would be abed at this point. He would not stand guard outside his sibling's door. He was not the same kind of king Cricket was, not as willing to get his hands dirty and inconvenience himself. So it had to be a soldier. Someone trained to fight, although how well, Takayoshi had no way of knowing. Another gamble. He did not like all of these chances they were taking with their lives and with the lives of the villagers. But perhaps his uncle was right about Takayoshi at least in this, he was far more impulsive than he had ever let on growing up.

Enough time wasting. Leo would run out of steam soon, and he and Estia needed to be clear of the village by that point. Takayoshi pulled the scarf tied around his neck up over his nose and mouth to hide his face and slid his hood further down over his hair. It was not common knowledge that Leo was officially a part of Cricket's court, not yet, but everyone knew about the romance between Takayoshi and the king of Lunette. Him taking part in this rescue mission might very well be seen as an act of war, and Takayoshi did not wish to speed things along any more than he had to.

An addendum to the plan that sorely hindered Takayoshi's ability to fight. He could not use the phoenix fire; he could not use his wings. But he could scale the outside of the house using the lattice, and climb through a window.

Moonlight poured in through the curtains as he brushed them out of his way, illuminating a room with a canopy bed, and animals painted on the walls. Tucked in the corner was a chest overflowing with toys.

An ache seized Takayoshi's chest, making his steps falter. He missed Becka as much as he missed Cricket, and this reminder of her left him more homesick than he had ever been.

The child was not there. The family must have been chased out of their home by Craven, and forced to take up residence elsewhere. Takayoshi hoped they had been able to take some of the child's favorite toys in their rush to leave, and that perhaps they were staying with someone who had a child of their own so that they could play together. It was a silly, idle daydream, and it cost him precious seconds that he did not have to spare.

He would ask after the family once they were free of this place. Not that there was anything he could do for them, but it would bring him some peace of mind to know they were unharmed, and hopefully happy.

His footfalls were silent as he crept across the room to peek through the crack between door and frame out into the hall.

Estia was being kept a couple of doors down, judging by

the guard pacing outside that room. The figure's stride was confident, and sure. Their shoulders back, their chin high. Either overconfident or highly trained.

Well. Takayoshi was about to find out which.

With careful movements he tucked himself behind the door, then kicked the door shut hard enough to make it slam.

He heard the guard on the other side jolt, but they did not yelp. Well trained then.

Their footsteps were cautious as they made their way down the hall to the child's room at the end.

Takayoshi shifted his weight, letting the floor beneath him creak, to draw them closer. Just a little closer. He just needed them a little closer.

Under normal circumstances, this would not have worked, Takayoshi recognized that. There should have been more than one guard. He should not have even been able to get close to the house, much less inside of it. Whether luck, arrogance, or the gods were on his side, Takayoshi did not know, and he did not care.

The guard turned the knob, and pushed inside to look about the room. From Takayoshi's position beside the door, their back was to him, and while it may have been dishonorable there was too much else at stake. Takayoshi brought the hilt of his sword down with all his might against the back of their head, and they stumbled under the force of the blow.

They spun, their own sword already unsheathed, swinging wildly at their assailant. Takayoshi had just enough space to step out of the way, the blade still managing to tear a hole in the front of his tunic. They stumbled again, steps faltering as the blow affected their balance. It gave Takayoshi the moment he needed to ram his shoulder into their sternum, sending them toppling to the ground where they hit their head again, this time on the edge of the bed.

They went down hard. Body thumping loudly against the

floor. Hard enough that Takayoshi worried maybe he had done more damage than he originally intended, but upon checking he found they were still breathing.

Relief rushed through him, but there was not a second to waste on it as Takayoshi rose and went for the hall.

The door was locked, but not in any way that would keep someone like him from busting through it. Which begged the question, why had Estia not tried to escape yet? His sword made quick work of the knob, and it swung inward to reveal a room without windows. A closet, more like.

There was only space for the cot pushed against the wall, and a narrow walkway.

What little light came from the hallway illuminated a shape under a thin woolen blanket.

"Estia," Takayoshi called. It could be a trap. He was not about to be caught unawares. His sword remained at the ready, and he did not allow himself to step inside lest someone shut the door behind him.

A groan came from the lump of blankets. Then, Estia sat up, peering at him through eyes swollen from lack of sleep, tears, or abuse, or perhaps all three there was no way to tell in the dim lighting. "Leo?"

"He is waiting for us outside of the village. You must rise, and we will go to him."

"Yoshi." Estia nodded to zirself as if understanding had finally dawned on zir. "We can't leave."

"Why not?" Takayoshi frowned, his grip on his sword tightening to the point that the hilt would leave imprints on his palm. This still may be a trap. He wanted to help Estia, but he was not foolish enough to think that Estia may not still be working with zir sibling. That the whole thing in the town square had not been staged to draw Leo out. What purpose that would serve, he did not know, but he was not about to trust Estia until ze had earned that trust again.

"Craven. . ." Estia panted a little, a hitch in zir breath making it obvious that ze was in pain. "He has my siblings. And he'll. . ."

"You cannot help your siblings from here." Takayoshi did not give Estia the chance to argue. He rushed across the small space, and pulled Estia to zir feet. Ze wobbled, whimpering softly at the pain of being handled so roughly. "You must take care of yourself first, then you can focus on others."

Estia barked a laugh, but the sound ended in another sob of pain. "Is that something your prince has taught you?"

"Yes. It is." Takayoshi began to lead them to the door, not waiting for Estia to agree or protest further. If ze had some issue with their plan, ze could take that up with Leo. Takayoshi's part was merely to get Estia to the rendezvous point. He would fulfill that obligation because he had promised Leo, and he took his promises very seriously.

"I'll only slow you down," Estia argued. Ze did not fight any further against Takayoshi's efforts to get them to the front door, which was good. They were quickly running out of time.

"Then we had better get started right away." The night had grown warmer, day fast approaching, but Leo's efforts to lead the guards away had not been in vain. Even with their slow progress, Takayoshi managed to get Estia to the tree line before the day broke.

"You don't have to save me, you know." Estia limped along beside him. More than once in their journey to the woods ze had nearly lost consciousness. Zir form going limp so that Takayoshi had to practically carry zir.

"I made a promise to Leo."

"He wouldn't hold it against you if you failed. He's good like that."

"I beg to differ." Takayoshi snorted softly, and continued on their way. He knew Leo well enough to know that if he had failed Leo may not say so out loud, but he most definitely would have held a grudge. Not that it mattered. He had not failed, and he would continue to not fail. Not where the people he cared for were concerned.

CHAPTER 9

"Usually, I would do this sort of tracking array in blood." Cricket squatted behind one of the many buildings at the edge of the capital, leaning his weight back against the wall. His legs were growing tired from all of this, but the array to track what where the magic from the land was going needed to be done in one go. They couldn't space it out over a couple of days. If any bit of the paint flaked away in the in-between it wouldn't work at all.

Claudia gave a soft questioning hum, not looking up from where she was working to paint the characters she'd been assigned for this cardinal direction.

"It makes the whole magic more effective." Cricket brushed his wrist against his forehead, mindful of the antlers and the scales that tended to itch. It had been a long couple of hours, and they were only about halfway through. He wished there was more than just himself and Claudia that he trusted to do this, but no one else was as well versed in magical theory, and he couldn't afford for this thing to do something it ought not to. It could be inert and do nothing, he was fine with that. But one wrong character and the whole of the capital could be sucked into a sinkhole , or set on fire, or disappear entirely. There was too much chance of something going wrong.

"Then there's some chance it won't work at all?" Claudia only sounded a little bothered by this prospect.

"Any theory has the chance of not working." Cricket stood, and stretched out his back with an exaggerated pop. One would think that being a celestial would mitigate some of the wear his body took after not treating it correctly—also known as sleeping at his desk, and yes he knew it was wrong, thank you Ignacia—but it did not. The aches and pains still settled deep into his bones. "You know that as well as I do."

Claudia nodded, pushing herself to her feet and gathering their supplies. The long handled rolling brush she'd created to draw the circle was a goddess send on their backs. But it did require a rather heavy bucket of paint which Cricket was in charge of pushing around in a wheelbarrow. One of the wheels screeched as they started up again.

"Don't let Ignacia hear you say that," Claudia said after they'd started walking again. "She finds this whole thing tedious, and then to find out we didn't actually learn what was leaching the magic from the land?" She shook her head.

Cricket couldn't keep down the laugh that burbled up his throat at the very idea. He knew Ignacia better than Claudia herself did, and the idea of her tantrum at finding out that this whole thing might be a waste of time was absolutely priceless. If he'd thought of it, he likely would have brought her along just for sheer amusement. But he hadn't. His head had been too full of all the things that could go wrong if they didn't get this sorted in a reasonable time. Of dead plants, and leeched soil. Of a kingdom on the brink of starvation and a war they didn't even know was coming. The thought sobered him a little, and the soft chuckle turned wry.

"Someone needed to stay behind to make sure Becka

actually attends her lessons." Not that he thought Ignacia was capable of making Becka do anything she didn't want to. She was a stubborn one, his daughter. He wondered where she got that from.

Claudia seemed to know this too because she barked a laugh.

"Also, Ignacia's magical theory work is subpar." Cricket paused in his pushing of the wheelbarrow to let Claudia dip the roller before they started again.

Claudia cut him a glare over the top of her glasses. "She has other skills."

"She does," Cricket agreed readily with a nod. It was nice to see that Claudia could be as protective of Ignacia as Ignacia was of her. He wished they had more time for him to better see their relationship, just to make sure it was what was best for both of them. But there wasn't, and so he'd just have to trust Ignacia's judgment on this. "You don't have to get defensive with me. Iggy's my sister, and I love her dearly. She's good at a great many things, but magical theory isn't one of them."

Claudia hummed, satisfied with this answer.

They stopped at the next cardinal point, and set to work on the characters that needed to be placed in the south.

"This is the last one," Claudia said, shifting onto her toes so she could better reach over the large 'vegetation' character she was constructing. "If it doesn't work, will we try again in blood?"

Cricket frowned and scrubbed at the tip of his nose, an anxious tick he'd never quite grown out of. "It would take too long, I think."

"Why? We can always get cattle from—"

"No. It has to be my blood." Cricket rubbed his nose again, no doubt making the skin red and irritated. It was amazing it wasn't raw with how often he'd been doing that of late, unable to quill the anxiousness that had settled into his very bones. It had only gotten worse since Takayoshi left. Like Cricket was missing the anchor that kept him from drifting away.

"Why?" Claudia looked up from her work, and frowned.

"There can't be any competing magical signatures. Not in blood magic." Cricket shook his head.

"But cows don't—"

"They do. Everything living does. Even the plants we used to create pigment in this paint." Cricket brushed his fingers along the tips of the bristles, rubbing the red between his fingertips in thought. "Even this has its own signature."

"Then should we be using it?"

"We don't exactly have any other choice." Cricket sighed tilting his head back to stare up at the sky for a moment. Clouds were rolling in, threatening rain. They had to hurry and finish this before then or all their work would be for not. "And besides, the magical signature in this is mostly faded. I'll be able to overwhelm it with a few drops of my own blood. It'll be fine."

Claudia didn't look entirely convinced, but she also didn't look like she wanted to argue with him over it, so she set back to her work. Cricket followed suit, and a while later they were finished.

Rocking back on his heels, Cricket brushed his hands together to clear away the dust, and cocked his head to look down at the last of the characters. "That should do it."

"Do what, exactly?" Claudia asked. She'd helped him create the array, carefully choosing characters that would draw on Cricket's magic to trace the spell sapping the land, but—

"Unclear." Cricket didn't really know what it would do either. It wasn't something anyone had ever used before, especially on this scale, and there was no knowing what form the information they needed would take. Would it be a line like on a map? Or would it be the persistent tug he had felt when he used something similar in Nishi all those years ago? "But we're about to find out."

"Should I stand back?"

"Couldn't hurt." Cricket pulled the dagger from his waist, and rolled up his sleeve to expose an arm marred with scales and scars. Teeth marks from hungry spirits, cuts from magic, and even a deep gouge from where his uncle had tried to end his life. He was a patchwork of scars these days. Marred by all the things he'd dealt with since the year he came of age. But he was stronger for all of them, because he had survived. Because he was still able to remain upright and protect his people. That didn't change how the bite of a blade in his forearm made him hiss.

Silence swallowed them up, broken only by the rush of his heartbeat in Cricket's ears and the *drip-drip-drip* of blood on hard, dried soil. It splattered, not even seeming able to soak in, casting droplets onto his boots, making them glisten in the fading light.

Cricket held his breath as he waited, letting the magic flow out of him along with the blood falling directly on the line they had drawn all the way around the capital.

He waited.

He waited.

And he waited.

"Your Highness," Claudia said, her tone gentle as if afraid perhaps she might anger him, "it's not working."

"It has to." Cricket practically choked on the words where they lodged in his throat. "It *has* to work."

But it wasn't, he could see that. There was no reaction at all when his blood and magic touched the paint. No faint glow of the spell taking shape. No gentle tug at his sternum to lead him where he needed to go. Nothing. Just the steady drip of moisture on soil stripped dry of everything it needed to grow new life.

"It's not." Claudia took his wrist and pulled a bandage from the bag on her shoulder. "It's a failed experiment."

"Then we'll try again." Cricket cleared his throat, made himself stand taller even as the weight of this failure settled onto his shoulders threatening to drag him to the ground. He couldn't stop. There was no stopping. He needed a solution, and he needed it before the rot reached the cities, towns, and villages beyond the capital. Before his people were hurt by whatever was going on here.

"We will," Claudia agreed, tying off the bandage carefully. "We'll keep trying until we have an answer. For now, let's head back. The rain will begin soon. And you ought to get cleaned up. Word is Yoshi and Leo will be returning shortly, and I don't particularly want to deal with all the fuss Yoshi will kick up if he comes home to find you bleeding all over the place."

"I'm not bleeding all *over the place*." Cricket rolled his eyes, but after a shared look, he sighed. She was right, Takayoshi would not be happy if he were to return and find Cricket injured.

"You're not the one he'd glare at over the dinner table." She dropped the brush into the wheelbarrow and started back into the capital.

"That's not entirely true. He's just as likely to turn that disapproving stare of his on me as he is on you." Cricket chuckled, shaking his head, then followed along beside her, pulling his sleeve down over his arm to hide the bandage. But the sleeve itself had gotten stained in blood somehow. He'd likely have to throw the whole tunic away, there seemed no way to dissolve blood stains caused by celestials. Strangely enough.

"Yes, but he finds it difficult to hold a grudge against you. Me, on the other hand? He's definitely likely to hold a grudge against me." Claudia was smiling a little, and the gentle teasing eased a part of Cricket he hadn't realized until that moment that he was holding still. His muscles relaxed, his shoulders fell away from his ears. It was nice, he realized, to be like this with people even when things were going wrong all around them. "And he can be awfully petty when he wants to."

"Nonsense, my future husband is beyond reproach," Cricket joked, his steps suddenly feeling lighter. Takayoshi would be home soon. And with one more person with a head for magical theory, they would work this out.

Claudia turned to look at him, one brow raised high on her face, the movement making her spectacles rise a little with it. "Beyond reproach you say? I suppose he's also a pillar of purity and manners as well?"

"Well, of course." Cricket nodded, his chin tilting back for a moment in a gesture that was decidedly arrogant. But it was hard to hold onto the pose for long and a moment later both he and Claudia were laughing. "Stop. Stop." He chuckled swatting at her.

Then something seized him, a thought he couldn't push away: he had failed today.

"Your Highness?" Claudia asked, seeming to notice the sudden shift in mood.

"I love him, you know," Cricket said softly, unable to really put words to the feeling of dread gripping his middle like ice. "I love him desperately."

"I know that." Claudia frowned. "Everyone knows that. Even him, although it took him long enough to realize it."

"It took me long enough to realize it too." Cricket rubbed at the bandage through the fabric of his sleeve.

"He doesn't hold that against you." Claudia stopped in the middle of the street, ignoring the people bustling around them to take his hands.

It was amazing how few people even seemed to notice them when Cricket wasn't dressed in full royal garb. Or maybe they were avoiding looking at him on purpose. There was no good way to tell.

"You know he doesn't."

"I just. . ." Cricket swallowed, his grip tightening on Claudia. "He's going to come back, and I'm going to have to tell him I failed at this."

"You only fail if you quit," Claudia said, simple as breathing, then she dropped his hands and started walking again. "And you haven't quit yet, have you?"

Cricket stood for a moment watching her back as she made her way slowly toward the castle, shaken by her words. She was right. He hadn't quit yet. And he wasn't going to. Not until he knew his people were safe.

CHAPTER 10

There was no fanfare when Takayoshi returned to the capital of Lunette. No parades. No hordes of people wanting to know how his mission had gone, and hear exciting tales. It was just Cricket standing at the gate with Becka beside him, her hand in his so he could keep her from running out into the street to greet Takayoshi. And Takayoshi found he honestly liked this better.

When he had returned to Helios after his first quest to help the common people, the crowds that surrounded him had been suffocating. Bearing down on him, even when their prince was widely known to not want that kind of attention. It seemed it could not be helped when one had once upon a time been the heir to the throne. He also wondered if perhaps his sister had something to do with it. A misplaced kindness.

"I didn't let the guard spread it around that you'd be home today," Cricket said when Takayoshi approached, his head tilted back to give Takayoshi a secret smile. Like they were sharing some kind of inside joke. It warmed Takayoshi to his very toes, making his clothing almost stifling in the late spring air. But he liked it just the same. Liked the warmth that radiated from Cricket, making Lunette feel like home in a way Helios never had.

"I appreciate that consideration." Takayoshi slid from his horse, and bent to scoop Becka into a hug that sent them both twirling into a circle. She laughed, her giggles filling the small space of the gate, lifting them up, and lightening the load of what Takayoshi would have to tell Cricket once they had retired to his offices.

"You're home. You're home," Becka chanted, her arms tight around his neck. She had grown in the week or so since he had been gone, which seemed impossible, but Takayoshi could tell the difference. Their little sunflower was sprouting up like a weed. She would make a fine queen one day.

"I am home," Takayoshi agreed, giving her one final squeeze before he put her on her feet once more. "And I have brought news."

"And a new friend, it would seem." Cricket tilted his head and narrowed his gaze on where Estia and Leo were sharing Leo's horse as if trying to see through the shadows that hid Estia from the world. "We have much to discuss?"

"We do." Takayoshi nodded. But that could wait a moment more. The war was not at their gates yet. He could take the time to greet his family, and to bask in the happiness of seeing them again. So he reached for Cricket next, pulling him close to his chest, and tilting his head back gently. "Have I missed much?"

Cricket's eyes darted away for a moment, clearly upset by something, but when they returned, he smiled gently. "Nothing that cannot wait until you've given me a kiss hello."

Takayoshi hummed, and dipped his head to press his lips to Cricket's. Before finding his soul mate, before gaining the powers of a phoenix and seeing color, Takayoshi had not been the type for such public displays of affection. He found he did not mind so much now. The press of Cricket against him, warm, and safe, and whole, added to the growing happiness in his chest, spreading through his veins like a drug and leaving him dizzy with it.

He was home.

"You better come inside before people start staring," Ignacia called forever and too soon later, drawing them apart. "We can't have them thinking you two have consummated your vows before your wedding."

Cricket pulled back to sputter, embarrassment coloring his cheeks rosy. "Not in front of the children, Iggy," he chided, and covered Becka's ears.

Ignacia raised a brow high on her face, her lips twitching a little at the corners as if she found this all very funny. "If you're talking about yourself, I'm afraid you're covering the wrong person's ears."

"Iggy!"

Takayoshi chuckled softly, the sound vibrating in his chest, his whole body buzzing with the feeling. But when he felt Estia and Leo at his back, he knew that Ignacia had a point. "She is right. Let us go inside, and we can catch each other up."

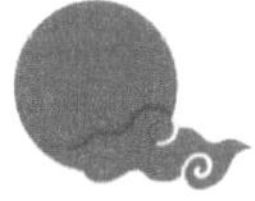

TAKAYOSHI WANTED nothing more than to scoop Cricket up into his arms, and hide him away from everything that was coming for them. For one whose personality was so large, Cricket suddenly seemed so small as they shared information, and the weight of what was to come settled heavily on his shoulders. Not that he wasn't holding the weight well, but the enormity of their problems seemed to dwarf them all.

"You will not be alone in this," Takayoshi said when the information was all shared. When he knew of the land being sapped of life and magic, and Cricket had heard of Estia and zir predicament. "You will have me, and our friends, and I will speak to my sister about sending reinforcements."

Cricket's hands squeezed into tight fists where they rested on the arms of his chair, and he sucked down a deep breath, struggling with something. "Would they even make it here in time?"

"I cannot promise that."

Cricket nodded, his shoulders sagging a little.

"But I can promise that even if they do not, we will make this work. We will protect our people. I will stand by your side. You will be the king you were always meant to be. And in the end, he will be painted as the villain." Takayoshi fully understood that the weight of expectation was crushing, but he knew too that somehow Cricket would not crumble beneath it. A marvel, that is what Cricket was. A miracle in elven form. And it was a privilege to stand by his side, to be there for him when he was in need. Takayoshi did not know how to say all of this out loud, the words lodged in his throat, getting stuck there, but he wished that he could. Wished he could do more than simply hold onto Cricket while the storm raged around them.

"He will try to paint me as *weak*." Cricket spat the word as if it tasted vile.

"The world will know better. Your people will see you as wise, for asking for help to protect them when you need it." Takayoshi desperately wanted to pinch the bridge of his nose to ward off the impending headache from being on the road for too long, but his hands were otherwise occupied in reaching for Cricket's to force his fingers open. He had squeezed so tightly that the nails had begun to dig bloody crescents into the meat of his palms. "And besides that,

Helios is family. We may not be married yet, but we very soon will be, and then my sister will be your sister."

"Do you need me to help draft the message?" Cricket asked with a world weary sigh, and a reminder shot through Takayoshi like a hollow ache of who Cricket had been before all this began. Of the silly little prince he had first met on the road years ago. Smiling, always smiling, and so bright that he outshone the sun. Takayoshi missed that boy sometimes, but the missing did nothing to dull the loving of the man Cricket had grown into. He only wished it had not wounded Cricket quite so much to become him.

"I think that would be best, my king." Although Takayoshi knew very well that if he were to ask Atsuko for help, she would have forces on their way come morning. But Takayoshi would not undermine him that way. They had built their relationship on mutual respect, and he could not go against that, would not. "But bear in mind that it will take time for Helios' forces to get here."

"I know. A month at best." Cricket nodded, his jaw working as if he were chewing on the inside of his cheek. "We will do what we must, even still. Let's handle that now, get it out of the way."

"Of course, my king." Takayoshi dipped his head, and pulled a mirror from his pocket which he set on the desk between them. With a single tap to the glass, and a murmur of his sister's name, their reflection disappeared and was replaced with that of Atsuko.

"Brother!" Atsuko's smile was wide, her eyes crinkling at the edges. "How are things?"

"Not well, I am afraid." Takayoshi shook his head, and leaned back to allow Cricket room to be visible as well.

"What's happened?" His sister's face fell, her dark eyes flicking between their faces.

"Craven is within Lunette territory," Cricket said, his

voice devoid of emotion as he relayed all they had spoken of in the last few minutes.

Takayoshi watched as his sister's face drained of color the longer Cricket went on, and when it was all through, she sat there, clearly unsure of what to say.

"All this to say," Cricket sighed, "we need reinforcements. I know it'll take time for them to get here, but the sooner they're on their way—"

"I'll send what forces I can," Atsuko agreed readily. "But," she inhaled deeply, chewing on the inside of her cheek, "my people were likewise hit hard by Sunil's attack. We are also still rebuilding. I can't guarantee that they will be enough."

"Anyone you can spare, we would greatly appreciate."

"Of course."

Even as they agreed, Takayoshi had the feeling that they would not make it in time. Not in time for the fight, at least. But they may make it in time to help with the ensuing clean up, and that would have to be enough. He shut the mirror after a brief goodbye, and they both slumped back into their chairs.

"What else was Estia able to tell us about Craven's plans? Did ze know anything about whatever spell is at work in the capital?"

"Ze just said it was something we had seen before." Takayoshi's stomach rolled at the reminder of that conversation, at how it had angered and terrified him all at once. "Ze said," he swallowed hard, licking his lips. He had wanted to avoid telling Cricket this part, because he knew it would upset him. But there was no avoiding it, and they had decided recently to be honest with one another whenever they could. This was something Takayoshi should not keep to himself. "Ze said that the curses you faced, and the monsters guarding the map pieces were all experiments. Craven was testing spells to decide what methods would best suit his war effort."

"He's been planning this that long?" Cricket paled, his hands going cold in an instant, enough that to touch them made Takayoshi's own joints ache. But he did not pull away, he could not, when Cricket looked so clearly distraught. "Since Sunil's first attack? That's been. . . Takayoshi, that's been at least five years."

"Yes, I am aware." Takayoshi's heart thudded hard against his rib cage. Five years. Craven had been preparing to take over Lunette for five years. "I believe the plan all along was to help Sunil kill Jaxith and unseat you, then take advantage of the turmoil left behind, and slay Sunil."

"Why?"

"I do not know." But he wished that he did know for certain. He wished he had an explanation for all of this that would make it make sense to them. That would make this feel less personal and more calculated. There was nothing. "Have you ever had any dealings with Craven before?"

"Nothing." Cricket shook his head. His fingers flexed in Takayoshi's hold as if he wanted to pull away, but Takayoshi would not let go. Not while Cricket looked so clearly upset. He would not leave him alone to drift. "I have not spoken to him anymore than any of the other nobles, which hasn't been much. Father always . . . Well, he let me play too much, I suppose."

Guilt drew Cricket's brows together, and Takayoshi desperately wanted to reach up and brush away the wrinkle that formed there. But that would mean releasing Cricket.

"I do not think that is a bad thing. You learned compassion for your people, and were unsullied by greed." Something Takayoshi could not say of many of their peers. He had not been quite so lucky to be kept away from court politics, and allowed to simply be a child as Cricket had. His uncle had been too busy trying to change his mind about abdicating the throne, and thus had forced him to interact with the other nobles. It was not an activity that Takayoshi had much cared for, but it did give him some perspective. "Craven is greedy. He saw an opening, likely from befriending Sunil. Sunil no doubt was more than happy to air his displeasure with someone he thought he could trust."

"Of course." Cricket's shoulders slumped under this realization. Expectation. A coming war. A kingdom in chaos. None of that had been enough to make Cricket curl in on himself, but the reminder that his uncle had never cared for him, had never seen him as family. It was a hard blow.

Takayoshi could not imagine what it would feel like to know that his own family had never loved him. It was enough to know that his uncle disapproved of his relationship with Cricket. But he knew that was nothing compared to what Sunil had done.

"And I'm sure he never shied away from telling everyone about the filthy parasite his brother was—"

"None of that." Takayoshi tugged on his hands, practically ripping Cricket from his seat, and pulling him into his arms. It was a tight fit, Cricket on Takayoshi's lap in the armchair in the corner of his study, but Takayoshi did not care. It was better to have Cricket there, safe, surrounded, than allow him to shoulder this alone. "What Sunil did was no reflection on you, or the love your father had for you. It was a reflection on the kind of person he was, and that is to say, not a good one. And perhaps Craven thought Sunil would be the weaker adversary, easier to overthrow once you and your father were out of the way."

Cricket made a soft sound of agreement, but it did not sound terribly convinced.

Takayoshi smothered the sigh that threatened to make him slouch as well. He would not give in to his own melancholy. He had done far too much of that throughout his life. So instead, he tilted his head down closer to Cricket's, and bumped their foreheads together lightly to draw Cricket out of himself. "We should go down to the training room and spar."

"We should?" Cricket perked up a little, his eyes suddenly bright.

"Mm. We should."

CHAPTER 11

It was late, far later than Cricket was accustomed to staying awake recently. He had begun rising with the sun to stay on top of the paperwork that seemed to pile up overnight, and to keep Ignacia from complaining about his sleeping habits. It wasn't right for a king to lay about in bed until past noon. But that meant going to bed earlier.

And now it was full dark, and the rest of the castle slept around them. Cricket had not realized how late it was while he and Takayoshi sat in his father's study discussing what came next. It was amazing how long they could talk now after so many years of silence spanned between them.

Cricket hadn't the faintest inclination when he dropped into the chair across from Takayoshi a few years—and a lifetime—ago, how their relationship and the stoic white knight would change. Takayoshi had looked at him like he was something vile then, hardly even seemed able to get a few words out to chase Cricket off from his mission. But now they spent hours together, discussing all they learned and planning for the future. And Cricket found comfort in the way Takayoshi spoke, in the cadence of his voice. He was so sturdy, and certain. Like he'd seen into the future and found them victorious.

It was more than Cricket could have hoped for from a partner, a husband. He had spent his entire life thinking one day he'd rule alone, and now he had this person at his side who kept him grounded, and reminded him every day that he could do this.

Someone who reminded him to have fun, even if that fun was sparring.

He had gotten terribly lucky.

Takayoshi left his side for a moment, going to the weapons cabinet to retrieve two practice swords. They could spar with real weapons of course, but it would likely be better if they didn't injure themselves, however minor, with a battle coming to their doorstep.

Cricket caught the practice sword by the hilt, squeezing the grip tight enough it dug into his palms. "It feels strange to be holding a sword again."

"Then you will be easy to beat." Takayoshi's eyes crinkled at the corners in a teasing smile, and Cricket was briefly breathless. This had been happening more and more as the weeks went on. They were able to joke, to laugh, to be friends as well as something more. And Cricket was struck silly by it.

It was funny falling in love with your husband.

Husband.

He could say that now. Because Takayoshi would soon be his husband, there was not a force on earth or in the heavens that would stop it. Craven could bring his war to their door, but he would not stop Takayoshi and Cricket from being together. And Cricket fell in love with Takayoshi a little more every day.

He laughed, startled by the happiness burning in his chest. It had snuck up on him. Made its way into his very bones without him having realized it. Just the way Takayoshi did now, striking out to slash at Cricket's torso while his guard was down.

Cricket yelped, and stumbled through a hasty parry. "Yoshi! We didn't say start!"

"Neither will our enemies," Takayoshi said in a tone so serious it almost belied the amused glint in his eye.

"You are laughing at me," Cricket accused, holding his sword up to point at Takayoshi. "You are laughing at your king."

"So what if I am?" Takayoshi batted away Cricket's raised sword with an easy strike, his movements smooth and unhurried. The grace of a man who had been using a sword since he was old enough to hold one. Cricket would never measure up to Takayoshi's skill, not when he hadn't taken his own practice half as seriously, but he had one thing Takayoshi did not, the willingness to fight dirty.

"Then I suppose I'll have to silence you."

Takayoshi lifted one pale brow, his lips twitching a little with a hidden smile, but Cricket did not give him a moment to consider what was to come next. He lunged, thrusting his wooden blade forward at the same time he stomped his foot hard against the floor beneath them. Ice spread from the sole of his boot, racing across the floor to climb up Takayoshi's leg, gluing down one foot while the other moved to evade Cricket's sword.

The movement caused Takayoshi to over balance, and even with his superior footwork he could not avoid stumbling back. Cricket retracted the ice quick enough to avoid Takayoshi breaking his leg, but not before Takayoshi skidded across the surface and fell flat on his backside in the middle of the training room.

Takayoshi huffed a laugh, letting his head fall to the floor when Cricket stepped over him to press the point of his wooden sword beneath Takayoshi's chin.

"Point in my favor, I think." Cricket grinned, a little bit of the mischievous wickedness that he'd known in his boyhood resurfacing. He felt like himself, for perhaps the first time in years. Takayoshi seemed to know this, to realize that this was what Cricket had needed all along, his expression turned unbearably smug.

"My king has gotten better since last we sparred." Takayoshi's words lilted in such a way to make him sound like he was forcing back a chuckle. It was adorable. And Cricket found himself hopelessly fond of Takayoshi and his antics. He bent to help Takayoshi to his feet, and fell back into his stance.

"His betrothed was simply distracted." It was false modesty, and they both knew it, but Cricket loved falling into the push and pull of a conversation with Takayoshi like this. It was like a dance, or a duel all its own. Each lunging and dodging with words while they circled one another in the middle of the training room.

"His Highness thinks too highly of my skills, I assure you." Takayoshi stepped lightly over the still frozen patch of floor, his sword never once lowering. For at the end of the day, even if this was a game, Takayoshi was a well-trained knight and he would not lower his guard for anyone who still held a weapon.

"So humble!" Cricket crowed, lunging out again. The blow landed, a strike against Takayoshi's arm that he merely grunted under the pain of. "You are clearly a credit to white knights everywhere."

Takayoshi huffed another laugh, shaking his head. "No more tricks, Your Highness?"

"Now, Yoshi," Cricket cooed, parrying his next strike with ease. "That would be telling."

"I have methods of my own."

"Yes, but our weapons are wood! If you were to use your fire, the duel would end here and now."

"And what a pity that would be." Takayoshi moved quickly, his feet flying across the floor as blow after blow landed against Cricket's blade, backing him across the floor. Cricket may have been tricky, and light on his feet, but he knew that of the two of them Takayoshi had the superior power behind his strikes. He had the strength in his arms Cricket didn't. And in a battle of stamina, or brute force alone, Takayoshi would always win. "Come. Come. Your Highness, where is your fight?"

"Maybe I'm just luring you into a false sense of victory before I strike."

Takayoshi hummed, disbelieving, and their swords locked, the blades pressing so hard between them that Cricket could hear the wood groan under the force. "If you were going to do something clever, now would be the time," he teased, his face pressing in so close to Cricket's that Cricket could feel Takayoshi's hot breath on his lips.

"Who said it had to be clever?" Cricket quipped and lurched forward to press his lips to Takayoshi's, drawing a groan from Takayoshi that made Cricket's toes curl inside his boots. It was exactly the distraction he needed to shove Takayoshi away again, and slice at his middle with his sword, catching the fabric with the blunt tip. "Point to me."

Takayoshi chuckled, dry, and quiet, but his eyes were lit up with the kind of happiness Cricket had not seen when they first met. He was having *fun*. The novelty that Cricket could be the source of it would never wear off. "I hope you do not intend to kiss all of your opponents. Your future husband would get very jealous."

"I think he'd understand." Cricket shrugged, tilting his head from one side to the other to crack his neck. "He's the kind of man that knows sometimes you have to fight dirty to win."

"Then I concede to my king's superior skills." Takayoshi bowed low, a smile ticking up the corner of his lips. "Please, teach me your ways."

"Later." Cricket laughed, throwing down his sword and pulling a dagger from his boot. The blade shone bright in the light, sharp, and wicked. But they both knew he had enough control over himself and the weapon that he wouldn't hurt Takayoshi, even as he thrust the blade under Takayoshi's bent chin and forced him into a corner. "Point in my favor. That's three of five."

"You win." Takayoshi dropped his own weapon, it clattered to the floor, but Cricket hardly noticed. "What will be your prize?"

"Hmm. I wonder." Cricket moved onto his toes and pressed another kiss to Takayoshi's lips.

"I DIDN'T GIVE it to him," Estia announced as ze entered the room in chains. Although Leo and Takayoshi had saved zir, Cricket could not take any chances that this was another trick. Estia had been more than willing to betray them all once before, Cricket would not put them in a position to be betrayed again.

"The pearl?" Takayoshi asked. He shifted beside Cricket, carefully cautious, and guarded. He had disappeared back behind his mask this morning, tucking himself away after they'd had so much fun sparring the night before. But Cricket could understand that. After all, wasn't he doing the same?

There wasn't space for feelings here. Not with so much at stake.

"Yes, the pearl." Estia frowned, lifting zir hands to scrub at zir nose. The shackles around zir wrists clanked together. Cricket barely restrained a wince. He hated this. He hated it more than he'd hated anything his entire life, but he recognized that Estia had left them no choice.

"Why?" Cricket asked when the others were silent for far too long. It wasn't because no one else was curious, he was sure of that, but maybe more because they were stunned by the announcement.

"I just. . ." Estia sighed, tilting zir head back to stare at the ceiling a moment before ze dropped zir gaze to meet Cricket's eyes. "I just couldn't. I knew what he'd do with it, and I knew what that would do to Takayoshi, and I couldn't. You understand?"

"Yes. I think I do." More than he wanted to, in all honesty. It would be easier for him if Cricket didn't understand what Estia was dealing with. If he could separate himself from this, and punish Estia the way any other noble would. It was likely a sign of weakness that he couldn't. And he was sure he would pay for it in the end, just as he had paid for it with Sunil. But it was the right thing to do, and he thought perhaps his fa ther would be proud of him for his mercy. "What would you have me do, as payment for not turning my very will over to your tyrannical brother?"

"I didn't do it for—"

Cricket cut Estia a glare, and ze shifted under his stare. "Answer the question. Takayoshi told me that Craven has your family. That was why you betrayed your friends to begin with, isn't it?"

"Yes." Estia looked down at zir boots.

"So you want assistance in rescuing them."

"Yes."

"And you wish to go along on the rescue mission?" Cricket could understand that request too. In fact, he could understand everything Estia had done to this point. Every last action made perfect sense to him as a man who would walk through fire to save his family and his people. Who had made an exile of himself to keep his daughter safe.

"I don't like this," Leo said, his voice deep and gravelly.

"You never like anything, Lionel, darling," Estia tsked and lifted zir head to frown at Leo. Leo did not relent under the glare. "You're too cautious by half."

"You shouldn't be going. You have information we can use." Leo shook his head, his eyes flicking to Cricket's as if begging for help in this. Cricket *could* do that. He could order Estia to stay put. But it didn't seem ze was likely to listen. It would be forced house arrest. And maybe he ought to, after all Estia was dangerous in zir own right. Ze could betray them all over again by leading their forces to Craven for the slaughter.

"If we let you go, you will retrieve the pearl and return it to us?" This was likely his worst idea yet, but Cricket couldn't help his soft heart. He wanted Estia to have zir family back.

"Of course, Your Highness. I will do anything you ask of me as payment. I'll walk into Craven's camp as a spy, and burn it down with me still inside. I just. . . I just. . ." Estia stuttered, stopped. Swallowed roughly around a well of emotion that made the next words come out choked. "I just need to make sure they're safe."

"I cannot send a full contingent with you." Cricket drummed his fingers on the desk in front of him. Even if he had a full contingent of knights, which he did not, he wouldn't send them with Estia. Not at the chance that this all might be a distraction to lead Cricket's forces away from home so Craven could attack. "We need everyone we have for when your brother brings his war to our door."

"I understand."

"I will go," Takayoshi volunteered, his hand gripped tight around the sword at his waist the only outward sign that he was upset by the situation. "There are children in trouble, we should take this seriously."

Cricket resisted the urge to rub at the ache forming between his brows. He didn't *want* Takayoshi to go. He wanted Takayoshi to stay right there in the capital at his side where Cricket could keep him safe. But he'd learned long ago that Takayoshi was the stubborn sort and there was absolutely nothing Cricket could do to keep him from running headlong into danger once he set his mind to something.

"Wasn't it you who once went running off to solve curses for his people to prove that the crown cared for them?" Ignacia asked, a smug note to her tone.

"Iggy, you're *not* helping," Cricket growled, forgetting himself momentarily, the mask of the king slipping beneath his annoyance. He cleared his throat and lifted his chin. "But you are correct. We have to show that we are not afraid of Craven, and his forces, that we're willing to take risks to do what's right. But Estia . . ." He paused, waiting for Estia to meet his gaze again. "If something happens to my future husband under your watch, I will bring the rage of a dragon down upon your head."

"Of course Your Highness. I would expect nothing else." Estia dipped zir gaze.

"I'll go as well," Leo said.

"We'll take no one else." Takayoshi leaned in close enough that if he had wanted to he could rest his weight on Cricket's shoulder from where he stood, but he didn't. Cricket felt the heat of him through the scant space between them anyway. It was a reassurance he very much needed. "A smaller force will have a better chance of sneaking in and out without notice."

Leo nodded his agreement. "And if we manage to take out some of Craven's forces, so much the better."

"Very well." Cricket sat up straighter in his chair. "Ignacia, you will be in charge of seeing they are well armed, and supplied. Claudia, I want you to go over their route with Leo before they leave. Estia, you will tell them where you left the pearl. I will not send them away without a firm destination in mind. Am I clear?" That last order was only partly because Cricket wanted to know where they were going, and mainly because if he needed to send reinforcements their way, he needed to know where to send them to.

"Yes, Your Highness." Estia lifted zir head, and there was a hopeful glint in zir eye. Blast.

"Takayoshi, you must say goodbye to our daughter before you're off again, and deal with the tantrum that ensues." Cricket couldn't help the smile that lifted his lips at that thought. "You only just returned home."

"Yes, Your Highness," Takayoshi said, but this tone was far less stiff, and full of respect than Estia's. There was a teasing lilt to it.

"And we must go over the message we'll send to your sister," Cricket reminded, without saying any more on the subject. He may have been willing to provide Estia with the forces ze needed to see zir siblings safe again, but he did not trust zir enough to know that he planned to ask Helio for reinforcements.

BOOK II
THE SLEEP

CHAPTER 12

Becka did not throw tantrums. She was far too old, and dignified for such a thing. She did, however, have very strong opinions about things for a seven-year-old, and the ability to argue those opinions until she was blue in the face. She took after Cricket that way, and Takayoshi could not be prouder.

"You can't leave," Becka said, her arms crossed, her nose wrinkled in that exact same way she had the last time he'd told her he was leaving. It was a posture Takayoshi was reasonably sure Cricket had used years ago when they first met in Totchli. Obstinate and proud.

"I am afraid that I have to." Takayoshi hated disappointing her. Hated even more how he had spent so many years wondering what happened to her after her village burned and he was forced to move on for fear of losing the thread of information about Cricket's dragon. He knew she survived, because they had not found her remains, but he had not known Cricket adopted her until he returned to Lunette and she was there in Cricket's arms. Smiling and happy as if she had not a care in the world. Cricket had given her something Takayoshi never would have been able to back then, security. He was glad of it. "Estia has siblings as young as you that need rescuing. You would not want me to leave them waiting, would you?"

"Why can't someone else go? Aunt Iggy has so many capable knights. Why can't one of them go? Why does it have to be you?" Her nose wrinkled further if that were at all possible, and Takayoshi swore that he heard Cricket choking back a laugh, likely enjoying this small argument far too much. Which was not helping at all, but Takayoshi did not have it within himself to scold Cricket for his delight in this. He had few things to smile about lately, and who was Takyoshi to take one of them away?

"Because none of them can do this." Takayoshi turned his hand over, palm facing upward, and a flame danced over the skin, crackling merrily like a bonfire in the autumn. It was not the only reason of course. There were others. But Becka was not of an age quite yet to understand politics, or at least to find them important. To her there was nothing outside of her family and her people that could possibly need the attention of either of her fathers. Least of all some feud between another kingdom's siblings. It did not help that they had yet to tell her a war was coming. Both agreeing that they should protect her from it as long as they could after all she had seen. "I think that makes me vastly more qualified for the job, do you not?"

"Overqualified, I think," Cricket could not seem to help himself. When Takayoshi looked up at him, he was smiling, his eyes twinkling a little with delight.

"Right! Papa is right. You're overqualified. You shouldn't go, you should stay here, with me and Papa." Becka grabbed his hand, heedless of the danger Takayoshi's fire posed her. Not that it would burn her, it did not seem to burn any of

Cricket's little family. Likely because the power derived from Cricket to begin with.

"That might be so." Takayoshi nodded, and squeezed Becka's hand, matching her grip with his own. "But being overqualified just means I will return sooner."

"It had better." Becka huffed. "You just got back."

"I know." But more than that, it had not been that long since they had beaten Sunil. It felt like Takayoshi had not been given leave to rest, and be happy for more than a few scant weeks before he and Cricket were thrust into another battle. Would it ever end? Or was this to be their lives so long as they were together? Was the universe going to consistently try to tear them apart? Perhaps this was part of his curse. . .

"You know," Becka repeated, a bit of petulance creeping into her voice. "So why are you going?"

"I told you, I have to." Takayoshi brushed a bit of her hair back from her face. She was not pouting, not yet at least, but it was well on its way. "Please do not make this more difficult than it has to be. I do not want to go, but I must. And I will return as quickly as I can, I promise."

"You swear?"

"With all of my heart." Takayoshi vowed, and pulled his hand from hers to offer his pinky to her. She looped her little finger around his, and shook it hard enough that it jolted his shoulder. Gods, she had gotten so strong in the time he had been away. Cricket had done well in raising her into a princess who would one day be a powerful queen.

"A promise, is a promise," Becka said. She sounded like she might be threatening him, but it was too adorable to really take seriously, so Takayoshi just nodded solemnly.

"It is. And I will not—"

"Your Highness," someone said from behind him, making Takayoshi still where he knelt on the ground in front of Becka. The urge was there to reach for his sword, but one glance at Cricket told him that was unnecessary. "Pardon the interruption, sir."

"What is it?" Cricket asked.

Takayoshi rose from where he was kneeling and turned to face the knight who had interrupted their goodbyes. They were young, face still innocent, and youthful. Many of the knights were now that Sunil had killed or sacrificed most of Cricket's forces. It made them no less loyal, but they were green in a way Takayoshi did not like. How effective would they be once war came to Lunette?

"I apologize. I know you were saying—"

"What. Is. It." Cricket's tone was crisp making it clear his patience had worn thin in a way it had not since before he had found his pearl. It made the hairs on the back of Takayoshi's neck raise, and his muscles twitched on memory alone to reach out to Cricket and soothe him. But he could not do that in front of one of Cricket's men.

"It's the pixies, sir. The ones in the garden? They. . ." the knight paused, licking their lips as if nervous. "Well, you ought to see it for yourself."

"Becka, go inside, it's time for your lessons." Cricket motioned for one of the maids to come and lead Becka back into the castle.

"But Papa, what's wrong with the pixies?" Becka frowned, her eyes darting from Takayoshi to the hall that would lead toward the gardens at the center of the palace grounds.

"I don't know yet, sunflower." Cricket brushed his hand gently through her hair. "I'm going to find out, and we're going to make sure they're okay. But to do that, I need you to go to the library and work on your lessons. Can you do that for me?"

Becka sighed. "All right."

"Good." He bent to kiss her cheek, then nodded toward the maid who Becka followed reluctantly. Once she was out of sight, Cricket and Takayoshi returned their attention to the knight. "Show us."

The youth nodded, and stumbled as they spun to head back the way they had come. They lead Takayoshi and Cricket around the palace, along the wall, to the gardens that rested between the library and the stables. There, on the carpet of fresh spring grass, lay at least a dozen pixies. All of them motionless on their backs. Their blue skin gone sallow with either fatigue or illness as they baked under the sun.

Cricket made a soft sound of upset, almost a sob in the back of his throat, and left Takayoshi no time to grab him before he rushed over to kneel in the grass by the nearest little creature. With such gentleness and care that it nearly broke Takayoshi's heart, Cricket lifted the tiny creature to check its breathing.

Takayoshi came to kneel beside him, heedless of the way the grass stained his knees, and seeped dew into his trousers. "How are they?"

"They're breathing, but it's shallow." Cricket laid the creature gently back on the ground, his fingers trembling. "How long have they been this way?"

The knight shook their head, shifting from one foot to the other. "We're not sure. The maids came out to let the bunnies out of the pen and found them this way."

"They weren't out here last night when we put the bunnies back in their pen," one of the maids said.

Takayoshi had hardly noticed that there were more than just the knight, Cricket, and himself in the gardens, but now that he was paying attention he found a small cluster of the castle staff. Although he did not care for being watched like this, he had to admit that it was nice to know that Cricket was not the only one who cared for the lower fae in his kingdom. That the staff saw the pixies as family as much as Cricket did.

"Are there any signs that they have eaten anything they should not? Spilled ingredients in the kitchen? Missing supplies?" Takayoshi did not know much at all about pixies. It was Cricket who understood all the different types of fae that lived in their lands. Cricket who spoke pixie and could recognize the markings of a goblin's claws on sight. Lower fae did not tend to inhabit colder climates, so it was no surprise that Takayoshi's education had not extended into that.

"Nothing, sir."

"It reminds me of Nishi," Cricket said, his voice rough with emotion. "Remember? The lower fae were the first to be affected. Next it was the . . ." Cricket's head turned, as if searching out Becka's small form, but Takayoshi was not going to give that worry any more power than it already had over them. Whatever this was, they would stop it before it had any effect on their daughter.

"The pixies in Nishi were attacking people. They had become violent. This is not the same."

"At some point they did. But how long? Were there symptoms prior? We don't know Takayoshi! We don't know!" Panic had settled into Cricket's gaze, making his blue eyes flit around the yard as if searching for something to channel his rage onto, looking for something that he could fight to protect his daughter and his people.

"Was there mist this morning?" Takayoshi asked, his tone forced into a calm he did not really feel. His heart pounded in his ears making it hard to hear anything around him, and his vision had begun to narrow to a singular point. That point being Cricket. Everything else was a blur of dark shapes.

"No, sir," someone said. Whether it maid or knight, Takayoshi did not know, and did not care.

"If there was no mist then this cannot be the same as Nishi," he reasoned. "The curse in Nishi traveled in the mist from the lake at the center of the town. There is no large waterway here that would produce a mist, so it is not the same."

"Fine!" Cricket bit out, his hands fisted in the fabric of his trousers. He leaned forward, his voice going low, a hiss. Which was likely for the best as Takayoshi was not sure how many of those around them knew of the war that was coming for them yet. It would be better if they not panic the common people. Not yet at least. "So it's not exactly the same. But you heard what Estia said, all those curses, those monsters you faced, they were tests. Experiments to find the best method of felling a kingdom."

"Yes. I did." Takayoshi pulled Cricket in closer, pressing his forehead to Cricket's so he could speak lowly and still be heard. "But the symptoms are different, and so is the method. It is possible that this is a curse we did not encounter on our quests. Perhaps this is one that dissipated on its own."

That thought seemed to calm Cricket a fraction. Not enough to completely will away the panic, but enough that his breathing returned to normal. Good. That was good. Another panic attack was not what they needed right that moment. "Anstice will have information on all of the other curses somewhere."

"I will have Claudia look, and if she cannot find them, she can reach out to Anstice at the same time we contact my sister for aid." Takayoshi's own fear eased now that Cricket seemed to be better in control of himself.

"We should have the knights check the city, see if there is anything new within our borders we haven't noticed." Cricket nodded, his head bumping almost painfully against Takayoshi's, but Takayoshi refused to move away. Not if he could provide some measure of comfort when there was something going wrong.

"I will put off my—"

"No. The sooner we rescue Estia's siblings, and I get my

pearl, the better chance we'll have against all of this. I need to be at full strength when Craven gets here. We cannot wait." Cricket's eyes blazed with fury, his forehead pressing harder against Takayoshi's as if he could force him to see sense through pressure alone.

"Then I will leave at once."

CHAPTER 13

"Bring the cots in here," Cricket ordered, motioning to the ballroom. It was dusty from disuse, but that was an easy enough fix. "And get someone in here to clean it before we bring in the patients."

"But your highness—"

He wasn't exactly sure who it was that was arguing with him, but when he turned to the small group Youta had chosen to help him perform this task, they fell silent immediately. "We aren't using it, are we?"

"No, Your Highness," the small maid at the front said, and dipped her head. "This room has not been in use since before His Highness left on his quest."

"Exactly." Cricket squeezed the doorknob a little harder than was necessary, the metal cutting into his hand. He hated the reminder of when he'd left home to save his kingdom from strange curses. Yes, it had turned him into the man he was. Yes, it had led him to Takayoshi. But it had also destroyed his family, led to his father's death, and was the first attack in a civil war that nearly rent his kingdom in half.

"It's just that there are plenty of rooms on the west wing that—"

"Yes, they'll be out of the way there," someone else said, but again Cricket could not tell who when he looked at the group. Although there was a youth in the back who was looking at their feet now, avoiding the glare of their king.

"I'm not worried about them being in the way." Cricket's tone had gone steely, his expression hard. The temperature in the corridor dropped a few degrees, and he waited in the ensuing silence as the small group grew steadily more uncomfortable under his stare. "Have I made myself quite clear?"

"Yes, Your Highness," the group said as one, not daring to raise anymore objections. Cricket wondered briefly how long it would take before he had undone the damage Sunil had inflicted on his reputation. It had only been a few weeks, but he didn't know how much more he could take of people questioning him every time he made a decision that went slightly against the norm. Like they believed he had lost his ability to think rationally. Like they didn't think he was qualified to make such decisions.

Years, he decided, it would likely be years before he had fully proven himself after what Sunil had done. It had taken a few months for Sunil to ruin Cricket in the eyes of his people, and it would take him years to recover from it.

"Good." Cricket nodded, forcing himself to release the doorknob when it felt like he might rip it from the door. "Then please ensure this space is as clean as possible, and that the lights are in full working order. We'll set up the cursed in here where myself, my advisor, and the healers can check on them. I want this done before the day is through."

"Yes, Your Highness."

Cricket stepped out of the way, and allowed the small group to enter and get started. He stood for a moment, watching them as they unloaded brooms and mops, their gentle chatter washing over him. It was like being a part of something while still being on the outside, and although he knew it was silly, it settled something inside of himself to know that this task at least, he could see to.

He couldn't find the cursed object right away, although he had men looking. He couldn't fight Craven when the man hadn't made a clear attack on Lunette yet. He couldn't go with Takayoshi to save Estia's siblings. And he had yet to find a solution for the dead land outside his city. But this? Ensuring those who were hurting had a clean, safe space to rest while he tried to find a solution? This, he could do.

Someone cleared their throat from behind him, and Cricket turned to find Ignacia standing there. Her armor gleamed in the warm lights of the hall, but it didn't soften her at all, didn't make her look any less dangerous. She'd taken to wearing her armor at all times after the battle with Sunil, like she was just waiting for the next to start. Or maybe it was because she didn't like the idea of being caught without it again. Cricket could understand that. It didn't mean he had to like it, but he could understand it. They had all been fundamentally changed by what Sunil did to them. Scarred in a way that would never be able to heal. Ignacia was no different.

"Have they found anything?" Cricket asked, hopeful, even as he knew that it would be near impossible to find a cursed object in a city as large as the capital. Especially when they didn't know what the cursed object would even look like. The only way he'd found the root cause in Nishi was by being affected by the curse himself, and using the water flooding his lungs to create a magical tether between himself and the object. But there was nothing to tether himself to now. No magical signature they could use. At least not yet, anyway.

"Nothing." Ignacia's brows were drawn together, her mouth pressed into a firm line. "But we're still looking.

Claudia thinks—" She stopped herself, looked over Cricket's shoulder where the small crew were still working on cleaning the ballroom, and tilted her head for him to follow her.

Their footsteps echoed off the stone walls, the silence between them settling squirmy and anxious in the pit of Cricket's stomach. It hadn't even been an hour since Takayoshi had ridden off into the horizon, and Cricket already missed having his steady presence at his side. It was easier to focus on things when Takayoshi was there. Easier to find a solution, and to remain calm, when Takayoshi supported him. Being separated this often had not been part of the plan after they defeated Sunil and took back Lunette. They were supposed to elope, raise their daughter, be happy.

Cricket wasn't happy now.

Ignacia didn't speak again until they were behind the doors of his father's study, the magic installed long ago to keep others from eavesdropping in place once they were closed, keeping them from being overheard. Cricket settled into the chair behind his desk, and let out a long breath.

"Claudia thinks the magic from the soil outside is being used to fuel whatever this curse is," Cricket said without Ignacia even having to tell him. "I had the same thought."

"What should we do about it?"

Cricket took a deep breath, forcing his nerves to calm at least for the moment. "There's nothing we *can* do right now, unfortunately. We just have to wait, and hope that some clue arises to tell us what we're dealing with."

"I don't like waiting."

"Trust me, Iggy, I don't either. But in Nishi we had the water in my lungs to lead us to the lake, here there's nothing. The healer can't even source why they're unconscious. I don't —" Cricket sighed, slumping back further in his chair, and scrubbing at his face. "I feel like we're just in a holding pattern until something worse happens. And by then it might be too late for them."

"It wasn't all of the pixies," Ignacia reasoned, as if this might soften the blow. "Maybe we can figure out what caused it by looking at what this group doesn't have in common with the others."

"Now there's an idea," Cricket said, pushing to his feet, his chair skidding across the floor.

He had his hand on the door by the time Ignacia caught up to the fact that he was leaving. She sputtered out a bewildered, "Where are you going?"

"To speak to the local pixie monarch of course." Cricket shrugged. It seemed a reasonable way to gather more information. Although the pixies were likely to be a little upset with the current circumstances, but he was sure he could smooth that over relatively easily. He just needed to remain calm, and use his words.

The garden was empty when they reached it, now that they had moved the unconscious pixies, it seemed no one wanted to be there. Like they worried they would be cursed too. Which wasn't a terrible assumption to make, but Cricket hated how fear hampered the lives of his people. Hated even more how there was nothing he could do about it. He didn't have answers, or solutions. All he had was the willingness to try to find them.

The old tree tucked behind the stables had gotten larger since the last time he'd climbed it. Its branches out of reach now. Which put the pixie's nest well away from where he could simply shout up at them. Not that he would have done that, it would be rude, and the pixies were very particular about manners. They were notorious for throwing things at people who shouted at them from the ground. Cricket should know, he'd gotten a black eye from an apple once. . . twice.

Inhaling deeply, Cricket closed his eyes, and reached for

the cold fire that lived under his skin now. The dragon was easy to connect with since finding his pearl, as if they were in sync, a singular being. In a way, Cricket supposed they were. Although he wasn't sure how long that was going to last so long as his pearl remained out of his grasp. He hadn't had any of the symptoms of the lack of it outside of the scales and antlers. But he was beginning to wonder if those were just going to become a permanent fixture. He certainly didn't mind them, even as they marked him as other. Not anymore, at least.

Still, the neat little trick of using the dragon's magic to levitate was certainly coming in handy. It had helped during battle, but as far as everyday life went, outside of a crisis situation? Being able to fly was actually pretty useless.

When he'd reached a height that brought him level with the pixie nest, he clicked his tongue in greeting, speaking in rapid pixie. "Hello. May I please speak with the monarch of this clan?"

Then he waited, the seconds ticking by into minutes. When no answer came after a few, Cricket frowned, moving closer to the nest. He had been keeping his distance out of fear that the pixies would think he was intruding. It wouldn't do to intrude on another noble's territory. Even if that territory happened to reside inside his gardens.

"Hello?" The inside of the nest was dark. Nothing moved in the shadows, and Cricket's stomach lurched. "I'm just here to discuss what happened earlier. Is there anyone home? I'd like to speak to your leader?"

Still no answer. And the closer Cricket got to the nest the more he was sure that it was empty. By the time he had his face pressed to the little entrance, his heart was pounding in his ears, palms growing cold with fear.

The nest *wasn't* empty.

There were bodies littering the floor of the nest. Tiny, and blue. Eyes closed, chests moving slow and labored, just like those that had been in the grass. Cricket scrubbed at his eyes, doing his best to suck back the tears that burned there.

"Ignacia! Get me a basket!" He called down, backing away from the nest so he could find a way to remove the roof from it. The pixies would no doubt throw a tantrum about that when they found out, but he had to get them out of there somehow so the healers could do their work.

"A basket," she muttered to herself, and ran into the castle to do just that.

She was back by the time Cricket had pried the roof off the nest, and set it gently on a branch, hoping the wind didn't knock it to the ground. Either way, he'd probably have to have someone help the pixies rebuild.

"Is this big enough?" Ignacia called back, holding up the largest picnic basket they likely had in the palace.

"I'll have to bring them down in groups." Cricket landed gently beside her and took the basket. "Go gather some men to help take them inside. The entire colony has been affected."

Ignacia nodded quickly, and Cricket levitated back up toward the nest to begin loading the pixies into the basket and bringing them down a few at a time. He was gentle with them, as he would be with any of his people. They *were* his people, even if they lived under their own monarchy. They lived on his lands, it was his job to protect them just as it was his job to protect everyone else.

And he had failed.

CHAPTER 14

The rot had spread even further since Takayoshi returned to the capital. He had only been home for a matter of days and already the tree where Takayoshi once hoisted Cricket to survey his kingdom had fallen. Nothing grew on the rotted wood, but it was slowly being broken down by something.

The image was unsettling.

There should have been mushrooms, some kind of fungus, or bugs, working to return the tree to the earth. But there was nothing

"We shouldn't stay here too long," Leo said, his fingers tight around the hilt of his sword.

They had stopped at the top of the hill to take a moment to inspect the rot. At least that is the excuse Takayoshi used. Really it was more about that tree in particular. The one he had once considered carving their initials into like some pre-pubescent boy in love. It was the first tree he had ever seen green leaves on, looking up at Cricket to make sure he did not fall, and seeing color all around him. Takayoshi remembered it still. It had been heartrendingly beautiful. If he had not been in love with Cricket already, that would have made him fall so fast there would have been no getting up.

The world was a wash of color around Takayoshi, verdant greens, lively browns, and the brilliant turquoise of Estia's hair. But the tree was none of those things. It was a muddy dead hue, turning gray as if the color had been seeped from it along with the life.

"Yoshi, did you hear me?" Leo asked, squatting down to rest next to him. "We need to leave."

"Does any of this look familiar, Estia?" Takayoshi did not budge from his spot, instead he turned to look at Estia over his shoulder. Ze had not moved since they came up the hill, zir eyes wide and frightened. "Do you know what this is?"

"No." Estia shook zir head. "He could be using the magic from the land to fuel any number of spells. There's no way to tell unless we find the source of the rot."

"Cricket climbed this tree," Takayoshi said, half to himself. "When he was on his first quest, and we were making plans to break back into the city to free his father from Sunil. I helped him."

"What?" Estia asked, and Takayoshi could hear the confusion in zir voice, even as he had returned his attention to the tree, his hand reaching out to touch it.

Leo snatched his wrist from the air before he could make contact. "I understand you're upset that this marker of your past is lost, but you're going to have so many great new memories with Cricket once we return home victorious." Leo gave his wrist a firm squeeze, a warning, and Takayoshi pulled his hand back slowly. "Let's not waste our time living in the past."

"You are right." Takayoshi nodded once, and stood. "The sooner we rescue Estia's siblings, the sooner I can come home to my family."

Family. He had not thought much of the word in his

youth. It was just something he called his sister and his uncle, the people he had grown up with. It took on a whole different meaning now that the word was used to refer to Cricket and Becka, and the small host of friends they had acquired through their adventures. They had found that family themselves, built it, forged it in the fires of battle, and it would withstand even what was to come next.

"Where is Craven keeping your siblings?" Takayoshi moved back toward his horse, only able to turn away from the city, and the people he had left behind because he knew he would be returning. And soon.

"WHAT DOES HE MEAN BY THIS?" Takayoshi's anger boiled inside of him, making his skin too hot, flames licking along his fingertips and catching on the tree where he, Leo, and Estia had set up their first watch of the village. It was a week's travel from the capital, closer than the village in the mountains, but still not close enough to be a problem. Not yet. But it would not be long. It was clear, to Takayoshi at least, that this was not mindless wandering, this was a path straight to the door of the capital. But why was he doing it *this* way? Why take his time?

Leo hissed like a wet cat, and patted out the small fires Takayoshi's anger had started. "Stop doing that."

Takayoshi ignored him, and turned his attention to Estia instead, looking for an answer.

"He means to get as close to the capital as he possibly can without anyone noticing." Estia was frowning, zir face twisted into something unhappy, and unsettled. It was understandable. Takayoshi could not imagine how it must feel to watch someone he loved tear down everything around him. Cricket and Estia had both suffered this now, and he wished he could do something to fix it for them. To take that pain away. He could not.

"Why do they not report it?" His own kingdom—Helios—was smaller population wise than Lunette, and the villages and cities were more spread out. Spanning from the bottom of the mountain to the top. Still, he could not imagine his own people not informing Atsuko of an invader in her territory. "He is an invader."

"He's not, technically." Leo shook his head, patting out more of the little fires Takayoshi had started with his irritation. Much of that emotion had bled away, replaced only with confusion. Why did Cricket's people not show loyalty to him? Why did they not send a message to the castle to let him know that an invading royal was in his lands? Craven had crossed the border days ago, by Takayoshi's estimate, but they had heard nothing of it at the capital. Did the people of Lunette not trust their king?

"How is he not? He is within the borders of Lunette with an *army*?"

"An envoy."

"Without giving notice to its ruler," Takayoshi continued, ignoring Leo who was being decidedly unhelpful right now. "It is rude."

"You did it," Leo mumbled.

Takayoshi cut him a glare, but Leo seemed entirely unfazed by this. Too many years of friendship, very likely. Takayoshi's fury had lost its effectiveness on a person who knew very well Takayoshi would never turn on him.

"You *did*." Leo shrugged.

"That is not the point," Takayoshi snipped.

"I think it is."

Estia cleared zir throat, and they all returned their focus

to the small fishing village where Craven had stopped to rest. He had not been there long, a day at most, based on the fact that his men had not taken the time to set up all of their tents yet. They were likely staying at the inn until they moved on.

"Would *you*?" Estia asked after a moment, zir fingers tightening around the tree where ze stood. "They need the money, and they're afraid. Craven probably threatened them." Estia's expression had gone stoney. "That's what he did up the mountain. And his men outnumber them, not by a lot, but by enough."

"It isn't an outright act of war," Leo said, his tone soft as he moved up to stand beside Estia. He did not reach out to zir, but Takayoshi could see how he wanted to. How it was hard for him to hold himself back when all he wanted was to be able to comfort the person he loved. Takayoshi understood the feeling all too well. That did not mean he was not a little bit annoyed by it. Honestly, they just needed to talk about their feelings, and get this whole dance over with. He knew from experience.

"Right." Estia agreed, although ze did not sound happy about it. "He's just visiting."

"He's a king. He's free to travel where he likes," Leo reminded, gently. "If anyone were to ask, he could tell them he means to visit with Cricket once he's closer."

"Where are they keeping your siblings?" Takayoshi shook his head, no longer wanting to discuss how there was nothing he could do about Craven's current movements. How the people of Lunette were scared of not just Craven, but their own king. He knew that was where this conversation would head next. To what Sunil had managed to do to Cricket's reputation by making him attack his own people, and then run away when he could do nothing to protect them. The way Cricket had battled against Sunil, and won—had cut down his own kin—would not have reached these smaller hamlets yet. It may never, if Craven burned the village to the ground before he left, leaving no one behind to warn his enemies.

Would he do that? Takayoshi was not sure, and he was too afraid to ask, honestly. Perhaps it would be better for the people here if Takayoshi and his small group of rescuers were to show their hand. To let Craven know that they had seen him here, and that any harm that came to this village's people would be seen as an act of war, kickstarting something Craven was clearly trying to prolong.

Why? Why was he putting it off? Why was he not simply charging in and starting the fight immediately? There was something else going on here. Something connected to the sickness of the pixies, and the spell that was rotting the land that surrounded the capital. Takayoshi had not been able to sort it out though. He did not have enough information. May not have enough until he was far too late.

That realization was terrifying. Roiled through him like a chill. Killing his flames. Making his hair stand on end.

"There," Estia said after some thought, and pointed to the inn itself. "He would not keep them apart from himself like he did with me."

Something lay under those words, a tone, an emotion that Takayoshi could not identify. He had learned much of how to read people in the years since he met Cricket, but not enough. He may never be able to find the hidden things behind Estia's eyes . There was pain, yes, but of a kind Takayoshi could not parse.

Leo took a step closer to Estia until his shoulder was pressed against zir's, but did not say anything.

"Night would be the easiest time to infiltrate," Takayoshi reasoned, turning his attention away from them and back to the inn. It was hard to watch the way they gravitated toward one another when his own sense of balance was so thrown off by the distance between himself and Cricket. A week's ride. What would have changed with Cricket by the time he was home again? How would Becka have grown?

"No. Daytime would be best." Estia shook zir head. "When they're on the road."

"They will be on their guard then, expecting an attack." Or at least, he would be. Logically when they were on the road was when they were the most vulnerable, but it was also when they would be the most prepared for an attack, for that very reason.

"We're less likely to hurt anyone in the village," Leo argued. "And it will give the children the ability to run versus getting caught in the crossfire."

"Very well." Takayoshi sighed. "We will attack when they are on the move once more. I need to know how the procession will be ordered."

"I can do that." Estia pulled away from Leo, grabbing the dagger from his waist on zir way to a tree with smooth bark. "They'll be on the move before the day turns too warm tomorrow."

"Then we had best prepare." Takayoshi pulled a map from his pack as well, to sprawl it across the earth at their feet. "What route do you think they will take?"

"An ambush." Leo smiled a little, approvingly.

"Oh! I love a good ambush!" Estia laughed, delight lining zir tone in a way Takayoshi thought he might never hear again from his friend.

Friend. Could they be that again? Could he find his way to forgiveness? He supposed he had already begun to in some small way. Else why was he here?

CHAPTER 15

"How many were there?" Cricket asked, a pad of paper in hand as he scribbled across it the numbers and species of those who had been affected so far. The numbers were stacking up. And with each new lower fae that fell to this affliction, he knew they grew closer to the upper fae also being affected.

"Twelve, Your Highness," the knight reported. Behind him those under his direct command were bringing in Goblins on stretchers. He hadn't even known he had goblins in his city. Apparently they lived in the kitchens where they were both a help and a hinderance in equal measure.

"And as with the others there were no signs of them ingesting anything that could have caused it?"

"No, sire."

Cricket scribbled this down before running his ink-stained hands down his face. It had been the Pixies first, then the gnomes who had made their homes in the gardens of the capital's citizens, tending to their vegetables, and keeping the pests away. Now the goblins. Goblins were child-sized. It was only a matter of time before—

He shook himself. He'd find something. He just needed more information. More time. Some fresh air would hopefully clear his head. With a nod, he gathered his things, and returned to his workspace in the gardens.

Cricket had begun to take his meetings in the gardens some days ago under the guise of looking after Becka while she played. Much of the staff was tied up in helping those poor creatures who had fallen under the spell of the curse, and Cricket would rather they worry about them than attending to his daughter who he could manage well enough on his own. Or that's what he said anyway.

Really it was mostly that he couldn't stand being so close to the ballroom. He had to walk past the open doors anytime he went from his study to another part of the castle, and the unmoving, silent faces of those affected haunted him. Their bodies so still it was almost no different than if they were dead.

Becka, for her part in this whole charade, was having a grand old time testing out her newly discovered Celestial form. Exhibiting remarkable control over the jackalope her Celestial magic had presented itself as. So much so Cricket was almost jealous.

"Don't leap so high, little sunflower," Cricket chided gently, but couldn't bring himself to really scold her. With Takayoshi gone for some days yet, and his kingdom on the brink of something terrible, Cricket needed some small happiness, and he could only feel a little guilty for finding that in Becka's sheer joy at her newfound power.

"I'll be fine, Papa," Becka called back as she took off at a run, changing mid-stride from a little girl to a gracefully leaping white hare. She trailed snowflakes in her wake that sparkled like stardust.

"Even still, take your time adjusting." Maybe it was because she was so young. Maybe it was because there were no barriers between herself and the creature her grandmother had gifted her with. Becka hadn't struggled at all in learning to control her new abilities. They had appeared, and she took to them like a fish does to water, not even having to learn to fly as a bird might. Like it was instinct. Second nature. It was glorious. Cricket only wished Takayoshi had been there to see it.

"Yes, Papa," Becka called back, but did not once slow down.

Cricket took a breath and returned his attention to the attendants who paced around the gardens with him. Each one of them looked as tired as he felt. Dark circles surrounded their eyes, and every step they took seemed to drag slower and slower. This curse, whatever it was, had not let them rest for more than a few hours at a time since Takayoshi left.

"It might be the elves soon," Ignacia said, her eyes flicking around to make sure no one outside of their small group was listening. Not that it mattered, Cricket was sure the people of the capital knew something terrible was coming, how could they not? But it was better if people didn't panic. If things didn't get to the point that they had in Nishi where every day citizens had to lock themselves behind closed doors when the sun fell, and lived in fear they'd be next.

"Have we *still* not found the cause?" Cricket was very near going out into the city and searching everyone's homes himself. He knew Ignacia's knights were doing what they could, and that she had chosen the best ones for the job, but none of them had encountered the curses Cricket had. They didn't know what to look for, not the way that he did.

But even if he did go out there himself, there was no way for him to search the entire city quickly enough. Not with everything else going on. If they just had something to tie a tracking spell to, that would be something. But so far the magic that had afflicted the lower fae remained stubbornly inert.

"No." Claudia frowned, her hands wringing. She was not wearing her glasses, but there were deep indentations left behind from the nose pads. Her clothes looked distinctly rumpled, as if she had slept in them, and Cricket didn't think he had seen her slouch ever the way she was slouching now. Even at the height of the war against Sunil, when all seemed lost, and they were all exhausted, Claudia stood tall.

He'd thought her unshakeable. He'd thought *all* of them unshakeable, himself included, his kingdom included. Craven and his attacks were proving him wrong. And every day Cricket was reminded that his hands were tied. His forces were small. His people were exhausted, and broken. He could not strike first for fear of proving Sunil right at every turn. There was nothing he could do, but wait.

Wait, and hope for answers. Wait, and hope the reinforcements Atsuko was sending would get there in time.

"We need to evacuate, Your Highness," another voice broke through Cricket's thoughts. He frowned to himself, and turned to meet the eyes of the older man who had said it. Lachlan had been one of his father's advisors since before Cricket was born. Cricket kept him around out of respect, but deep down he thought they both knew that perhaps Lachlan should retire. He'd only ever known peace, and he did not seem capable of dealing with their current issues.

"And where would you have me send them, Lachlan?" Cricket asked, his head tilted so his short dark hair fell into his eyes. He missed his braid a little more every day. Missed how easy it had been to brush all of his hair out of his face, and ignore it for a little while. He also missed the days when his fingers didn't end in talons and get caught in his tunic as he was putting it on. Things had only gotten worse without access to his pearl, since Takayoshi left.

What would he think when he came home and found Cricket like this again? More beast than elf in the last few days? Would he think him ugly? Would he turn away? Of course he would. Cricket could hardly look at himself in the mirror anymore. And how much of this was permanent?

"I—" Lachlan frowned, his face twisted into something that looked distinctly sour. No one else said anything, all seeming to realize that Lachlan had spoken out of turn. That he was about to be reprimanded in the gentlest way possible.

Gods, Cricket hated this part of being king. Hated how it all came down to him, rested on his shoulders, and he was *helpless. Useless.*

"You don't know, do you?" Cricket pressed. He didn't mean for it to come out as cold as it had, but he couldn't seem to stop it. He was furious with himself for being unable to protect his people. With Craven for attacking them. With Sunil for making the situation so dire. And with his father for not teaching Cricket a better way to handle things.

"Of course you don't," Cricket continued when Lachlan just gaped at him. "Because there is nowhere to send them if we evacuate them from the city, is there? Their homes were destroyed. There isn't a city in Lunette large enough to house this many refugees outside of the capital. And to send them to our allies in Helios would require supplies we do not currently have." Cricket's hands tightened into fists at his sides, the sharp nails on his fingers cutting crescents into his palms that left them damp and bloody. He did not shy away from the pain though. The pain was the only thing keeping him from shouting at Lachlan.

"Well if you'll forgive me for saying so, Your Highness."

Cricket had learned a long time ago that when an elder started a speech like that, they were about to say something that would make him absolutely furious. His eyebrow twitched as he stared down Lachlan, hoping the other man would get the message that he should stop before he'd begun with just a look alone.

He didn't seem to.

Cricket envied Takayoshi the ability to silence people with a singular glance.

"It's not safe for them here."

"I can't just turn them out." Cricket forced himself to take a deep breath, forced his tone to remain even and measured. He was not a tyrant king, and he would not be mistaken for one simply because his temper was running a little high at the moment. "And I won't. Evacuation is not an option unless you can find me someplace to send them that will provide them with the resources we're able to here."

Lachlan looked as if he wanted to say more. Perhaps he meant to accuse Cricket of condemning his people to this terrible curse simply because he was stubborn. There was never any way to really tell what might come out of someone's mouth before it did, but Cricket had had enough. He didn't want to hear it.

And didn't he know already that the decision he was making was a dangerous one? He understood that the curse would spread eventually to the upper fae, that it would begin affecting his people next. Starting with the children. He'd seen it with his own eyes.

But what other choice was there? Neither option was a good one. Either he risked them being affected while he searched for a solution, or he sent them out into the wider world with little more than the clothes on their backs, and hoped they found someplace that would accommodate them, or that Craven didn't cut them down on the road. And who was to say the curse wouldn't follow them? Who was to say whatever was causing this sickness wasn't already in their blood streams just waiting to eat away at their magic? He had no way to know that it wasn't. It would be worse if they were to leave, and fall ill on the journey.

"I've made my decision," Cricket said when the group was silent for too long. "We will not evacuate the city. We will continue to care for those who are affected here in the castle. I will not discuss this further. Have I made myself clear?"

A murmur of assent traveled through the group, and Cricket did his best not to show how his shoulders relaxed, falling away from his ears at the confirmation that this would not be brought up again. He didn't have the energy to keep rehashing this, especially not when they didn't have anything new to discuss. If they had some more information maybe—

A thud rang through the gardens, silencing any thoughts in Cricket's head.

He turned slowly to see what the noise had been, terror clinging to his spine, something in his stomach telling him not to look. Maybe if he didn't look it wouldn't be true. But he had to. Because he had to know.

Becka lay on the ground, her chest rising and falling in harsh pants, eyes unblinking where they stared up at the sky.

"Becka? What's wrong?" Cricket took a step toward her, then another, then another, and soon he was running across the open grass, heedless of the plants he trampled in his rush to get to her. Because Becka wasn't answering. She wasn't answering, and she wasn't moving. Usually when she got like this, when she fell, she would either cry out for attention, or push herself to her feet and declare herself just fine Papa, don't worry, with a smile so feral and sharp Cricket swore she'd gotten it from the gods themselves.

But now there was nothing. No crying. No wailing. No wanting hugs, and reassurances. And certainly no picking herself up off the ground to show how tough she was. To prove that she could be just as strong, just as brave as her fathers. She just laid there. Eyes unblinking.

"Becka." The word broke in Cricket's throat, catching on something sharp. The ground jolted his knees where he landed beside her, reaching for her to check her pulse, to make sure she was breathing even when he saw her chest rising and falling. She was alive, still. But there was no response. No indication what had happened.

Cricket pressed his fingers more firmly against her wrist, and reached with his magic to check on her, the same as he had with the pixies, and the goblins, and the gnomes. The same as he had with every creature who presented these symptoms.

The magic inside Becka was not still, and dormant the way theirs had been. It was a riot of anger, and fight. Snarling, and snapping against whatever was attacking it. Trying to burn it away. There was some relief in that, but not enough. Not near enough.

Cricket scooped Becka up, holding her close to his chest. "Call the healer, I want them to come see her," he ordered without once taking his gaze away from his daughter's face. Her eyelids, which he had previously thought were frozen open, were fluttering as if she were fighting for consciousness. "And send men out into the city, check on the other children. Tell them to spread the word that any instances of this curse should be brought to me directly. I need to examine everyone more closely."

He'd been putting that off as best as he could since the first pixie had fallen ill. Trusting in the healers and doctors of the castle to find a cause. But hadn't he always known that in the end this would come down to him? That he would have to be the one to find the common thread?

"Your Highness, is that—"

"That wasn't a *suggestion*, Lachlan. I will examine the others." Cricket lifted his chin to meet the gaze of the advisor.

Lachlan opened his mouth to argue further, and Cricket thought he knew what the man wanted to say before he could even say it. How could Cricket, who had no formal training, find an answer where the others had failed?

"His Highness has seen many things on his travels," Claudia provided, her words steely and sharp enough to cut. "I trust in his guidance with this."

Another murmur of agreement spread through the small group of attendants, and Cricket didn't wait to see if Lachlan had anything else to say. He pushed through the doors into the corridor, his footsteps hurrying toward Becka's room.

CHAPTER 16

It was two days before Craven and his men set off again. Two days of waiting, and watching, and planning. Two days during which Takayoshi grew steadily more anxious. Every minute he was away from home was a minute wasted. Every second he was not at Cricket's side was a second too long.

Anything could happen while they were away.

Yes, they had the enemy in their sights, so he could not personally lead a charge against the capital, but that would not stop him from launching all manner of other attacks. Craven had not even been close by when the rot started. And he was a week's ride away when the first pixie was found.

"You need to stop pacing," Leo said, not once taking his gaze away from where they had stationed themselves to watch Craven and his men load up.

"I am not pacing." Takayoshi was unclear on how else to shake out the nervous energy that made the muscles in his legs burn. Movement seemed the only method. So he had taken to doing short walks across the forest behind where Leo and Estia rested. That was not pacing. That was simply—

"You are," Estia argued, also not turning zir head to watch him. "But don't be too hard on him, Lionel. He just wants to get home to his husband."

"I'm not being hard on him." Leo grumbled something else under his breath, but Takayoshi could not hear it from where he had once again crossed to the large oak some feet away. Not that he wanted to hear it anyway. Leo had grown steadily more grumpy while they waited. Which was no doubt caused by his own anxiety. "We should go over the plan again."

"There is no need." They had gone over the plan backward and forward several times over. Takayoshi could probably recite it in his sleep at this rate. He knew it paid to be prepared, but Leo seemed to be over-preparing in Takayoshi's opinion. Still, he could not fault anyone else for how they dealt with nerves. And Leo no doubt was struggling with seeing Craven again so close by. "Do we perhaps want to discuss what is really bothering you?"

"No. We do not." Leo shifted his weight, the brush beneath him crunching a little.

"It'll be all right," Estia soothed, zir hand lifting from where it had been in zir lap as if ze wanted to touch Leo's shoulder. But ze stopped just short, zir fingers opening and closing for a moment before zir hand fell away.

Takayoshi had tracked the entire motion, and it made something unsettled, and unhappy stir in his chest that he could not put a name to. Heartbreak, maybe, at seeing his two friends dance around each other in a way that was wholly unnecessary. But Leo had yet to forgive Estia for what ze had done, and even once he had, he could never forget. May never be able to trust again. Takayoshi could not blame him for that. It was perfectly logical.

"They're on the move." Leo rose from where he had been

resting on the forest floor, pushing against his cane when the motion clearly pained him.

Estia's hands twitched again at zir sides, as if ze wanted to reach out but did not think ze had the right. Especially when the injury had been caused by Estia zirself.

Takayoshi shook himself. He did not have the time, nor the energy to spend on the tragedy that was Estia and Leo. Especially when he had learned from his time traveling the world, that one day they would either sort themselves out, or they would go their separate ways entirely. There would be no in between. All he needed to do was wait, and be there for his friends no matter the end result.

"Get into position," Takayoshi ordered, and took off at a run through the trees, leaving Estia and Leo behind. It was a gamble, one he would not have taken some years ago, to leave Estia with Leo. To believe that Estia would not shout and reveal their position. He wanted to trust Estia, he did. Was that foolish? Yes, he knew that it was. And the Takayoshi of the past, the one who had not yet met a prince and fallen in love, would not have. He would have left Estia in that cell, and never thought twice about saving zir or zir siblings.

Love did strange things to people.

By the time he reached the place where he was meant to wait for Craven's procession, Takayoshi could feel heat trickling down his spine. Sweat coated his collar. He was not breathing hard, and although his muscles burned, it was a pleasant burn. Action, not anxiety.

Now, all he needed to do was wait.

It took him a moment to climb a tree just off the road, movements uncertain, and a little clumsy. He had watched Cricket climb enough trees, he should know how to do this by now, but he did not. And he feared using his phoenix abilities lest he set the whole forest ablaze.

His balance was precarious for a moment on the branch

he had chosen until he found his footing. Then Takayoshi settled in to wait.

Craven was at the front of the contingent, his head held high, his armor shining in the dappled sunshine as if it had not seen a single day of battle. It likely had not. Takayoshi wondered what Craven would do when it was rusting with the blood of his men, slain by their enemies. He supposed he would find out.

The thought that it would be easy, simple really, to fall from the sky and burn this entire troop to cinders, was almost *too* appealing. They would still be a week's ride away from the capital. Cricket would still be safe. He could end this whole thing before it even really began. Remove their enemy from the equation. Damn the consequences.

But . . . well, there would be consequences. Now that their engagement was common knowledge, Takayoshi could not do anything without his actions reflecting back on Cricket and his own kingdom. The assumption would be that Lunette attacked first, waged war on Cytherea. It would invite questions and criticism. It would paint Cricket and Takayoshi as tyrants. With Cricket's reputation only beginning to rebound, they could not afford it.

Takayoshi let out a breath, his hand gripping his sword tightly. He could not put an end to this, not yet. Not until Craven had completely shown his hand. Until then, he would wait, and keep himself ready. His blade would be sharp when the time came to drive it through Craven's heart and put a stop to him.

What followed was a small host of soldiers. By army standards, the group would not put a dent in the Helion forces, but with how Lunette's force had been left by Sunil's civil war, it would not take much to fell the capital. If Lunette did not also have the Celestials on their side, the kingdom would be torn to shreds by this meager showing.

Takayoshi shook himself, and focused once more. It was a mistake to have the prisoners in the back, only guarded by a handful of soldiers, but Craven was arrogant, or maybe just ill-informed in the ways of battle tactics. Or maybe he simply did not care what became of his siblings. Either way, Takayoshi spotted the small group of horses surrounded by soldiers more than halfway through the group. Estia's siblings looked tired, and wan. They had not been beaten the way Estia had, but there was little doubt that they had been mistreated.

The grip of his sword cut into his palm as Takayoshi tightened his hold. He could not ever imagine treating his sister this way, least of all when she was still a child. The youngest of Estia's siblings were not more than twelve. How long had they been living under Craven's rule? How long had he been hurting them? Had this been going on when Takayoshi and Claudia visited Cytherea all those years ago? Could he have stopped this?

A tree fell in the forest, landing with a loud bang, and drawing the attention of the group at the back for a moment. Not long enough to completely separate them from the pack, but enough that it would take more than a couple of seconds for the soldiers from the front to rejoin the battle at the back. Especially with how narrow the pass was.

A sharp, shrill whistle rent the air. The signal that Leo and Estia were in place. And then the first arrow went flying, burying itself into the shoulder of the largest guard in the lot. Which only seemed to anger him, as he shouted a war cry to the trees.

They had to be quick. Reinforcements would be on them in seconds.

Takayoshi leaped from the branch straight into the center of the circle of guards, his sword already drawn. The horses with Estia's siblings riding them kicked up a fuss, upset by the surprise. Someone shouted, likely one of the guards to call for more men. But the sound was cut off by a gurgle, and Takayoshi only had a moment to realize it was because Estia had shot the person in the throat.

He was suddenly very glad they were on the same side.

With a swing of his sword he cut two of the siblings loose. They were sharing a horse, and finding themselves separated from the others they both turned to him with wide eyes.

"Go." He grunted his sword clashing with a knight who had wheeled around and meant to strike him from above. A dirty tactic, but then so was falling from a tree and catching one's enemy by surprise. Takayoshi could not feel shame for that, surprise was all they had.

"Go where?" the little girl whispered, terror making her voice tremble. "He'll follow us."

"He can try," Takayoshi smiled, although it was not more than a twitch of his lips he could feel it just the same. Knew how it cut into his cheeks, and would have made Cricket laugh for the sharpness of it.

Then as another knight swung their weapon toward his head, Takayoshi dropped to the ground, and lit fire to the underlying brush, drawing a half circle around Estia's siblings, and the remaining knights. It would not hold Craven and the rest of his forces off for long. But the smoke that billowed from the damp leaves Leo and Estia had littered in the area created a screen that was nearly impenetrable.

Between Estia's arrows, and Takayoshi's sword, they felled the rest of the soldiers guarding the siblings, managing to save the horses. Takayoshi helped Estia's siblings loose of their bonds, leaped onto one of the dead soldier's horses and without another word turned their group around.

Estia also dropped from the trees above, landing on the horse behind Takayoshi, zir hands around his waist as ze leaned back to smile at zir siblings.

"Don't worry. We'll get you to safety." Estia gave a little wave, then stopped, leaning back further in the saddle. "Where's Damian?"

Takayoshi turned to watch as the small group sank under Estia's stare. The royal family of Cytherea had nine children total. One being Craven, another being Estia, but there were only six faces before him. He had not noticed in the scuffle. But why would he? They were not his siblings to keep track of.

"Where is Damian?" Estia asked again, fear slowly crawling into zir tone.

"He's with Craven," one of the younger siblings spoke up, her voice shaking a little. "He's been with Craven this entire time."

"He's there. . . He's there willingly," another said. A brother. Takayoshi did not remember their names, there were too many of them, and he had not spent enough time in court to learn them

"*Willingly*?!" Estia shouted. "But why would he. . . "

Betrayal flashed across Estia's face, crashing onto zir features so hard it nearly knocked zir from the horse. It should have made Takayoshi feel vindicated. After all Estia had betrayed him and his more than once. But all it left him feeling was sad and hollow

"Estia, we must leave. The fire will not keep them at bay for long." Already Takayoshi could hear shouting through the smoke. Craven's men were regrouping. They needed to be far from this spot, out of sight, by the time Craven turned his forces around.

"But he has my brother." Estia's voice had gone choked, and when ze turned around Takayoshi could see the pain and stress lining zir eyes. "We have to save my brother."

"We will," Takayoshi promised. "But not today."

"But—"

"Leo will be waiting for us."

Estia sighed, zir shoulders hunching, and nodded. Then ze turned zir attention to the group of six behind them, and ordered "stay close" before turning back in the saddle and nudging Takayoshi's horse to move.

Their horses sped down the path through the forest back the way they had come, but not toward the village. Instead they circled around, taking a lesser traveled road, one that had not been on any map, and would lead Takayoshi home to the capital, to Cricket.

Leo waited for them at the head of the trail, his horse stamping her feet in the undergrowth.

"All present and accounted for?" Leo asked, his lips curling up a little at the sides. There was something jovial about his expression now. Likely feeling the high from this small victory.

Takayoshi was feeling it too. It hummed through him, making him sit up straighter in the saddle. It would not win them the war, he knew that. But it would give them the means they needed to do so, and would strike a blow against Craven that he could not admit to anyone lest they find out he had been holding his own siblings hostage.

"No," Estia said zir voice sick with concern, bringing down whatever small height they may have climbed to with this successful rescue mission. "He still has Damian."

"Damian?" Leo frowned, his gaze flicking from Estia to the group behind them. "Your twin?"

Estia nodded zir head, zir shoulders drooping further.

"We'll get him back, Estia." Leo's fingers tightened around his reins, his eyes flicking back the way they had come as if he meant to ride off and retrieve Damian right then.

"We need to leave first," Takayoshi said, hating himself a little for how he had to speak sense. He knew what it was to want to go back for someone he loved. Knew how it could ache. But they did not have the forces they would need to save anyone else, not right in that moment. And they could not risk those they had already rescued.

Leo's gaze landed on his, and Takayoshi saw the decision settle behind his eyes. "Yoshi's right. We need to get your younger siblings to safety first. We will come back for Damian."

Estia released a sound that was half strangled by emotion, but ze nodded just the same.

"Let us go home." Even with the knowledge that they had not been completely successful, even knowing that they would have to save one more, there was happiness still. It lifted something that had been pressing heavily on Takayoshi's chest for what felt like years. He was going home, finally. To Lunette. To Becka. To Cricket.

And this time he would hopefully get to stay.

CHAPTER 17

There were so many of them. Far too many. More than even had been affected in Nishi all those years ago.

A sea of sleeping faces.

Cricket's heartbeat drowned out the sound of his boots on stone as he paced the halls of his castle, trying to clear his head, to think.

The ballroom was full up with pixies and goblins and gnomes and hobs and all manner of lesser fae. To the point it was overflowing into the great hall, and the receiving hall where he now sat.

The only sound that surrounded him was the soft scuffle of the maids tending to the sick. Providing them with water, and changing their blankets. There wasn't much else they could do for them. Sometimes Cricket would catch one of Youta's daughters reading to them. That was nice. But he didn't know that it would do anything aside from leave a hollow ache in his chest.

Becka was just the same. She had been the first to fall ill of the elves, but she was not the last. And soon whatever was affecting those more densely packed with magic would begin to affect the adults. He didn't know this from experience, but it was the next logical step.

A solution. He needed a solution. A way to track what was happening to his daughter and to his people. A way to cure them all.

"You Highness," Youta said, her voice gentle as she came up behind him. "You should get some rest."

"I'll rest when I've figured out what is going on in my kingdom." Cricket gripped his trousers tightly, his talons poking holes in the fabric. The talons he could do without, he decided. They were a nuisance. Maybe having his pearl back would leave him with enough choice and control to get rid of them. The antlers and the scales he could deal with, even if they did make him see a monster when he looked in the mirror. But the talons were just annoying.

Youta sighed, and moved to stand beside him, reaching out for him for a moment, before pulling her hand away.

"How is the most recent victim?" he asked, throat tight, the sight of Becka falling still burning behind his eyelids every time he closed them, followed by a sea of other faces. Children. So many children.

The most recent had been a little boy. Not even five yet.

The child's parents had been given accommodations, and food, while Cricket and his army of healers and doctors looked him over. He was smaller than Becka. And he'd been struck down in the middle of the street.

Convulsing.

Becka hadn't convulsed, thank the gods, Cricket didn't think he could handle that.

It had been a struggle to peel his mothers away from him, Cricket could understand that.

She shook her head after a moment.

"I need to check on Becka," Cricket said after a moment

too long of silence. His boots creaked under him as he spun to head that way and while he half-expected Youta to stop him, she did not. She let him turn, and leave his sick citizens behind in favor of his sick daughter.

The door to Becka's room creaked open. He had been meaning to have the hinges oiled for ages now, but Becka seemed fond of the sound. Every time she heard it, she knew someone was coming to visit her, and she would light up like a sunflower, turning toward the sun.

No squeal of happiness accompanied his entrance now. Just the creak. Which seemed to echo in the silent room, bouncing off walls, and leaving the space all the more hollow for it being the only sound.

"Oh Becka," Cricket said, the words escaping on a long exhale as he settled at her bedside. She looked tiny laying there like that. Which was strange. She had grown so much since coming to him a few years back, but now she reminded him so much of that little girl he'd found hiding in the rubble of her home. Her grandmother's body beside her. A white cloak protecting her from the fire and the debris. He'd known she belonged with him when he'd seen that, something in his mind telling him that she was his just the way he had always been King Jaxith's.

The white cloak probably had something to do with that, he'd only found out later that it was Takayoshi's. Given to the child after they'd bonded.

But now she looked small again. Swimming in a sea of pale colored bedding, her blankets pulled up to her chin. She hated sleeping like that, he knew that. Would often kick the blankets off in the middle of the night when her body temperature rose too high. Not that it had ever stopped her from seeking out cuddles from her father.

He gently folded the blanket away from her neck, pushing

it down under her arms so he could take one of her little hands in his own, and give it a gentle squeeze.

"Whatever am I going to do with you?" he asked.

There was no answer, which just made him hold her hand a little tighter. Normally such a question would have had Becka laughing, delighted in her mischief, the adorable little gremlin that she was. But now there was nothing. Except—

Except a quiet thrum of magic along his fingertips where they rested near her wrist.

No. That couldn't be. He'd checked her magic nearly every hour since she'd fallen ill. It had been just the same as the others. Still, and silent, dormant. But this, this wasn't dormant at all. He pressed his magic into her wrist to feel along the veins, testing the waters, and her magic fought back. Howled at the invasion. Snarled at something else that lingered on the edge of awareness.

Something Cricket almost recognized. Although he couldn't see it, he would describe it as . . . green.

Like plant life. Like forests and undergrowth. Like moss.

It was green, and it was *retreating*.

Cricket's own magic turned at his will, facing away from the snapping jaws of Becka's to stand against this vine threatening to strangle it. He latched on. Magic cold as ice freezing the vine in place, turning it blue, and brittle. Then Becka's bright magic struck, and it shattered into a million pieces. Turning to not more than dust under their combined attacks.

Becka gasped, her eyes flying open, and she sat up so quickly she nearly smacked her head against her father's. But she was awake, and Cricket would have taken any pain that was caused by it without a single complaint.

"Papa?" she asked, her voice scratchy from days of disuse. "Papa what happened?"

"I don't know, baby." Cricket scooped her into a tight hug, his face pressed into her hair. "I don't know, but I'm going to find out." And now he had a place to start. Something to look at. A connection between the rot and the unconscious victims.

Becka coughed, burying her face into his shoulder. It sounded dry, and wretched, and once she got started she couldn't seem to stop. Cricket pulled back, reaching for the cup of water on her nightstand, and held it out to her.

Becka wouldn't take it, not even as tears streamed down her face, and her little body shook with each ragged cough. It lasted for far too long, tiny specks slipping between her fingers with the force of it, and when it finally stopped, and she pulled her hand away it was coated in a layer of tiny seeds. No mucus. No crimson. Just seeds.

She took the water from him, and drank heavily while Cricket reached for the seeds, scooping them into his own hands to examine more closely. "How do you feel now?"

"Better." Becka nodded, although her voice came out as a croak. "Papa . . . I'm not sick like you were, am I?"

His chest tightened at the memory of that illness. At the reminder that this was eerily similar to when he'd been coughing up entire flowers. But it hadn't started with seeds. It had begun with petals and leaves, indications that something was actually growing in his lungs.

"I'm not sure yet, sunflower, but I'm going to find out." He would have to do some research. Maybe have one of the healers do a scan of Becka and be sure that there was nothing growing in her lungs. But there was a difference in what he'd felt inside of Becka versus what he'd dealt with on his own. It wasn't quite the same. It was of a similar vein. Botanical in nature. But not the same. And there were a number of curses and spells having to do with plants.

But it would narrow down the search. He just had to hope that this magic was not something exclusive to Cytherea. He slid the seeds into a handkerchief, folding it carefully for closer examination later, and returned to doting on his daughter.

HOURS LATER, after Beck had fallen back into a more restful sleep with Ignacia at her bedside, Cricket slipped into the library where he found Claudia half slumped against a table.

"Nothing still," she said when she heard the door open, not even bothering to look up.

"I might have something, actually." Cricket pulled the handkerchief from his pocket and opened it to show her the seeds. They looked like the ends of a dandelion, so small they could be scattered on the wind.

"What is this?" Claudia scrubbed at the bridge of her nose, pushing her glasses up into her hair as she pulled the handkerchief closer to get a better look.

"Becka coughed these up. Almost the same way as when I coughed up the water in Nishi. I need your help creating a tracking array to find their source."

"Now?"

"Yes, now."

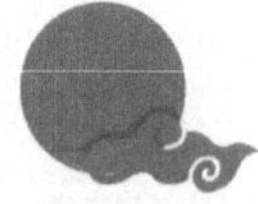

"IT ISN'T WORKING, why isn't it working?" Cricket muttered to himself, looking once again over his notes from the arrays he and Claudia had tried the night before. Array after array. All giving back the same result.

"I don't know." Claudia frowned, her ink-stained fingers tapping nervously against the woodgrain. "But we need rest."

"Once more." Cricket shook his head. "I have another idea."

He took another of the seeds from the little glass dish where they'd put them. They were running dangerously low, and many of their experiments so far had destroyed the seed they used for them. Even if his own magic wasn't failing him from exhaustion, they would have to stop soon.

Slicing open the tip of his finger, he worked an array onto the sheet of paper where the seed rested, working the characters out from the center as he had once down with the diagram for his own body many years ago. Balance, and order. Attention paid to the negative space. This one would work. He knew it would. It had to. There were no other options.

With the array written out, he waited a moment, taking a breath as his head spun, and said a little prayer to Selene. *Let this work. Let me find a way to save our people. Let me put an end to this curse.* Then he pressed a clean finger to the edge of the paper, his magic flowing from him to light up the bloody characters. They glowed warm at first, but as he pushed more and more magic into them, they burned brighter until they were near blinding.

He hissed, his eyes watering with the sting, but didn't look away.

After several moments, the light lifted from the paper, spinning, spinning, spinning like the magnet in a compass. Searching for the source. Seeking a direction to send Cricket in. A place to start, that's all he needed. A path to head down to find the source of their trouble. Somewhere he could send his knights to hunt down the cursed object they needed to find.

But the light just continued to spin, and spin. And the longer it did, the deeper Cricket's stomach dropped. Until finally the light faded entirely, and all that was left was a burned up piece of paper, and no answers to be had.

Cricket shouted, slamming his hands on the table hard enough that Claudia jumped, but she said nothing.

"You should go to bed," Claudia said after a long silence.

"I'm going to keep searching," Cricket responded, and pushed back from the table to head into the stacks. He had missed the answer. It had to be there somewhere.

CHAPTER 18

The rescue mission was not a total victory, Takayoshi understood that. Was reminded of it every day that they traveled back toward the capital. Estia was happy to have zir siblings back, but the loss of zir twin sat heavy on zir shoulders, coloring every word ze said in something a little less vibrant than it should have been. Tension was thick as fog between them, a question of "what will we do next?" rested on every tongue.

That knowledge did weigh on Takayoshi, did make the hum of pleasure at their success just that much less, but it could not completely diminish it. They were one step closer to the retrieval of Cricket's pearl.

All Takayoshi could hope was that knowing zir siblings were safe would make Estia less likely to betray them again in the end. It was hard to trust zir after everything, but Takayoshi did not see where they had much choice. Besides that fact, Estia had given them all ze had on Craven's plans. Which was not much, but it was more knowledge than they could have gathered with just observation alone.

"We'll be back this time tomorrow," Leo said from where

he was riding next to Takayoshi. They had taken to bringing up the rear of their little group to ensure that no one could surprise them, they said. But Takayoshi knew it was because Leo worried, like he did, that Estia and zir siblings would run away. That this whole thing was some huge farce that would end in them both dead.

"We will." Home. It was a good thought. It settled warm in his stomach, fluttering there with every inhale. He would be home tomorrow. Holding his little family in his arms, where they belonged.

"You're happy," Leo accused.

"I am." There was no denying it. It was clear in the smile on his face, and Takayoshi would not deny it even if there were any reason to try. It was good to be happy once more. Good to be settled in some small way. After everything they had been through, he and Cricket were finally on the same page.

The war was not over, Craven would be at their door soon, but the battle was won. They were together, and they knew that they loved each other. Takayoshi was grateful of that. They just had to fight this one last battle.

"It looks good on you." Leo nodded, then clicked his tongue and nudged his horse forward to move to Estia's side. But not before calling over his shoulder, "Maybe your prince will have a hero's welcome waiting."

The thought made Takayoshi smile more, the expression feeling almost foreign on his face. A hero's welcome would look different for him than it did for anyone else, but Leo was aware of that. He knew all Takayoshi wanted by way of a grand welcome was his husband and daughter there with a smile.

WHATEVER TAKAYOSHI HAD BEEN HOPING for, it was not this. The capital of Lunette spread before them quiet as the grave. It had not exactly been bustling before they left, with so many killed during Sunil's attacks, the capital was only half full. But closer to the castle at its heart, people had settled, and even begun to return to normal life with markets, and laundry, and children laughing in the streets.

There was no laughing now. No fresh smelling sheets. No first of the season's produce. Just a stillness that made Takayoshi's heart stutter in his chest, fear crawling along his nerves.

Were they too late? Had Craven already enacted his final spell on Lunette's people?

"What— What happened?" Rowan asked. He was one of Estia's middle siblings. A tall young man, with deep black hair. "Where is everyone?"

Rowan had come into his own a little on their travels, letting Leo teach him sword work, and offering to help with the younger children. Not old enough yet to be of any real use in a battle, but Takayoshi could see how one day he would make a fine leader. Kind, and caring.

"Head toward the palace, we will find out." Takayoshi nudged his horse to pick up her pace, unable to bear looking around them any longer. Besides, they would not find answers here. The only one who could provide answers was Cricket himself. Takayoshi prayed to the goddess that he was still all right. That whatever had happened to hide the people away in their capital had not been the slaying of their king.

By some miracle he managed to keep control of his fear long enough to not tear through the city on his horse, or worse yet, light anything ablaze as he rode past. Takayoshi could feel the heat simmering under his skin, just waiting to be let loose.

But all of those worries vanished at the sight of the gates into the palace.

They were open, and waiting. And there, standing in their shadow, was Cricket. Becka was not beside him, and as Takayoshi drew closer he could see that Cricket had grown pale in the time he had been away. Dark rings circled his eyes. And although Cricket stood tall, and did his best to hold an official air about him, clear exhaustion hung off his shoulders. His posture less careless slouch and more sleep-deprived hunch.

"You're back," Cricket said a little breathless, as a smile overtook his face.

Takayoshi hummed his agreement as he slid from his horse. "I am back."

Takayoshi closed the distance between them, and it was easy to wrap Cricket in his arms, pressing his nose to his hair. To know that he was safe, and that all of this had not been for naught. With Cricket's arms around his neck, and Takayoshi's hands pulling Cricket in flush against his chest, Takayoshi could finally breathe fully for the first time in weeks.

Cricket was whole.

Cricket smiled a little, pressed his forehead to Takayoshi's and let his eyes squint in his joy. Takayoshi pulled back just enough to press his lips to Cricket's brow, inhaling deeply the smell of his hair. Incense, the salt of the sea, and home. Takayoshi wanted to pull him in closer, to press his lips to Cricket's in a kiss far more passionate. But there were too many watching eyes, and he knew very well how inappropriate that would be. At least . . . until they were wed. Then no one would be able to say anything about the appropriateness of their affection.

Takayoshi could not wait. But he would do his best to be patient.

"And you brought friends." Cricket shifted on his feet so he could peek around Takayoshi and see who was with him.

Takayoshi grumbled softly at the inattention, but allowed Cricket to move around him and inspect the small group. There would be time later for a proper greeting, and to check in that Cricket was all right. To sit him down and make him eat a proper meal, and get some proper rest. In the meantime, they had to deal with Estia and zir siblings.

"Your Highness," Leo said, dipping into a respectful bow. "May I present the royal family of Cytherea."

Cricket's smile was broad, although it did not hold the same happiness he had turned on Takayoshi. There was an ugly, covetous part of Takayoshi that reveled in that knowledge, but he did not allow it to show on his face.

"As I'm sure no one said this to you when you crossed my borders, welcome to Lunette." Cricket swept his arms out in a motion that Takayoshi was sure was second nature. As if showing off the beauty and liveliness of his city. Then a moment later, Cricket seemed to realize what he was doing, and he dropped his hands awkwardly to his sides. "Forgive me, we're in a bit of a state of. . . well. We're in a state."

"What has happened?" Takayoshi murmured gently, only just loud enough for Cricket to hear. Cricket shook his head, a signal that they would discuss this later.

"Come with me, we'll get some food ready, and rooms prepared. You'll have to. . ." He paused a moment, licking his lips, a tell Takayoshi was beginning to realize meant he was hiding how upset he was about something. Takayoshi wanted to ask what it was. To sit Cricket down and force him to talk. But now was not the time. "You'll have to excuse our mess.

We will have to eat in one of the smaller sitting rooms. The dining hall is currently in use."

"In use for what?" Estia asked, pushing for answers the way that Takayoshi himself wanted to.

Cricket turned to lead the group back into the castle without answering. Instead he said, "Right this way."

Leo tilted his head at Takayoshi as he passed with them. A simple gesture to ask if he was coming as well. Takayoshi shook his head, then lifted his chin in a subtle motion. An indication that he would be along after a while. He needed to know what had Cricket so upset first.

Takayoshi had become so a part of the palace of Lunette and Cricket's family since the battle with Sunil, that no one stopped him in the halls. They did not even seem surprised at all to see him without Cricket at his side. As if the palace was as much his as it was Cricket's. It was not. Not yet, anyway. But Takayoshi allowed this knowledge to leave him feeling at peace.

"Your Highness," Youta dipped into a bow where she was carrying a tray away from the dining hall. She, like Cricket, looked tired, and drawn. Whatever had happened in his absence had not just upset Cricket, it seemed, it had worn on all of them. Fear returned, and Takayoshi straightened his back against the looming feeling that made him want to hunch.

"Youta." He dipped his head out of respect. "I've returned with most of Estia's siblings. No doubt Cricket will be asking you to prepare rooms for them soon."

"Oh good." Youta's face brightened into a smile, then it faltered a little. "Most?"

"We were unable to retrieve Estia's twin, Prince Damian. It seems he has fallen in with Craven." Or worse, but Takayoshi was hoping that it was simply a matter of Damian not understanding the situation fully, of him being manipulated, for Estia's sake.

"Oh." She frowned, her head dipping to look at the tray in her hands. "I suppose you're here to see the victims."

"Victims?" Takayoshi glanced behind her, and in the crack between doors, he could finally see the cots lining the dining hall, each full with a person. Pixies, and goblins, and. . . *children.* There were *children* in there. His heart plummeted. He had not seen Becka. Where was Becka? Had she been affected?

"The pixies were affected shortly after you left. Then the gnomes and goblins," Youta said, turning to open the door further so he could see, and shaking her head a little at the sight before them. "It's been a few days since. . ." when she turned back to look at him there was a sadness in her eyes Takayoshi could not begin to process.

"Since what?" He was reasonably sure he did not want the answer to that question.

"Becka was the first to fall ill, Your Highness. She—"

Takayoshi did not wait to hear anymore, he did not let Youta finish telling him what happened, he spun from the door and tore through the halls. He knew this path well, had trod it several times since returning to Lunette. For story time at night, and music lessons in the afternoon. For simple things, like checking in on how her other lessons were going. Takayoshi had been given his own quarters, and most of the time he was not there. Most of the time he was either with Becka in her rooms, or he was at Cricket's side.

He bumped someone on his way, a maid carrying a load of laundry, and only had a moment to offer her a hasty apology even as the linens went everywhere. Because he had to see for himself. He had to know what had happened to his daughter.

By the time the door creaked open, and he found Becka sitting at her desk, her head bent over a book, his heart was beating so quickly he was sure it would leap from his chest. But there she was. His little girl. Studiously going over whatever work had been assigned to her.

"Shishi?" Becka asked, her head tilted when she spotted him. "What's wrong?"

"Nothing." Takayoshi let out a long slow breath, trying to calm his racing heart. "Nothing is wrong. I am home."

"You are." Becka's face brightened. "To stay this time?"

"Yes. To stay." He nodded and bent to hold his arms out to her as she raced across the room to hug him tightly.

CHAPTER 19

Cricket was pacing. His steps furious and unsettled. The other children hadn't woken up yet. Becka hadn't been unconscious for more than a couple of days, but the child who had been affected right after her was still sleeping. The little boy's eyes closed tight. His breathing had finally settled, and there were no more fits. But that didn't actually make Cricket feel any better.

What if that was because his magic had stopped fighting? What if it was because his body was giving up? How could Cricket look into the faces of his parents and explain to them that Cricket didn't know what the difference was. Or rather he did, but the thing that had pulled Becka from her sleep wouldn't wake any of the other children.

Still, Cricket sat by the boy's bed, and he tried. He pressed his magic into the boy's veins and fought against the curse that had settled into his blood. He endured the snapping, and the thorns that dug into him not leaving physical scars, but magical ones. Pain that ebbed beneath the skin like a bruise, but never made itself visible.

"You can't keep doing this," Claudia said, her tone hushed

as she looked about the room to make sure no one was looking at them. "You're going to burn yourself out. Let one of the others try."

"No one is as powerful as I am." That much was true. Cricket was the first Celestial, and he was most closely related to the source of their magic. Takayoshi was a close second, but even he had been unable to rail against the vicious vines that tightened around the children's magic, threatening to suffocate them. What would happen if it did? Would the children die? Cricket didn't want to think about that. Couldn't afford to. It would be too easy to give up if he did.

"Take a step back from it," Claudia advised. "Let's come at it from another direction. When brute force doesn't work, there has to be a different solution."

"But we haven't found one yet. We can't find the source. We can't find a cure. We've got *nothing*." Cricket choked on the words, almost a sob. It was true, they hadn't found another approach yet, nor any writing on this kind of curse at all. Whatever it was, it was new, or it was Cytherean magic that he didn't have access to. He didn't know which option scared him more, was more hopeless, left him more helpless.

"But we will." Claudia nodded to herself, her words measured and sure. She had faith in their abilities as a team. Trust in Cricket. So many people did now. So many of his subjects were putting their lives in his hands. "Estia and zir siblings might know something of this. We'll have them look."

"Yes, let's leave this up to the traitor," Cricket hissed.

Claudia jerked as if she'd been struck, but she didn't move away from Cricket. Didn't let the venom in his words drive her from her chair and the room as some might have. "You don't mean that."

"Don't I?" He wasn't sure that he didn't, actually. Cricket

hadn't been there when Estia had betrayed them all, but he was still angry on their behalf. And then there was the matter of Estia holding his pearl hostage. It was hard not to be a little bitter. Hard not to let that bitterness fester into something more.

"You don't. Because you're too smart to let something as foolish as a grudge ruin relations with another noble family." Claudia sounded oddly like Mawra in that moment, and the longing that panged through Cricket's chest nearly had him doubling over with it. Mawra. Father. How many more parents would Cricket lose to this infernal war? All of them, for those had been all he had.

"Your Highness," Claudia called, her voice firm, pulling him back into the present. "We cannot snub our noses at whatever help we're given from Estia. Ze is trying to make up for past wrongs, and we should allow zir to do so."

Gods, when had she gotten so good at advising? Hadn't he just appointed her no more than a fortnight ago? "You're right." Cricket sighed scrubbing at his face. He knew there were dark circles ringing his eyes. He knew he looked sallow and wrung out. But there didn't seem to be any helping either of those things. "What time is it? Don't we have a meeting with the others soon?"

Claudia nodded, tucking a pocket watch back into her pocket. "We should be going, actually. If you're done here? I didn't want to interrupt your work."

Cricket bit back a sarcastic response with another long exhale. It was kind of her not to treat what he was doing like it was pointless. To allow him to continue to try as if he could learn something new in his attempts, even as she sat beside him and watched the curse sink its teeth into him and drain him. If he didn't stop this, he would fall unconscious just like the others soon, he knew that. He needed rest. He needed time away. He needed to recuperate.

"I don't think there's anything more that can be learned today," is what Cricket said instead of all the nasty spiteful things that sat like bile on his tongue. His continued failure to find answers wasn't her fault, it was his own.

If Claudia noted the anger in his tone, she didn't comment on it, just rose from her seat and led the way to the door. Cricket forced himself to stand taller, his chin held back, as he walked through the corridors of his castle, even as the weight of everything threatened to make him hunch, make his back bow beneath it.

"We will find an answer, Your Highness," Claudia said, her tone steady and sure. She'd learned to read him over the weeks since the final battle with Sunil. Learned to see him in his entirety the way only a friend could. Cricket wanted to shrink back from that knowing gaze, to put distance between himself and Claudia, to hide from her. But Claudia, like Takayoshi, and Anstice, and Ignacia, seemed to see right through him. How had he surrounded himself with people who found him so frighteningly transparent?

Cricket didn't answer, and it didn't seem like Claudia expected him to, for the silence between them was comfortable, not fraught with unanswered questions as they walked the rest of the way to his father's study where the others waited.

When they entered, Ignacia stood by the door, her mouth pressed into a firm line. Estia and Leo were sitting in the chairs on the one side of the expansive desk. And Takayoshi stood just off the right side of the large chair opposite them, as if waiting for Cricket. It lit something warm and liquid in Cricket's chest to see Takayoshi waiting there for him. Ever the vigilant sentinel. Ever the loyal knight. Ever *Cricket's* in a way he would never be anyone else's.

"I hope I haven't kept you waiting long," Cricket said. He hesitated for a moment at the corner of his desk, unsure if he wanted to sit in the chair behind it—his father's chair—or somewhere else. In the end, he compromised and came to lean on the front lip of the desk, maybe a little too close to Estia and Leo for their comfort, but he didn't care. He wasn't there to make anyone comfortable, least of all Estia.

"Not long," Takayoshi assured. Cricket could hear his boots creaking behind him, as if he were shifting his weight subtly. Likely trying to decide if he should join Cricket or remain where he was. Adorable, honestly, how easily now Takayoshi adapted to Cricket's impropriety. He didn't scold Cricket about it. He didn't try to bend Cricket to the rules that had been instilled in him. He tried to accommodate Cricket's tendencies to the best of his abilities.

Cricket held up a hand over his shoulder, staying the movement, and making the choice for Takayoshi. He was fine where he was, this meeting would hopefully not be long.

"So," Cricket began, leaning further back against the desk. He liked that in this position he stood a little above them both, even though Leo was impressively tall. It made him feel more like he had a handle on this conversation. "We have held up our end of the bargain, now it's time for you to hold up yours."

"Your pearl," Estia said, not a single question in zir tone. Ze knew what Cricket wanted, how could they not?

The talons on Cricket's fingers dug into the meat of his arms, reminding him what he looked like now. How much closer to a monster he'd grown over the days that passed. He should have had control over this. The dragon was no longer fighting him for dominance, they had merged into one being. But his shifting abilities were lacking without the magic of the pearl to . . . what? Ground them? Replenish them? Focus them? He wasn't even really sure what the point of the pearl *was*, but he knew that without it he looked like *this*.

"Precisely." Cricket smiled a little, one sharpened tooth on display as he peeled his lips further back. No one seemed frightened of him, not yet anyway. But how long before his appearance resembled too closely the demon prince Sunil had painted him as for people to ignore it? How long before he lost control enough that something else slipped? His mental state was fine, for the moment. But how much longer would that last?

"I'm sorry. I can't give it to you." Estia shook zir head, but although the words were contrite, the tone and the expression on zir face was anything but.

Cricket's jaw clenched so hard his teeth ground together, and he saw Ignacia move out of the corner of his eye. Her hand falling to her sword, ready to defend him should he need it. He shook his head, and Ignacia stood down.

"Why not?" Cricket asked through his teeth. Anger froze in his veins, turning his fingertips so icy they felt like icicles through his tunic sleeves.

"I cannot give it to you until my twin is returned to me." Estia lifted zir head, clearly trying to hold some of the ground ze had lost in this conversation. But Cricket was rapidly becoming tired of this game. Another king was leading an army to his door. The children of his city were sick. And this *person* was keeping something from him that might be vital to putting a stop to it all.

"Cannot? Or *will* not?" Cricket leaned in further, the congenial mask of civility slipping away from his face. Did Estia know the cost of holding something so valuable? Didn't ze see how this could ruin all of them? Zirself included!

Estia met his eyes, but didn't say anything. Instead ze jutted zir chin out defiantly.

Cricket lashed out, not even thinking before he grabbed Estia by zir jaw, his talons digging into the skin there. Everyone jumped into action at once. Leo grabbed for his sword. Ignacia leapt across the room. Claudia let out a startled sound of protest. And he could hear Takayoshi making his way around the desk, footsteps measured, even.

"I need that pearl," Cricket said. Fury spread like frost from Cricket's fingers into Estia's skin, but ze didn't so much as flinch. "I need it to save all of us. To protect my daughter. To stop the coming war. To cure this affliction . So answer me this: cannot, or will not?"

"Cannot," Estia bit out, but refused to look away from the anger painted across Cricket's face.

"Why *not*?" Cricket snapped, jerking zir head.

Instead of answering the question, Estia narrowed zir eyes on him. "It doesn't matter why not. The point is I can't. And neither can anyone else. It is unretrievable for the moment, and will remain so until my twin is safe in the capital with me."

"So he has it then." Cricket didn't need to ask, and he knew even if he had, Estia wouldn't confirm it. "You left the thing that can *control me* in the hands of your brother who has turned tail and joined Craven?"

The ice was spreading along Estia's skin, turning zir lips a blue tinge. Zir next words were said through chattering teeth. "It is on his person, but he'll never find it. I only have to be within a few feet of him to get it back."

"And what if he discovers it?"

"He won't," Estia assured. "You're safe. It can't be used against you."

"Cricket," Takayoshi said, soft and calm as he reached out to grasp the wrist of the hand holding Estia's chin still in a vice grip. "You need to let zir go."

"Let zir *go*?" Cricket croaked, a disbelieving laugh on his tongue. "Why should I? Do you know what ze has done?"

"I do. But this is not the solution." Takayoshi's hand was warm around Cricket's skin, thawing the ice, and chasing away the chill. "Come. Let us get some rest. In the morning things may look better."

"They won't." But Cricket let Takayoshi tug his hand away from Estia's jaw, pulled his magic back to reside under his own skin again, leaving Estia's skin the normal burnished ochre color it was meant to be.

"They might."

"I apologize." Cricket sighed heavily, his shoulders slumping. "I shouldn't have attacked you like—"

"No apologies necessary." Estia shook zir head. "Were I in your shoes, I'd react the same. But Takayoshi is right, Your Highness, you need some rest. We all need to be in peak form when Craven gets here, but you especially. Please," Estia practically begged, "allow your family to take care of you."

Cricket nodded numbly, and let Takayoshi pull him from where he was leaned against the desk into his arms. Let the warmth that lived under Takayoshi's skin heat his own. Let himself be led from the study.

CHAPTER 20

"I understand why you are upset," Takayoshi said, but he did not take his arm away from Cricket's waist as he led him down the hall toward his quarters. Cricket's response was a perfectly reasonable one to what they had just found out. Takayoshi, likewise, was angry with Estia for zir deceit. But he could also understand why Estia had lied to a certain degree. Because if Takayoshi had known Cricket's pearl was in Damian's custody, he would not have stopped until he had it in hand again. Damn the consequences.

He would have left Leo and Estia to bring the rest of the Cytherean royal family back to the capital, and spent his time trying to get the pearl away from Damian. He may have even struck out against Craven directly. That would have caused trouble for all parties involved, but Takayoshi could hardly leave something that could control the man he loved so close to someone who clearly hated him. Maybe that was not true. Maybe Craven did not hate Cricket. Maybe he was merely an opportunist. The fact still stood.

"But?" Cricket asked, leaning more heavily against Takayoshi. He was tired, Takayoshi could see it in every sluggish movement. How many days had he spent at the bedside of their daughter? Of those affected by Craven's curse? Had Cricket even been eating properly? Takayoshi had left Cricket in the care of their little family, had trusted them to ensure that Cricket would take care of himself. But they all had their own duties to attend to. And of course when the curse hit, things would slip through the cracks. Cricket's needs seemed to be one of those things.

"But ze is right, perhaps the safest place for that pearl is away from everyone. Us included." At least Takayoshi hoped that was the case. He could not imagine a world in which Craven had control over a dragon. What little he knew of the king of Cytherea did not bode well for him having that kind of power. It was a lot of trust to put in someone who had already betrayed him more than once, but Takayoshi was willing to let Estia prove zirself. And ze did seem earnest, more so than ze had ever been before. "We have to trust that ze knows what ze is doing."

Cricket snorted, rolling his eyes. "How do we know this isn't all some elaborate trick? How do we know Craven doesn't already have my pearl in hand?"

"If he did, he would not hesitate to use it against Estia and zir siblings." Of this Takayoshi was certain. He had seen the look of hate in Craven's eyes more than once when he looked at Estia. He remembered how Craven had treated Estia before they left Cytherea in search of information on Cricket's dragon. There was a bone-deep knowing in all of it. A recognition that he had not put together then, but understood all too well now. Craven had looked at Estia the way Sunil had looked at Cricket. Like ze was an obstacle, and nothing more. "I trust zir."

Cricket stopped, his movements jerky and uncoordinated in his exhaustion, and tilted his head back to look up at

Takayoshi. "How can you trust Estia after what ze did to you? To Leo? To Claudia?"

Takayoshi hummed, tilting his head back to look up at the ceiling in thought. It was hard to put his emotions into words, always had been. And this one was even more difficult to pin down than some of the others. It was perhaps . . . hope? "I do not know."

"You don't?" Cricket tilted his own head to the side, inquisitive and perhaps a little amused.

"I do not." Takayoshi shook his head, looking back to Cricket with a soft, gentle smile. "But I have faith in the person who was one of my friends during a time in my life when hope was limited."

"So you just. . . *want* to trust zir?" Cricket was smiling a little now, his eyebrows raised high on his face as if he had just discovered something delightful.

"I suppose so." Takayoshi nodded.

"Hope is a dangerous thing you know? It's often dashed." But Cricket did not sound like he was discouraging it. Rather the words sounded like something he had heard before and was now repeating to Takayoshi. Perhaps it was something someone unkind had said to him as a child, someone like Sunil. Words that someone else had tried to drill into his head that Cricket had never put much weight behind himself.

"I think I have heard that before." Cricket's tiny smile was infectious. It spread like wildfire through Takayoshi's veins, making him warm all over. "Do you think I should take it to heart?"

Cricket barked a laugh, his eyes dancing, and Takayoshi hardly resisted the urge to lean in closer, to taste that laugh on his tongue. Then, shaking his head, Cricket said, "I never do."

"Then I will not either." Takayoshi felt his grin spread wider across his face. He bumped his forehead lightly against

Cricket's needing the closeness if just for a moment. "Come. You need rest. Remember?"

"I feel better now." Cricket poked out his bottom lip.

"Perhaps you do, but how long will that last?" Takayoshi got them moving once more, not allowing Cricket to dig his heels in even a little as they rounded the corner to Cricket's rooms.

Cricket stopped just outside of his door, his hand lifted to press flat against the door. His fingers curled, scraping talons against the wood, his head ducked to hide whatever expression he had on his face in his hair, but Takayoshi noted the rigidity of his shoulders, the unsettled air about him. Something was wrong. Something other than Estia's potential betrayal. He did not say anything right away. He just stood there. His hand on the door.

And Takayoshi waited, knowing well enough that if something was wrong, Cricket would tell him. They communicated now. They did not hide things. Not anymore.

"I do not want to be alone," Cricket said after what felt like a moment too long. "I have. . . " He sighed, his shoulders slumping a little, and he leaned forward to press his head into the wood just above his hand. "I have nightmares about the curse. About what happened to Becka. They wake me up at night. And sometimes I cannot tell what is real and what isn't."

Takayoshi made a soft sound of understanding. "Is that why you have not been sleeping in your own bed?" Takayoshi lifted a hand to grasp Cricket's shoulder, and pulled him in close to his chest, folding him in his arms as if that alone could protect him from the ghosts that haunted the both of them. It could not. They would never be entirely free of the horrors they had seen, or the terrors they had known.

"It's foolish, I know." Cricket sighed, his hot breath ghosting across Takayoshi's neck, the skin raising in gooseflesh where Cricket had pressed his face in close, hiding away from the world. "I should be over this. I am a king. A Celestial. A dragon. But I just—"

"It is not foolish," Takayoshi said, gentle but firm. "We have all been through many trials. We have all known trauma unlike any those who raised us could have foreseen. We were not brought up to fight a war, and yet we must." He lifted his hand to thread through Cricket's hair, rubbing gently at the back of his neck. "I think it would be strange if we did not suffer some. . . consequences for this."

Cricket made a soft, wounded sound as if unhappy with being so *seen*. But he did not move out of where Takayoshi held him. They stood there for a moment in the quiet of the hall. The whole of the castle was either asleep, or busy elsewhere. No one would even know about the impropriety of Takayoshi joining Cricket in his quarters. Not that he thought any of their family or friends would have a problem with it. Takayoshi and Cricket had made their intentions for one another very clear, it was only the absence of adequate time for a full ceremony that was holding them back from marrying.

"I will stay with you," Takayoshi said, pressing a kiss to Cricket's forehead, careful of his antlers. "You will not have to wake up alone." *Never again*, Takayoshi did not say, but he vowed it in his head. He would not leave Cricket to that kind of fear. Not so long as he could help it.

"You don't have— you don't have to." Cricket lifted his head, his eyes wide. "I know it would make you—"

"It will not make me anything. I will stay with you." Takayoshi shook his head. "I just need to go to my own quarters and prepare for bed, and then I will return. In the meantime, you should change and perhaps *bathe*?" A little smile ticked up the corner of Takayoshi's lips on the last word.

Cricket blinked a moment, and then he was laughing again. "I always forget how funny you are sometimes, Yoshi."

"Hmm." Takayoshi could not resist leaning in for another kiss to taste that laughter. It was warm like sunshine, and twice as sweet as the first of a new season's fruit. "Off with you. It will not take me long."

Cricket nodded quickly, and turned back for his door.

IT DID NOT TAKE Takayoshi more than fifteen minutes to clean off the grime of the day, and change into a more comfortable pair of pants and tunic made of soft fabric. Then he was back at Cricket's door, knocking lightly on the wood.

Cricket flung it open a moment later, his hair still dripping from the bath, and color high on his cheeks from the heat of the water. "That was so *fast*."

Takayoshi hummed his agreement, and stepped over the threshold into Cricket's rooms when he moved out of the way. He had been here a time or two since returning to the capital, but walking into Cricket's private rooms always left his nerves buzzing a little. A reminder that perhaps he should not be there after all sat heavy at the back of his mind. It sounded oddly like his uncle, and he pushed it aside. There was no room for his uncle's rules in this space.

"Sorry everything is kind of a mess," Cricket laughed, the sound high, and nervous as he stumbled in front of Takayoshi to make it to the bedroom first. By the time Takayoshi made it to the door, Cricket was trying to right the blankets, his hands fluttering nervously as his talons caught on the covers.

"It is all right." Takayoshi shrugged off the long robe he had put on over his sleep clothes, and laid it carefully in a chair by the door so it would not wrinkle. Then he moved to take Cricket's hands in his own, stilling their movement. "Come. Rest," he murmured softly, and guided Cricket gently until he was sitting on the bed with Takayoshi. Once there, Takayoshi pulled the blankets up over Cricket's legs, and nudged him lightly to lay down. "I am here, and I am not going to leave you alone."

Cricket nodded with a loud swallow, but he let himself curl up under the blanket, his eyes following Takayoshi the entire time as he came around the other side of the bed and lay beside him. "What if—" Cricket cut himself off, pursing his lips a little. "What if I move in my sleep? What if—"

Takayoshi did not roll his eyes, but it was a near thing. Instead, he reached for Cricket and pulled him in closer, allowed Cricket to curl around his side, his chin resting on Takayoshi's chest. "Is this what you were concerned about?"

"Sorta." Cricket's cheeks were ruddy with embarrassment in the low light of the moon coming in through the windows. It was impossibly endearing.

"Then do not be concerned. It is fine." Takayoshi curled his arm comfortably around Cricket, and leaned back into his pillows, content. "Now. Rest."

Cricket grumbled, squirming a little as he tried to find a way to lay that was most comfortable to him, and Takayoshi let him take his time to find it. All the while keeping his eyes closed so Cricket did not think he was bothering him. When Cricket finally found a position that suited him, he settled entirely. Once he had, his breathing evened out quickly, and Takayoshi was able to find sleep himself.

TAKAYOSHI HAD BEEN TRAINED from an early age to be a light sleeper. The monks in the mountains of Helio said it was a means to keep himself and his fellow knights safe. They taught him that if he did not sleep lightly, it was more likely he would be overrun by their enemies.

Sleeping beside Cricket was no different. And when the bed dipped under Cricket's weight, when that weight disappeared. . .

Takayoshi roused quickly.

"Cricket? What is wrong?" Takayoshi slid from the bed, and followed Cricket to the door, only pausing a moment to grab his discarded robe and wrap it tightly around Cricket's shoulders to ward off the chill.

Cricket did not answer, and when Takayoshi finally managed to get out ahead of him in the corridor outside of his rooms, he found Cricket's eyes open but unseeing, a blank expression on his face.

Sleep walking. When had he started *sleep walking*?

Without another word, Takayoshi followed Cricket through the halls.

BOOK III
THE WALKERS

CHAPTER 21

Someone was calling Cricket's name. Their voice soft and leading, like the final warm breeze of summer before autumn set in. Although he'd only heard Selene speak a handful of times, he would swear that it was she who was calling for him. Leading him through the sprawling streets of his capital.

There was a light up ahead.

It pulsed softly. Dimming and brightening seemingly at random. It was beautiful. A lure. Cricket wondered what would happen when he reached it. Would he be warmed by its light?

"Cricket," she called again. "Come."

He'd never seen his mother in person. There were depictions of the goddess Selene, surely, but those were artist renderings dreamed up by people who had never set eyes on her before. He wondered what she would look like. Would she have his eyes? He was created of her, with no father to speak of, at least not one of blood. So there was no one else he *could* look like. But that didn't mean she wouldn't have borrowed features from people she cared for. The brows of her first believer. The nose of the most devout priestess. The lips of the goddess who was her best friend. She could have put together his face like a child played with clay, built a baby out of a rainbow of her favorite colors.

Someone else said something. Their voice deep, and worried. But Cricket couldn't make out the words. It was as if they were speaking at him through water, or glass. Separate, and far away.

He *knew* that voice, though. It was familiar, and aching. Something tugged at his chest, tried to draw him back the way he'd come. A line he could only just resist because he was following the trail of his mother.

"Cricket. Come to me," his mother's voice broke through his thoughts again, pulling his attention back to the light. "Come to me, my son."

His chest swelled with warmth. *My son*. He hadn't known he wanted that until now. How many years had the longing for those words lived beneath his ribs? Had it always been there? Or was it new? How hadn't he noticed it before?

"I'm coming," he called back to her, taking another step toward the light. Stars, she was beautiful, even as he couldn't make out her features. Her long hair danced around her, sparkling with stardust. And her arms were held wide. Ready to give him the embrace he'd always wanted. "Mother. I'm here."

"That's it," she cooed, approval heavy in her tone. "My son."

Another step.

The ground was cold beneath his bare feet, which was strange wasn't it? Why would he be walking the streets barefoot? And how had he gotten into the streets to begin with?

"Cricket!"

He shook himself. That didn't matter. All that mattered was getting to his mother. The cold was negligible when compared to the warmth of her presence. Just like the other voice—they were shouting now, but he still couldn't make out the words—was nothing compared to her voice.

Would she embrace him? Would she take him away from all this? Let him know peace?

Stars. It had been so long since he had known peace. Five years or better. Not since before he left home the first time. Oh that he could go back to that time. To not knowing what war looked like. To not knowing how blood could glimmer on the blade of his sword. He missed those days. Missed that innocence. When his biggest concern was enraging his uncle. When he hadn't had a single doubt that he was a good and worthy king. A good and worthy man.

"Cricket!" There was that voice again. Right near his ear this time, so loud it made him jerk. And then there were vice-like arms around his waist tugging him back from his mother. Pulling him away from—

The ledge of a rooftop. The step he'd just been about to take was out into the open air. The building wasn't so tall that the fall would have definitely killed him, but there was a chance. Especially if he had been alone.

"Cricket," Takayoshi begged again, giving him a little shake before he grabbed Cricket closer, and spun him around. "Are you awake?"

"Yes. What— How did I get here?" He thought he knew the answer already, and honestly, it was frightening.

"Sleepwalking." Takayoshi's hand moved to the back of Cricket's head and held him closer. "For an hour at least. I followed you here all the way from the castle. I could not wake you."

"I'm okay now, Yoshi," he said, but even as the words left his lips they sounded a lie. They shook on the exhale. He had to be fine. He had to be all right. They didn't have time for him not to be. "I'm fine." But a question lingered in the back of his mind, did this have anything to do with the cursed citizens? He'd never sleep walked before. Why now? It had to be connected. Nothing in this world was coincidence. "Let's just go home."

Takayoshi's hands were shaking a little, ruffling Cricket's hair, but Cricket didn't say anything about it. He'd clearly frightened Takayoshi enough for one evening.

Taking a deep breath, Cricket willed down his own panic. "I'm fine," Cricket assured again, wrapping his arms tight around Takayoshi's waist. He didn't know how else to reassure Takayoshi. Especially as there was no brushing off what had almost happened. "We'll just have to make sure that I lock my door from here on out."

"This is not a joking matter." Takayoshi hugged him tighter, the embrace near crushing.

"I know. I'm sorry."

"You could have been hurt."

"I know." Cricket sighed, and rubbed his forehead against Takayoshi's chest, letting the warmth of him seep into his skin, warding off the chill of the night. When he tilted his head back, he pressed his chin into Takayoshi's chest.

"Are you not afraid?"

He was. He was so afraid every part of himself shook down his toes. But he could not put the energy into this. Not with everything else. And in the end he just wanted. . .

"Let's go home. Please."

Takayoshi looked for a moment as if he might argue, his brows pinched together just the tiniest fraction. Cricket was sure that he wanted to say they needed to look him over for injuries before they made the journey back, but a shudder racked down Cricket's spine at the threatening chill, and that seemed to still Takayoshi. He frowned, his lips pinching together.

"Yes. Let us go home," Takayoshi agreed. "We will examine you there."

Right. Because Cricket was looking forward to *that*. He nodded, and let Takayoshi lead him back to the edge of the roof where a ladder waited for them to return to street level. Had he climbed that while he was still sleeping? It was amazing he hadn't fallen. No wonder Takayoshi was so shaken.

Cricket's toe caught on something in the dark, and he pitched forward, only just missing going face first into the hard rooftop thanks to Takayoshi's firm hold. "Careful, my king."

"I was. I just. . ." Cricket frowned down at his feet. There was something uneven on the roof. Something lumpy and. . . Green? He leaned forward trying to get a better view of it in the moonlight. When he reached to poke it, it moved away from him like it was living. "Yoshi, I need a little—"

A small orb of magic floated down to rest in his palm, and Cricket turned his head to smile up at Takayoshi. He could have done that himself, surely, but he was still drowsy, and stars only knew what that bout of sleepwalking had done to his magic. Best not to push his limits. When he tilted his head to smile up at Takayoshi in thanks, Takayoshi just nodded. "What is it?"

"I think it's a vine." Cricket frowned and reached for it again, but it squirmed away from him, acting differently than any vine he'd ever seen. "It won't let me get a hold on it."

"Maybe it is best that you do not touch it. We do not know why it is here."

Cricket hummed thoughtfully. "Do you see any buds or anything?"

Takayoshi was silent for a moment, a second light bursting to life over Cricket's shoulder, and Cricket heard him move away to search the rest of the rooftop while

Cricket tried to coax the vine into allowing him to peel it off the roof. But every time he reached it squirmed a little further away.

"No flowers," Takayoshi reported. There was an unsettled quality to his tone though.

"What is it?" Cricket turned to look at him. There was a crease between Takayoshi's brows as he made his way back to Cricket.

"We should return home."

"You noticed something. What was it?" Cricket pushed himself to his feet, giving up on the vine. He would return in the morning when the chill lingered less against his skin, and he could see better. Then he'd get his samples to run his tests.

"There is something familiar about this plant." Takayoshi reached for him again, his hand fisting in Cricket's sleep clothes, the grip tight enough it made the seams creak. "Please. Let us return home."

"Familiar how?"

There was tension across his shoulders. Fear, Cricket realized, perhaps a little too late, fear that mirrored his own. Takayoshi was afraid of this plant, afraid of the implications. And it frightened him more than anything else since Cricket was coughing up blossoms and choking on his feelings.

"Okay." Cricket breathed, flicking his wrist so the light floated above his shoulder and he could pull Takayoshi in by his face. "Okay, we'll go home."

With a thought, his talons turned knife sharp and he cut through the vine, retrieving a chunk of it to shove into his pocket.

Takayoshi nodded, leaning to press his forehead to Cricket's for a moment, his eyes closed. There was stress around his eyes, the lines only just visible to Cricket because he was looking for them. Takayoshi opened his mouth to say something else, maybe to explain the danger they were in, but whatever he was going to say was lost to the sound of crashing coming from the street below them.

"What was that?" Takayoshi asked, his eyes remaining closed for a moment.

"I don't think we want to know." But Cricket pulled himself away from the embrace anyway as a shout rent the air, and looked down on the street. Below, there were a handful of people, shuffling down the cobblestones. One of them had broken a window, and the others were helping him to drag everything out onto the street, and pile it together. Someone had lit a fire on what was already there. "Are they. . ."

"Sleepwalking," Takayoshi confirmed. "Their eyes are open, just as yours were, but there is no indication that they are seeing anything."

"Hey!" Cricket shouted, throwing a pebble at one of the sleepwalkers.

There was no response. They just continued about as they had been.

"Hey!" Cricket tried again, desperation clawing at his throat. "Wake up!"

"It is not working."

"We need to stop them." Cricket rushed to his feet, and darted across the rooftop back to the ladder, heedless of his bare feet, and lack of weapons.

"How? We cannot wake them." Takayoshi was beside him a moment later, keeping pace, and not letting Cricket get too far out of his sight.

"We'll have to create a containment circle." Cricket didn't even pause as he started down the ladder, fully expecting Takayoshi to follow after him, and he did. "Do you have your dagger with you?"

"I did not grab it on my way out the door."

The cobbles were rough on his feet, and pain shot up from his right heel as he stepped down on a sharp bit of stone. But there was another crash from the street around the corner, and there was no time to treat the cut even as it bloomed hot against his heel.

"Let's just hope they're the only ones who have been affected so far tonight," Cricket said, rushing around the corner with Takayoshi following closely behind. He stopped at the end of the alley that opened to the street on the other side, and peaked around it. "When I was sleepwalking, did I notice anything?"

"No. You were completely unresponsive."

"So theoretically, I can make the circle around them without them noticing. Provided we're not too loud." Cricket leaned back against the wall of the alley, and lifted his foot to examine the injury there. It had stopped bleeding for the most part, if it had ever bled enough to do what he needed.

"You are hurt." Takayoshi knelt before him, taking his foot into his hand to examine it.

"It's nothing, Yoshi. Leave it alone. I just wish it were deeper, then I could use the blood for the containment circle." He shook Takayoshi's hold and put his foot back on the ground, then moved to look around the corner once more. There was plenty of glass. If he could find a shard large enough it would do what he needed.

"Can you not make the circle with something else?"

"What would you have me use? We don't exactly have ink or chalk in our bed clothes." Cricket pinched the bridge of his nose. "And who knows how long before they grow bored and move on to the next business, or turn violent. We have no idea what they're being told to do. We have to be quick."

Takayoshi let out a breath, low and slow, and when he opened his eyes again, he nodded as if he had a plan. "I will keep them contained. Does the circle have to be completely closed unto itself to hold them?"

"Well. No. Obviously if I had walls, I could scrawl the

characters onto the walls, and they could connect to one or two arcs and—" He stopped, understanding dawning, then nodded in turn. "I'll work fast."

"Please do," Takayoshi said, the words more order than suggestion as he started at a run into the open street. The sleepwalking citizens didn't notice him at first, and that gave him the moment he needed to grab a chunk of broken glass, and kick it toward Cricket.

It skittered just shy of the alley, leaving Cricket to reach out and grab it. With a deep inhale, he cut into his wrist, and got to work. The arc at the back of the alley was the first to go down. It was sloppy, and shaky, but it would hold. He knew it would. The characters on the walls were not much better, but he could feel the power burned into his blood.

There was a muffled cry from the street, and although it was not Takayoshi's voice, Cricket couldn't help but worry what the sleepwalkers would do to him if he tried to stop them from destroying more property.

Quicker. He had to be quicker.

But the light was dim. And his mind was still slightly hazed over from sleep.

Blast it all to Styx!

Cricket's head spun from blood loss or exhaustion, he couldn't tell anymore. But he was almost done. He was almost there. Then they could lock them in this alley and everyone would be safe until he had come up with a more permanent solution to the problem.

His knees scraped against the ground as he shuffled across the cobbles to create the final arc, muddying his sleep pants, and scratching the skin. But it was fine. It was all going to be all right. He knew that now, as the magic snapped into place and his head spun.

"Yoshi! Now!" Was his voice weak and thready? Stars, he

hoped Takayoshi didn't hear it that way, it would only worry him.

"Yes, Your Highness!" Takayoshi called back, and then he was hurtling the small group of sleepwalkers toward Cricket, leaving Cricket just enough time to shuffle out of the way and lean heavily on the wall outside the alley. His breath coming in hard pants. Gods. He was tired.

He leaned his head back against the wall, and closed his eyes and promptly lost consciousness.

CHAPTER 22

Cricket listed heavily to one side, and Takayoshi had to make a choice: keep Cricket from cracking his head on the cobblestones, or get the last of the sleepwalkers herded into the alley.

He could only hope he made the right decision as he lunged to grab Cricket by his waist, and tug him in close, allowed himself to sink carefully to the ground with the weight of Cricket in his arms. And handled him like the precious person that he was.

The last of the sleepwalkers stopped mid-shuffle into the alley, and tilted their heads as if listening to something, their eyes still strangely vacant. Then they turned, and dashed back the way they had come, their steps far quicker than before. Takayoshi knew he should rise and chase after them, for fear of them hurting themselves or someone else. But the heaviness of Cricket against Takayoshi kept him from giving chase. There was something more important, far more important, right in front of him.

Cricket may very well be angry by the choice Takayoshi made, but he would never make another one, he realized. He had spent far too much of their time together choosing to do the right thing, choosing to be the good knight. Perhaps it was time he allowed himself to be selfish. To bask in the love he had found. To take care of his person most dear.

Cricket was warm in his arms. Warmer than he should have been. Takayoshi frowned, leaning forward to press his cheek to Cricket's forehead. The difference in his temperature was alarming.

"Fever."

Takayoshi said, and rested Cricket across his lap so that he could tear off a part of his own sleep shirt, and bandage the still seeping cut on his wrist. He wished that Cricket had asked him for blood for the containment circle instead. But it would have made their plan to gather the sleepwalkers more difficult, he supposed, and he knew that Cricket was far better at that type of magic than he was. Still, they had no idea what kind of harm that choice would have on Cricket, and Takayoshi did not care for the unknown of it.

Cricket mumbled in his sleep, snuggling in closer.

It was sweet, and Takayoshi wished he had longer to lean into the soft feeling in his chest at seeing Cricket this way. But he did not know if the sleepwalkers would return, or if there were more of them about, and Cricket was vulnerable like this. They needed to return to the castle before more trouble befell them.

Bending down further, he scooped Cricket up into his arms, and started back the way they had come. Careful to stick to the edges of the road in case he needed to duck into an alley and hide.

Which happened far more than he would have liked. Takayoshi did not make it but a couple of blocks before he came upon another small group of sleepwalkers causing trouble. There were no broken storefront windows this time. But they had started a fire out of someone's cart that they had left outside overnight.

"Go home," Takayoshi ordered, even as he knew that the order would go ignored.

The small group of seven turned as one, their eyes blank and unseeing, but somehow fixing on him just the same. And then a snarl went through them, seeming to echo from one to the other to the other. Showing teeth that were blunt, but no less dangerous.

And the first lunged.

"Oh. That's not good," Cricket mumbled from where he was still resting in Takayoshi's arms.

"No. It is not." Takayoshi tightened his hold on Cricket, backing away quickly before turning to run as the group moved in a unit to chase him. He wished, suddenly, that he knew the capital of Lunette as well as he knew his own. That he could run blindly through the streets and make it home without too much trouble. But that was not an option. Maybe one day, he thought, maybe one day this place would be as much his home as Helio had been.

Something caught on his leg, and he when he glanced down he saw a hand clasped around his ankle. The sleepwalker's face was turned up to snarl at him as fingernails cut into the skin through his thin sleep pants.

Takayoshi shook them off quickly, and picked up his pace.

"I could make another—"

"No." Takayoshi shook his head. "You are too weak, and I am not taking the risk that you will get hurt. We will stay ahead of them."

"Then put me down at least," Cricket reasoned.

"Not a chance." Takayoshi dipped his head to offer Cricket a smug little smile, then spun on his heel and darted back the way he had come. The sounds of footsteps behind him told him that they were being pursued, but he did not look back, he did not slow. "The fastest route."

"What?"

"The fastest route home, and quickly, please," Takayoshi breathed deeply, trying to keep his heart rate steady, but it pounded in his chest against his wishes, fear trickling down his spine. What would the sleepwalkers do if they caught them? There was clearly some violence being ordered of them. But how much? Would they rend flesh? Or would they simply hold Takayoshi and Cricket hostage until something worse came along? Takayoshi was fairly certain he did not want to find out.

"This way." Cricket pointed down an alley. "We should be able to loop back around, if the street on the other side is clear."

"Let us pray to Selene that it is." He should not have come out unarmed, he felt naked without his sword to protect himself and Cricket. And he could not use his phoenix fire to fight here, not for fear that he would harm one of the unaware civilians. An act that he was sure Cricket would find unforgivable.

"We could fly back," Cricket offered.

"I have never flown with a passenger before, and I am unsure what the fire of the phoenix would do to you in this form." Takayoshi shook his head. Although it was a reasonable suggestion. "Let us keep that as a last resort."

His booted foot caught on something in the dark of the alley, and he stumbled forward, just barely keeping his grip on Cricket in his arms as he regained his footing. The snarls of the sleepwalkers grew closer still, gaining.

"What was that?" Cricket asked, wriggling a little in his hold as if to get down.

"Stay still."

"We should investigate."

"No, we should not. They are right behind us. We will have to return in the daylight to investigate properly, when we have more soldiers to keep us safe."

"I don't need a soldier to keep me—"

"Cricket," Takayoshi chided, softly. He was well aware that Cricket was perfectly capable of defending himself, but not against his own citizens, and not in such large numbers. "I am trying to focus on getting us back home safely. Please do not make this harder than it already is."

"Turn left here." Cricket huffed, his arms crossing over his chest in a petulant pout as Takayoshi swiveled quickly to turn down the next street.

But as he spun to face the direction of the castle, his breath lodged in his throat. There was another group of sleepwalkers milling about here too. "Stars."

"Has *everyone* in my city been infected?!" Cricket threw up his arms wildly, almost smacking Takayoshi in the face, and sending them both reeling. "Sorry. Sorry."

"It is alright. Just, be more careful." Takayoshi ducked into another alley and kept running. His breath was growing more labored the longer they ran. All the training and the magic in the world could not account for running full speed along uneven cobbles with a full-grown man in his arms. "Where next?"

"I don't know, Yoshi. They're everywhere." Cricket's tone had grown distracted, and upset, and Takayoshi did not have to look at him to know he was sinking into his own head. Would he find a solution there? Takayoshi was not sure, but he also knew that they did not have time for Cricket to shut him out, not right now.

"Cricket, pay attention," he ordered, perhaps a little too firmly.

Cricket made a soft noise as if he were listening.

"Where next?" he asked again, hoping this time the

answer would be different, but as they crossed over into another street, he found yet more sleepwalkers. It was not the entire population, or at least he hoped it was not. But it seemed that they had all been drawn to Cricket and himself by whatever they were seeing. Likely led there as some kind of trap.

And every time he got within a certain distance of them, they turned as a unit and started after him. Making fear trickle down his spine in a cold sweat.

"What do they want, do you think?" Cricket asked, pointing down another alley, then toward a street that would lead them to the outskirts of the capital, away from the castle. It was not the direction Takayoshi wanted to go in, but it seemed there was little choice, and he needed more room if he was going to try utilizing the phoenix to fly them home. He wondered if he could shift just enough to allow him the wings but none of the other features of his phoenix. Did he have that level of control?

"We will discuss that more when we are safe," Takayoshi said in between breaths.

Cricket hummed. "There's a small town square up ahead. They usually hold the market there during the spring. It should have enough room for you to shift."

"I told you I was unsure if I could carry you in that form." Even if it did seem that Cricket had read his mind, because he had just been thinking there was not enough space, had he not? And they were very much out of other options. He could not turn and fight the citizens, as he did not have a weapon. They were blocking all routes to the castle. And he would soon run out of breath to continue running at this speed.

"I have faith in you," Cricket tilted back to fix Takayoshi with a heart-rending smile.

"Very well." Takayoshi nodded. "Show me the way."

"Left again."

TAKAYOSHI'S LUNGS burned from a lack of breath by the time they reached the square. His muscles had yet to start aching, but he was sure it would not be much longer before they did. And come morning the exhaustion would hang heavy around his neck.

"Have we put enough space between them and us?" Takayoshi asked, sucking down air where he had paused in the middle of a small gathering of buildings.

"Just enough, I think." Cricket looked over his shoulder, his fingers still tight in the collar of Takayoshi's shirt. He had not shown fear this entire time, but Takayoshi knew it had to be there, lingering under the surface. "Put me down, let's make this quick."

Takayoshi's arms did not want to release Cricket, but he forced himself, mentally telling the muscles to lower Cricket carefully to his feet. Then he reached for the fire living beneath his skin, and let it heat every fiber of his being until his bones became lighter, his skin sprouted feathers, and he stood ablaze before his prince, a beacon in the night. He wished he had time to experiment more with the change, but he didn't. This would have to do. He would simply have to hope that his fire did not burn Cricket.

"I always forget," Cricket said, holding out a careful hand. "How lovely your phoenix form is."

We do not have time for that, Takayoshi chided lightly.

Cricket laughed, swaying a little on his feet, exhaustion still evident. "That tickles when I'm not a dragon."

Takayoshi huffed out a breath of relief, and glanced behind Cricket again. He had put some distance between them and the sleepwalkers, but not enough, not nearly enough.

Stop playing, let us go.

Cricket smiled broadly at him. "How do you want to do this? Just pick me up with your talons? Or should I—"

Takayoshi did not give him time to question it further, he bent his neck low, and scooped Cricket up onto his back. Cricket's legs splayed wide, his thighs pressing into the tops of Takayoshi's wings.

Is the fire catching? Am I burning you?

Gods he would never forgive himself if he hurt Cricket that way. But instead of answering, Cricket let out a soft whoop of excitement, and leaned forward to wrap his arms tight around Takayoshi's neck. "Get us out of here, Yoshi. Take us home."

And Takayoshi, fool that he was for anything that made Cricket happy, could not stop the satisfied hum that vibrated his beak as he pushed off from the ground just before the sleepwalkers leaped at them. Takayoshi lifted his talons higher to keep them from burning themselves on accident.

"I'm not too heavy, am I?" Cricket asked, his mouth pressed so close to Takayoshi's ear that even with the heat of his fire burning along his skin, he swore he could feel it still.

No. My prince is perfect.

"Stop flirting, we don't have time." Cricket chided with a barely restrained laugh, swatting him lightly on the neck.

Takayoshi let out a soft huff of laughter as he rose above the buildings of the capital, and started toward the center of the city. Toward home.

CHAPTER 23

The heat of Takayoshi's phoenix fire was only just bearable to Cricket's elven skin, but he wasn't going to complain. It was much like a hot bath after spending too long in the snow, aching and burning, but at the same time warding off a bone deep chill that Cricket had not known was there up to that point.

And the view! There was nothing at all that he could compare the view to, apart from when he had flown over the capital himself as a dragon. But then it had been rushed, and harried, panic making every sight ugly and jarring. He still wasn't able to fully appreciate it, not with the sleepwalkers below them starting fires, and causing damage to the city. One day, after all of this was over, after everything had settled down, he'd have to have Takayoshi take him flying like this without the threat of his kingdom falling apart nipping at his heels.

You're very quiet, my prince, Takayoshi's voice hummed through his mind, a gentle tickle at the back of Cricket's mind. There was a softness to it that Cricket was never able to tease out when Takayoshi spoke out loud. Likely because he was so used to keeping himself stiff, and upright, he was still learning how to be soft. But in the quiet of his own mind, Takayoshi seemed so much more at ease with himself.

"Just enjoying the view, dear," Cricket said with a little laugh when he saw Takayoshi duck his head either in acknowledgement or embarrassment. He liked to think that Takayoshi's fire burned a little brighter at the endearment, but there was really no way to tell. "I wish the streets were better lit. I'm worried there might be more vines crawling through the dark alleys." Another thought struck him a second later, one that nearly stilled his blood, making him break out into a cold sweat despite Takayoshi's warmth. "And what trouble the sleepwalkers are causing where I can't see them. You don't. . ." He swallowed roughly. "You don't think they'd hurt anyone, do you?"

Takayoshi hummed. *I do not know.* And he sounded as afraid by the thought as Cricket was. *There will be time once the sun comes up to find answers.*

Cricket didn't want to wait for that, they both knew it. But he understood Takayoshi's reasoning, and even more, he understood the fact that Takayoshi wasn't going to let him run off into the night to chase down mysterious vines when his own people had turned violent and were after him. So he kept such thoughts to himself.

When they landed in the courtyard between the gate and the front of the castle Cricket found even this part of his home not untouched by the chaos of the capital.

"You're Highness," a young knight said, sweeping into a hurried bow. "There are citizens at the gate. What would you have us do?"

"What do they want?" Cricket straightened his sleep shirt, hoping to look at least half as in command as this young man seemed to think he was. Thankfully, the knight seemed a little distracted by Takayoshi molting beside him, his feathers turning to ash, leaving behind a man in a ripped sleep shirt.

Takayoshi tilted his head, annoyance making his brow twitch just the slightest at being stared at. "I am going to check on Becka," he said after a moment.

"Good idea." Cricket nodded, and waited until he was gone before turning his attention back to the confused knight. It would take them all some getting used to, Cricket supposed, being ruled by Celestials. "What do the citizens at the gate want?"

The young man seemed to shake himself, and returned his attention to his king. "Nothing, as far as we can tell. They don't speak. But they've been knocking at the gate for well over an hour now, trying to get inside."

"The gates are locked tight?" That would be enough to stop the average citizen of Lunette. Although if Craven were to launch an attack at this very moment, Cricket knew they would be lost. All he could hope was that Craven and his army were still far enough away that they would not be a problem until he had solved this latest issue. Of course the fact that he hadn't solved the one before that wasn't terribly encouraging. Blast, he was a terrible king, wasn't he?

"They're sleepwalking," Cricket said, and he hoped that by speaking out loud it would silence his inner voice long enough to at least get away from where his knights could see him panicking over this. Fat chance.

"Sleepwalking?" The knight frowned, but he didn't stop Cricket as he made his way toward the gate for a better look. More were coming still, likely following the trail of Takayoshi's smoke through the sky. "Their eyes are open."

"Yes, but they aren't conscious of what they're doing. They're being led by something." Why, he still didn't know. Nor did he know *how*. Takayoshi's reaction made him think that maybe Takayoshi had some inkling.

"How do you know that?" The knight asked.

Cricket stepped up within reach of one of the people at the front of the crowd and they took a swipe at him, reaching for his collar. He heard the clang of weapons being drawn around him, and he stepped back, holding up his hands to show his knights that there was no harm done.

"Stand down," he ordered, and waited until all swords were sheathed before he turned his attention to the knights gathered around him. "It doesn't matter how I know, what matters is that I do. They're sleepwalking. They're not in control of themselves or their actions. And anyone who intentionally harms a citizen of the capital while they're in this state will face repercussions at my hand. Have I made myself clear?"

"Yes, Your Highness," the assembled knights agreed in unison, and Cricket relaxed a little knowing that this at least he could do. He couldn't find a solution to their problem until he better understood what their problem *was*, but at least he could keep his soldiers from hurting his people on purpose.

"All measures taken to contain them are to be nonviolent in nature," he continued, his voice carrying through the courtyard. "For tonight, I will not be sending any of you out into the city. But that will likely change, so be prepared."

Cricket looked around the little group. They were all either nodding, or watching him intently. No one seemed bothered by this edict. Which was good. He didn't want to send knights out into this mess who weren't in the right place mentally to deal with such a thing.

"In the meantime, do not open the gate unless someone is hurt. And send word to me if anything changes. We have a couple more hours until sunrise, hopefully they'll wake up then."

"Yes, Your Highness."

Cricket nodded to himself, and waited until the crowd parted for him to make his way inside the castle. The doors shut behind him, and Cricket sagged in relief. Without so many eyes on him he was finally able to listen to his body a little more. And his body was telling him that he'd been run down by a blasted carriage. The bottoms of his feet burned with cuts, and scrapes from walking barefoot through the streets. His muscles ached with the strain of using magic when he hadn't had enough rest, left on his system. And he was beginning to wonder how he was even upright anymore with the exhaustion that threatened to drag his lids down over his eyes.

Cricket leaned against the wall near the door, letting himself breathe a minute. He just needed to rest, just for a few scant moments before he turned his attention back toward the problem in front of him. There was little doubt that this might be the only rest he got for the next few days.

"My king," Takayoshi said, his boots scuffing against the floor of the foyer just outside the little entryway.

"Yes. Just give me a minute," Cricket sighed, scrubbing at his face. His eyes were heavy, and fuzzy, dry from the air of flying and from being open too long. Styx, had he even blinked when he'd been sleepwalking?

Takayoshi made a small sound of acknowledgement, and did not approach Cricket, allowing him to remain in the shadow of the entryway. The privacy was nice. The dark shadow of the lowered ceiling was nice. The only thing nicer would be his bed surrounded by pillows and blankets, with his face smooshed against Takayoshi's chest. Funny how a few scant hours of sharing a bed together had already embedded itself under Cricket's skin, and made a home for itself there.

Once Cricket had a better hold on himself, he slunk out from the shadows. Whatever Takayoshi saw, did not make him happy, if the pinched wrinkle between his eyebrows was anything to go by, but they didn't really have time for that right now. "Have you gotten everyone out of bed?"

"The guard had already awoken Ignacia and Claudia." Takayoshi held out his arm for Cricket to lean on without a word, and Cricket took the support gratefully. It didn't do much to ease the strain of his muscles, but it was a nice gesture, and at the moment he was too tired to fight against his need for small comforts.

"Good. That's good." Cricket let out a small breath as they started walking. He wondered if Ignacia and Claudia had been together when the knights had woken them. Probably not. They were too careful for that. A notion that he found positively silly, but he would badger Ignacia about stopping this sneaking around business later. When his kingdom wasn't on the verge of burning down around him.

"Claudia of course then went to wake Leo."

"Of course." Cricket had to shake his head, and bite back the little smile at the way Takayoshi said that. As if he were very tired of their little family's antics, but also found them deeply amusing. Stars, Cricket loved this man. "And Leo woke Estia, I'm assuming."

"My king knows his people well," Takayoshi murmured with a note of pride in his voice. "They are waiting for us in your study."

"Just them? Or has Ignacia roused the entire house to deal with this crisis?"

"Just them." Takayoshi's lips twitched at the corners.

"Are you laughing at me?" Cricket gasped, clutching his heart, and stumbling enough that Takayoshi had to grab him by the waist to keep his legs from giving out on him entirely. "My husband is laughing at me!"

Takayoshi hummed good naturedly, and refused to relinquish his hold on Cricket until they reached the study where their friends waited. No one was sitting this time. But Leo and Estia were still in their sleep clothes, looking rumpled and tired.

"Cricky," Ignacia said on a sigh, already crossing the room to take his hands, and look him over like an overprotective mother hen. "Takayoshi said you were sleepwalking?"

"I was. But I'm fine. Everyone sit, we have much to talk about." Cricket motioned to the chairs, and forced himself to walk as normally as he could with the cuts on the bottoms of his feet to his own chair behind his father's desk.

Takayoshi frowned at him as he came to stand beside him.

"We'll send for the healer once we've filled everyone in," Cricket promised, not even needing to know what the frown wrinkle was about this time. It was getting increasingly easy to read Takayoshi's expressions and his moods. With Takayoshi's nerves soothed, Cricket turned his attention to filling everyone in on what happened to them that evening. It was somehow more distressing to repeat the events to the people who loved him most than to live through them. Or at least, for Cricket it was.

"I'm fine," he tried to assure them, but the words didn't make Ignacia's face look any less pinched.

"You said it used your mother to lure you out?" Claudia was frowning too, her fingers tapping against the pad she'd pulled from somewhere to take notes while they spoke. Cricket was glad at least one of them was treating this as a research opportunity instead of a traumatic event. It allowed him to distance himself from it just a little. "It shouldn't have been able to mimic the form of a goddess. There's magic in place that—"

"When I said that, I mean I *thought* it was Selene." Cricket sighed, rubbing a hand down his face and hoping no one noticed the hint of shame in his voice. He *should* be ashamed of himself. Was he so starved for affection that he allowed himself to be tricked into thinking some creature was his mother? And how could he say such a thing in front of people who clearly cared for him.

"If it is what I think it is," Takayoshi spoke, his words carefully measured as always, "then it is not uncommon for it to use the visage of a loved one to lure someone in."

"But it wasn't luring him in," Ignacia pointed out. "It was luring him off a roof."

"Were there any blooms? Anything to indicate that it is. . . that?" Leo asked.

Cricket raised his brows at Leo. He, Takayoshi, and Claudia seemed to be talking around a shared experience. Some monster they were afraid to name.

"No but it did not have blooms then either. It utilized the foliage of the forest to disperse its pollen." Takayoshi tightened his hold on Cricket's chair.

"Yes, but when it attacked us," Estia said, "It was trying to lead us to a pod in the forest, so it could use us for fertilizer. You in particular," ze nodded to Takayoshi.

"Yoshi. What is *it*?" Cricket pressed, not willing to be in the dark any longer.

"When I traveled in search of information about the dragon, we entered a forest just outside of the village where Becka lived. We stayed overnight on the edge of the wood, but in the morning when we woke, the forest had surrounded us." Takayoshi did not look at him as he spoke, his eyes stared into the middle distance as if he were remembering something particularly distressing.

"Shortly after we started hearing voices," Claudia said, picking up where Takayoshi left off as if she seemed to realize there was something he did not want to discuss. "Afterward, we determined it was something in the pollen allowing a magically enhanced plant to penetrate our thoughts, and draw us closer."

"But this is only affecting those who are asleep." Cricket tapped at his nose in thought.

"The plant was fairly mature by the time we encountered it. It had already feasted on the flesh of a number of people. Maybe this is something it did early on." Claudia kept her tone careful and scholarly, not letting her emotions get the better of her.

"It was big enough to swallow Yoshi whole by the time we found it," Leo added, seeming not to care for beating around the bush.

"So it could have been there for months by that point," Estia continued, following the thread. "And if my brother went into the woods, I've no doubt he went in search of any seeds that might have survived."

"So. . . how do we combat this?" Ignacia frowned, her hands tucked behind her back where no one could see how her fingers curled into fists. But Cricket knew they were clenching, because he knew his sister.

"Facial coverings to filter the air," Claudia proposed. "But even that isn't a guaranteed solution. It's a stop gap at best."

"We need to find the plant and destroy it." Leo leaned forward, his elbows resting on his knees.

"We will begin our search at first light," Takayoshi nodded. "There are vines in the city, perhaps they will lead us to the source."

Leo murmured his agreement and rose. "Well, then, we should all get a little more sleep in the time being, yes?"

"Agreed." Claudia nodded.

"Ignacia, you'll organize some knights we can trust to help with this," Cricket said, not rising from his father's chair. He wasn't sure if he could at this point, if he were honest. His legs had gone oddly jelly-like. "And tomorrow evening we will be instituting a curfew until we have this matter settled. So see to it that the citizens know."

"Of course." Ignacia dipped her head in acknowledgement, and they all filed out.

All apart from Takayoshi, who's wrist Cricket grabbed when he made to move away. "You said the creature used loved ones to lure you in."

Takayoshi made a soft sound to let Cricket know he was listening.

"It used me against you, didn't it?" Cricket didn't actually think he wanted the answer, but he'd asked the question just the same, and he knew Takayoshi well enough to know that he wouldn't hide anything from him.

"It did." Takayoshi did not meet his eyes. "But it was a paltry imitation at best."

Cricket smiled softly, and tilted his head back to look up more at Takayoshi, giving his hand a little tug. "You're going to have to kiss me for that."

"That is entirely fair."

CHAPTER 24

"Sunil must have planted it when he had free run of the capital," Leo said, his tone soft, and serious. It was the tone of a man who had seen enough battle to know what was coming next. And it unsettled Takayoshi, set his teeth on edge.

"Hopefully it's just the one," Claudia added. She was just as antsy, just as uncomfortable with this discussion as Takayoshi was. He could not see her mouth, but he could see the way her brows had continued to pinch closer and closer together since breakfast.

None of them had slept at all the previous night. Too wound up, too upset by what lay ahead of them. Takayoshi did envy the others who did not know what they were facing. They did not understand the way the creature could twist everything around, and turn something a person loved into something that would kill them.

He had not lied to Cricket the night before when he told him that the monster had used Cricket against him. But he had not told him the full truth either. Had not laid before Cricket how his love for his prince had been what nearly killed him. How the monster had tricked him into thinking he was safe, and cared for, had given him a glimpse of everything he had ever wanted with his soul mate. How that glimpse had almost smothered him. Cricket did not need that on his conscience, especially when he was not to blame for it. And Takayoshi knew him well enough to know that Cricket would blame himself. Better that he not know at all.

"We should start at the edge of the city," Takayoshi said, hoping that some direction would make this whole thing feel easier, feel less insurmountable. It did not. Takayoshi was beginning to wonder if anything would.

The vines were everywhere. He had not been able to see them as well in the dark, had simply thought the streets of the capital uneven and in need of repair. He had ridden them enough times one would think he would have noticed something amiss. But who noticed the street beneath their feet when it was not an obstruction?

"Do you really think we're going to be able to track the vines from here toward the source?" Leo's lack of faith in this plan was not helping. He had to know that. But Takayoshi could not fault him for his skepticism, and irritation at their lack of a more solid plan. It was bothering Takayoshi as well that they were simply walking the city and hoping to stumble upon this creature. They needed more clear direction, but at present, there was none to be had.

"Cricket said that the tracker spell he has used in the past will not work with this creature as the magic innate in it attacks his own any time they interact." Takayoshi's hand twitched to reach up and pinch the bridge of his nose. A new habit he had likely acquired from Claudia who was frequently rubbing at the marks her spectacles left behind.

"Yes, but there has to be something *else*." Leo shifted at his side, his hand far too close to his sword. It had been that way for what felt like weeks now. And again, Takayoshi could not blame him for it. They were all on edge. They were in a holding period, waiting for the next bad thing to happen. He did not like it.

"We'll try this, and if it turns up nothing, we'll go back to the drawing board," Claudia reasoned.

"You know if we let it draw one of the sleepwalkers in and just follow—"

"The only sleepwalker it seemed even interested in leading anywhere was Cricket." There was more bite to Takayoshi's words than there needed to be. He knew that. It was unfair of him to be angry with Leo for suggesting a plan that he likely would have proposed himself in any other situation. As if that were not enough to silence Leo's plan, Takayoshi reminded, "And that was to lead him off a roof."

"Why do you think that is?" Claudia asked. Takayoshi was sure she was just trying to waylay the oncoming storm between he and Leo, but he allowed the subject change.

"Unclear," he said, skirting around another makeshift pyre left by the sleepwalkers the previous night. Cricket's men were working to clear them away, but they could only move so quickly, and by this evening there might be more.

"It's just. . ." Claudia bit her lip in thought. "With you, it wanted to consume your magic. But it couldn't consume his magic if it just killed him."

"Maybe it has something to do with the way its magic reacts combatively to Cricket's," Leo suggested. When they both turned to look at him, he frowned. "I know I'm not as well versed in magic theory as you, but it just seems like good battle tactics to take out the biggest threat to it, right? And what bigger threat than a dragon king?"

"But none of the other Celestials have been affected." Claudia shook her head. "By that logic, wouldn't Ignacia and Yoshi also be as big a threat to it?"

"Neither of them have faced off against it directly, yet," Leo reasoned.

"So we're working under the premise that it doesn't have memories of the previous creature. That it is in fact a whole new monster." Claudia tapped her chin thoughtfully, nearly stumbling over a thick vine. Takayoshi caught her. "Thanks."

Takayoshi rubbed at his chin thoughtfully, a gesture oddly similar to Cricket's own thoughtful ticks. "I think it is reasonable to assume it is an entirely different creature as it is not acting the same way the previous one did."

"So maybe Craven. . . altered it?"

"Let us hope he did not make it stronger in the process." Takayoshi's little scouting group all fell silent at that thought. What if he had in fact made it stronger? What if that was why it was coming at them differently? They would not be able to predict it based on the prior creature's behaviors. Takayoshi did not like this. At all. It did not bode well for them. "We will know more once we find the pod."

"I could collect some samples. . ." Claudia's hand twitched to her satchel over her shoulder. "We'd get a better understanding of the creature if I just examined it a little closer."

"Would we? Or do you just want to play scientist with the monster?" Leo teased.

"Be quiet." Claudia huffed.

"I do not want to cause it to retaliate against us anymore than it already has," Takayoshi said, breaking up the argument before it could even properly start. He cared for his friends, dearly, but he knew how they could be when they got to bickering, and sometimes it was just better to not let them start at all. "

Claudia grumbled a quiet "fine" and they continued on their way.

The more he saw of the city, and the state of it, the more Takayoshi thought perhaps it would be wise if they did contact his sister for reinforcements. Cricket's small army was not enough to deal with a problem of this size alongside the coming war. Something would have to give. And they were rapidly running out of time to find solutions before—

"No," Leo hissed, ducking back behind a cart on the edge of the city, his shoulders rigid.

"No what?" Claudia asked.

The answer came by way of she and Takayoshi looking off into the distance and seeing a camp set up some yards away. A much larger camp than Takayoshi had anticipated when he first encountered Craven and his men.

"He got here sooner than I expected," Takayoshi said more to himself than anyone else, his hand tight on the hilt of his sword.

"That's more men than we saw with him when we rescued Estia's siblings." There was an edge to Leo's words that might have been fear, or anger, or something else entirely. It was hard to tell with the way that Takayoshi's heart was slamming against his chest, his pulse so loud in his ears he could hardly hear them.

"We don't know that it's Craven," Claudia reasoned. "It could be—"

"What? Some other army come to attack Lunette's capital?" Leo hissed, and turned to glare at her. "The Hermes royals I suppose. Or maybe the Helio—"

"Not now," Takayoshi chided gently. "We do not have time for you two to fight now." Goddess above, he was so very tired of this entire thing already. It seemed that events were transpiring non-stop recently. All he wanted was a quiet moment to himself to spend time with his soon to be husband. To plan their wedding, and make everything official. Could Craven and his bid to take over a land that did not belong to him not wait until after that had happened? "Leo, I need you to run back to the castle and tell Cricket what we have seen."

"But we need to find—"

"Claudia and I will continue searching for the pod. We cannot deviate our focus from this entirely when we do not know what the night will bring." Takayoshi knew they were spreading themselves thin by splitting their focus like this. He also knew that if they simply abandoned their efforts to solve the issue of the pollen invading the lungs of the capital's citizens, then they would be in for more trouble. Craven's army was not an immediate threat, not yet at least. The creature was. "Go."

Leo dipped his head in understanding, and rose from where he had crouched behind the cart to turn on his heel and head back toward the castle at a run. For all his bickering, and complaining, when it came to it, Leo was just a soldier in want of a commander. And he had chosen Takayoshi to be that commander.

"What if we don't find it before sunset?" Claudia asked.

"I will not return home empty handed. There is too much at stake." The notion that he might have to return to Cricket a failure made Takayoshi physically ill. Cricket was counting on him to find the creature and dispatch it. To protect their people in a way only he could.

"But what if—"

"Claudia." Takayoshi narrowed his eyes on her.

"Right. We'll cross that bridge when we come to it." She nodded. "For now, I think following the thickest vines would be our best bet. They'll give the creature the most sustenance and should lead us directly to it."

Takayoshi let out a soft breath, and dipped his head to examine the vines at his feet. It was hard to tell which of them was the thickest when they were clearly so far from the source. "Do you think they are all like this?"

"What do you mean?" Claudia asked, picking one seemingly at random and starting in the direction of the castle with Takayoshi following behind.

"The vines out this far are all thin, and spindly. If they are like this all the way around the edge of the city, it would point to the pod being more centered than otherwise."

Claudia stopped, her head tilting in thought.

"I want to be clear," Takayoshi said with a frown. "I am not suggesting we waste time walking around the edge of the city and measuring the widths of all the vines to see. I am just curious."

"Oh but you know how I love to sate my curiosity." Claudia grinned, tipping back on her heels a little.

"I do. But we will not be doing that now." Takayoshi could not help but laugh a little. "Come, we must find the pod before sunset. I will follow this vine, you follow another. Hopefully we will find something soon."

Claudia sighed, but set off in the direction he indicated.

With his friends no longer by his side, Takayoshi had more time to think. Which was unfortunate, because his mind ran rampant with all of the things that could, would, and had already gone wrong.

Craven was at their gates. He could attack at any moment. The children of the capital were still sick, along with many of the lower fae inhabitants. And now there was the pollen affecting the adults, making them sleepwalk. How long before all of these things culminated into the fall of the capital? Into the end of Cricket's rule?

Takayoshi took a breath, and straightened his shoulders. He would not let that happen. He would die fighting if he had to, but he would not let that happen.

CHAPTER 25

Sleeping seemed an unnecessary luxury at this point. One that Cricket may never get to indulge in again. Maybe one day he'd get to lay down beside his husband and just rest, enjoy the feeling of someone warm and solid beside him.

Today was not that day.

Tomorrow wasn't looking so good either.

"No one is fighting back against the curfew," Ignacia reported. She was still upright, and alert, in spite of the circles around her eyes that signified she hadn't slept.

Gods if Craven's plan was to utterly exhaust them so they'd be asleep when he attacked, it was working. How much longer could they keep this up before it broke them? And who would break first? Would it be one of the staff? Or Cricket himself? He wasn't sure, and he didn't think he wanted to find out.

"Cricky," Ignacia called, tone gentle. "Are you listening?"

"Hmm?" Cricket lifted his head from where it had been resting against his palm to blink his heavy lids at her. "Oh yes.

No one has a problem with the curfew. Good. Good. I'm not sure how much help it'll be."

He rubbed his face, trying to will away some of the exhaustion as he sat up straighter. "Have we heard anything from our allies in the north? I know they are a month's ride at best but—"

He hadn't checked up on that situation yet, and he felt a little badly about it. But with everything else going on, whether or not Atsuko's forces made it to Lunette in time had fallen to the wayside.

"They left a week ago, but we have heard nothing from them since."

Chewing on the inside of his cheek, he sighed a little. This was such a mess. He was drowning in problems, and no one seemed able to offer a life raft. Or maybe they were simply unwilling. . .

Yes. They want to see you drown. All of them.

Cricket shook himself, frowning a little, and forced his mind back to the discussion at hand. "What progress have we made on clean up?"

"It's slow work." Ignacia sighed. Cricket wished she would sit down and take a rest, but she stayed standing where she was, at attention. Like a soldier giving their last report to their commander. Honestly, she looked like she might fall over soon if she didn't take the time to sit down. He could order her, he supposed, but he'd never really liked forcing Ignacia to do things. She was his sister after all.

His sister. . .

Who not but a few years ago was so happy and carefree. Yelling at him to get down off the wall surrounding the castle, then following him over when he said he wanted to go off adventuring.

"You took that from me."

"What?" Cricket's head jerked up, unsure of what he'd just heard. Ignacia wouldn't say that to him, right? But. . . but if she did, she'd be right. He had taken that from her. He'd taken that and more from Anstice; her mother, her home. And what had he given back to his dear sisters, to his most loyal friends? Nothing.

"I said, I'm worried the clean up will come to nothing, and we'll just have to do it all again tomorrow." Ignacia frowned at him, taking a step toward him as if she were going to reach for him. "Are you all right?"

"I'm fine." Cricket forced a smile onto his face that he knew she would see through, but couldn't seem to stop himself. "Fit as a fiddle. Why wouldn't I be?"

Ignacia's jaw worked a moment, as if she were chewing on the words she wanted to say, then she swallowed them down. "No reason." She shook her head. "You should try to get some rest before Claudia and Takayoshi return."

"Really, Iggy, I'm fine. And besides, there's too much to see to still. I'll rest once all of this is settled." Which might be never, now that he was thinking about it. Craven might attack before he could solve the issue of the curse, and the plant creature attacking them. And then all of this would be over. He was starting to wonder if that might be better for everyone actually. . .

Ignacia opened her mouth, her brows drawn together in upset, but just as she was about to give voice to whatever was on her mind, Leo burst into the room.

"Your Highness, they're here." He rushed across the room, the doors slamming behind him once more with a loud bang that made Cricket's ears ring.

"Who's here?" Ignacia's expression morphed from one of pinched concern to one of pinched annoyance. The shift was subtle, but Cricket had known her long enough to recognize the signs.

And you've annoyed her enough over the years to see the shift, haven't you?

Cricket shook himself. He wasn't sure where all the intrusive thoughts were coming from lately, but he wished they'd stop. They were more a distraction than he could afford at the moment, and if he didn't get a handle on things they might get someone hurt. Maybe Ignacia was onto something about him needing to rest.

"Craven and his army." Leo leaned over, clutching his knees as he panted.

"Already?" Cricket stood from his chair, the legs scraping against the wood floor. "How could he be here *already*?"

"I don't know." Leo shook his head, straightening up once he finally caught his breath. "Yoshi sent me to tell you. But I need to head back and help them—"

"No." Cricket sighed, scrubbing at his face as exhaustion weighed more heavily on him. "I need someone to go and see what his forces look like." Not that it would matter much, Cricket reminded himself. He had what he had. He couldn't just make soldiers magically appear. And he was not going to force his citizens into service if they didn't want to fight. "I have to know what we're up against. And you're the best person for the job."

Leo faltered, his eyes flicking from Cricket to Ignacia and back, unsure. Cricket could understand why. Takayoshi had given him an order, and now Cricket was giving him a different one.

"You can check in with Takayoshi and Claudia on your way out of the city," Cricket amended, his tone gentle. "But I need a report on Craven's forces before supper."

Leo dipped into a deep bow, then spun on his heel and exited as quickly as he'd come without another word.

"You can't let Takayoshi undermine you like that," Ignacia said the moment the door was closed. "He is not king."

"He will be, one day."

"Even then, you'll be in charge." Ignacia's lips pursed a little more in displeasure. If she hadn't been the one pushing them to make their union as public as possible not but a week ago, he would worry she was upset because she didn't approve of Cricket's relationship. But that was silly. He knew better. Ignacia liked Takayoshi as much as she liked anyone. So there was no reason for him to start worrying that she didn't approve now.

"We'll rule together." Cricket settled back into his chair, his muscles strangely tense. He should be out in his city doing something about all of this. He should be hunting down the creature. He should be spying on Craven's forces. He should be checking in with his citizens. He should be helping with clean up. Anything. Everything. But instead he was stuck behind his father's desk giving orders. Because he was king, and the king didn't get his hands dirty directly, he had other people do that for him.

"You will. But in the end, all decisions will come down to you," Ignacia insisted. "You know that. . . don't you?"

Was that judgment lining her tone, or was he imagining it? Gods, he was so tired he couldn't even tell anymore.

"Of course I do," he said, even though he didn't actually believe it. He wanted he and Takayoshi to rule together. That meant sharing decisions and making compromises. But he was starting to wonder if he wanted that not because he loved Takayoshi, but because he just didn't want to do this alone. He didn't want to have the final say. He didn't want it to be all his fault when things went wrong. Could anyone blame him for that?

"I can," Ignacia said, her tone a snarl.

Cricket jerked his head up to look at her, but she wasn't. . . she didn't look angry like how she'd sounded. "You can what?"

"I didn't say anything." Ignacia wrinkled her nose, her eyes growing more concerned. "Are you sure you're all right, Cricky? Maybe you should go back to your quarters and lie down if just for a couple of hours. We can manage things here in the meantime."

"Maybe you're right." Wasn't she always? Cricket didn't know when he'd stopped listening to everything that Ignacia said, but clearly he'd been an idiot to think he could go without her advice. Maybe *she* should run the kingdom.

"We don't need you anyway."

Cricket jerked at the words as if he'd been slapped. That was right too, wasn't it? They didn't need him. Sure, he was king but it wasn't like he was really *doing* anything with his crown. All he was doing was making more of a mess of things. Maybe it would be better if. . .

"Right," he said, clearing his throat. "I'm just going to. . . I'm going to rest for a bit. Have someone come get me when Leo or Yoshi return. I want to know immediately." He lifted his chin, hoping to make himself look a little taller, a little more certain of his position as king. All it did was make him feel smaller. "Understood?"

"Of course." Ignacia dipped into a bow, and left the study without another word.

And then there was only silence in his father's study. Silence and the weight of realization that Ignacia was right. They didn't need him. He was just making all of this worse. Without him there things would be so much easier. They would be able to—

"I'm going to bed," he told himself, cutting off that train of thought before it could get any worse. Everything would make more sense once he'd had some real sleep. Maybe he'd even understand what Ignacia was getting at when she said those things. Because surely she couldn't have meant them the way they sounded. She knew him too well, knew all his little insecurities, to have said such things carelessly.

Which was more reason why she did mean them. Wasn't it? She wouldn't have been so careless as to say something like that to him accidentally. She wouldn't say it if she didn't mean it. Ignacia had always been careful with her words that way. Ever since they were children. Because she was the older sister, and she took that duty seriously. Because she didn't want to trample what little confidence Cricket found.

He shook himself. To bed. He needed to go to bed.

The walk to his quarters seemed to take a decade, a century, more even. The hallway stretching and twisting in front of him, going on and on forever. The floor tilted beneath his feet, sending him sprawling into a wall.

His shoulder slammed against the stone, sending an ache through his body, and drawing a short gasp from his lips.

"Your Highness," a voice called from behind him, and when Cricket turned his head his vision darkened.

Stars, how often was he going to lose consciousness? It seemed like every other day recently. He shook the spots away and Estia came into focus.

"Are you all right?" Estia's voice came to him as if through water, all warbly, and indistinct.

"I'm fine." What other choice did he have? He had to be fine. He couldn't be anything but, not right now. Not until he knew his people and his family were safe. "I was just going to lie down for a little while."

"Let me walk with you." Estia moved up to his side, zir hands stuffed into the pockets of zir trousers. "I was headed that way anyway."

"I said I'm fine," Cricket snapped.

"And I said I was headed that way anyway." Estia tilted zir head, bright aqua hair falling into zir eyes. Their shoulders bumped together a little as Cricket swayed down the hall, but it seemed to swerve around less with someone else walking beside him.

"How are you?" Estia asked after silence had settled between them a bit too long.

"I'm fine, like I said," Cricket repeated, his teeth clenching together. But he forced himself to take a breath and release the tension. There was no reason to snap at Estia, ze was just trying to help. Or was ze? "How is your family?"

"They're settling in nicely." With a brief pause in zir stride, Estia turned to fix Cricket with a blinding smile. "I want to thank you for taking us in. For offering us sanctuary."

"You're welcome." Cricket squirmed under the sincerity. Or perceived sincerity. He didn't know Esta well enough to know if ze was lying or not. "Well this is me," he said when they reached his door, and pushed inside without even a goodbye.

The door shut behind him, and in the darkness of the drawn curtains, Cricket saw a face he never thought he'd see again in this life.

"Hello, nephew." Sunil smiled, sharp and sinister. "I see you're letting traitors into my home now."

Cricket leaned back against the door, trying to quell the nausea crawling up his throat. The room was spinning again. His feet unsteady. Nothing helped. He couldn't get far enough away. Couldn't escape. He scrambled for the knob to the door but it had disappeared.

"This isn't real. You aren't real." Cricket breathed in through his nose, making the conscious effort to try to calm his racing heart. "I killed you."

"And yet. . . Here I am."

CHAPTER 26

The vine led Takayoshi through the streets of the capital for upward of an hour, snaking down alleys and up pathways he had never seen before ending at an abandoned temple. Takayoshi's hand fell to the hilt of his sword before he pushed in. He knew full well he should bring reinforcements, knew what trouble he could get into facing this thing alone.

But his friends had been unable to fight its pull before, and none of them had the fire of a phoenix living beneath their skin like he did.

The door to the temple creaked open loudly, as if it had gone long untended to. A sentiment backed up by the darkness and debris Takayoshi found inside. The windows were coated in a layer of dust so thick he could not see the sky through the glass.

He wondered how long this temple had sat vacant for it to be covered as it was. Surely this was not the work of just the couple of months since Sunil had taken over the capital and chased Cricket—and many of his supporters—out of the city. This had to have come before that.

But as he drew closer, the light through the still cracked door shining a line across one of the votives just inside, he noticed that the dust was not dust colored at all. It was a mustard yellow in color, almost like. . .

"Pollen," he rasped to himself, adjusting the mask on his face. Had he walked right into the creature's lair? Or was this just a result of this place being abandoned and left open to the elements?

There was no way to really know without looking. So Takayoshi tightened his grip on his sword, and continued onward.

Past the little alcove where the door was located there was a wide open hall with a high ceiling, and windows cast in stained glass. He could just make out the image of Selene cut from pale blue shards, and pieced together. Stilling for a moment, he squinted at her through the dimness.

She was beautiful, but she looked nothing like Cricket. There was not so much as a hint that they were related based on this imagery. Which, he supposed, made perfect sense as most artists had never seen the goddess in person, nor did they know that Cricket was her son. Still, Takayoshi had been hoping for some indication, some sign, some vague passing resemblance. Silly maybe, but Takayoshi had long since given up pretending to be sensible. Sensible men did not fall in love at first sight with ridiculous princes, after all. Or so he had been raised to believe.

Drawing his gaze away from the image of Selene on the far wall, Takayoshi focused instead on the room as a whole. There were no benches in neat rows, as he was accustomed to from the temples of Helio, but instead there were small round cushions, all evenly spaced around five or six square tables among the vines.

The space looked more like a meeting hall or a community

center than the temple it was meant to be. But then, Takayoshi realized he had not visited a temple dedicated to the Lady Selene before. His god had always been Helios, as he was from Helio. That had changed in recent years, but he still had yet to visit one of her temples. Would she think him impertinent? Calling upon her for favors, and marrying her son, without paying homage to her as a goddess first? He hoped not. Either way, he would have to rectify that once he was sure this temple was clear.

Thankfully, because there were no benches nor a pulpit, there were very few places for a creature to hide. At least in the main room.

The soft sound of his sword being drawn echoed through the vast emptiness, but as expected there was no answering sound of weaponry. There would not be, if the creature held true to its nature, but thus far it had been just different enough to put Takayoshi on edge.

He stepped carefully over the vines, and around the tables and pillows, in the hopes that he would avoid the creature's attention. But there was no way that it did not already know he was there. The question was, was it lying in wait? Or had he simply chosen the wrong location?

It was possible that the creature was hiding somewhere else. There were plenty of buildings in the capital that were left abandoned after they had defeated Sunil. There simply were not enough people to fill them, even with the refugees pouring in from around the kingdom. Sunil had killed too many, used their corpses to fuel his war machine.

But this one had good lighting, and based on the soft dripping sound Takayoshi could hear as he drew closer to the altar at the back of the temple, access to water. It was an ideal environment for a plant.

But this creature was not just a plant. It had other needs. Otherwise why would it be draining the surrounding land of its magic? That would be something to take into account if today's search turned up nothing.

In all honesty, maybe they should have thought of that before. They were all reasonably minded people, intelligent, clever, but panic had seized Takayoshi by the throat seeing Cricket out on that ledge. And he found himself unable to think of another solution besides charging in and slashing at every vaguely plant-like thing in sight with his sword.

He had a little more self-control than that, but it was a very near thing.

Fear and love could make a person reckless when experienced separately, but when experienced together? They had the power to turn even the calmest of people into someone entirely unable to think rationally.

The space behind the altar was darker than the rest of the temple. A thick curtain acted as a barrier between the main space, and a short hall beyond, blocking out any light from the windows above.

Here is where it would hide, if it were in this building at all. Tucked into the dark, away from prying eyes, and the threat of lower fae whose primary diet was vegetation.

With sword clutched tightly in one hand, and a fire burning bright in the other, Takayoshi stepped into the dark. He allowed the sound of dripping water to lead him deeper down the hall, with the hopes that the creature would be near the water source.

The first door on the right was already open, pushed so by the vines, or so it seemed.

Takayoshi moved quickly, ducking inside of the room to look around. A vacant classroom, nothing more, and the vines seemed less abundant here than out in the main hall. Still, Takayoshi took his time inspecting the room to be sure there was nowhere for the creature to hide. It would help if he knew what size it was now.

The following two rooms were much the same. Desks and books left to gather pollen as the people meant to fill them had been driven from their homes. Takayoshi's stomach turned at the sight of them. How many of these people—adults, elders, *children*—had been pushed from the city in a bid to escape Sunil's evil? How many of them had not made it to safety?

There had been no children amongst the hungry spirits that Sunil raised to fight against his nephew, but that did not mean that children had not lost their lives in the battle. And those that did not had lost parents, and loved ones. Had been orphaned just as Becka was once upon a time.

When this was over, after he was married, and crowned, that would be his first project as Lunette's new king, to find out what happened to the people who had come to this temple. There had to be records somewhere. If not here, then in the castle, surely. Anstice would know how to find them, he would contact her, then he would do his best to send help to those who survived, and bring peace to those who had not.

The door at the end of the hall did not sit ajar like so many of the others. It was closed firmly, and as none of the others had turned up the source of the mysterious dripping sound, Takayoshi had to assume that was where the water was located.

The hilt of his sword dug into his palms, his fire reacting to the tension swimming in his bloodstream, heating his skin. Singing below the surface, waiting for him to let it loose on some new foe. The doorknob was cold beneath his overheated hand, oddly so, but then that might have just been because he was so on edge that his skin was practically burning up.

He turned it, or tried to anyway, but there was no give.

Locked.

Taking a deep breath, Takayoshi raised his sword,

prepared to bring it down hard on the knob, and force the door. But as he swung his blade downward something wrapped tight around his ankle, and yanked.

Pain shot up his leg. A bone too close to being snapped. Maybe it had been. He could not be sure. What he could be sure of was whatever grabbed him was dragging him away from the door. Back through the dark of the hall. He lost the hold he had on the flame in his palm, and could not seem to regain it with the way the world spun around him.

This entire situation brought back entirely too many memories for Takayoshi's liking. Although at least he was not unconscious.

Yet.

He hissed as the vine slammed him into one of the walls, his ears ringing from the impact.

And he had not lost his sword this time. The hilt was cutting into his palm enough he was sure there would be a bruise, but he was not letting it go. If the creature meant to drag Takayoshi to its pod, he would be ready for it when he faced it.

He crashed through the altar , sending the long bench skittering across the floor, and he sent up a silent apology to the goddess whose temple he was being forced to desecrate. She would understand, he was sure. After all this was in the name of protecting her son.

His ankle was starting to throb now. *Definitely sprained, probably broken*, he thought, adjusting his perception of how long that would take to heal. There would not be time for an extended rest in bed, but Takayoshi was sure he could get one of the healers in the castle to help him. They all seemed very qualified.

Another wince was torn from Takayoshi's throat as his head smacked against the leg of one of the tables. He lifted his free hand to rub at the place, and his fingers came away bloody.

Blast. If he let the creature continue to—

It twisted. Slinging him into another table. His head bounced off the hardwood legs, and sent the piece of furniture sliding across the room.

Was it trying to make him lose consciousness?

A muffled gasp left him as it flung him into the air. And he had just enough time to curl into himself, protecting his head, right before he was slammed down into another table with enough force his vision briefly blackened.

This one shattered under the impact. A splinter of wood lodged into his shoulder through his back. The searing pain of the wound ripped through him until it was almost all he could comprehend.

Before he could draw in a pained breath, the vine wrapped around his injured ankle again. The pressure so intense Takayoshi's vision began to swim from the pain.

Why was it not taking him back to its pod? Why was it abusing him thusly, and not dragging him away to be digested? This made no sense. Unless. . .

Unless he was on to something with this temple. Unless behind that locked door the creature resided.

He had to get up. He had to go see what was behind that door.

Takayoshi swung his sword at the vine, but it jerked at the last moment, flinging him once more against a wall. He grunted. Pushing himself to his unsteady feet, sword held in two hands now as they had begun to shake. But he would not allow it to sneak up on him again.

The door to the temple flung open, spilling fresh daylight into the darkness, and he was momentarily blinded.

Which was all it took for the creature to grab him again and fling him so hard he lost his sword then slam him back onto the floor, and grab at his other ankle and wrists with bruising force.

"What are you doing?" Ignacia shouted, her boots slapping against the floor as she chopped through the vines holding Takayoshi down.

"Clearly I was playing a rousing game of tag," Takayoshi replied dryly.

"This isn't time to be funny." Ignacia glared at him, but offered her hand to help Takayoshi up just the same. The vines slithered back to where they had come from, as if they thought they were outnumbered.

"I think it is in here," Takayoshi said. He winced as he put weight down on his injured ankle, and fire shot up his leg, but that was not going to stop him from—

"I'll investigate here, you head back. Cricket needs you." Ignacia ushered him back out into the street where their horses waited. "He's—" Ignacia pressed her lips together hard enough they lost all color. "He's not well, Yoshi."

"Find Claudia," Takayoshi ordered, climbing onto his horse. "I think it's in the back room, behind the altar . It would not let me enter."

"I'll check." Ignacia nodded, then she looked up at him with an expression he never thought he wanted to see on her face again. Fear. "Hurry."

CHAPTER 27

"I'm not afraid of you anymore," Cricket said, but the words sounded trite, even to his own ears. Of *course* he was still afraid of Sunil. He would be afraid of Sunil until the day he died. His uncle had made sure of that.

"Are you sure about that?" Sunil tilted his head, a grotesque smile tugging up the corners of his bloody lips. Cricket hadn't noticed the blood at first, the way it dripped from his uncle's mouth in a slow dribble, gathering on the floor.

"Yes." But the word came out forced, and tight.

Sunil clicked his tongue. "You haven't changed at all have you? Still the stubborn boy playing at being stronger, and more worthy than he is. You've an invader on your doorstep and instead of handling it, you're hiding in your rooms like a child."

"I need rest."

"You can rest when you're dead!" Sunil spat, then laughed, his dark eyes glittering with malice. "Which might happen sooner than you think."

"Why are you here?" Cricket forced himself away from

the door, his legs oddly stiff as he passed his uncle on the way to the small settee set before the fire of his private sitting room.

"You tell me." Sunil shrugged, following after him. "You're the weakling dreaming about the man who always hated him. Why are you punishing yourself, Cricket?"

Cricket didn't answer. He stared into the fire, and hoped that if he ignored this specter of Sunil he would just go away.

"Not that you don't deserve it." Sunil moved again, positioning himself between Cricket and the fire so Cricket was forced to look at him. "I'm just curious as to why this time."

"I am not punishing myself," Cricket bit out, his eyes flicking up to meet his uncle's gaze.

Sunil snorted. "Keep telling yourself that kid."

"This is the work of the pollen. Yoshi told me about the creature and what it could do. It's in my head." And as much as he knew that to be the truth, he still couldn't force the image of Sunil away. Couldn't silence the dripping of blood gathering in a pool in front of his hearth at the feet of the man he'd killed some few weeks ago.

"Would it make you feel better to know that it was? Would that absolve you of the guilt you feel over my death?" Sunil tilted his head, the stream of blood dribbling down from his mouth sliding across his chin to his cheek.

"I don't feel guilt for what I had to do. You forced my hand!" Cricket clenched his teeth together to keep from screaming at Sunil, because that's all he wanted in that moment—maybe all he'd ever wanted—was to scream at his uncle. To cry, and wail, and tell his uncle all the ways in which Sunil had hurt Cricket. All the ways in which he had made Cricket's life harder, and worse than it had to be.

"Did I?" The slow smile that crawled even further up Sunil's face was a rictus, an imitation, and it chilled Cricket to the bone. "And while we're on the subject of your darling

Takayoshi," Sunil said, changing the subject, though not to Cricket's relief.

"He's out in the city, trying to hunt down the creature." Cricket crossed his arms over his chest, defensive.

"Oh? You mean the thing *you* ought to be doing? Out there protecting *your* people?"

"Our people," Cricket corrected, but his stomach lurched.

"Point stands."

"I'm the king, I can't just. . ." Cricket bit down hard on his tongue, unable to finish that sentence. Hadn't he just been thinking the same thing not but an hour ago? That he should be out there, protecting his people? That he'd traded one type of prison for another by defeating his uncle?

"Can't just what?" Sunil leaned in closer, the metallic scent of blood growing thicker. "Can't protect your people? Can't fight the battle to come? Can't put your own neck on the line?" Sunil snorted. "How many people have to die for your arrogance, nephew? How many have to lose their lives so that you can be safe, and happy? Is it worth the cost?"

Was it? Cricket wasn't so sure anymore. "That's not what this is. I'm not *hiding*."

"Do you think the people around you believe you worthy of their sacrifice?" Sunil continued, ignoring Cricket's outburst.

"Or maybe they know, just like I always did, that you're nothing but a scared little orphan with no place to—"

"I am the son of a goddess!" Cricket stood abruptly, his chin lifted. "I am not an orphan. My mother loves me, and she left me here to protect her people. I am the son of the moon herself, and you would do well to treat me as such."

Sunil barked a laugh in delight, his hands lifting to clap happily. "There is the arrogance I know so well. The spoiled little prince who always thought himself right even when everyone else told him otherwise. The one who ran off half-cocked into a trap."

Cricket huffed, standing up straighter.

"It's easy to stand up to a hallucination, nephew." The fire glinted crimson against his bloody teeth. "But what of facing off against the truth?"

"The truth?" Cricket faltered, his hands twitching at his sides. "What *truth*?"

"Come and see, nephew, what they really think of you," Sunil said, soft and condescending. "Follow me, and I'll show you how it really is."

Then he turned and started back for the door to Cricket's quarters. Cricket knew he should ignore him. He knew he should go into his bedroom and lie down, just like he told Ignacia he would. He knew that he needed rest, he hadn't had any in what felt like weeks. But what if Sunil was telling the truth? What if the others did think badly of him and they were just hiding it out of fear of the dragon?

He had to know. Even if the knowledge might kill him. He had to know.

So he followed the ghost of his uncle to the door, and out into the hall. Let the man who had tried to kill his father, and rip away everything he had ever loved, lead him toward the soft hush of voices. People trying not to be overheard.

No. Not just *people*. Takayoshi and Estia.

"I'm telling you," Estia insisted, zir tone hard to decipher with how ze was whispering, "there's something not right about him today. I know you said the plant was affecting him, but he's not asleep, Yoshi, and still it seems—"

"The pollen affected our waking hours in the forest as well," Takayoshi said, cutting Estia off. A strange new habit he'd developed since coming back from Helios that Cricket found unbearably charming. "You may not remember, because you were the most afflicted by it, but you heard voices even when you were awake. You rushed out into the forest, and Leo ran after you."

"I know." Estia sighed. "But this feels different. I'm not. . . I'm not sure what the end goal of the creature is in all of this. At first it seemed like maybe it intended to make Cricket hurt himself so that he wouldn't be a threat to it. But now . . ."

"Now, what?" Takayoshi's voice dipped lower, fear edging his tone.

"Now I worry he'll turn against us," Estia said it so quietly that Cricket almost might have misheard. He almost might have been imagining it. But he wasn't.

Sunil was right! They didn't trust him. Worse yet, they were plotting *against* him.

"See what I mean?" Sunil whispered close to his ear. "They don't have any confidence in you to be able to overcome this thing. And why should they? Everything you've done, you've had help to accomplish. You've never done anything on your own. How can they count on you to rule when they can't even count on you to protect your capital?"

"Leave me alone," Cricket growled, swatting at the ghost of the man who had never cared for him, never loved him as family ought to.

"Your Highness?" Estia asked at the same time Takayoshi murmured, "My King?"

Sunil laughed low, and dark in his ear, but the shape of him disappeared. And Cricket was forced to lift his chin, and march himself around the corner where he and Sunil had been hiding.

"I was unaware we were having secret meetings to discuss my mental state now." Cricket's spine went rigid, his shoulders tense. But he did not back down. He couldn't. Not after everything Sunil said to him. "How are you finding it? Do I meet your standards?"

He didn't actually think he wanted an answer to that question. Whatever Estia and Takayoshi said would either be a lie to placate him, or would be the truth and would ruin him. Still, he was not a coward, and he would not back away from this.

"No?" He asked when they remained silent a little too long for his liking. Their eyes flicking from him to each other and back, a silent conversation happening in those momentary glances that left him isolated and raw. "Well, I suppose we all can't be the picture perfect king trained by the monks of the mountain and—"

Takayoshi cut him off by stepping forward, his body heat suddenly so very close it simmered along Cricket's skin, and took Cricket's face into his hands. Sword calloused fingers brushed over his cheeks. Cricket fought tooth and nail against the urge to lean into the comfort that touch provided.

"Who has been speaking to you?" Takayoshi asked, his golden eyes meeting Cricket's, the expression in them so deep, so worried, Cricket nearly crumpled under the weight of it. "What lies has that creature been feeding you, my king?"

"Is it lies if I catch you talking about me behind my back in my own castle?" Cricket shot back, shrinking away from the raw care and love he found brimming in Takayoshi's gaze. It was all still so new to him, to see the light of love shining in Takaoyhi's eyes when he had spent so many years certain all Takayoshi felt for him was disdain.

"It is if you did not hear the whole conversation and are taking things out of context." Takayoshi's thumb brushed gentle, and slow against the skin beneath Cricket's eye, as if wiping away a tear. He wasn't crying was he? He couldn't tell anymore, he was so tired. "Who has been speaking to you?"

"My uncle said—"

"Sunil was a treasonous liar in life," Takayoshi practically snarled, his brows creasing together in anger instead of concern. "Why would you ever listen to him in death?"

Because I killed him.

"He said I'm weak," Cricket said instead of giving voice to his thoughts. "That I should be out there helping my people. That I'm *hiding* in my castle to—"

"Listen to me." Takayoshi leaned farther forward, pressing his forehead hard enough against Cricket's that he swore it would leave a bruise. "You are our greatest weapon against the war that is to come. King or not, we cannot risk you getting hurt doing something reckless. Am I understood?"

Cricket swallowed, his throat suddenly tight. Sincerity had always been something he struggled with facing head on, and Takayoshi's sincerity was even weightier than that of his sisters or his father's.

"Am I understood?" Takayoshi repeated, bumping his forehead lightly against Cricket's.

"Yes." If he thought that would make Takayoshi's gaze less intense, it didn't. All it did was draw a soft smile from him that crinkled the skin around his eyes just so, and made him look all the more handsome for it.

"Next time Sunil comes to call, I want you to seek one of us out," Takayoshi instructed, but it sounded more like a plea. A gentle urging for Cricket to take himself, and his mental health seriously.

"Okay." Cricket's tongue was too thick for his mouth all of the sudden. Unwieldy and slow.

Takayoshi closed his eyes, and inhaled deeply. Then he pulled back, releasing Cricket's face, and looked him over from an arm's length. Thus giving Cricket a moment to really see him for the first time since finding them in the hallway talking.

Blood dried and flaking on a wound along Takayoshi's hair line. A section of white blond hair caked with yet more blood.

Favoring his one side. And a red stain creeping over his shoulder from his back.

"You're hurt," Cricket choked, reaching for him again, his hands fluttering anywhere and everywhere he could reach. "Let me see."

Takayoshi hummed, but let Cricket walk around him and inspect his injuries. "I had a run in with the creature. Or at least, some of its vines."

"Have you been to see the healer?"

"Not yet. I wanted to check with you first."

Cricket huffed a little. "Come into my room, and sit," he said, taking Takayoshi's wrist. "I'll call for them. Estia will you—" He paused, frowning. Estia was gone. Likely disappeared to give them some privacy. That was oddly. . . kind. Cricket shook himself, and continued on his way with Takayoshi trailing behind him.

Watching Cricket suffer through the torment of the creature's pollen was enough to make Takayoshi want to grab his sword and tear through the capital until he found it and cut it into pieces so small they were invisible to the naked eye. Knowing it was using Cricket's guilt at having to slay his own uncle against him, just made that desire burn that much hotter.

But he had to stay where he was. He had to remain at Cricket's side, and keep him close. No one else seemed able to get through to Cricket when he got caught up in his own head, and Takayoshi was not going to leave him to fight against his own subconscious alone.

So after Cricket finished tending his wounds, and the healer had looked him over, Takayoshi sent someone to the library to gather as many books on botany as they could carry, and bring them back to Cricket's quarters.

There were stacks and stacks piled up around the couch where Takayoshi sat with Cricket sprawled in his lap, head resting on his thigh. His fingers carded carefully through

Cricket's hair, while Takayoshi's mind worked methodically through the reading material.

There had to be some answer here.

Claudia's insight, and keen researching skills would be helpful in this instance, but she had yet to return from her scouting mission into the city to find the pod. Although Takayoshi had not said as much to anyone else, he was beginning to worry for her. The sun would set soon, and there was no word of her return. All he could hope was that she had simply gotten caught up in her work as she so often did. Her mind moving along while time slipped by around her, unnoticed.

If that were the case, maybe by the time she came home, she would have an answer for him. There was hope in that, and Takayoshi decided to lean into it, because not doing so was too bleak.

Cricket snored softly where he rested in Takayoshi's lap. He had been helping in the research for a little while, but eventually his energy flagged, and he gave himself over to sleep.

That was for the better. He would have a harder time fighting off the vindictive visions of the plant without proper rest, Takayoshi knew that from experience. Lack of sleep would muddy the senses, twist the world around him, and lead to irrational thinking, like the thoughts he had expressed earlier.

There was not a world that existed in which Takayoshi would not need Cricket at his side. Not just need, *want*. Cricket was everything Takayoshi had ever hoped for in a soulmate, and more. And the poison that creature was filling Cricket's mind with could not change that, would not change it. Takayoshi just had to ensure that Cricket had no cause to doubt it.

A task easier thought than accomplished. For as kind as

Cricket was, he rarely showed that kindness to himself. And as clever as he could be, his mind was also able to twist itself into knots just to hurt him. Many of Cricket's best qualities could also be termed a curse if left to turn against him as they so often did.

Takayoshi was learning that was why Cricket kept himself constantly busy and surrounded by people, now more than ever. It was a tactic to quiet his mind, and take him out of his own head. A tactic that was failing him, unfortunately. And Takayoshi was unclear on how to make it work better.

Especially after Estia told him that Ignacia reported something about Cricket seeming to ask questions about things she had not said. So even with his sister in the room, he was being harassed by the creature.

This did not bode well.

A knock at the door drew Takayoshi's attention back to the page that he had been staring at for quite some time now, and he realized he had not absorbed a single word of it. Perhaps he should heed his own advice and get some rest. But he could not leave Cricket alone. And what if he woke up from another of his nightmares? Or what if he took to sleep-walking again? Takayoshi was unwilling to take that risk, even if sleeping would speed up his healing.

The knock came again.

"Come in," Takayoshi called softly, hoping his voice carried just enough, but did not rouse Cricket. His eyes flicked down to the man in his lap. Cricket's mouth was open, and he was beginning to drool. But he showed no signs of waking. Good.

Ignacia entered a moment later.

"Anything?" he asked, although he was almost certain from the crease of her brow and the set of her jaw, that she had found nothing. It was strange to have been around this small group of people so long now that he was beginning to pick up their tells. To be able to read their expressions before they even spoke. He had not had that prior to Cricket coming into his life. He liked it. It felt like . . . *family*.

"Nothing." She shook her head. "If it was there, it was gone by the time I went back to look. Can it move like that?"

Takayoshi released a long slow exhale to steady himself, placing his finger in the book he had been reading to mark his place, and shut it to give Ignacia his attention. "When we encountered a creature of this type before, it was not able to move from where it had been planted. It had to use its vines to bring its prey to it."

"But that was a first draft, as it were." Ignacia relaxed a little as she spoke, pacing over to the hearth to place another log on the fire.

"Yes, that is the running theory. That Craven has made changes to its magical makeup since then." A theory he did not much care for, as it left them with far too many unknowns. He hoped Claudia returned soon, and when she did, she came bearing something more than what he found.

Ignacia's rigid posture, and the soft grunt of annoyance seemed to mirror his thoughts. "What does it want with Cricket, do you think?"

"Estia thinks that it means to sew discord amongst us."

"But?"

"But I do not agree." Takayoshi set the book he had been reading onto the stack beside his legs. He would likely have to start with it at the beginning now that he was thinking about it anyway, he could not remember anything he had read. "The creature we encountered before was manipulative, and cunning. But it was living on its base instincts. All it wanted was to hunt, eat, and spread."

"Then why try to lead Cricket off a roof?"

"Leo's theory, and I tend to agree, is that because Cricket fought the creature's magic to free Becka, the creature views him as a threat. Any animal, if backed into a corner, will attack. Cricket has backed it into a proverbial corner." But these were all just theories, and in the end, Takayoshi could not be certain how many of them were correct. They *seemed* correct based on the creature's behavior. But as Claudia would say, they were working with a very small sampling at current. To have more answers they would need to have more attacks, and Takayoshi was not willing to put Cricket up as bait to satiate his own curiosity.

"And the reason Craven unleashed it upon us with no way to control what it does?"

Takayoshi's hands itched to lift and rub at his temples. He did not know why Ignacia was in here bothering him. He had research to do, and if she wanted answers about the plant she could just as easily go and ask someone else. "His reasoning is to sow discord among us and our people. Very likely he has found some way to protect his own army against the pollen, which means it is only us and our citizens that are affected."

"Which makes us easy targets." Ignacia concluded, turning back to him from the fire, and there he saw it. Real worry creased her brow.

"Especially with Cricket struggling to know what is real and what is not," Takayoshi confirmed. "But you knew all this. Or if you did not, you could have easily found it out from someone else. Youta, I think, is very much up to speed. So why are you here, Ignacia?"

She frowned at him, her eyes flicking down to the sleeping king in his lap, and all at once he understood.

"We know what he is suffering through now. We know the signs. And now that we do, all of us can keep him from slipping again. We will not let that creature continue to torment him as it has been doing. I promise you." He appreciated, though, how much she cared for her brother. How much all of them cared for Cricket. It was a relief to know he would not be alone in helping Cricket stay himself until they could find a solution to this.

"Do you know where Claudia is?" she asked, instead of acknowledging what he said.

"No. But I told her to return home before dark. Hopefully she will have news for us when she does." He was unclear what he would do if she did not. "Any news from Leo?"

"Not yet. I'll send him your way as soon as he's back."

"Thank you."

Ignacia dipped her head in a little bow, and exited the way she had come without another word, leaving Takayoshi to his reading and his thoughts.

SUPPER TIME ROLLED AROUND, and while Cricket was awake again, and a little more well-rested, there was no sign of Claudia.

"Did you not see her on your way back through the city," Takayoshi asked Leo, but he knew it was too much to hope for. The capital was vast. Claudia could be anywhere.

"No." Leo frowned down at his plate, his hand flexing around his fork. "I could go out and—"

Cricket frowned, he didn't like the idea of sending anyone out into the streets after sunset, but Claudia was missing. He couldn't let her stay out there, not at the risk that she might be injured and dying. "Yes. Take some men with you, and keep to the back streets. No lights. Do your best not to draw attention to yourselves. Do you understand?"

Leo nodded, but his shoulders had gone a little rigid. His gaze flicked about the table to Estia, and zir siblings, and his jaw clenched as if he wanted to say more but he knew he should not with so many extra ears listening.

"After supper, you and Ignacia will form a search party." Cricket continued, chewing on his lip in thought. "And I'll need you to report in before you leave."

"Of course, Your Highness."

The rest of dinner passed in a tense silence. All of them on edge waiting for news of Claudia, and the moment when they were able to tuck themselves into Cricket's study and discuss what Leo had discovered when he spied on Craven's forces.

Finally behind closed doors again, Leo slumped into a chair near the window. "We were right, his army is much larger than we originally encountered when rescuing Estia's siblings. It's at least three times the size, maybe more."

"Too large for our own army to handle," Ignacia shifted her weight from one foot to the other. "Even with the help of the Celestials."

"I would rather not send the Celestials into a fight with common elves." Cricket leaned forward, holding his head in his hands as his fingers fisted in his hair. "I don't want to run the risk of hurting innocents."

"So we're just supposed to sit back and let him destroy us because we won't use our best weapon against him for fear of what people will *think* of us?" Ignacia scowled at him, her fingers tightening into fists. "Think clearly, Cricket. He brought war to our doorstep. He cursed our people. He deserves this."

"Is there any way to undermine their forces before they reach our gates?" Takayoshi asked, hoping for a solution that would not put Cricket in battle again if he did not want to go.

"Nothing that I can think of." Leo shook his head. "He's placed his forces out in the middle of a field. There's no attack routes we can take that he won't see coming to pick them off one by one. And when he breaches the city perimeter. . ."

"We need to get the citizens inside the castle walls before that happens," Cricket said, suddenly lifting his head. "Tonight, if we can."

"You think he will attack so soon?"

"I think he's not just going to sit out in a field and *bake* for the next week." Cricket growled a little, his jaw clenching, but Takayoshi knew that the anger was not directed at him. "He will be inside of the city before tomorrow evening, if not by tomorrow morning. I want our people safe before then."

"And how would you have us do that?" Ignacia turned back from where she had been looking out the window to eye him. "You've said so yourself, we shouldn't be out in the city when the sleepwalkers are—" She stopped, understanding seeming to settle on her all too quickly.

And then a moment later Takayoshi understood as well. "Cricket, we will not use you as bait. It is too risky."

"It's a risk I'm willing to take." Cricket rose from his seat. "Ignacia, prepare the knights. I'll need them to gather the citizens who haven't been affected by the pollen yet too. They should have created a roster of a kind while they were dictating the curfew. They can use that to gather everyone up. I'm not leaving them to the mercy of Craven."

"Yes sir." But she did not sound pleased with this order.

"Leo, you and your search party can use this as the distraction you need to search for Claudia. But I want you back before morning, to report at the very least. I need to know what you've found even if that isn't Claudia."

"Of course." Leo dipped into a deep bow.

CHAPTER 29

Choices. Everyone made them, and Cricket was making this one. He was actively choosing to put his life in danger to bring his people home. To make sure they were safe from Craven's army.

The creature who borrowed his uncle's face to torment Cricket had gotten so much wrong. His family wasn't turning against him. He wasn't weak. But one thing it had gotten *right* was the fact that Cricket needed to stop asking others to put themselves in the line of fire for him. He needed to stop *hiding*.

He had cowered behind his title long enough. And that was not the kind of king Cricket's father raised him to be, nor the kind he wanted to be. He was better than that. He would not allow Craven to make him curl up in a corner while his people suffered. Not anymore.

"I do not like this plan," Takayoshi said, pressing himself even closer to Cricket where they were both on the same horse. His breath was warm against Cricket's ear, sending a shiver down his spine.

"Yes. You've made that very clear, Yoshi." Cricket couldn't help but laugh a little. "If you have another plan, I'm all ears."

Takayoshi huffed, clearly disgruntled, and Cricket patted his hands where they rested around his waist. "You have nothing to prove by doing this."

"No. Maybe not." Although Cricket was sure that he did. He had to prove to his family that he was not so fragile as needing taking care of the way they were trying to do so. And to himself that he could still do this. That he was strong enough to fight the battle that Craven brought to their door. "But it's the right thing to do. It'll keep my people safe."

"There has to be another way."

A less dangerous way, he didn't say, but Cricket heard it all the same. It was sweet how worried he was for Cricket, but it didn't change the facts. And the facts were, "if there is, we don't have time to find it. Craven has seen to that."

Takayoshi nodded, his head bumping against the back of Cricket's. "You will remain safe."

"I'll do my level best. That's all I can promise." Cricket laughed a little, nerves making him jittery. He knew the trouble this could cause him. The gods only knew what the creature was telling the sleepwalkers to do with the prince if they caught him. He would just have to be faster. There wasn't any other choice.

He slid down off the back of the horse they'd brought out to the edge of the city. It was one of the horses generally used by the knights. Trained for combat, ready to run as fast as her legs would take her. She would be reliable, and quick, and that's what Cricket needed from the horse that would carry Takayoshi to safety.

Takayoshi shifted, ready to join him, and Cricket stopped him by putting his hand on his knee. "No. You stay with the horse."

Takayoshi frowned, his brows pinching together. "I would like to be at your side, in case you need me."

But even as he said the words, Cricket could see how his injuries were taxing him. How riding a horse even was almost too much. He'd be no good to Cricket running through the streets in the condition he was in. In fact, he might actually get them both hurt if Cricket let him come along. Better not to risk it.

"And I would like to know that you're safe." Cricket patted his knee lightly. "It'll put my mind at ease to know that you can get back to the castle quickly and easily."

"Let me ride along beside you," Takayoshi pleaded. His golden eyes had gone large, and round.

Cricket sighed. "Stars, who taught you how to do puppy eyes?"

"I believe I learned that particular skill from you, my king." And he sounded decidedly smug about it. Because of course he did.

"Yes, well. The deal was that you learn it and you not use it against me."

"My apologies" Takayoshi dipped his head, but there was the lilt of a smile at the corners of his lips. He wasn't sorry at all, whatever he might pretend.

"I should have just left you at home." Cricket scrubbed at his face. It was quiet in the street still, but he didn't know how long that would last. Likely not as long as it would take for Cricket to convince Takayoshi to go home. Gods but he loved this man to distraction, didn't he? Yes. Yes, he did. So much. "Fine. But you stay out of the way, and you do not draw your weapon on the civilians. Have I made myself clear?"

"Yes my king." The smile that crinkled the corners of his lips turned victorious, and Cricket groaned.

"One of these days, Yoshi. You and I are going to have a serious discussion about how frequently you make fun of me using my title."

His smile only seemed to widen at this. "I look forward to it." Then Takayoshi readjusted himself on the horse, and turned his attention back to the street. "Incoming."

And Cricket was forced to turn his attention to the approaching group of sleepwalkers. The number had grown exponentially. Cricket sucked in a deep breath to keep himself from crying out in panic. They were ill-equipped for this. But they would make do, just as they always had in the past.

The sleepwalkers shambled toward them, much the way a hungry ghost might, but Cricket was not fooled. He knew just how quickly their slow, stumbling movements could turn to knife-like precision.

He waited, his breath lodged in his throat. Unable to move. Unable to think while they slowly got closer. The waiting was worse, Cricket decided. The uneasy tension of *how much longer* and *have they not noticed me yet*, worse than anything else that would come his way that night.

But still he stayed, his legs burning with the need to run, to flee.

"Should I shout to them?" Cricket asked.

"Perhaps. But I do not think they would hear you. I think the creature is trying to catch you off guard."

"It might be working." It was definitely working. The longer he stood there, the more unsettled he became. And with that uneasiness would come mistakes. "Do you think it knows what we're planning?"

"If it does, I do not think it cares. Its priorities are not the meager battles of men, but the feasting that can be had from them."

"I really wish you wouldn't put it that way." Cricket chuckled softly, shaking his head. But some of the tension had eased from his shoulders. Although he wanted to protect Takayoshi, it was good to have him at his side again.

"What way?" Takayoshi tilted his head in question, but the crinkling of his eyes gave him away. He knew what he'd done. And he'd do it again if it brought Cricket some peace.

"You know exactly—"

One of the sleepwalkers lunged for Cricket, and he scuttled back last minute, keeping just enough distance between them that he'd be able to lure them back to the castle.

"Well, my love," Cricket said, dancing out of the way of another reaching sleepwalker as they bypassed Takayoshi entirely. "You have your marching orders."

"As do you," Takayoshi said, not giving a single bit and allowing for Cricket to run off on some hare-brained scheme without him. Not that Cricket thought that he would, he knew enough of his soon-to-be husband by now to know that Takayoshi was beautifully stubborn. And he had set his mind to remaining at Cricket's side through all of this, which is exactly what he would do whether Cricket wanted him to or not.

Cricket laughed, high, and bright, and delighted, and took off in a run. His steps unhurried and loping along, as he looked over his shoulder to make sure the sleepwalkers were pursuing him.

"They are very close behind you," Takayoshi called. Based on the sound of hoofbeats, he was bringing up the rear of their strange little parade.

"Make sure they stay that way, would you?" Cricket shouted back, and returned his attention to not tripping over a vine and falling on his face.

"Yes," was all Takayoshi said, and Cricket trotted along

happily, leading the little group of sleepwalkers on a merry chase through the capital toward the castle.

It didn't take him nearly as long as he thought that it would to get the first group where he wanted them. But the group wasn't very large, and that was going to prove to be a problem.

Another ten minutes and he was inside of the castle, trotting along through the corridors toward one of the many receiving halls with two doors. He went in through the front door, and waited a moment, dancing out of the way, and side-stepping reaching hands until everyone was inside.

With a loud, shrill whistle, the guards on either side outside the doors shut them, and Cricket slipped out the other side of the room.

"How many was that?" Cricket asked, bracing himself on his knees as he panted.

"Twenty," Ignacia deadpanned. "You can't do this all night, Cricky. You'll burn out."

"I'll be fine." She was right though, and he knew she was. He couldn't do this all night. He would burn himself out if he kept this up. There had to be another way, a faster way. "Maybe if I wind my way through the streets a bit more I'll garner more attention and pull in a bigger catch."

"I don't think that's the take away from this." Ignacia was frowning, he could hear it in her voice even if he wasn't looking at her.

"Maybe if we use the potion Claudia made to trick Sunil when you escaped, we could lure more sleepwalkers to the castle," Takayoshi proposed.

"Only one problem with that," Cricket said, then winced when the sleepwalkers started banging on the door of the hall when they heard his voice. He tilted his head, and led the others away from the hall back toward the front gates. It was going to be a long night and he didn't have a moment to waste.

"And that problem is?" Ignacia asked, all impatience. Not that Cricket could blame her, every minute they spent arguing was a minute they didn't spend getting his people to safety.

"We don't know how they're identifying me." Cricket reached for the reins of the horse he and Takayoshi had ridden to the edge of the city not but a half hour ago. "We don't know if the plant is seeing through their eyes, and thus is seeing me. Or if it's given them orders, and they're working off sight that way. Or if the plant is sensing me by some other method. My magical signature perhaps."

"All very valid points," Takayoshi conceded, climbing into the saddle with Cricket's help.

"Very valid." Ignacia rolled her eyes. "But we have to try something Cricket, we don't have time—"

Cricket held up his hand and reached for the dagger at his side. He lifted it to cut a lock of hair and held it out to her. "Try it. But don't waste too much time with it if it doesn't work immediately. We don't have the seconds to spare to be fiddling with magic we can't guarantee will work."

He didn't wait for a response, he climbed into the saddle in front of Takayoshi and nudged the horse back through the gates. From there they took off at a gallop through the streets, back toward the edge of town.

And just as Cricket didn't wait for Ignacia to say anything to stall him leaving any longer, he also didn't wait for Takayoshi to argue with him again running along beside him.

"Perhaps riding the horse would—"

"If I'm too quick, I'll lose them." Cricket shook his head. "Come on, let's get this done."

Then he took off at a sprint down the street, twisting and

turning through narrow alleys and main throughways, gathering at least fifty sleepwalkers as he went.

"I think I'm getting good at this!" Cricket laughed, delighted.

Between this group, and the people the knights were able to round up, maybe they were getting closer to having all of his citizens safe behind the walls of the castle. If he could keep this up, then by first light, they should all be tucked away where Craven couldn't touch them. He just. . . he just had to keep this up. In spite of the burn in his muscles. In spite of the catch in his lungs. In spite of the fatigue.

"Here come some more," Takayoshi called.

Five more joined their parade from a side street, and Cricket smiled to himself. This was working. It could work. He could get them all where they needed be. This would all be—

Three figures darted from the alley on the other side. They grabbed at the sleeve's of Cricket's tunic, and he stumbled, tripping over a vine. Cricket yelped, only just catching himself, grateful suddenly for all those footwork lessons where Ignacia drilled the importance of steady footing into his head.

But they kept coming. Slashing at him with hands curled into claws. The vines were no issue for them, like they knew exactly where every one of them was. Like the plant was controlling them.

"Cricket!" Takayoshi was still behind the large group, trying to steer the horse through them so that he could get to Cricket, but he couldn't seem to get around them. Cricket was just glad he wasn't forcing it, he didn't want any of his people hurt.

"Yoshi, look at the street signs!" Cricket dodged another attack. His heel caught on a vine that he would swear was not there a moment ago, and he went down, finally. His knees and hands scraping against the ground before he could roll to his feet again.

"What?"

"The street signs! Where are we?"

"Crescent street," Takayoshi called back. Cricket was grateful he hadn't asked why he wanted to know. Hadn't even argued that the information was irrelevant in the face of what was in front of them. "It looks like we are near a cobbler's, but I cannot make out the sign in the dark."

"I'll be able to find it." Or at least he hoped so. He skittered back again, only just managing to stay out of reach of his assailants. Three, he could handle. But the longer he stumbled along, staying an arm's length from them, the more riled up the others seemed to be getting. "Do you think you can loop around and pick me up on the next cross street?"

"What about the horse being too quick?"

"We'll have to keep her at a trot! But I can't— *Blast*." He hissed as he tripped over another vine and landed hard on his hip. It jolted his joints, made everything ache. And then they were on him. Not just the first frenzied three, but more. All ripping at him. Tearing. Grabbing his clothes. Scratching his face. Pulling his hair out.

Cricket's arms went up to fend them off, at least until he could get his feet back under him. But the ground seemed to move beneath him.

Vines.

The vines were moving. Twisting and turning to keep him unsettled.

He swatted at the sleepwalkers, trying to get them away from him without hurting them, but nothing he did seemed to deter them. Taking a deep breath, Cricket reached for the dragon and the ice that came with it, hoping if all else failed he could make the cobblestones slick enough that the sleepwalkers would fall. They might get hurt, but not as badly as if he attacked them.

The ice settled at his feet, and began to spread outward, creating a little patch and—

And then a hand grabbed him by the wrist and hauled him bodily up onto a horse.

Cricket's shoulder screamed from the movement, but Takayoshi didn't give him a moment to complain. He wheeled the horse around and started them back to the castle at a brisk trot, only looking back once to make sure they were being pursued.

"We will be using the horse from now on," Takayoshi said, and Cricket could tell he would broker no argument.

Cricket decided to just ignore the order instead of argue about it. "I think we were close to it back there. That's why they started attacking me like that. It was trying to defend itself."

"We will inspect the area in the morning."

"If we have time," Cricket muttered to himself, and turned to look again at the people shambling along behind him. "They've slowed down now."

Takayoshi hummed his understanding and pulled the horse's reins to slow her down. "Hopefully, Ignacia's potion idea has worked."

"Yes, hopefully." Cricket couldn't take his eyes off the people following behind them at a slow pace again, his mind worked. They'd slowed down almost as soon as it was clear that they'd scared Cricket and Takayoshi away from that area. How close had he been to the pod? Was it on that street, or the next one over?

"It plays tricks too," Takayoshi said, seeming to know exactly where his mind was. Then he told Cricket about the vines in the temple. "We cannot trust everything we see."

"Still, it's a place to start."

"Yes. It is a place to start." But as Takayoshi fell silent, Cricket sensed there was something else on his mind as well. Something else bothering him. Something they didn't have time to delve into right that moment as they turned the corner and trotted through the gates of the castle again.

Two trips down. How many more to go before the sun rose?

Not too many, he hoped.

BOOK IV
THE WEDDING

CHAPTER 30

The first young rays of the sun were just breaking the horizon as Takayoshi pushed the horse faster through the gates of the castle.

There was so much joy to be had. A victory. A triumph.

"We did it!" Cricket shouted, lurching forward to wrap his arms around Takayoshi's neck and nearly toppled them both from the saddle.

"We have not claimed victory yet." But even as the words left his lips, Takayoshi could not quiet the swell of happiness in his chest.

The war was not over, no. Craven would be at their gates likely before breakfast had even been cleared away, if Leo's intel was correct. But this was a small win in and of itself. For they had saved Cricket's—*their*—people from being decimated by another war. They had gathered everyone from the list the knights provided. All they could do was pray that was everyone. It was not perfect, it was not the end to this conflict that they all needed, but it was something, and as Takayoshi had learned of late, sometimes one needed to celebrate the small triumphs.

"But we will soon," Cricket said, his tone low in Takayoshi's ear, warm breath tickling the sensitive skin, but so very sure it made a chill run down Takayoshi's spine.

"Yes. We will soon," Takayoshi agreed, turning his head to press a kiss into Cricket's cheek. He would see to that himself if he had to. "For now, let us get these people somewhere they can rest."

They turned to look over their shoulders to survey the confused group behind them. No longer sleepwalking, they all seemed bewildered as to how they had wound up inside the gates of the castle. But at least they were awake and thus no longer a danger to themselves or those around them.

Cricket shifted so he could better face the citizens behind him, lifting his chin up, looking every inch the king he was. "We have brought you here for your protection," he declared. "War will soon be at our gates, and I will not see any more of mine fall to it so long as I have a say. While you're here, all your needs will be met, including a protective detail. And once we have defeated this current foe, you are free to return home." He slid down off the horse now that he had their attention, stepping toward them, his hands spread wide. "In the meantime, my home is your home. Please make yourself comfortable."

Takayoshi watched him for a long moment, letting Cricket save face even as he leaned heavily against the horse, needing her strong legs to steady him after the night he'd had. When the knights came forward to help usher the people away, he slid down and stood behind Cricket, his hands carefully and subtly on his waist until they were alone just inside the gates.

Then he pulled Cricket into his chest before crouching down and scooping him up in his arms, and off his feet. "And now—"

"Takayoshi, put me down," Cricket laughed, breathless and exhausted. "I can walk. I'm fine."

Takayoshi ignored his protests, and took the long way around to the side door toward Cricket's wing. "Now we rest," he finished, still not putting Cricket down, although he noted that Cricket had largely stopped struggling after his initial protests. Instead leaning into him, letting Takayoshi bare his weight.

"One of us needs to be in the guard tower." The words came out mumbled from where Cricket pressed his face in so close to Takayoshi's neck. His voice a warm tickle against Takayoshi's skin. "I don't want us to look unprotected. Ignacia isn't enough, it needs to be the king."

"I am not king yet."

"Do you want to change that?" Cricket asked around a giggle that made him sound half-delirious.

"What?" Takayoshi stopped, his body going so still he might have been sleeping. At least externally. Internally he was a riot of emotions. His heart slamming against his chest. His ears ringing, half sure he had not heard Cricket correctly.

"The entire capital is inside the castle." Cricket's voice went terribly soft, as if he were unsure all of the sudden.

And that was enough to get Takayoshi moving, dropping his head to press in close to Cricket's face, pressing a kiss to his lips that almost sent them both to the ground. Because how could Cricket ever doubt his feelings? How could he ever be unsure of what Takayoshi felt for him? There should never have been a single doubt in Cricket's mind that Takayoshi loved him with everything he had, and that he had wanted to wed him from the moment they met.

"Is that a yes?" Cricket's laugh had gone high and nervous.

"Ignacia is going to throw a tantrum," Takayoshi warned, but that was not going to stop him.

"Very likely." Cricket's grin widened, and now as so

many other times, it seemed he was reading Takayoshi's thoughts. "But she wanted the whole capital to see, didn't she?"

"We do not have more than an hour." Takayoshi's feet sped up. They had a lot to prepare if they were going to be married before Craven moved his forces into the city. "Possibly two."

"Plenty of time," Cricket insisted. Then he wriggled again, more insistent this time. "But if we're going to get everything done in time, we'll need to split our attention. You're in charge of Youta and the decorations?"

Takayoshi hummed his agreement, placing Cricket carefully back on his feet in the grass. His hands still on Cricket's waist, he hesitated for a moment. "Are you certain this is what you want?"

Cricket took hold of his face, offering him a soft, almost sad smile. Fear flashed through Takayoshi, making his skin prickle with cold, but he held onto Cricket, because he would never let go of him. Not again. Not so long as he lived. "When we go to fight Craven, I want to be married to you. Just in case."

He did not have to say just in case of *what*, Takayoshi understood immediately. Just in case one or both of them did not make it to the other side of this infernal war. "Then when we meet Craven on the battlefield," Takayoshi ducked his head, his words dipping low, "it will be as husbands."

Cricket sighed, relieved. "Good. Now go. We don't have any time to waste." But before he could send Takayoshi off, he moved onto his toes and pressed a kiss to Takayoshi's lips. Slow, and lingering. Then he pulled back, and gave Takayoshi a gentle shove with a little laugh. "Leave Iggy to me. She can hardly say no to her baby brother after all!"

Takayoshi nodded, and turned toward the direction of the entrance to the kitchens, certain he would find Youta there.

"THIS IS NOT near enough time to do this properly," Youta said, and although the words were like a scolding, the tone was anything but. A smile split her face so wide, Takayoshi worried it might crack. Already she had Takayoshi in one of the larger halls left unoccupied by their sleeping citizens, clearing space, and putting in neat rows of chairs.

She had a small horde of staff helping, busy bees all delighted to see their king happily wedded. Takayoshi worried for a moment that maybe this was not the right time. Maybe they should not do this with so much darkness lingering over them. But Cricket was right. If this battle should be their last, he wanted to go into it knowing that Cricket was sure of his commitment to him. He wanted to go into it knowing that they had gotten to at least be married.

"For one thing," Youta continued her not-quite tirade, "what will you wear?"

"I am hardly concerned with that." Although maybe he should be. He did want to look his best, did he not? He shook himself. There was not time for foolish vanity. And beside that fact, Cricket would marry him even if he were wearing rags. "I just want to be married to the man that I love."

Youta stilled for a moment, something she had not done this entire time, then she let out a soft, happy little chuckle. "Very well then. We'll do our best, won't we?"

"We will." Takayoshi nodded. His heart soared. Soon. Soon he would be married to the man that he loved. Soon they would be able to say that they were united as one. It would lift the curse, but that was very much just a bonus to the ability to call Cricket "husband". To know that his best friend would be linked to him until the day that he died. His best friend. . . Claudia! "Excuse me, I need to check on something."

He did not wait for a reply, he tore off at a run toward Cricket's study. The door flung open, and Takayoshi ignored the affronted squawk from Ignacia to enter, and step up to Cricket's desk.

"Has Leo returned with Claudia?"

"Not yet. We have only just returned, he hasn't checked in yet." Cricket frowned, glancing out the window as if to check the time.

"Claudia is not here. She was to be my best-person. She is my best friend. I want. . . " He bit his tongue, eyes burning with tears. He wanted to marry Cricket so badly it ached. But at the same time, how could he without Claudia there at his side? She had been there for him through all of this. How could he make the vow, and say the words without her there? He was frozen with indecision. "And my sister. Atsuko should—"

"Okay." Cricket's voice was soft from where he was suddenly at Takayoshi's side, his hands taking Takayoshi's own in a gentle hold. "Okay. Tell me what you want to do, and we will do it."

"I do not. . . I do not know." Was he letting Cricket down in not being able to do this? What effect would that have on him in the battle to come? "Tell me what to do."

"I can't. You know I can't. This has to be your choice but —" Cricket squeezed his hands tightly, bringing him up to press kisses into the backs of his knuckles, "know that whatever choice you make, I support it. If we need to wait for Claudia and our sisters to be here, then we will. I can wait. I would wait centuries for you, if I had to."

Takayoshi took a breath, and tried to quiet his mind. It was a struggle. He had experienced so many different emotions all in the span of a half hour. And every one of them conflicted making the choice that was ultimately his that much harder to make.

"A compromise," Ignacia said, but it sounded like it cost her to say as much. She was rubbing at her temples, her expression tight and tired. Takayoshi had forgotten, momentarily, that while he was missing his best friend, she too was missing someone. Claudia and her had grown close over the months that they had aided he and Cricket in their fight against Sunil. And now Claudia was missing.

Something dark, and vicious twisted in Takayoshi's stomach. This had been a bad idea from the start. Doomed. He should not have agreed to wedding Cricket with the war so close to their door. Their happiness could not supersede what was going on around them. And yet, he wanted nothing more than to cling to what limited joy he could find. He wanted to go into this final battle, with his husband at his side in more than just name.

"We're listening, Iggy." Cricket tilted his head to face her, never once letting go of Takayoshi.

"Right." Ignacia nodded to herself. "We'll have the formal ceremony just for a small selection of the staff and knights, just enough to make it official. We'll use the basic vows, and rights. Then, when all of this is over, and we all come out on the other side, we'll do a more personalized ceremony. Something just for our family. Will that suit everyone?"

"I like it," Cricket declared. "It allows for us to solidify our union before the battle so as to counteract any lingering issues from Venus' curse, but also have a more meaningful ceremony later for those we hold dear. Yoshi? Thoughts?"

Takayoshi opened his mouth to answer, but before he could, Cricket pressed a finger to his lips.

"Do not agree to this if it is not wholeheartedly what you want," Cricket warned. "I am not pressuring you into this decision. If we must wait, then we will wait. Understood?"

A soft hum left Takayoshi as he nodded his understanding.

"Now you may answer." Cricket grinned brightly, pulling his hand away. He still looked so tired. Stretched thin and brittle by a lack of rest and an evening spent running away from his own citizens. But there was happiness there too, mixed in with the fear. He wanted this. He loved Takayoshi and he wanted this.

And Takayoshi wanted it to. "Let us be wed."

"Excellent!" Cricket tilted his head back to laugh, his throat bobbing with the motion.

"Great, now get out. We still have a lot to do, and only about . . ." Ignacia consulted her pocket watch. "A quarter of an hour to do it in."

"And it's bad luck to see the groom on the wedding day," Cricket chimed, pushing Takayoshi toward the door.

"Right, and you two could use all the luck you can get," Ignacia grumbled.

At the door, Takayoshi spun around for a moment. He dipped down and stole another kiss. "For luck," he reasoned, then he was gone. Back to completing preparations for their wedding.

Their wedding.

In a few scant hours, he would be married.

CHAPTER 31

Cricket had never actually thought he would be married. He had been too young to think of marriage when he'd first met Takayoshi. And by the time he was of an age to consider it, he was at war. Spending every day fighting for his life. So no, he'd never actually thought he'd get to a point where he would have someone to call his own. Where someone would call him husband. And even if he had thought of it? He could never have seen Takayoshi coming.

Takayoshi was everything Cricket had never allowed himself to think that he wanted, and then some. He shone so brightly he put even the sun to shame. And the best part? The most awe-inspiring part? The part that frequently stopped Cricket in his tracks? Was that Takayoshi didn't even know it.

The fact that Takayoshi didn't seem to realize how wonderful he was consistently knocked Cricket sideways. Because it meant he was all of those things: strong, brave, true, funny, but also *humble*. Somehow.

The fact that Takayoshi existed at all, was a small gods-given miracle. The fact he wanted to marry Cricket was something else entirely.

Cricket who was messy, and scattered. Cricket who didn't sleep enough, and needed to be reminded sometimes to eat. Cricket who was the opposite of Takayoshi in almost every way.

And yet, there Cricket was, studying himself in the mirror in his bedroom.

"You look handsome papa," Becka said, a little smile on her face. He couldn't have his entire family there, the thought still tugged at his chest, made him wonder if perhaps Takayoshi had a point in putting a stop to this. But he had Becka, Ignacia, Youta, and Leo. And above all, he had Yoshi. That would have to be enough. It *would* be enough. At least for now. Until he could gather his family all together again.

"Thank you sunflower." Cricket met her eyes in the mirror, and grinned back at her, although it was a little forced. There was an ache behind his eyes that didn't seem as if it would ever go away, and every muscle in his body screamed from fatigue. He needed sleep, Takayoshi had been right about that. But he knew the moment he allowed himself to sit down it would all be over. An object in motion stayed in motion, and once Cricket stopped moving he wouldn't be able to get himself up again for at least a couple of days—if not, longer.

"Shishi is lucky." She tilted her chin up, a habit she had learned from him, but the tone was all Takyoshi. Decisive, and leaving absolutely no room for argument.

"Is he now?" Cricket couldn't help but tease.

Becka hummed in response, another thing she'd learned from Takayoshi over the last few weeks.

"Do you want to hear a secret?" Cricket whispered, turning from the mirror to look at her.

Becka nodded eagerly, scooting off the bed so she could get closer to him, her eyes wide and interested.

He met her halfway, crouching down so they were of a height. Then he murmured into her ear, grinning all the while because it was the absolute truth, "I'm terribly lucky too, I think. Don't you?"

"Definitely," Becka agreed readily. Her little arms hugged his neck so tightly he was half afraid she'd strangle him, but he didn't push her off. Couldn't. It seemed like it had been so very long since they'd been close like this. Since they'd had time to just be father and daughter. He pressed his face into her hair, inhaling the soft scent of grass, and little girl that lingered in her hair. "Papa."

"Hm?"

"I think I'm happy. Are you happy?"

"I don't know that I could be any happier, Becka." And that was true too. Nothing was going his way lately. Everything was falling apart around him. But he didn't think he could possibly be any happier. He had his daughter, and soon he would have his husband. What more did a man need, really? "Now," he pulled back to get a better look at her, "let's do something with this hair of yours."

"Papa," Becka groaned, her head falling back with a healthy dose of dramatics, "My hair is fiiiine."

"I beg to differ little miss. When was the last time you brushed it hmm?" He tapped her nose. "Come on, let me braid it for you. Just like I used to."

Before everything happened. Before his father died. Before his uncle returned and ripped his kingdom apart. Before he fled into the night like a thief with his daughter on his back. Before he showed up on Takayoshi's doorstep and begged sanctuary. Before. . . well. Just *before*.

"Do I have to?" She sulked, flopping down into the chair as he guided her by the shoulders.

"Yes, I'm afraid you do." He tapped her lightly on the head with the brush, then got to work. "Now, none of your lip, little lady. It's my wedding day, after all."

THE HALL WAS BEAUTIFUL. Not half as grand as what he was sure his family would have liked, but Youta had worked some kind of magic that not even he could compete with.

The medium-sized hall Youta chose was a wash in swaths of pale blue draperies that Cricket had never seen before. Were they curtains? Sheets? Were they in storage until that very moment? He didn't know. He also didn't think it really mattered.

The point was, it was beautiful. More than he could have hoped for given their circumstances.

So much more.

Stars, he really was lucky, wasn't he? And not just that Takayoshi was waiting for him at the beginning of the aisle, a soft smile crinkling his eyes. But also in that he had people who loved him enough to throw all of this together. That they saw how important this was to him, and they came together to make it happen. No one was as lucky as he.

"Are you all right?" Takayoshi asked, his voice husky, and quiet as he dipped his head to Cricket. He looked startlingly handsome, cast in a warm glow by what had to be hundreds of candles and votives Youta chose to light the room in instead of using the magical lights. Cricket wasn't sure where the deep blue tunic had come from, it might have been one of his own, but it made Takayoshi shine all the more. "We can put a stop to this still."

"I wouldn't dream of it." Cricket shook his head, and

scrubbed at his eyes. Oh gods, he was crying. He was crying, and Takayoshi probably thought it was his fault. "I'm just overwhelmed is all."

Takayoshi turned his back on the gathered people, and crowded in so close to Cricket that all he could see was the midnight blue of Takayoshi's tunic. "Take a minute."

"Everyone's waiting." Leaning forward, he rested his head against Takayoshi's chest. It was a nice, sturdy chest.

"And they can continue to wait. We are not walking down the aisle until you are ready."

Cricket let out a delighted little laugh. He forgot sometimes how Takayoshi cared little for what other people thought, or said. His primary concern was first and foremost always what was right. And right now, what he believed was right was to shield his soon to be husband from the knowing eyes of those around them.

With a deep inhale—for the first time since they'd been back—Cricket allowed himself to rest. He closed his eyes. He sucked in lungfuls of Takayoshi's sandalwood and snowfall scent. And he let his mask drop. It felt good.

"I know we are not married yet, but would it be inappropriate for me to embrace my husband?" Takayoshi asked, his tone nearly as flat as ever, but when Cricket lifted his head he saw the curve of a smile on his lips.

Cricket threw his head back and barked a laugh that no doubt startled everyone around them. "Somehow I always forget how funny you are, my dear."

"I am glad you forget sometimes," Takayoshi said, his voice whisper soft. "I delight in reminding you. And will continue to do so for the rest of our lives."

"Yoshi!" Cricket gasped, clutching his chest dramatically as he rocked back on his heels, only just avoiding stumbling as Takayoshi grabbed his elbows. "You didn't tell me you were a romantic."

"I would have thought that obvious." Takayoshi huffed a laugh, reeling Cricket back in. "Now, are you ready to get married?"

"So ready." Cricket chuckled, delighted.

With a nod, Takayoshi turned back around, settling at Cricket's side easily, and held out his arm. Cricket took it, and let Takayoshi lead him toward where Ignacia, Youta, and Leo were waiting for them.

The altar to Selene was just as beautiful as the rest of the room. Dripping with candles, and soft fabrics. Cricket didn't know his mother well, but he thought she would approve.

Ignacia nudged him lightly, and passed him a pale silver votive, as yet unlit. She looked like she might be a little teary eyed, but he wasn't going to tell anyone. At least not so long as she didn't tell anyone about the tears in his own eyes.

Youta shifted to standing in front of them, her back to the room, a heavy leather-bound volume in her hands. "Are you ready?" she asked softly, so no one but they could hear.

Cricket nodded, and out of the corner of his eye, he saw Takyoshi nod too.

"Good. Then repeat after me." She cleared her throat, and tilted her chin back so she could be heard by even those who were behind her. "I Cricket, king of Lunette do take Takayoshi to be my partner in all things. To protect. To cherish. To find new beauty in the everyday with. To love."

Cricket's words caught in his throat, right along with his heart. He coughed a little, dislodging them, and smiled up at Takayoshi. After that, it was the easiest thing in the world to repeat the words. Easier still to hold his votive out for Takayoshi to light with the tip of his finger, and place the candle beside Takayoshi's before bowing once to the statue of his mother.

Takayoshi swept Cricket into his arms, dipped him backward, and kissed him so deeply Cricket worried he might fall to the floor. But Takayoshi held him fast, and a whoop went through the gathered crowd. By the time Cricket stood up again, he was dizzy with giddiness, and joy. It tasted like fizzy stuff on his tongue.

They spun to face the room full of his— *their* citizens, their hands still clasped. Cricket looked to Takayoshi one last time, his heart stuttering at the smile split across Takayoshi's face. It was definitely large enough that anyone could see it, not just someone who knew him well enough to know where to look.

A real smile. Stars. He was brilliant.

Then they both, as one, dipped into a bow to their people.

Just as they were turning to take the third, and final bow, the one they would give to each other as a sign of respect to one another. . .

The doors to the hall burst open.

"Can't we finish a single ceremony in this kingdom without someone bursting in dramatically?" Ignacia grumbled under her breath as everyone turned to watch the young knight stumble up the aisle.

"Apologies Your Highness. . ." he hesitated a moment before adding, "es." As he dipped into a low bow that almost sent him to his knees.

"What's happened?" Cricket asked, cutting straight to the heart of the matter.

"Craven is at the gates." The knight rose, his lips twisted into a scowl. "He has hostages."

"Hostages plural?" Cricket's heart clenched in his chest.

"He has the Lady Claudia, Your Highness."

Cricket cursed under his breath, and he felt Takayoshi tense beside him. He turned to Takayoshi and offered him a tense smile. "One last bow, my love, and then we go to war?"

"Yes. One last bow."

They bowed to each other, then turned as a unit back to the knight.

"Youta," Cricket called over his shoulder, "get everyone settled, and make sure Becka is safe."

"Ignacia, you are with us," Takayoshi finished, not even having to hear Cricket say it to know what he was thinking.

"I'll gather a small contingent of soldiers." Ignacia nodded, turning on her heel to exit through a side door and do just that. Leaving Cricket and Takayoshi to head toward the gate themselves.

CHAPTER 32

The guard tower gave Takayoshi a strange sensation of vertigo. Which made no sense. As a phoenix he flew without a single care for the height at which he soared. And even before then when he had just been an elf, he had never once struggled with a fear of heights. In fact, the distance to the ground did not even register most of the time.

Things were different now. He was not moving, but he swore he was spinning, spinning, *spinning* out of control. And his ears had taken to ringing, a loud high-pitched sound that made him more than slightly nauseous.

Of course during those times he was not looking down at his best friend held at sword point, her mouth gagged, her eyes pleading with him to do something, but nothing too rash, as he was now. That seemed to make all the difference.

Just beside her was who Takayoshi could only assume was Estia's brother, Damian. His hair swept into his face to hide his eyes. But there was no mistaking the rigidity of his shoulders. The posture screamed betrayal, hurt. Whatever deal he had thought he had with Craven, he had clearly been proven wrong. Takayoshi wondered how long before Craven made it clear that he was in this for himself, and himself alone. That he would not be sharing his throne with anyone, least of all his adopted brother.

Maybe not long after they saved Estia's other siblings, and left Damian behind with Craven. Maybe not until this very moment. Either way, Takayoshi pitied him, but also envied his ignorance. How peaceful it must be to believe oneself above the horrors of others. To feel that one was superior even to one's own family.

Claudia jerked in the man's hold, the blade cutting ever so slightly into her skin, leaving behind a red smear.

Takayoshi's chest was tight with something, panic maybe, and even Cricket's steady presence at his side did not seem to help. Although the coolness of Cricket's palm pressed firmly against his own, his fingers tight around Takayoshi's at least made it clear he was not alone in this. The grip seemed to say *I'll fix this. I'll make sure she's safe* without a single word having to pass between them. Takayoshi had never been so grateful for the way Cricket seemed to read him like a book as he was now.

"There was no need to get all dressed up to meet with me," Craven called. Takayoshi could not see his face well enough to make out the expression, but he imagined that Craven was smirking. That seemed the thing people like him would do when they thought they had the upper hand in a situation such as this. An assumption that was patently false.

"You interrupted our wedding," Cricket responded, tilting further into Takayoshi's space, their shoulders bumping together lightly. "So I hope whatever you called us out here to discuss is worth it."

"Your wedding?" Craven tilted his head, and Takayoshi would swear that his smile grew.

Claudia jerked beside him, but Takayoshi could not look at her, because if he did he knew that the guilt would overwhelm him entirely, the guilt or the strange sensation of the ground tilting forward under his toes, threatening to throw him from the wall. She should have been there. She was his best friend. She should have been at his side. But they had done it without her, because to not do it would have been worse. Because he needed to go into this knowing that he belonged to Cricket and vice versa. Because with the curse of Venus hanging over their heads, she could take this excuse to strike them down.

"Yes," Takayoshi said. He allowed the gentle pressure of Cricket against him to ease some of his own aches. He was loved. He was safe. And together they would bring Claudia home.

"Then allow me to be the first to offer my congratulations." Craven dipped into a low bow that screamed insincerity, and it took everything Takayoshi had to not hurl a ball of flame at his feet just to watch him dance. He could not chance that one or both hostages would get caught in the crossfire of the ensuing fight should he allow his temper to get the better for him.

"The second, actually." Cricket's grin had gone sharp, and biting. "But who's counting?"

"What was that?"

Takayoshi had to swallow back a chuckle, but Claudia did not seem to feel any need for such restraint, for she barked out a laugh. It was muffled through the gag, but Takayoshi heard it just the same.

"Thank you." Cricket's tone was equally sarcastic, and the chill of his magic bit more firmly into Takayoshi's hand. He was angry. Maybe more so than he had ever been in all of their acquaintance.

Craven, for his part, did not seem to recognize the fine line he was treading upon. A mistake Takayoshi hoped he did not live to regret.

"Now"—Cricket released Takayoshi's hand so he could clap once, sharp and echoing—"please tell me that you've interrupted our ceremony to inform me that you're planning to return home? You're just dropping Claudia and Damian off on your way out, right?"

"I'm afraid not."

"Shame. That would have been a worthy wedding gift, wouldn't it?" Cricket turned to look at Takayoshi, his brows raising at the jest. His tone to that point had been carefully light, friendly even, if a little sarcastic, but Takayoshi saw it for what it was. Cricket was trying to keep the situation from escalating, trying to keep Craven from getting angry and lashing out against Claudia and Damian. For all his false cheer, this was still a hostage situation. They could not forget that.

"I hate to disappoint, especially on such a happy occasion." Craven ducked his head in some kind of false apology that made Takayoshi grind his teeth.

"Liar," Cricket hissed under his breath.

Takayoshi could not help but agree. It was very evident, even to him, a person who struggled sometimes with understanding people and their social cues, that Craven was delighting in this. To the point where if Takayoshi were a betting man he would say—

"He knew about the wedding somehow." It was a deeply unsettling thought. Especially given that the wedding had been the work of a couple of hours. How could anyone have known? Takayoshi's hands opened and closed at his sides, longing for the comforting grip of a sword. "A spy."

"Or he has some kind of mental link to the plant creature, and it's feeding him information via the sleep-walkers." Cricket murmured, not taking his eyes off of Craven, but he reached for Takayoshi's hand again, and gave it a firm squeeze. "The question is does that make me as much of a liability to our cause as it does our people?"

Takayoshi decided abruptly he did not like this line of thinking, and promptly disregarded it. For all that it was possible, he would not allow himself to follow down that path. Cricket would not betray them involuntarily or otherwise. Even if the creature did have access to a person's thoughts that way, and could share them with Craven, the dragon's magic would protect Cricket from that, surely.

"There's only one way to find out." Cricket tilted his head, his fingers tapping against his chin, but he did not expand upon that thought. Instead, he returned his attention to Craven. "If you didn't come to return our loved ones to us, then why *are* you here Craven?"

Craven seemed to have been waiting for this exact question, for when it came he crowed happily, his whole posture changing as he bounced on his toes like a child excited for the winter solstice. It was disgusting. "I am here," he said, still bouncing a little on the balls of his feet, "to let you know that you have exactly one day to cede to my demands. If they have not been met by the time we break our fast tomorrow. . . I burn your capital city to the ground. Which would be a pity since you've only just rebuilt, wouldn't it?"

"Kind of him to give us one whole day," Cricket muttered.

Takayoshi hummed his agreement. He wondered how much longer Craven would keep them there playing this foolish game. Wasting what little time they had to come up with a better plan to rescue their friends. Especially given the fact that they were in all likelihood surrounded.

"I do not think he will actually give us that time," Takayoshi murmured back. "He will attack before then, in the hopes that he will catch us unprepared."

"Of course he will. Dishonorable wretch." Cricket's grumbled words were a balm, although Takayoshi was unclear on why. Maybe it was just nice to know that he was not alone in finding this entire situation to be a nuisance. "And what are your terms?" Cricket called down to Craven.

"Now, there is no need to be so irritable Your Highness." Craven tsked, shaking his head.

"He says as if he is not holding our friends, and our entire kingdom hostage." Cricket's little asides were terribly endearing. But even more enthralling was the way Cricket used the word *our*, already considering Takayoshi to be the king of Lunette, at his side. Takayoshi would have to kiss him about that later. "Are you going to tell us what you want? Or are we going to stand here all day? Waiting."

The waiting was making Cricket antsy, Takayoshi could see it. His toes tapping beneath them, his weight shifting ever so slightly from one foot to the other. The only solace in this was that Takayoshi knew Ignacia was at their backs, and had secured the castle long ago. If Craven was trying to distract them, he could keep them there as long as he liked, his people would not breach the castle walls.

Takayoshi had been expecting it, for what else could Craven want in exchange for his hostages, but it still caught him off guard when Craven said, "The dragon pearl."

"Now what do you want with—"

"You give me the dragon pearl, and I will leave your land in peace," Craven said, not allowing for Cricket to lean into the act Takayoshi saw him building up. To convince Craven that the dragon pearl was meaningless. That it was just another trinket with a fancy name. Instead of what it was, the key to controlling Cricket, and using him as a weapon against anyone and everyone who chose to stand against the one holding it.

"And how do I know that you won't take it, and then turn right around and use it as a weapon against my throne?" Cricket asked, the words carefully selected. How much did

Craven really know of the pearl? How much did he really know of the dragon? Was he basing all of this off of Sunil's information, or did he have Estia's too? In spite of Estia saying ze'd given him nothing. They had to know, and the only way to get that information from him was to keep him talking. Theoretically.

Craven seemed to realize this too, because he shrugged, disinterestedly. "I suppose you don't. But you do know that if I don't get what I want, I will kill your friend here, and raze your city to the ground."

"I see." Cricket's jaw ticked around the words, his hands going icy in his rage, fingers turning blue at the tips where his talons still had not returned to normal, blunt nails. The chains someone had strung between his antlers jangled a little as he tucked his chin in an expression of determination.

"Ultimately, Your Highness, the choice is yours. You give me the dragon, or you watch your city burn."

Takayoshi's heart hammered against his rib cage painfully at the wording, and he whispered, "he does not know."

He hoped Cricket understood what he meant.

"No. It would seem he doesn't," Cricket agreed softly. There was some relief in Craven not knowing that the dragon was Cricket, although not much, it meant he did not understand the full power he held over Cricket and by extension Lunette. "I'll wager he doesn't know about the other celestials either. How quickly do you think Anstice could get here?"

"Not quickly enough. But we still have Ignacia, and myself." Even with Anstice's celestial powers, she could not fly as he and Cricket could, and thus would have to run the entire way from Helios to Lunette's capital. That was a month travel by horse, maybe two weeks at the speed which a kitsune could run. But that would be without rest, and they both knew Anstice could not keep up such a grueling pace.

"Give us a week," Cricket called back.

"Twenty-four hours, and not a second more." Craven's tone had gone harder, as if he was reaching his limits for pleasantries, as unpleasant as they had been.

"Forty-eight."

"You test my patience, Prince Cricket," Craven hissed, and raised a hand.

"It's King Cricket, actually."

The soldier holding Claudia slid his blade across Claudia's arm, drawing a thick stream of blood.

"All right. All right. Twenty-four hours!" Cricket held up his hands in surrender, unwilling to push Craven further. "We'll meet at the square at the foot of the clock tower near the edge of the city. A nice open space, so I can be sure no one is lying in wait for me."

"So glad we understand one another." Craven dropped his hand and the soldier's blade fell away, but they left Claudia bleeding. She had enough knowledge to patch herself up, but if they did not get to her quickly enough, and she was not treated, there would be a danger of infection. "Oh, and see that my delightful younger sibling delivers it, won't you? I have so missed zir."

Then he spun on his heel, and he and his men marched away from the gate.

"We need to find out where he's holding them." Cricket frowned, watching them go. They disappeared around a corner a couple of minutes later, and Takayoshi lost sight of them.

Takayoshi hummed his agreement. Getting the hostages out of the crossfire would help, but he was not sure how much. "We will mention that when we sit down to discuss our plans with the others."

Cricket nodded, his lips pursed in a troubled expression.

"My King, what is wrong?"

Cricket turned to him, and he seemed to make the conscious effort to clear the expression from his face so that he could smile at Takayoshi. "Why don't we change that to husband, huh?"

"Husband," Takayoshi repeated, his chest blooming with warmth.

"Come on. We don't have much time." Cricket held out his hand.

CHAPTER 33

"What *else* didn't you tell him?" Cricket asked, a growl in his throat.

"You know you're not really supposed to be mad at someone when they *don't* spill your secrets, right?" Estia crossed zir arms over zir chest, meeting Cricket's glare without a trace of fear in zir gaze. Which was infuriating, because he was trying to be intimidating here! He was angry, not just with Estia, but with this entire situation, and he needed answers. Now. Before things got worse.

"We just need to know what Craven is and is not aware of, Estia," Takayoshi said, his words calm and steady. He was angry, just as Cricket was, Cricket knew that, he was just handling it better. Which was a real shame, if you asked Cricket, because there was something undeniably attractive about a Takayoshi who let his rage carry him through. It wouldn't be helpful in this current situation, and Cricket recognized that, but that didn't mean he couldn't find it a pity that Takayoshi was keeping himself so tightly wound at the moment.

Estia released a long slow breath, and brushed zir hand

through zir hair. "I didn't tell him anything I learned from the archive.

"Why not?" Ignacia stared hard at zir, as if she didn't believe it. Not that Cricket could blame her, it was a tough sell.

"Because I'm not an idiot." Estia lifted zir shoulders once, before letting them drop into a slouch. Cricket didn't envy zir what ze was struggling with, but he did understand it. After all, he'd been there himself, hadn't he? Had a family member who just wanted to use him to their own advantage. Who would willingly kill him if he didn't give them what they wanted. In many ways, he and Estia were the same. In many ways, they were also different. Cricket didn't think he'd be able to betray his friends to save his own skin but . . . if he had to do it to save Becka? To save Takayoshi? Well, that might be a different story.

Ignacia huffed a breath which was all annoyance.

"He had no reason to keep me and my siblings alive once I told him, did he?" Estia shifted uncomfortably in zir chair, and Cricket saw Leo mirror the movement out of the corner of his eyes. They hadn't spoken since he and Takayoshi had returned from the wall, and he wasn't sure if it was because they were mad at each other over something, or there was some other reason. He meant to ask Takayoshi if Leo and Estia made up after they came back, but there never seemed to be time. And he didn't really think it mattered, in the grand scheme of things. "The plan was to keep the information to use as a bargaining chip for our release."

The noise Ignacia made in response to that was a snarl. Her hand dropped to her sword, and she took a step forward, only stopped by Leo stepping in between them. "Get out of my *way*, Lionel."

"I know you're angry. I know you're worried about Claudia," he murmured to her, his arm out to keep her from advancing. "But attacking Estia isn't going to solve anything. And ze isn't the one you're really upset with."

"What happened?" Cricket asked, nodding to Ignacia when she glanced at him for instruction. The single motion could have meant anything to anyone else, but Ignacia seemed to understand him. Her hand fell away from her sword, and she stood down, albeit with a disgruntled press of her lips.

"We were at an impasse." Although zir voice was light, Cricket could see how it pained zir to say so. And he knew what that was like too. Sunil had been unreasonable, unwilling to be bargained with. Had left them at a standstill until all that was left was war. "I refused to give him what he wanted without certain assurances, and he refused to release us until I had."

"So all Craven knows is what Sunil told him." That was something of a relief to Cricket. His uncle hadn't known everything there was to know about the dragon, although Craven had to know who he was, and what the pearl could do.

"Not even that much." Estia grinned a little, the expression sharp, and feral. "Your uncle wasn't willing to give all of that up either. You were a weapon to him, one he wanted to keep very close to his vest. Explaining what the pearl could do, and who the dragon was would have given Craven too much power."

"So what *does* Craven know?" Ignacia had relaxed a little, her shoulders dropping from where they had been up around her ears in upset.

"Only that the pearl is linked to the dragon. He's gotten it into his head that the dragon is inside of the pearl somehow. That it's a weapon in its own right, not the key to one."

"And if what he said when confronted at the gate was a true representation of all he knew, then that means the plant wasn't providing him with any additional information." They could use that, Cricket realized. Estia had provided Craven with just enough rope to hang himself with his own arrogance. Now. They just had to find a way to best utilize this advantage. "Did you show him the pearl after you stole it?"

"He saw it at a glance, but I never let him hold it. I wasn't willing to risk him not giving it back." There was a tightness about Estia's eye at those words, as if it pained zir to think of zir brother turning on zir in such a way. But as Estia didn't mention it, neither would Cricket.

"Then how did he know it was the real thing?" Ignacia's frown had returned, thoughtful, her mind already working through the problem ahead of them.

"He just had to take me at my word." Estia shifted again in zir seat. Cricket wondered what it had cost Estia for Craven to do that. If he had tortured his own sibling to ensure ze wasn't lying. He would like to say that he didn't believe it, they were family after all. But he had seen enough of what family could do to a person without even so much as a blink of remorse.

"Where is it?" Leo asked. He sounded like maybe he already had his suspicions, and when Cricket looked over at him, his brows were pulled down and his eyes were narrowed on Estia.

Cricket's gaze flicked back to Estia who shrank a little under Leo's knowing gaze. Then ze flapped zir wrist and said much too flippantly, "Around my idiot brother's neck."

"And he doesn't know?" Ignacia's tone was disbelieving. Although she didn't know anything of the Cytherean royal family, Cricket did. Damian had never been the sort to think overly much about anything. He was very much the leap first, ask questions later type. So it would make sense that he wouldn't look too hard at a gift given to him by his own twin.

Leo was the one who answered. "The amount of magical

knowledge Damian has could fill a thimble." And there was a note of approval in his voice. "How did you get it on him?"

"I just gave it to him, as a gift. He's been wearing it around for weeks, and has no idea." There was a little tremble of laughter to the words. Estia met Cricket's gaze, zir eyes sparkling as if they were both in on some very big joke. "It's tucked away in a pendant of course, but. . . well." Ze shrugged.

"All right." Cricket inhaled deeply, working his mind around all that he had learned so far. "Then what we need is a decoy. Since Craven doesn't know exactly what it's supposed to look like that part should be easy, the trouble will be in creating something that gives off enough magic to convince him it's the weapon he's been looking for."

"Claudia would be the best person for this job." Takayoshi's tone was flat, to anyone else, but Cricket detected the subtle dip in it. The upset, and sadness, and how he missed his friend.

Cricket reached for him, giving his hand a firm squeeze. "Even without Claudia, we'll make this work. I think Estia and I should be able to come up with something between the two of us. We'll start work at once."

Estia nodded. "I can draw up some sketches of what it should look like to be the most convincing to him."

"Perfect." Cricket straightened his spine a little more, stretching his neck from one direction to the other. He was tired still, hadn't even taken a minute to eat breakfast. But there was work still to be done, and he would rest when this was all over.

"My King," Takayoshi said, then frowned, his jaw working a moment when Cricket looked up at him, raising a dark brow in question. "Husband," Takayoshi corrected.

"Yes?"

"I would request permission to go on a rescue mission. If

we can free the hostages then we do not run the risk of them being caught in the crossfire." Takayoshi kept his words slow, and even, carefully measured as if afraid that showing Cricket how much he wanted this he would convince Cricket he shouldn't have it.

Cricket didn't like it. The idea of sending Takayoshi behind enemy lines without him there to back him up didn't sit right with him. There were too many ways it could go wrong.

And, "I can't lose you," Cricket rasped, his throat suddenly tight. "No. Denied. Not with everything that's going on. And Yoshi we just—" He cut himself off, forcing himself to breathe through the panic clawing at his throat. "We were just married. We haven't even been able to properly celebrate it yet."

"We will celebrate when we have won." There was such confidence, such assuredness, in those words. As if Takayoshi didn't doubt for a single second who would be standing when the dust cleared. Cricket wished he had that kind of faith in their plan.

"I can't lose you too," Cricket whispered.

Takayoshi let out a breath, not a sigh, just a short sharp exhale, and closed the space between them. He leaned down to where Cricket was sitting behind his father's desk, and pressed his forehead to Cricket's, their noses bumping a little.

"You will not," he promised, a vow, said just as serious, just as sternly as when they'd promise themselves to one another during the wedding. "I will be right back."

"Okay." Cricket nodded, reeling himself back in. It would be too easy to give himself over to the fear of losing someone else he loved. To let that fear paralyze him and keep him from acting. And right now, they couldn't afford that. So he buried those emotions to be dealt with later. "Who will be going with you?"

"Leo." Takayoshi brushed his thumb, calloused from sword work, over Cricket's cheek before he pulled back again. "We will leave shortly."

"Shouldn't you wait for the cover of darkness?" That seemed a reasonable thing to do. Wait until it was night time and then no one would see them sneaking through the streets.

"If we are able to bring home Claudia and Damian then we will want to launch our attack on Craven and his forces in the evening when his people would be less able to combat our soldiers who know the layout of the city better." Reasonable. Annoyingly so, that's what that was. But Cricket couldn't see a fault in the logic. Takayoshi was exactly right, that would be their best option. Get in. Get their people out. Attack before Craven even realized he'd lost his hostages. Curse him for being so reasonable!

"Fine." Cricket sighed heavily, leaning back in his chair until his neck ached from the strain of looking up at the ceiling. "But in the meantime—"

"You will work on the pearl decoy." Takayoshi nodded sagely. "It will be good to have options should my plan go awry."

"I want you back before we have to meet with Craven."

"I will do my level best, husband." Takayoshi dipped to press a soft kiss to his lips, then he turned, nodded to Leo, and the pair of them swept out the door.

"All right." Cricket clapped his hands, sitting up in his chair again. "Estia, and I will work on the decoy. Ignacia, I want you to go over the maps we have, see if there is anywhere our soldiers can hide and act as back up for this meeting. I don't want Craven to go back on his word just because he thinks Estia and I are easy targets."

"Of course." Ignacia's lips ticked up in a smirk.

"They could be anywhere in the city," Leo hissed, annoyance dripping from every word, as if Takayoshi were not perfectly aware of that fact.

It was a fool's errand, he knew that too. That in all likelihood they would find nothing, and he would return home to his husband empty handed. But he had learned to hope over the years that he had fallen desperately in love with Cricket. Learned to see the glimmer of possibility where once he might have disregarded such a slim chance as nothing at all. They might find nothing at all. They might find Claudia and Damian and bring them home before any harm could befall them. He was willing to try.

"This is going to take forever, maybe we should split up," Leo suggested from where he stood at Takayoshi's side looking out of the mouth of the alley. They had slipped from the castle into an alley across the way, one that Takayoshi recognized more than he would like. It was where he had hidden with Cricket not so long ago when they had returned to find Sunil on the throne, and Jaxith Ill. So much of the capital brought back memories, not all of them good.

"We are not splitting up."

"Yoshi." Leo sighed, brushing his hand through his dark hair, and ending the motion with a scratch at the stubble lining his scarred jaw. "The fastest way to—"

"We are not splitting up, Leo." And not just because he had promised Cricket that he would not go alone. "With Craven and his men somewhere in the city, we should not travel without someone to watch our backs."

He did not say that the last time he had split up, one of his friends had gone missing and inevitably been captured. He did not say that the lack of that friend sat a hollow ache in his chest. Or that he feared he might never see her again.

But Leo seemed to hear all of those things anyway. "We should go in a circle, starting in the arc closest to the castle walls. I can't imagine he'll have wanted to go far from his inevitable target."

Takayoshi nodded, letting out a relieved breath as his shoulders relaxed. It was good he had brought Leo along on this. Leo knew Craven, knew his tactics, at least in part. The only one who would have been better was Estia, but ze was not trained in battle the way that Leo was, and besides that fact, Cricket needed zir. To forge a decoy that would trick Craven into thinking he was holding the real thing. To make their back up plan viable.

"Any other parameters we can use to search?" It was wishful thinking, Takayoshi knew that. There were too many options for places to hide. Still, if they could narrow it down.

. .

"I'm afraid not."

"Then we best get started." Takayoshi pushed off from the wall he had been leaning against. "I would also like to check in on something on Crescent street before we head back."

"What?"

"Cricket thinks that is where the creature might be hiding. Are you ready?" It was a silly question. Whether they were ready or not, this is what they were doing. They did not have another choice.

"We could still go home," Leo said, but his tone was teasing.

Takayoshi hummed, but gave no other reply as he stepped out from the alley where they had been hiding to begin their first circuit around the castle walls.

THE SUN CREPT across the sky as they searched, Helio's light haunted Takayoshi with all the time he lost. Not that it was time wasted, he wanted to find Claudia, and any time spent in that pursuit was time used well. But there were only so many hours available to him before their meeting with Craven, and he needed to be at Cricket's side for that.

Takayoshi and Leo kept through the deep shadows and darkened alleys provided to them by the summer sun, avoiding being seen only because Leo had spent a number of weeks mapping out this city when he was left in charge of watching over Cricket. They worked in an ever widening circle around the castle, peeking through windows, ducking into doorways, and coming up with nothing.

"He would not have hidden himself away on the outskirts surely." Takayoshi huffed, his fingers tapping against his sword.

"You're getting impatient, Your Highness," Leo chided. "Your husband is rubbing off on you."

"Perhaps." Although not nearly enough, for Takayoshi was sure Cricket would have found Craven by now. "We are close to the place where Cricket thought the creature might be hiding, we will check there next."

"I don't think he'll be hiding near the creature."

"Perhaps not. But if we can eliminate that particular threat from the equation, it might up our chances of winning this war." Not that he had any doubt they would. Things seemed dire now, but Cricket was not the kind of man to be beaten. Takayoshi loved that about him.

Leo grunted his agreement, and they slipped out onto Crescent street after checking that it was barren of anyone who might see them. The vines which had been all over the city were thickest here, covering more of the cobblestone street than not.

"Maybe Cricket is onto something with this," Leo murmured to himself, stepping lightly over the vines as best he could.

"I never doubted him." Takayoshi wondered how the creature would sense them. There were not trees with leaves to feel the vibrations as there had been in the forest, and without the shared conscious of the sleepwalkers, perhaps they would be safe from the creature's aggression.

"You never do," Leo said, but if Takayoshi were to wager, he would say that it sounded fond. Which was a nice thought. One that he did not have time for because a moment after he too stepped out onto the street, a vine lifted from the ground, ripping dust and stone from the street, and hurled itself toward his middle.

There was no time to think, nor to act, all he could do was tighten his muscles and take the blow at the center of his stomach, releasing a grunt of pain as the bruising force of the creature hurled him from his feet.

"Yoshi!" Leo leaped after him, his sword swinging to cut through the vine, and put an end to its attack. But there were too many of them, Takayoshi could see that now. They had walked right into the creature's den, and they were unprepared to deal with it.

The vine holding him to the ground went limp, but before it could even hit the ground, another latched onto his wrist. Takayoshi reached for the heat in his veins, feeling the fire blaze as it crawled along his skin like it might a dry forest floor. He grabbed onto the vine, his grip tight, the flames flowing from his fingertips onto the green, green vine and bur—

Not burning. The vine was too fresh, too damp. All he managed to do was sear it before the moisture made the fire spit, sputter, smolder, and eventually turn to nothing but acrid smoke.

"They are too moist for me to burn!" Takayoshi gasped against the sharp pull of a vine taking hold of his wrist as he reached for his sword, and yanking his arm over his head. It tore at something in his shoulder. Something he was certain was not supposed to be moved that way.

Leo hacked at the one latched on his arm, and Takayoshi was able to pull his arm free, to reach for his sword once more. But it was not more than a single heartbeat before another vine replaced the first, holding tighter, grinding the bones together so hard they might break.

And as Leo raised his sword for another swing, a vine latched onto the blade and ripped it from his hands, flinging it down the alley, just as a thick rope of green lashed around Leo's neck, squeezing tight enough his face began to turn red.

Takayoshi struggled more, fighting against the hold they had on him, but it was useless. There were too many of them, and without his fire, he could not fight back enough.

"I'd stop struggling if I were you," a cool, detached voice said from down the street, footsteps treading carefully over the cobbles until Craven was in front of them. "My little friend here doesn't like it when its vines are destroyed."

"Craven," Leo hissed, his eyes narrowing, but he had stopped fighting against the vines, and as he had, they had loosened around his neck.

The ones pinning Takayoshi to the ground forced him to his feet, tying his wrists behind his back in a motion that made his shoulder scream. He gritted his teeth against the pain.

"Lionel," Craven greeted in return, his eyes crinkling with a false smile. "I thought you were dead."

"Yes, well. I do so love to disappoint."

"Hmmm. Might have to rectify that." Craven lifted his hand and motioned for the soldiers behind him to move in. "Bring them back to camp. I have some questions for His Highness, and I'm sure the Lady Claudia would love to see her friends one last time before I skin them alive."

"You will not kill us," Takayoshi said, his chin held high in a gesture he had learned from Cricket. Subtle arrogance, regal, and assured.

"Won't I?" Craven tilted his head, amusement thick in his tone. "Why not?"

"Because, the more hostages you have, the easier it will be to convince my husband to hand over the pearl. You will not kill us until after he has done so." And that would buy them a little bit of time. Not much, but a little. Takayoshi would just have to think of a way out before then.

"Perhaps," Craven murmured. "But that does not mean I have to leave you entirely unharmed until then."

"Is it wise," Leo asked, his smile sharp and cutting, "to take the king's new husband as your hostage?"

"Very," Craven said simply. "It will keep His Highness from doing anything foolish during our meeting." Then he turned to his men. "Take them away."

Takayoshi kept his chin high as he and Leo were dragged back to Craven's camp, retaining as much dignity as he could manage what with being tied up by vines. It was not an easy task, but as he was now one of Lunette's kings, he could not see doing this any other way.

The room they threw he and Leo into was cold, and lacked any kind of furnishings. Likely, it had been used to store dried goods at one point, or to keep vegetables fresh through the warmer months.

"Yoshi! Leo!" Claudia lunged toward them, gathering them both up into her arms in a hug so tight it made breathing difficult.

He hugged her back just as fiercely, glad to see that she was safe at least for the moment. How long that lasted would depend on what Cricket did next. "I am glad you are safe."

"And you're *married?!*" She pulled back so she could glare at him, her mouth twisted into an expression he could not give a name to. It was not a scowl, or a frown, but it was also not a smile. It was a cross between the two. As if she were both happy and furious at him for something. Very confusing.

"I am." Takayoshi nodded, and the expression shifted to something a little more angry. "It was very rushed, and last minute," he said, trying to placate her.

"Was it now?" Claudia asked. Her tone sarcastic, and annoyed, her hand fisting in his tunic so tightly he feared she'd tear it.

Takayoshi hummed his agreement. "Ask Leo."

"Oh no." Leo stepped away from them, laughing a little to himself. "Don't drag me into this."

"Traitor," Takayoshi and Claudia grumbled at the same time, then they were both laughing, holding each other tightly again. And it was like no time had passed at all. Like nothing had changed between them even though Claudia had been taken hostage, and Takayoshi had been wed without her at his side.

"Tell me everything." Claudia grabbed his hands and

pulled him over to sit on the floor against the wall, and Takayoshi obliged.

BY THE TIME Craven's men came to drag Takayoshi from the cell with the others, he had devised a plan. He was going to start a fire while they tortured him, break free, then he'd go back to get the others out. It would be quick, clean, and efficient. He would have them all back to the castle before supper time.

Someone clapped a set of iron shackles onto his wrists, and Takayoshi felt his fire die in his veins.

That will pose a problem.

Still, he could do his best to cause a distraction and get free. Maybe he would be offered an opening. He sent up a silent prayer to Selene that he would. But there were no hopping rabbits, or gentle breezes to tell him if she had heard or not, so he allowed the soldier to drag him down the corridor of the building Craven had holed himself up in.

It was a court house, or a town hall, perhaps. Takayoshi was not sure, and he had not spent enough time out in the city since returning to tell. He would need to rectify that soon, now that Lunette was his home. But for the moment, he set his mind to drawing a mental map of the place.

The room they brought him to was small, and empty, just as the cellar had been. He wondered if Craven's men had cleared it out, or if the people had when Sunil had taken charge of the capital. There was so much of Lunette that had not yet been rebuilt, but they would have time for that after Craven was defeated, and things had settled. Of this, Takayoshi was certain.

He was forced to sit in a chair where the shackles around his wrists were bound to the back of it, keeping his arms immobile. Then they bent to tie his legs to the chair as well. He wondered if they thought he would struggle, maybe he ought to. But this was not his opening, and he was not going to waste his energy on it. Better to let them think he would continue cooperating, to lower their guard, then he could attack.

"Are you ready for our little chat?" Craven asked, a sly smile splitting his face, but showing no teeth.

"I suppose I have no choice." Takayoshi tugged a little on his bindings, just to make Craven think that they would hold. But he did not test them with his full strength, not yet.

"No. You don't." Craven shrugged. He gave a nod to a soldier at his side, and the man moved forward, his hand curled into a tight fist which he hurled against Takayoshi's jaw. Pain burst behind his eyes, making stars dance across his vision.

"Are you not supposed to ask a question before you start hitting your captive?" Takayoshi asked, his head tilted in curiosity. There was blood on his tongue, metallic, and hot from where his teeth had cut his cheek, but he swallowed it, not willing to let Craven see him bleed. Not if he could help it.

"I figured I should set the tone for this conversation." He nodded again, and the man hit Takayoshi once more, his ears ringing with the force of it.

Measuring his breathing to quell the sense of nausea that came with the pain, Takayoshi lifted one pale brow high on his face. "Very well, you have set it. What is it you want?"

"You will tell me what your husband's plans are for our meeting." It was not a question, it was an order.

Takayoshi did not respond well to being ordered to do things. Anyone who knew anything about him knew that. Of course, it was unlikely he would give Craven what he wanted even if that were not the case.

"No. I will not," he said simply.

Craven flicked his wrist, and the man landed a hard blow to Takayoshi's stomach, right where the bruise had begun to form from the plant's abuse. He felt a rib crack in his chest, and he coughed, blood dribbling down his chin.

"You will," Craven insisted. "If you don't, this will continue."

Lifting his chin once more, Takayoshi met Craven's gaze. "You are welcome to try to force me," he said, words evenly measured, if a little raspy for his fresh injuries. "I am sure my husband will be delighted to reward you for the treatment you have shown me while I was in your care. I would be willing to wager he will not hesitate to return it tenfold." And then he smiled, teeth bloody, and steeled himself for the beating that was to come.

CHAPTER 35

A puff of smoke plumed from the pearl nestled carefully in a bed of fabric on the desk. Cricket coughed, waving it away with his hands.

"Just missed my eyebrows that time," Cricket crowed.

"I told you to wear the safety goggles." Estia flapped them at him once more, but he waved zir away.

"They push on my antlers." Bending down, he poked at the pearl with one taloned finger. It didn't do anything, just sat there. Nothing he did seemed to work, and they'd tried all manner of objects to act as a decoy. Silver, and copper, gold. An actual pearl had seemed too obvious, but he'd been willing to try it as a final, last hope. "It's not taking the magic."

"Why are we trying so hard?" Estia rubbed at zir forehead, smearing soot across the skin. Cricket's face probably wasn't fairing any better, but it didn't matter.

"Because it has to hold up against Craven's scrutiny at least long enough for us to get the hostages away from him, and out of firing range. Ideally, at least behind the gate." It was by no means a perfect plan. Haphazard and full of holes. But it was the best they had with what they were given.

Granted, he could turn into a dragon and go in there claws flying, but Selene only knew who would get caught in the crossfire, or be hurt under Craven's order once he had, and that wasn't a chance he was willing to take.

"I've tried everything I can think of. . ." Cricket chewed on his lower lip in thought, one sharpened tooth catching the skin. He was missing something. He always seemed to be missing something. This would be better if Claudia were there to help. Her magical knowledge far outweighed his own as she was more well-traveled and well versed in the magics of other kingdoms. But she wasn't there.

Still, he thought maybe if he could just think like her, he'd find their solution.

What would Claudia do?

"Why are you helping us?" Estia asked after what might have been a few minutes or an hour of Cricket just pondering in silence. It was hard to really tell when he got caught up in his head like that.

"Hm?" Cricket lifted his head, brows raised high, confused by the question.

"Me and my siblings. Why did you help us? Why *are* you helping us? You could have just turned us away at the gates. You could have me locked up in your dungeons, torturing me for answers. But instead, my siblings are in a nice suite of rooms, taken care of perhaps better than they ever were at home, and you've let me sit in on every meeting so far to help you figure out what to do with my brother. Why?" Zir brows were drawn together in the center, a frown creasing their mouth.

"Seems the right thing to do." Cricket shrugged, and ducked his head back to his work. It really was as simple as that, always had been. Yes, he had been betrayed in the past. Yes, Estia had shown that ze had the capability to turn on zir own friends. But Cricket had always believed that to earn trust, one had to give it, and if Takayoshi—who had been the one betrayed, by the way—was willing to forgive Estia and give zir another chance. Why shouldn't he? Still, he shot the question back, curious. "Why are you helping us?"

"Oh." Estia stilled entirely, as if stunned by the realization that maybe Cricket was just that type of person. Cricket didn't look up to see what zir face was doing. He was too busy working through all the other things he could try to make this work. "I just. . . I uh. . . because you're the only one who can defeat him. Craven. I've tried. I've tried everything I can think of. And nothing has worked."

"So you're using us," Cricket said, although not totally bothered by the notion. If Estia needed them, then ze would be less likely to betray them. Still, he'd rather Estia was doing this because ze cared about zir friends, and wanted to find a place among people who actually looked after each other. But nothing in this life was perfect, he was beginning to realize.

Either way, he didn't have the time nor the energy to ferret out if Estia were lying or simply putting up a front.

Iron wouldn't work. It would just absorb the magic and negate it. Zinc maybe? No. Gods, they could be there all night trying different minerals if he went down that road. But now, he was sure it was something more obvious. Something more simple. Something—

"I—"

"A scale!" Cricket announced suddenly, his head lifting to smile brightly at Estia.

"What?"

"We need to use a dragon scale as the decoy. It's the only thing that'll be able to absorb my magic without melting under the force of it because it's a part of me, a part of my magic. We can glamour it to look like the pearl, and when Craven holds it, it'll put off enough power to fool him into thinking he has the real thing."

Estia's face paled. "Won't that. . . won't that hurt?"

"Definitely." Cricket nodded firmly, but the thought of a little pain didn't sway him away from the idea. "But it's the best we've got. Come on, we'll go find Ignacia, she can help you extract it."

"Me?" Estia squawked. Cricket didn't wait for zir to get a hold of zirself, he spun on his heel and headed out of the room in search of his captain of the guard.

"I don't like this."

"You say that all the time, Iggy." Cricket rolled out his shoulders as if readying for a fight. It wouldn't do any good to waylay this any longer than he already had, but he couldn't help procrastinating a bit. He knew what it would feel like to have a scale ripped from his skin. Knew how it would sear through him like fire, and make him weak with the after-shocks. But he really couldn't see any other way, and he wasn't willing to put Claudia and Damian in danger by doing this halfway. "Just make it quick. One clean slice. And go for one of the smaller ones. That'll be easier to glamour."

"I don't like this," Ignacia repeated.

"Good thing you don't have to." Cricket bared his teeth at her. "Think of it as an order from your king."

"Isn't that exactly what it is?" Estia asked.

Ignacia and Cricket ignored zir, instead staring at one another, each refusing to be the first to blink until Cricket's eyes began to burn from being open for too long. Ultimately it was Ignacia who looked away first, her lips turning down into a frown.

Cricket nodded to himself, took another deep breath, and

shifted. The cold bite of the dragon's ice slipped over him so quickly it made him shiver. When he next opened his eyes the world was sharper, and colder, like someone had cast a blue light over everything. And the room was much tighter.

There should be some small ones down at the end of my tail, he said, and avoided looking at it. He hadn't looked at it at all since he'd defeated Sunil. Didn't want to know if the tip had grown back, or if it remained a blunt end after Sunil's torture. Much better not to know, he'd decided.

Ignacia moved around him to look when he refused to pull his tail forward for her. Probably better he not look at her while she do it anyway, he was liable to pass out or lash out. Neither of which did they need right that moment.

"Yeah, there are," she confirmed, and he heard the soft *shink* of her blade pulled from its sheath.

Just make it fast.

"I'll do my best." She sounded like she was concentrating very hard. Which could be a very good or a very bad thing, Cricket wasn't sure which, and he didn't have the presence of mind at the moment to really think about it. "On the count of three.

Okay.

"One. . . Two. . ."

Blinding pain shot through him, white hot, and burning through all other thoughts as he ripped his tail away from her, curling it up towards his chest to protect it from further abuse, and roared.

"Are you all right?" Estia asked, coming around to check on him.

Cricket snarled at zir, snapping his jaws, his whiskers vibrating with the motion. Estia took a step back, holding up zir hands in surrender. With a forced inhale, exhale, Cricket calmed himself down. The floor under his tail was stained red with his blood. But he'd chosen the room that would remind him the least of the cell where Sunil had kept him not but a few scant weeks ago.

Pale marble floors, not cold stone. Bright lights, plenty of windows, open so he could smell the fresh air. Anyone could have looked in on what they were doing. But he needed all of those things if he wasn't going to spiral.

Even then, it was a near miss as he could feel his mind slipping back into the cold, dank cell, the iron collar heavy around his—

"Cricky." Ignacia put her hand on his muzzle, heedless of how easy it would be for him to snap at her and rip her arm off. "You're okay," she said, voice firm.

Did you get it?

"Yes." In her bloody hand she held a midnight blue scale, about the size of her palm. "Now what do we do?"

Now we make a decoy, and pray to the goddess that Craven doesn't look at it too closely.

He shook out his shoulders again, this time the motion was lumbering and nearly knocked Ignacia off her feet. Then he took a deep breath, closed his eyes, and shifted back. Shrinking down to the size of an elf once more. Vulnerable, and small. He didn't think he liked it much, not with everything going on. And there was a place on his back right above his bottom that rubbed raw against his tunic.

"Let me patch that up for you, and then we can get to work," Estia volunteered, already pulling bandages from a kit one of them had wisely thought to bring along.

"Thank you," Cricket breathed, and stood still while ze did zir work.

THE DECOY WAS READY. The sun had set. And Takayoshi was not back yet.

"He'll be fine," Ignacia insisted. "He can look after himself."

Objectively, Cricket knew this. He knew that Takayoshi was more than capable. But that didn't quiet the worry that ripped through him every time he looked outside and saw that the night was deepening and there was still no sign of his husband.

"He has Leo with him."

"What will you do if they're not back by morning?" Estia asked, because apparently ze was the only one looking to say anything useful at this point in time.

"We'll have to go anyway," Cricket responded even as bile crawled up his throat. He did not say that they would have to hope that nothing had happened to Takayoshi and Leo while they were away. He did not say that in all probability they had been captured. Because they all knew the truth of what Takayoshi and Leo not returning meant.

"And if they've been captured by the enemy?" Ignacia asked, because she was pragmatic. A trait Cricket was finding *very* annoying at the current moment.

"Then Craven had better hope not a single hair on my husband's head has been harmed. I killed my own uncle for less." And when he smiled back at her, his teeth were sharp, and his eyes were glowing with the fury of a dragon.

CHAPTER 36

Everything ached by the time Takayoshi was returned to the cellar with his friends. None of the injuries were permanent, they would all heal within the week, but that would not help him come morning when he was dragged out to meet with his husband, unable to fight back, or protect the people he loved most.

"Cricket will come," Claudia assured him, her fingers gentle as she assessed his condition.

"He will," Takayoshi agreed. Although at this point he was not sure if that would be for the better or worse. He had made himself into a liability by not listening to Cricket's advice. He had been arrogant enough to think he could go out, find their friends, and return home unharmed, and he had been proven wrong. "I was foolish. Naive."

"I don't think he'll hold that against you." Leo stretched his legs out in front of himself where he was sitting on the floor. It was clear the cool air and the lack of proper seating was playing havoc on his leg. Would he even be able to walk when they were carted from the cellar to be used as a living shield for a coward?

"Maybe he ought to." Anger bubbled in his stomach, making his skin prickle with heat. He should have listened. Now, he would not be at Cricket's side when he faced off against their enemy. Now, he would be on the other side, instead, and thus would be in the way. Not to mention the wounds that had been inflicted were going to cause a problem. "Can we get the iron off?"

"No. I've tried already." Claudia rubbed at her own wrist which was red and raw with chafing from the metal. "And with it on there's no way to access our magic."

"I don't know why you lot are even bothering," a rasping voice said from the shadowed corner. When Takayoshi looked over he found Damian there, curled in on himself, his body curled around his knees. He looked so small, so young like this. When in truth he was not much younger than they were. A year, maybe two. "He's going to get what he wants. He always does."

"Be quiet, Damian," Leo hissed. "You don't know anything about these people or what they're capable of."

"No. But I know what my brother is capable of." Damian lifted his head, and when he did, Takayoshi could see that his eyes were ringed in darkness from lack of sleep, and bloodshot from tears very likely. "And so do you, Lionel. He'll get what he wants, he always does. And when he does, we're all dead."

"Well with that attitude." Claudia scoffed.

"It's not an attitude, it's the truth." Damian unfolded a little, coming out of himself in his agitation. It was a shame that the spark of defiance and fight he was exhibiting now was only to tell them that their cause was hopeless. Only to pressure them into feeling as defeated as he was. "Craven cannot be stopped."

"Craven has never before come up against Yue Cricket." Leo smirked a little, his eyes growing bright, pride and faith lacing his tone in a way Takayoshi did not think he had ever heard from Leo before.

"Underestimating Cricket was Sunil's first mistake," Claudia nodded in agreement. "And it will be Craven's last."

Damian shook his head, curling back up a little more as if dismissing them and their foolishness. "He will have the pearl, and he will have Lunette. And once he has Lunette he will go after Hermes, and Helios, and all the other kingdoms."

"He is welcome to try to take Lunette," Takayoshi said. The hard floor made his injuries ache more, but he swallowed down every noise of protest. He would not show pain, or fear in the face of someone who clearly lacked faith. He would only show the foolishness of a man in love. A man who knew that his soulmate would come for him, and when he did, Cricket would burn everything that stood in his way. "He is welcome to try to take everything from Cricket. But everyone who has ever made the attempt has failed."

"You think he's that weak?" Damian lifted a brow incredulous.

"No." Takayoshi's lips twitched into a smile. "I do not doubt his strength, or his capability. I do not think for a single second that he will not put up a fight. I just know that my husband is stronger, and that he will not stop until he has saved his friends, his family, his people, and me. Your brother will be lucky to make it out of this fight alive, but I doubt he will be given even that much mercy once Cricket sees what he has done to me."

Damian scoffed. "You put an awful lot of faith in a king who is not much more than a boy."

"And you put a lot of faith in a man who has shown time and again that he cares little for the lives of others." Takayoshi did not shrug, but he did tilt his head to one side slightly, a mocking curiosity. "The want for power can only take a person so far. The need to protect the things one loves will take them much farther. What does your brother love?"

"Himself."

"Then he is weak." Takayoshi's chin lifted in an arrogant tilt, one he had seen his husband wear so many many times that repeating the motion himself made his chest throb a little. "And I pity him."

Damian clicked his tongue. But he did not argue further. And when he was silent for long enough, Takayoshi nodded and returned his attention to the shackle at his wrist.

"Claudia, do you have any hair pins?" He had never picked a lock before, but there was a first time for everything, and Takayoshi was not above trying.

Claudia just stared at him, clearly annoyed.

"It was worth asking." Takayoshi offered her a small smile. "If we cannot pick the locks, our next option is to contact Selene."

"The goddess?!" Damian gasped, his head suddenly flying up.

"I think I have the prayer wheel memorized." Takayoshi ignored the outburst, narrowing his gaze on the floor. It was dim in the cellar, but he could make it work. And besides, he had done this particular set of characters so many times now, they were practically ingrained into his muscles. "I will just need some blood."

"You're just going to call upon the moon goddess?" Damian was fully unfurling himself from where he had been curled into a ball now.

"She's not going to be happy about this," Leo warned.

"She rarely is." Takayoshi could not help but agree. She would be furious, not at him for having reached out, but at him having waited so long to do so. At them allowing things to have grown so dire before they did.

"And she'll answer?!" Damian's tone was full of disbelief, his eyes wide as he watched them.

"It'd be rude for his mother-in-law not to." Claudia snickered. "We might be able to sharpen my belt buckle enough to use it."

"That will do." Takayoshi nodded.

"Mother-in-law?! That makes Cricket. . . that makes him. . ." Stuttering in his disbelief, Damian moved to wobbling feet so that he could cross the cellar to them.

"The son of a goddess, yes." Takayoshi lifted his head from where he had been focusing on the floor to figure where the best place for the wheel would be. It would likely wind up being a wobbly circle, but that would be fine. The one he had drawn as a child had been far from perfect. He smiled a little at Damian. "Care to rethink your stance on Craven's assured success?"

"I—"

"Here." Claudia handed the belt buckle to Leo who began to grind one edge against the stone floor to sharpen it.

"I'm not going to be able to get it as sharp as a blade," Leo warned. "You should let me provide the blood, you're injured enough."

"No. It will be stronger if it is my own. I will not have her ignoring my prayer simply because she does not recognize the magical signature sending it." What was one more wound? He had survived far worse. And what was a little more blood spilled in the name of his love? Takayoshi had thought to himself once upon a time that there would never come a time when he would not open a vein to provide Cricket with what he needed, and that proved as true now as it ever had.

"Yoshi—"

"Leo. I have made my choice. Just get it as sharp as you can."

Leo grunted, clearly displeased with this answer, but did

not fight him further on it, returning his focus to the task before him.

"She will likely be awaiting my prayer." Because he knew well enough that she was watching the events unfold in her kingdom, her son's kingdom, as closely as she could. She could not interfere, but she would want to stay informed on if things were going terribly wrong for her son.

"She can't do anything," Claudia argued, her lip between her teeth. "You know she can't."

"No, but perhaps she can get a message to Cricket for us." He was not sure how much good that would do any of them, but he did not want Cricket to walk into the meeting in the morning without knowing what had become of Takayoshi and his friends. It would only increase his worry. "We will not tell her about my injuries, it will only make him worry more."

Claudia scoffed.

"It's done. Or as done as it can be." Leo held out the rough piece of metal. One side of it was jagged, but it should be sharp enough to tear through skin. The scar it left behind would likely be the worst yet. It would be worth it.

The pain was white hot, racing along Takayoshi's nerves in a way that would not be ignored, just had to be born, as he dragged the metal deeper into the skin of his arm. But also oddly grounding, familiar. He knew this pain. It was an old friend. It cleared his racing thoughts, and settled his mind.

The drips of blood against stone echoed in the silence of held breath, all of his companions watching, waiting as a cold sweat crept down his back. What if this didn't work? What if they hadn't gotten the symbols right? What if—

Then a blinding light lit up the circle, burned the shapes into his eyes.

"I had hoped when next we spoke it would at your wedding to my son," Selene greeted, irritation in her tone.

"I had hoped that as well, my lady." Takayoshi ducked his head in respect. "Apologies that that is not the case."

Selene harrumphed, an oddly mortal noise, but Takayoshi would allow it as there was every reason for her to be upset at the current moment. "The fact that it is not does not bode well for you sun prince."

"Again, I apologize." What did she want from him? He could not change the circumstances, no matter how much he wished to.

Selene clicked her tongue, clearly disapproving, but the sound was so achingly familiar, and so much like Cricket, that Takayoshi could not fight the twitch of his smile. "As you are not contacting me to discuss your wedded bliss with my son, what is it that you do want, sun prince?"

"Assurances."

"I cannot provide certainty that you will win this war, as you know I cannot interfere in any way." She did not sound happy about that though, and Takayoshi could understand why. If it were his child, his Becka, he would do anything within his power to make sure she came out on the other end unscathed.

"Not for me." Takayoshi shook his head. "For my husband. I want you to speak with him, tell him that we are all right, sooth his worries. He should not go into this final fight with his mind full of untruths and uncertainties. We are fine. We will return home soon. Anything else will only slow him down."

"Craven tortured you," Selene hissed, and he could imagine her eyes narrowing as Cricket's might, her lips pursing. "And you would have me tell my son otherwise?"

"He will know soon enough how I was treated here, there is no point in him getting himself worked up now. Tell him to rest, conserve his strength. He will need it."

"I don't approve of this."

"I will take note." Takayoshi smiled a little more, unable to stop himself. He wondered if Selene realized just how similar her son was to her. "But you will do this anyway. It is for the safety of your son as well as Lunette."

"Yes. I will do it anyway." Selene huffed, petulant. "Is there any other messages you'd like me to ferry along while I'm playing carrier pigeon?"

"Just that I love him, and I have faith in him."

"Very well," the words left her on a sigh, all anger retreating in the face of Takayoshi's undying devotion. "In the meantime, take care of you and yours where you are, Takayoshi. He would never forgive me if something were to happen to you under my watch."

"Yes, my lady." He dipped his head again, and a moment later the light faded, and all he could see was darkness. He squeezed his eyes shut, trying to get the spots out of his vision, but it did not help.

"My brother is going to die, isn't he?" Damian whispered, almost as if he did not actually want an answer, and Takayoshi was not going to give him one. He would find out soon enough.

BOOK V
THE WAR

CHAPTER 37

"He does not want you to worry," Selene said, her voice kind in a way Cricket had never thought a god's could be. But then, he supposed, the fact that she was his mother made all the difference. Of course she would be kind to him, if no one else.

"A little late for that." Cricket laughed, the sound too high, and a little panicked. Echoing hollow through his chest. Very late for that, actually. He had been panicking for hours by this point. Once the decoy was created, and everything else was set in place, there was nothing to do *but* worry.

"You should rest, son," Selene pushed. The word son sat heavy in his ears, settling around him in a way Cricket had never thought it would before. A warm blanket weighing him down. Her approval, her care, felt too good, and he didn't deserve that comfort. Not now. Not with his husband in the enemy's hands, and his kingdom on the brink of war.

"I *can't*. Can't he see that I can't?" Takayoshi couldn't see anything, because he wasn't there. He was locked away somewhere in the city, far enough out of Cricket's reach that

Cricket ached with the loss of him. "Can you tell me where they are? Maybe we can stage a—"

"You will risk your pearl if you do that, as well as a worse assault on your lands. Don't rush things," Selene chided gently. "It will all work as it is supposed to. Trust in fate."

"Yes, because fate has been *so* kind to me so far."

"Hasn't she?" Cricket couldn't see his mother either, but he imagined her tilting her head curiously. A mirror image of the way he reacted sometimes to people. How alike were they actually, and how much of this was wishful thinking on his part? "She brought you Takayoshi. She gave you a daughter."

"Yes. Yes she did." And then she threatened to take all of those things away, but he didn't say that. Arguing with a goddess—even if she were his mother—didn't seem wise. "Well thank you, mother, for ferrying his message along. You didn't have to do that."

"Of course I did." She sighed as if perhaps she wished she could reel him in close, and sooth his worries herself. He imagined what it would be like to be held by his mother, finally, finally, finally. But that was not to be. "But son, I would do all this and more, that I could."

"I know, mother." Cricket scrubbed at his face. "I should rest."

This conversation was making him more tired than anything else he'd dealt with thus far. Why was it so hard to talk to her? It should have been easy, they had so much to talk about. But every interaction felt strained. Maybe one day things would be different. Today, they were not.

"You should," she agreed. "I will be here, when the time comes, watching over you both."

"Thank you, mother." He dipped his head, and the light faded away, his mother leaving him to his solitude once more.

HE SHOULD SLEEP. He should sleep. He should sleep.

But he could not. No matter how he exhausted himself with pacing. No matter how he knew his people needed him at his best in the morning. He could not.

So instead, he paced back and forth from one wall to the opposite one in his father's study, running his hands through his hair over and over again, making it stand up in all directions.

His husband was in enemy hands. His friends were in enemy hands. The only thing protecting his people were the walls surrounding his castle. They could stay inside, but for how long? They did not have enough rations to feed this many indefinitely. Not that Cricket wanted to. What he *wanted* to do was tear through Craven's camp and leave only destruction in his wake. What he wanted to do was to prove to Craven just how foolish it had been to come here in the first place. To punish him for daring lay a finger on what belonged to Cricket.

"It's time," Ignacia said from the door.

He lifted his head to blink at her, confused. Had he spent all night pacing? She nodded toward the window, and when he looked, he saw the first watery rays of daylight filtering in through the trees outside.

"So it is." Stars, he had wasted the night doing the exact thing Takayoshi had told him not to. "Are the knights in place?"

"And awaiting your signal." Ignacia dipped into a little bow as he brushed past her out into the hall. "I'll be joining them in a moment, once I see you and Estia to the gate."

"Thanks for this Iggy." He grabbed her by the shoulders

and pulled her into a tight hug before she could stop him. "I love you."

She groaned at the intrusion of her space, but let it happen, patting his back awkwardly before she pushed him away gently. "Stop acting like you're marching to your death."

Cricket just smiled at her, and started down the corridor again. The truth was, maybe he was heading to his death. Maybe this would be the thing that finally ended him. But there was no stopping it now. He had been headed this way for over five years, and if he had to make the same choices all over again? He wouldn't hesitate, not for a single second. The journey had hurt. Broken his heart. Torn him apart. But it had also pieced him back together bit by bit. It was all worth it for what he had found. A family he had not known he needed. A husband he had not known he wanted. A strength he had not known he had.

"Are you ready?" he asked Estia once they reached the front doors where ze was waiting.

"No, but it's too late to change the plan now." Still, Estia smiled at him, sharp, and pointed, ze was ready to go to war whatever ze might say to the contrary.

"It is," Cricket agreed, and pushed through the doors, across the courtyard, out of the gates.

From there, it was a short trip via horseback, and the clocktower came into view. Cricket's heart pounded against his chest, fear making it erratic. What would he find when he slid off his horse? And would their plan work?

Only one way to find out.

"Ah good," Craven said, stepping into the middle of the square, his hands held out to his sides in what he likely thought was a gesture of harmlessness, of peace, of congeniality. Cricket was not fooled. "You made it."

Cricket slid from the saddle, and walked with Estia to meet Craven at the center of the square. There was no one else there, not yet, but Cricket wasn't fooled by that either. He could sense the eyes on them. They were surrounded, whether they could see Craven's forces or not.

"Where are our people?" Cricket didn't let his eyes waver from where his gaze was locked with Craven's, a battle for dominance.

"Which people would those be?" Craven's smile crawled up his face, clearly pleased with himself, thinking he had the upper hand, thinking himself clever. Gods, Cricket wanted to rip all of the teeth from his mouth and see how he could smile *then*. "My brother, and your advisor?" He gestured with one hand and Claudia and Damian were dragged from one of the surrounding buildings.

It was a clear show of superiority, an intimidation tactic, to show that Craven had gotten here before them and thus had control over the area. Cricket wasn't worried. His knights would be close. And they knew the city far better than Craven's men ever could.

"Or your husband and the traitor?" Another sweep of his hand and Takayoshi and Leo were dragged from a separate building. Takayoshi's jaw was purple, and he was walking with a limp, favoring one side, clearly battered.

Cricket's anger flared, fingers turning icy. "What did you *do* to him?"

"He'll be fine. I assure you." Craven's smile widened, delighting in seeing Cricket upset. Sadistic. "So long as you give me what I want."

"And the rest of them?" Estia asked. "Lionel, Claudia, my brother? You'll hand them over too?"

"Lionel was never part of the deal." Craven lifted a brow, tilting his head in question, an amused tilt to his brow. The realization made Cricket physically ill. To think Craven hated his own siblings so much that he would use the people they loved against them. "The deal was only ever for Damian and the advisor. But out of the kindness of my heart, I'll return your husband. I'd hate to start a war over something so trivial."

Trivial?! A scream crawled up Cricket's throat. He swallowed it down with some force.

As i f the lives of the people he loved were not more than pawns for Craven to move around on the board, to do with what he would. As if the atrocities he had already committed were not enough to go to war over. Clearly, he thought in returning Takayoshi 'in good faith', he would keep Cricket from attacking.

He was *wrong*.

"And what of Lionel?" Estia insisted. Zir hands were clenched at zir sides, tension tightening zir shoulders, making zir stand stiffer, taller.

"I see no reason—"

"The deal was you return *all* of my people," Cricket cut in. He was not playing this game with anyone, least of all Craven. He was tired. His husband was hurting. And he just wanted to take his family home and hide them away for the foreseeable future. "Leo is one of mine as well."

"He is a traitor to the crown of Cytherea," Craven hissed, the smile slipping from his face, the first real emotion he had shown throughout this entire conversation. Cricket wished he was in a better headspace to enjoy it. "You would harbor a traitor to my crown? *I* would see him punished for—"

"I'll trade myself for him," Estia volunteered, taking a step forward. "An even exchange, I think. You let Lionel and the other hostages return home, and I'll go back to Cytherea with you."

Cricket's jaw ticked with irritation. That wasn't part of the plan, but he didn't have time to argue about it now. His gaze fixed on Takayoshi, one brow twitching upward in question. *Are you all right, my love?*

Takayoshi dipped his head in affirmation, and Cricket tore his eyes away, forcing himself to look over the rest of them. When he came to Damian, he saw that the pearl was still there, embedded in a pendant around his neck. Good. At least *part* of this was going to plan.

"Very well." Craven clicked his tongue, annoyed. "But first, the pearl."

Cricket nodded to Estia, and ze stepped forward to hand over the decoy. Craven's hands clutched it tightly, holding it up to the light as if to check its authenticity. Which was amusing as Cricket knew he had no way to tell if it were real or not. But he allowed Craven the act.

"Now, the hostages," Cricket ordered. "You set them free."

"Not until I have Estia in irons." Craven's shrug was unhurried, and he hardly took his gaze away from the pearl long enough to fix his sibling with a disgusted look, the greed so clear in his gaze it made Cricket's stomach roil. "Say your goodbyes."

Estia didn't turn to look at Cricket to check with him as ze made zir way toward the hostages, but he noticed a subtle shift in zir posture, and he understood what ze was going to do before ze did it.

Ze went to Damian first, zir hands careful, and slow as ze wrapped zir arms around his neck, pulling him close.

"Goodbye little brother," Estia murmured, zir hands fiddling with something at the base of Damian's neck. Cricket watched the pair from the corner of his eyes. Waiting. Craven didn't seem to notice anything amiss, neither did the guards standing behind Damian.

But there was a twisted expression forming on Craven's face. His brows drawing together, his lips curling in upset. As if perhaps he was beginning to put something together, beginning to understand. Or maybe he was realizing that the item in his hand was a fake...

A moment later, Estia spun and tossed the pearl Cricket's way, counting on him to catch it. Only it fell short, not heavy enough to make it all the way to him. It bounced against the street, light flaring from the little orb at the center of the pendant, leaving behind a crack in the cobblestones, drawing Craven's attention. And even if he didn't know what it was, he knew it must be important, so he dove for it.

Cricket scrambled across the distance as well, dropping to his knees so quickly it sent pain shooting up his spine. But that was fine. Nothing else mattered outside of getting the pearl.

"What is this?" Craven hissed, grabbing the chain, and lifting it up to get a better look at it.

Cricket didn't give him the time he needed to examine it, he lunged at Craven, tackling him to the ground. There was a struggle. A fist connected with Cricket's jaw. He jammed his knee into something soft, maybe Craven's stomach. His back scraped hard against the cobbles, drawing a hiss.

"You *tricked* me." Craven spat, pulled a dagger from his belt to slice at Cricket in his bid to get the pearl.

Cricket's fingers wrapped around it, tight.

With a yelp, Craven's dagger sliced through the muscles in Cricket's forearm, and it was only reflex to let his fingers fall loose. Giving Craven just enough time to scoop the pearl up. But Cricket grabbed for it again in a flash. Ignoring the blood and the slick sweat in the harried need to get it back from Craven. To keep his people safe. To keep himself safe. To keep his *family* safe.

Neither was winning. Neither was losing. But Cricket wasn't going to give up. He couldn't afford to.

Cricket elbowed Craven in the throat, making him cough, choke, wheeze, then he scurried back, the pearl clutched tight to his chest. Safe, and out of harm's way. Away from the hands of the man who would use it to turn Cricket into a weapon against his own people.

His breaths left him in cold puffs, fogging in the air. Whiskers brushed his cheeks. Cricket reached up to touch his face and frowned. He had half shifted in the struggle. His face elongating and squaring off into a muzzle, his cheeks covered in scales. He didn't have to touch them to know his antlers had grown.

"You're the dragon," Craven hissed. "Of *course* you are."

"Surprise?" Cricket hated how his voice shook on the word. Was he laughing or crying? Was he scared or triumphant? Even he couldn't tell. But at least he had the pearl in his hand. His people, the ones he loved, they were safe from him, if only for the moment. But not safe from Craven. Who's men had taken hold of Estia as well, and now held Cricket's nearest and dearest by sword point.

"We've been tricked! Bring me his husband!" Craven ordered, tightening his hand around his dagger. It still dripped with blood, and although he didn't say it, the intent was clear.

"No!" Cricket screamed.

CHAPTER 38

Takayoshi was shoved from behind.

The sounds of his friends crying out, struggling against their captors, accompanied his stumble forward over the uneven cobblestones. His legs still a little numb from an entire night sitting on a stone floor, and the wounds inflicted by Craven's torture. Each step a study in struggling to remain upright, to keep his chin held high. He did not want Cricket to be upset by what he saw. But there was little choice in that, wasn't there?

Then he was on his knees in front of Craven, finally close enough to Cricket to see the color of his eyes again. Gods, he looked tired. Dark circles ringed his eyes, and there was distress creasing his brow. Everything in Takayoshi screamed to reach out to him. To bring him peace. The iron cut into his wrists as he struggled against his bonds to do just that, leaving them raw.

"Husband," he murmured softly, not looking away from Cricket. No one else mattered in that moment. Not their enemies at his back. Not their friends held tight by those enemies. Not their kingdom on the tipping point of war. All that mattered was that Cricket was before him, and he was *hurting*. "I am all right."

"No you're not." The words came out choked, Cricket's eyes already brimming with tears. His own hands twitched at his side, the desire to reach for Takayoshi clear in every tiny movement. "What have they done to you, my love?"

"Nothing that cannot heal." It was the truth. He would be fine in a matter of weeks, possibly days, they just had to make it through this first. And they would. Because there was nothing Craven could do that would bring their story to an end. They were fated to be together, Takayoshi knew it in his bones. Their love was one that was written in the stars, given to them by the gods. Let Craven test that. Let him try it. He would find it steadfast, and hearty, unbreakable.

"Enough of this!" Craven shouted. He grabbed Takayoshi by his hair and shook him, making Takayoshi's head lull a little before he regained control over himself again, tugging at the roots in a motion that was painful, but not unbearable.

Cricket snarled, bearing teeth gone sharp like fangs. A dragon's teeth, made pointed and brutal for hunting prey, and killing enemies. Craven would live just long enough to see those teeth up close, Takayoshi was sure of it. And he would revel in the knowledge that Craven had paid wholly for what he had done to everything and everyone Takayoshi cared about. Cricket had shown himself without mercy once already.

"You will give me that *pearl*." The cold bite of steel pressed into the soft palette beneath Takayoshi's chin, but he did not hiss or struggle in the hold. He remained steady, and kept his eyes on Cricket, hoping to tell him everything he needed to with just his eyes. To hold fast. To wait. To find his opening.

"He will not." There was not a world in which Cricket would put everything and everyone they loved in danger for just the life of one man. Takayoshi may be his husband, may be the man he loved, but he was not worth that. He hoped Cricket understood it as well as he did.

"Yoshi," Cricket said, a plea. Takayoshi did not have to hear his thoughts to know that he was begging Takayoshi to not have to make this choice. He was begging the world, and the gods, to not make him give up one of the things he loved most just to protect the rest. Takayoshi wished that he could give him that, if just to relieve the distress in his voice, but he could not.

"He will not," Takayoshi repeated, giving no quarter. There was not another option to be had in this situation. If only he could access his fire. If only the iron was not blocking his magic. If only his body were not stiff, sore, and exhausted. Craven would not stand a chance against him in any other situation. But Craven had played this well. Cut Takayoshi off from his power, beaten and bloodied him to the point of weakness. Takayoshi hated it. He should never have become a weakness for his husband. He should always have been his *strength*.

The blade bit into his skin, a hot trickle of blood flowing down his neck.

"Give. It. To. Me. Or I slice his throat here and now." Craven bared his teeth, the blade pressing harder against Takayoshi's skin.

Takayoshi hissed involuntarily, but still did not lean away from the dagger. Let Craven follow through on his promise. Let him make the mistake of spilling his blood on Lunette soil, and see what would come of it. Cricket would *end* him. Cricket would—

In between one blink and the next, Takayoshi saw Cricket's eyes spark murderous. He had never seen them narrow that way before. Never seen that curl of his lip. He had seen Cricket angry plenty of times, but never like this. Never before had he been *afraid* of what Cricket might do next. But now uncertainty and fear crawled along his nerves, lighting them up with anxiety. What was Cricket planning? What would be the inevitable fall out?

"Release him, or face the consequences." It was not a suggestion. It was not a plea. It was not a question. It was an order, one that if Craven did not heed, he would regret. Anyone who knew anything about Cricket could hear that in his tone, but Craven did not know him. Had not seen Cricket as he grew into the king he was today. He would not understand the danger he was putting himself in.

"Cricket," Takayoshi gasped, a warning. *Do not do anything you will regret, my love.*

Cricket was not listening. Instead, he was panting frantically , his eyes jerking about in an erratic pattern that Takayoshi could not follow. He was thinking, doing the calculations, and whatever he was coming up with was not in their favor.

"Foolish boy." Craven scoffed. "You can't order me. Bring me the pearl, and this will all be over."

Suddenly, Cricket came to a conclusion, and he met Takayoshi's eyes. Whatever choice he just made, Takayoshi would not like it, he knew from simply looking at Cricket's set jaw, and narrowed eyes. It would be foolish, and risky. Someone would likely get hurt. But it was likely their best chance.

"You want it so badly?" Cricket asked, his head tilting curiously. He lifted the chain into the air, dangling the pearl before his face, a mocking gesture. "Come and get it," he said just before he opened his mouth, tilted his chin back, and swallowed the pendant, chain and all.

The gulp seemed to echo in the square.

Takayoshi's heart lurched into his throat, panic seizing his ribs. What did this mean? What would happen next? What was Cricket planning? He could not tell. He could not follow this line of reasoning. And that made everything so much worse.

"No!" Craven screamed. His surprise, and fury, made his hand shake, the dagger digging in further to Takayoshi's neck.

"You'll have to kill me to claim your prize." Cricket grinned, sharp and feral, and then he was laughing, the sound so high, and so jagged it threatened to cut Takayoshi to pieces. To scatter those pieces to the wind, and leave him nothing left. Because this was a sacrifice he could not save Cricket from. This was something he could not undo.

"Very well." Craven's hand tightened around the dagger, Takayoshi's only warning what was to come next. Not that he could do anything about that warning. He could not fight back. All he could do was struggle against his bindings, and try to move away from the cold heat of the blade. Craven pressed it in closer, forcing Takayoshi's head back against his stomach. "You have made your choice. Now you will live with the consequences of *your* actions."

Then several things happened all at once.

Craven pulled the blade away from Takayoshi's throat, and lifted it as if to plunge it into his chest.

Cricket screamed, the sound a heart rending, and lunged forward, claws at the ready to rip Craven apart.

And Craven, seeing the attack coming just as Takayoshi did, yanked Takayoshi up by his collar, using him as a bloody, fleshy shield.

Cricket's talons dug into Takayoshi's chest, the pain a ripping, tearing, burning sensation that had him choking, coughing. Blood coated his tongue. Filled his lungs. Made it hard to breathe. Hard to think. Someone screamed, but his heart was pounding so hard in his ears he could not tell who. Was it him? Was it Cricket? Was it one of their friends?

It did not matter now. What was done was done.

But there was Cricket above him already, his face cracked open with anguish, tears streaming down his cheeks.

"My husband," Takayoshi managed to force the words out past a tongue grown thick with exhaustion. He reached up to take Cricket's face into his hands, but his hands shook. The strength it took him to do so left his lids heavy. He had not been so tired in all his life, like all of the years of exhaustion had caught up to him all at once, making every part of his body weigh more than it ever had before.

Gods, he just wanted to sleep. Rest. He needed rest. And then he would be fine, surely. Because this was fate. He was meant to be with Cricket. Nothing could rip them apart. He knew that, had always known it, had never doubted it. So he was not dying. This was not the last of him. This was just. . . this was just a wound.

His heart gave a sickening lurch, a warning maybe that he was fooling himself, but Takayoshi ignored it. He would be fine. He had to be. There was no other option.

"Nononononononono." Cricket repeated the word over and over again, not even a breath in between them. He held onto Takayoshi. His hands gentle. His chest hitching with sobs.

"Cricket." Takayoshi smiled a little, his eyes crinkling at the corners. Stars, even like this, Cricket was beautiful. Cracked open like an egg. Terrified, and shattered. Even like this, Yue Cricket was a vision. Painted in starlight, and so alive it made Takayoshi ache. He loved him. So very much.

Cricket leaned forward, his forehead pressing to Takayoshi's, the battle seemingly forgotten. Or maybe it was already over. Takayoshi was not sure, he only had eyes for his husband. And he could not hear anything beyond Cricket's ragged breathing, and hitched sobs.

"I'm sorry," Cricket rasped, the sound wrecked, and wretched.

And then there was darkness.

CHAPTER 39

The world was pain.
Life was empty.
Existence was futile.
All that was left for him was vengeance.

Cricket came to all of these realizations as the blood pooled around him, soaking into his trousers, growing cold.

Takayoshi was gone, and there was nothing left for him to do but to rip out the heart of the man who had taken Takayoshi from him.

"No. No. No. No. No. No. No." He didn't know how many times he'd said it by now. It couldn't take back what he'd done. It couldn't bring back what he'd lost. But he couldn't seem to stop himself from saying it just the same. From wishing that just that one word would make what had happened untrue.

But the blood was now cooling on his talons, turning thicker, congealing, crusting over just as it had when he'd killed Sunil. Takayoshi's body was heavy, and lax where it rested across his legs. And although his eyes were open, still golden and beautiful, they were unseeing. His expression frozen in something peaceful, and at ease with the end coming.

Which just made all of this worse. Because how dare Takayoshi be all right dying this way. How *dare* he be willing to leave Cricket behind?

"I told you not to cross me!" Craven crowed as if what he had just done would assure his victory. As if it were not the death knell of a man who had already long overstayed his welcome in this world. And he was standing over Cricket like some kind of triumphant warrior instead of the murderer he was.

"You told me, did you?" Cricket asked, his tone soft, deadly. His hands moved slowly, gently, as he lowered Takayoshi to the ground. Took his time to close Takayoshi's eyes, and brush his pale hair back from his face. He was beautiful. Even in death. And it wasn't fair. "I'll be back, my love," he murmured softly. Maybe he'd even join Takayoshi when he returned. Lay down on the cobbles and let the world move along without him. That seemed the best thing at this point. "I just need to deal with this refuse, first." Then he rose slowly, his breath leaving him in freezing puffs of air. Heartbreak giving way to fury.

"You told me," he said again, advancing on Craven, every step freezing the ground beneath him, but leaving the space around Takayoshi untouched. He would not allow his Phoenix to freeze, even in death, but let everyone else suffer for what had happened. Let everyone else know the cold fury of the dragon. "You *told* me."

The dagger clattered to the ground, Takayoshi's blood still staining the tip. "Men! Seize him!" Craven shouted, ready to cower behind his soldiers, but the world around Cricket had faded to nothing. What did their lives matter when the one he loved was gone? What did anything matter? Was his heart even still beating? It didn't feel like it was.

"Now," Cricket said, the word quiet, but echoing. An order to the knights Cricket knew Ignacia had hidden around the square, ready for his signal. They had not moved before then. Maybe they should have. But it was better this way. Better they waited until Cricket was ready for them.

And then the battle began in earnest.

One swipe of Cricket's hand threw the first of the soldiers brazen enough to follow their leader's orders to the ground. His skull hit so hard against the street below, Cricket swore he heard a crack like an egg. That didn't matter either. Their lives were petty. Trivial.

Swords clashed around him. His knights cutting through Craven's forces, even as they were larger. Getting the hostages out of the way to leave Cricket to follow Craven's retreat across the square.

Craven was backing up, panic setting in.

Good.

Cricket wanted him afraid when he killed him.

The next two men came at Cricket as a united front, but Cricket had already shifted into the dragon. His massive size taking up so much of the space in the square that there was hardly any room left for those trying to fell him, and the soldiers fighting amongst themselves.

Arrows whizzed through the air toward him. But they bounced off of his scales, clattering to the ground. Harmless.

Something crunched beneath his back paw, and it was only the dying scream that told him it had been a person unlucky enough to get in Cricket's way as he advanced toward where Craven had tucked himself into a corner.

Foolish, foolish, mortal.

All of them were. Willing to die for a man who cared nothing for their lives, would use them as cannon fodder to protect himself. They would not live to regret their allegiance if they had not begun to do so already.

There was a row of soldiers in front of him suddenly, the last few still willing to follow their king's orders, willing to die for him. Their weapons raised high. Swords, and spears, and bows. But they were easy enough to dispatch with a swipe of his tail, little tin soldiers he could bowl down with nothing more than a thought. Then Cricket was looming over Craven, his breath so cold it made Craven's teeth chatter, his lips go blue.

"Mercy. Mercy please." Craven cowered, his hands pressed together in prayer, and held above his head where he crouched by the wall. It was a shame Cricket was so heart-broken and angry, or he would find seeing the once arrogant man curled in on himself amusing. "It was a mistake. A mistake! I did not know!"

You did not know what? Cricket hissed, blowing out more frigid air along with the words. It didn't matter what Craven said. His begging was useless. He had killed the one person in the world who might have saved him, and now there was no one left to calm Cricket's anger. *You did not know that this land did not belong to you? You did not know that that man was my husband? You did not know that you should not pick fights with people more powerful than you? Which of these facts are you pleading with me over?*

None of them would save him, but Cricket was not going to tell him that, he would think that would be obvious.

"All of it. All of it! It was a mistake. A mistake!" He wasn't making any sense anymore, and Cricket was beyond caring. Because this would all end soon enough.

It was *a mistake,* Cricket agreed. *But mistakes have consequences. And your mistakes, your greed, cost me much this day.* He dipped his head so he could better meet Craven's eyes. The king of Cytherea was terrified. His eyes so wide, his pupils so tiny in fear that the white nearly consumed them. *What do you think the consequences should be for you?*

"Mercy!" He begged again. "Mercy. You are a merciful god."

I am not a god. Cricket snapped his jaws at Craven in warning, and the man fell silent, his body visibly trembling now. *Gods are forced to show mercy to mortals like you. But I? I am just a man. A man whose husband you have stolen. A mistake which will cost you your life!*

Then he opened his maw, and grabbed Craven by his middle. After a few crunches of bone, and screams, and gushing blood, Cricket swallowed Craven whole in one fierce gulp without a second thought. The man's screams didn't stop until he hit Cricket's stomach, and then maybe it was only because Cricket could no longer hear him through the lining.

That done, Cricket turned his back on what was left of the Cytherean soldiers and his own knights battling it out, and returned to his husband's side. The scales melted away, sloughed off, so that by the time Cricket dropped to his knees at Takayoshi's side again, he was no longer a dragon, he was just a man. Just a man who had lost too much.

"You need to come back," he whispered, pulling Takayoshi into his arms again as a sob wracked his body. "You're a phoenix. Phoenixes rise. You can too. You can come back." But he was begging a dead man. Begging someone who was beyond hearing at this point. What use was there? Still, he couldn't stop himself. Couldn't help but press his face into Takayoshi's hair, and inhale the smell of him that lingered, even above the metallic tang of blood.

"Come back to me, my love. Come back," he begged, again and again. Pressed his tears into Takayoshi's hair until it was wet and clumped. Held him so close he hoped to imprint the feeling of Takayoshi on his skin.

He still felt warm against Cricket. His skin still holding onto the fire that sang through his blood in life. Enough that Cricket could almost convince himself it was true. Convince himself that Takayoshi was still alive. A phoenix just waiting to rise from the ashes. But maybe those were just stories...

The warmth seemed to be growing. . .

No. That had to be his imagination. Wishful thinking. Cricket's subconscious trying to ease the pain in his chest so it wouldn't kill him. There was no hope of that. He would die there with Takayoshi in his arms. Whether it be at the point of a blade or from exhaustion, it didn't matter. He would not leave.

Something flickered out of the corner of his eye, and when Cricket looked he found that a flame had started on the crown of Takayoshi's head. Burning brightly, licking through his hair, spreading like wildfire. Engulfing every part of Takayoshi, and starting to spread to Cricket as well. Hot, and burning. Like standing too close to a bonfire.

"Cricket! Cricket let him go!" Ignacia shouted. He wasn't sure where she'd come from, but he felt her grab his shoulder and try to rip him away. Someone else was trying to pull Takayoshi from his arms, to separate them. But the fire burned them both and they had to retreat lest they turn themselves to ash. And even if they hadn't, Cricket would not allow it. He would stay. He would let Takayoshi's fire consume him. It was a fitting end to the dragon.

"Your Highness! He'll burn you up! You have to let him go!" Claudia shouted.

He wouldn't. He was never going to let Takayoshi go again.

Cricket bent his head, and let the flames engulf him. Let them dance hot and threatening along his skin. Let him burn.

CHAPTER 40

All was peace.
All was silence.
All was light.

Which was strange, because a moment ago there had only been pain, and screaming, and anguish, and battle. But now all of that seemed far far behind him. Takayoshi opened his eyes, squinting against the brightness of the room around him.

"Cricket?" he asked, wondering where his husband had gone. He had been there a moment ago. Shattered to pieces as he watched Takayoshi's blood spill at his hand. Lost to his pain. And now Takayoshi was alone. Alone and in someplace unfamiliar. But not afraid.

"No. Just a goddess." A woman stepped into the room.

Or perhaps it was less of a room. There appeared to be no walls. No doors. Just a vast emptiness. Just nothing and nothing that seemed to go on forever. Nothing except this woman who seemed to have stepped out of nowhere. No door. No entrance. Just not there one moment, and there the next.

He recognized her voice, although her face was not one he had seen before. "Selene."

Now that he had said the name he could see the similarities she had with her son. The shape of their mouths were alike, the curve of their smiles the same. The nose was different, perhaps she had borrowed that from someone else. But their eyes sparkled the same moon rise silver-blue, and her hair, just like her son's had once been, was long enough to trail stardust in the wake of its midnight-blue. She was lovely, but not as beautiful as the many paintings and sculptures depicted her. Not ethereal in that way. Better, he thought, actually, more real. And her similarities to Cricket made him ache.

"I have died," Takayoshi said, coming to the conclusion rather abruptly. The knowledge hurt more than it likely ought to. To be dead meant he had left others behind. It meant Cricket and Becka and his friends were mourning. It meant he had lost. Craven had won. It did not seem fair. Not when he had not done all of the things he was meant to. Not when his life, his happiness, was just beginning.

"In a manner of speaking." Selene stepped forward, but did not reach for him the way he had assumed someone might in these situations. Which was good, Takayoshi did not want, nor need her comfort. What he wanted was to go home.

"What does that mean?" Why could no one ever speak clearly on these matters? Was he dead or not? Would he have to watch his husband and their daughter mourn him for the rest of their lives from afar or no? There was no in between. Either he would open his eyes to the man he loved, or he would have to face years without him.

"You're a phoenix. I'm sure you know what that means."

He did not, actually. He had spent so much of his time trying to better understand the dragon and what it meant for

Cricket that he had hardly given any thought to his own abilities, his own nature. He understood that he could cause fires. He knew he could fly. He and the bird living inside of him had come to an understanding, both of them having the same goals. But that was about it.

Something on his face must have shown his confusion, because Selene let out a delighted little laugh. It reminded him so much of Cricket that he had to draw in a short, sharp breath. He lifted his hand to rub at the ache in his chest where before he had died, had been a gaping wound left by Cricket's talons.

"Apologies." She dipped her head, but she was still grinning, and the word did not sound half as apologetic as she maybe meant it to. Not with amusement still curling around the edges of it. "It's just it's been so long since I've been able to teach someone something. Centuries, in fact. I've missed it."

Takayoshi wished she would get to the point so that he could get on with whatever was next. Not reincarnation, he would not allow himself to enter the cycle of rebirth so long as his family was still alive. So long as there was still the chance that he might be able to watch over them, and protect them from afar. Nor would he risk the chance of going back to find love somewhere else. There was no where else for him, no *one* else for him. Only Cricket.

But. . . something came next. He knew that much.

"What does it mean?" he asked, hating how it sounded on his tongue. Like he was inept. Not knowing something had always irked him. If Cricket were there, he might have delighted in the annoyance that curled his lips just a little into a frown. Might have laughed at the idea of Takayoshi admitting defeat in this small way.

"How is it that my son knows more of your own nature

than you do?" Selene shook her head, exasperated, her midnight blue hair falling into her face. There was no anger or annoyance there though. "You are a phoenix, son of Helios. You may have died, but now you have a choice to make."

"What choice?"

"You can return home, to your husband, to your daughter, to your people, and face the grueling recovery of your injuries. Face all the pain and misery that comes from living a mortal life."

Her hand moved through the air, an orb appearing to show him the blood stained cobblestone square where his body still remained. So many dead. So many wounded. All in the name of greed. And he had to admit, returning to that alone was not appealing, but returning to Cricket? To Becka? To the home they were building together? That, he would not give up for anything.

"Or you can stay here, and become one of the gods." Selene swept her hands out at her sides as if to gesture to something all around her, but Takayoshi could see nothing. Just the ever expanding white. And even if he could, there was no choice to be made. She seemed to realize that, seemed to know the answer before she had even spoke, if the little smile curling up the corners of her mouth told him anything. He had seen that expression enough on Cricket to know what it meant, and thus he did not dally.

"Send me back." The pain. The misery. The long road to recovery. All of those things would be worth it if he also was able to hold Cricket again. To read stories to Becka. To research with Claudia. To spar with Leo and Ignacia. There was nothing he would not give to return to the happiness he had found. Even godhood, he would give up. There was not a question.

Selene nodded. "I'd hoped you'd say that. Just be cautious, son of Helios. You will be weakened in your newly risen state."

And then he was falling.

CHAPTER 41

By the time the fire had begun to die away all that was left of the king of Lunette and his husband were a dragon curled tight around the smoking form of a man.

Cricket nudged Takayoshi's hair with his muzzle, inhaling again, hoping to suck down the last traces of the man that he loved still clinging to his skin. If this was all that was left. If he had to say goodbye when he pulled away, then he'd just never pull away. He'd just never let Takayoshi go. He would stay there forever wrapped around the man he loved, and let the rest of their world crumble around him without a care.

Except. . .

Except. . .

Except. . .

Takayoshi's eyes were squeezing shut, as if he was preparing to open them. And his mouth opened to let out a soft, weak groan.

Yoshi? Cricket thought the word, sending it to Takayoshi's mind via his dragon's telepathic abilities, his tone full of reverence, and hope.

"Give me a moment." Takayoshi brushed his fingers along Cricket's muzzle without opening his eyes. "Just a moment. It is taking my eyes time to adjust."

Cricket nodded, pulling back a little, and letting the dragon fade, shifting back so he could hold Takayoshi close to him. So he could press kisses into his skin. Prove to himself over and over again that his husband was alive. That he had not lost him in the end.

But in doing so, he was no longer wrapped tightly around Takayoshi. No longer protecting him from the world around them. And it left Takayoshi open to one final attack in his weakened state.

A vine leaped up from the street and wrapped tight around his middle, then yanked, ripping Takayoshi from Cricket's arms.

Cricket reached for him in an instant, all instinct, but he wasn't fast enough to grab onto Takayoshi before the creature dragged him away. All he could do was run after him, give chase, and hope he wouldn't be too late by the time he caught up to Takayoshi.

They wound through the streets of the capital, Takayoshi's eyes wide, mouth twisted with pain, but he did not release a sound. Not that it mattered, Cricket was doing enough screaming for the both of them. Screams of rage, of fear, ripping from his throat over and over again as he tore after the love he'd only just gotten back.

There was a loud crash, and when Cricket turned the corner, he found that the creature had dragged Takayoshi through a door and into one of the businesses along Crescent street. The wood lay in splinters around the frame, and Cricket slowed his steps, approached more carefully.

He had no weapons, but he didn't need them so long as he had his talons, and his teeth. The dragon would do the work for him.

The floor creaked under his weight as he entered, the boards giving way a little beneath his feet. It took a moment for his eyes to adjust to the gloom beyond. Every window it seemed had been covered, whether by the creature or by the former occupants, he wasn't sure. It made the inside of the building dark even with the bright morning sunshine hot on his back.

There would be no sneaking up on the creature, Cricket knew that. It knew he was coming. It had likely led him there on purpose, otherwise it wouldn't have stolen Takayoshi right from his arms. This was a trap.

"What do you want from me?" he called as he stepped further into the building. The first floor was one big open room, which didn't sit well with Cricket. It meant there was no place for him to hide. It gave the creature the advantage.

There was no answer, just the sound of the building settling around him. With his eyes finally adjusted, he was able to look around and find no sign of the creature or Takayoshi. Although, to be fair, he wasn't really sure what he was looking for when it came to the creature. Takayoshi had made some mention of a pod, but that didn't really tell him anything.

"Are you going to come out and face me?" Would challenging the creature get it to show itself? Maybe. Maybe not. But Cricket was not above such tactics.

There was movement out of the corner of his eye. Cricket whipped around, but by the time he did whatever it was, was gone.

"Didn't I already prove what a mistake it is to take my husband from me?" His hand tightened into a fist at his side, talons digging into his palms. Blood dripped down from the wounds, joining the slow trickle still coming from the gash on his forearm. If he were not still running on adrenaline he was sure that he would have passed out by then from sheer exhaustion and blood loss. That was a problem for later.

"You should just give up here," a voice said from off to his right, and when Cricket whirled around, he found nothing. Not even a shadow. But he'd recognized that voice.

"Are you going to continue to use my mother against me? It won't work!" The creature had to be hiding somewhere. If not on the first floor, then perhaps the second. Or maybe . . .maybe it was under the floorboards. But then it would have had to drag Takayoshi down there, and that would mean there would need to be a hole in the floor big enough for him to fit through. There wasn't, not that Cricket could see from where he was standing in the center of the first floor. But maybe the creature was hiding it. Making him see things that weren't there.

How would he be able to tell?

"You're right," another voice said, deeper, angrier, Sunil. "Besides, you don't deserve a peaceful death."

"Who wants a *peaceful* death?" Cricket mocked, spinning on his heel to look around him. There was no manifestation of Sunil in the room with him. But that didn't mean that he wasn't being shown things that weren't real. He stepped carefully over the floor, going by what he felt instead of what he saw, praying that the creature couldn't trick all of his senses. "I want to go out in battle, protecting the people I love. Knowing that they're safe because of what I've done."

Sunil snorted. "Always seeking glory, aren't you nephew? Never happy with what you have. Always reaching. How long before that reaching loses you everything? Your kingdom. Your family. Your husband."

"Are you going to come out and face me or continue to hide in the shadows like a coward?" This whole thing was getting old, quickly, and Cricket was beyond ready to take his husband, and his people, and just go home. To sleep for the next month until all of this was nothing more than a memory.

"You'd know all about cowardice, wouldn't you, nephew? Running away with your tail tucked between your legs the moment things get hard. No wonder your husband went off without you in search of his friends. He knew you'd never be able to save them."

"That's not true!" He knew it wasn't. He knew that Takayoshi hadn't gone out alone because he didn't think Cricket was capable. It was because they needed to split their forces. Because they needed more than one plan to assure they made it out of this victorious. The only time he had ever run from a fight was to protect Becka.

"Isn't it? Have you asked him?"

"I don't need to!" Cricket snarled, his lips peeling back from teeth gone pointed with anger. It would be easy to shift into the dragon and rip the house to shreds until he found the creature, but he might hurt Takayoshi in the process, and he wasn't willing to risk that again. Not so soon after he'd gotten him back. "Show yourself!"

"Why should I? You're hardly a worthy opponent." Sunil scoffed. But there was something else in his voice this time. Like a second voice on top of the first, hollow and echoing. A hint of the creature. Was Cricket getting closer to it? Was that why he could hear it better now? He kept moving across the floor, each step carefully measured so he could feel out in front of him. "Not a worthy opponent. Not a worthy king. Your father would be ashamed."

That stopped him short. Cricket stilled, a growl in his throat, but doubts clouding his mind.

"He would not!" But. . . but what if he *was*? Lunette had been at peace for all of Jaxith's rule, but the moment Cricket took the throne, it was thrown into chaos. People died. Homes were destroyed. Families were separated. Why?

Because Cricket wasn't capable of maintaining order? Because he wasn't the king his people needed? Because he wasn't good enough? Wasn't worthy? Like Sunil said.

"He would," Sunil jeered, joy curling around his tone as it rose in volume either to taunt him further or to hide the underlying echo of the creature, Cricket wasn't sure. And it didn't really matter. "You're a failure to his legacy, and to your people. Look how much of your kingdom was destroyed in just the first month of your rule. Much of it by your own hand!" Sunil cackled.

"You forced me! I had no choice!" But that wasn't an excuse, was it? He should have been willing to sacrifice his family—himself—for his people, for the greater good. But time and time again he'd put the people he loved above his duties as king. Jaxith would not approve. Jaxith had always taught him that the people came first. Cricket had proven he couldn't remain objective that way. He couldn't separate what he cared about from who he was.

"You're selfish," Sunil said the words Cricket had been thinking, and they rang true. "Unwilling to give up the things you care about for the greater good. What kind of king is that?"

"I love my people!" But the protest felt weak even to himself. *Could* he say he loved them when he'd been willing to let them die to save his daughter? When not even a half hour ago he'd been willing to leave them behind in favor of following his husband into death? What kind of king did things like that?

"Do you? Prove it."

"How?" Cricket didn't know when he'd fallen to his knees, but the floorboards were hard through his trousers, digging into his skin. He'd do anything to prove that he cared for his people as much as he was supposed to. To prove he was worthy of being their king. To live up to the name of his father.

But. . .

He *had* lived up to that name, hadn't he?

Memories flooded his mind as if planted there by someone else, maybe his mother giving him a hand, maybe Takayoshi reaching for him. There was no way to tell, but they pulled him out of the muck and the mire before he drowned in his own insecurities.

Days of sleepless nights at the bedside of the people afflicted by the pollen.

Grueling hours spent leading his people to the castle where he knew they'd be safe.

A fight with Sunil that ended in blood dried so hard under his nails he thought it'd never wash away.

Weeks of burying the dead, and offering them the peace his uncle had stolen from them.

He had sacrificed time, sleep, his own health for his people. Done everything he could to protect them, to make sure they were safe. And when this was all over. . . when the war was settled and there wasn't another battle on their horizon, he would spend years—perhaps the rest of his life—rebuilding. Making sure that they had everything they needed to live long, prosperous lives.

His rule thus far may not have looked exactly like his father's, but that didn't mean it was wrong. That didn't make him a failure. The circumstances surrounding his rule were vastly different than those surrounding Jaxith's. Jaxith had been a king in a time of peace. Cricket had come into his crown in a time of war. They were not the same. And he was sure his father would be proud of what he'd done with what he'd been given.

"I am a good king," he said finally, more sure of himself than he had been in months. "I am worthy."

"Die!" The creature snarled.

A vine broke through the floorboards, and wrapped around his wrist, yanking him to the floor so quickly his chin smacked against the wood, teeth cutting through his tongue so the hot metallic taste of blood coated the inside of his mouth.

He couldn't see Takayoshi, but he heard the soft whine that accompanied his own pain, a sound of distress, and then a shouted, "Cricket! Behind you!"

And Cricket? Cricket had had *enough*.

He didn't even bother to whirl around and meet the barbed end of the vine, he shifted, fast as a blink. The thorn bounced off of his scales, the creature hissing from somewhere below him. Under the floorboards then, just as he had thought.

With a swipe of his paw, the wood fell away, and he dropped down to the cold floor of the cellar below. Ice spread from his paws, making any and all vines in his wake shatter, shards flying through the air. Slicing his cheek. Drawing blood. The creature whimpered. Cricket spun, and found a plant pod open like a mouth, Takayoshi caught in its maw, his arms bloody from where they were covering his face. He was struggling, his mouth twisted in pain.

Cricket lost any control he might have had over his temper. He leapt forward, his scaled back knocking against what was left of the floor above, breaking away more of the boards and sank huge, pointed teeth into the pod. Ripping it apart. Giving Takayoshi only a moment to roll to the floor out of the way of the attack.

He was still shredding it, sending pieces of plant viscera around the cellar like a dog with a rag, when he felt the warmth of a hand on his shoulder.

"Cricket," Takayoshi murmured. "Let me finish it."

Then he reached for the vines at their feet, and fire spread from his palm, a blaze that would burn their city to embers if it weren't tightly controlled. But it *was* tightly controlled, only catching on the vines, and what was left of the pod, reducing it to ashes in a blink

"That won't be the end of it," Cricket gasped, slipping the dragon off like one would a cloak.

"No." Takayoshi agreed, his voice a little breathless in his exhaustion and pain. But he was standing under his own power, and he was alive, that was more than Cricket could have asked for. Still, Cricket moved to shore up his side, by pulling his arm over his shoulder. "There will be more cleansing to do. But without the pod to control it, the vines are no longer a danger."

"Rebuilding will take years."

"Yes, but we will not be doing it alone." Takayoshi offered him one of those soft smiles that made Cricket's heart lurch in his chest.

"No. We won't be."

EPILOGUE

The day saved, the kingdom on the mend, the two men returned to their castle, to their people, and saw to their wounded. The sleepwalkers had awoken, a little worse for wear having bumped into and tripped over things in their sleeping state, but mostly unharmed. Those who had been cast to stillness by the curse, would have a longer road to recovery. The days spent in bed meant weeks regaining their strength, but Cricket and Takayoshi were committed to seeing their people healthy, and happy once more.

And when all of that was said and done. . .

People came from all over the kingdoms to witness the official royal wedding of King Cricket and King Takayoshi. To see them pledge themselves to one another, and watch as the sun and the moon became one.

But in the end, it was only the royal families of Helios and Cytherea that were allowed to attend the private ceremony. Well, the royal families and... a few other guests.

"Grandpa!" Becka shrieked, and ran past Takayoshi and

Cricket so quickly neither of them had time to scoop her up and keep her from further ruining the braid Cricket had put into her hair. There were flowers woven into the strands, just as she'd asked, but none of that mattered at all once she saw the figure of Jaxith in the doorway.

"Father?" Cricket spun, his eyes wide, his heart pounded. "But you're—"

"Visiting, son. Just visiting." Jaxith grinned, lifting Becka into his arms to press a kiss to her cheek. He looked younger than he ever had in Cricket's life. The lines around his eyes still there, but much fainter. And there was a rosy glow about his cheeks that Cricket couldn't remember seeing since before Sunil's initial attack on Lunette. "I couldn't pass up the chance to see my son get married."

"Again," Ignacia grumbled from behind them, her hands on her hips.

"A pleasure as always Ignacia." Jaxith's smile widened, then he winked at Cricket and added, "Yes, again."

"Only this time, I'm going to officiate," another voice came from the door, and when Cricket whirled to see who it was his jaw dropped. Selene was standing in the doorway, a long, sparkling gown hanging from her shoulders. Her own midnight-blue hair braided carefully.

"Mother?!" Cricket squawked.

"Surprise, surprise." Selene laughed, giving a little twirl. "Come now, son. Let's get you married."

Takayoshi was at his side, a smug little smile on his face as if he'd known this would happen all along, but Cricket could hardly pay attention to that. The goddess Selene had brought his father home to attend his wedding. He would have all of the people he loved in one room for the first time in years.

"Before we get to that, I want to have a little chat with you, son." Jaxith passed Becka off to Takayoshi, and tilted his head toward the door before leading Cricket out into the cool night air.

"If this is about everything that happened..." Cricket took a breath, ready to tell his father that he'd done his best. That he wasn't ashamed of how he had handled things. That in the end, he was the king he was meant to be.

Only Jaxith surprised him, putting a hand on his shoulder and giving it a gentle squeeze. "You have done well, my son. Do you know that?"

Cricket swallowed around the thickness of tears in his throat. "Believe it or not, I do."

And Jaxith's smile was so bright it could outshine the sun. "Good. Now, I believe you have a wedding to attend."

THE CELEBRATION that followed the wedding of King Cricket and King Takayoshi was perhaps not the largest Lunette had seen, but it was most certainly the most joyous. The people of Lunette honored their rulers who had done everything they could to protect them in the way only a kingdom still healing from war could, with abandon, with the knowledge that any day could be their last. There were parades, and dances, and many an engagement in the weeks that followed.

And if there was some gossip among the people that the Lady Selene herself had descended from on high to bear witness to their union, neither the kings, nor their new allies would confirm nor deny. And to be fair, the kingdom didn't care one way or the other, so long as their kings were happy. So long as their princess was smiling. Their lives would be bountiful.

And should their people or their friends need them at all in the future, they were safe in knowing that the kings of dusk and dawn were never afraid to rise up and protect those they cared for.

That the dragon and the phoenix would be there.

ACKNOWLEDGMENTS

First off, thank you—the reader—for joining Takayoshi and Cricket on their journey . The Heir to Moondust was something I started during the pandemic, and one of the projects that made being stuck inside a little easier. I hope it has brought you the same wry amusement, and smiles it brought me to write.

Although this book is over, Cricket and Takayoshi's story is far from finished. Their world has so many more stories to tell. So rest assured, this is not the last you've seen of Yoshi and his new friends.

Next, I'd like the thank my small hoard of beta-readers. You guys gave some excellent insight, and I really appreciate all of your hard work!

And last but certainly not least, thank you to my small writing support group at MTP. Tiss, Elle, and Jasmine—without you there would be no Lou.

ABOUT THE AUTHOR

Born and raised in a small town near the Chesapeake Bay, Lou Wilham grew up on a steady diet of fiction, arts and crafts, and Old Bay. After years of absorbing everything, there was to absorb of fiction, fantasy, and sci-fi she's left with a serious writing/drawing habit that just won't quit. These days, she spends much of her time writing, drawing, and chasing a very short Basset Hound named Sherlock.

When not, daydreaming up new characters to write and draw she can be found crocheting, making cute bookmarks, and binge-watching whatever happens to catch her eye.

Learn more about Lou and her future projects on her website: http://louinprogress.com/ or join her mailing list at: http://subscribepage.com/mailermailer

facebook.com/LouWilham

instagram.com/lou.wilham

MORE BOOKS YOU'LL LOVE

If you enjoyed this story, please consider leaving a review.

Then check out more books from Midnight Tide Publishing!

Secrets of a Rose by Adina Chiles

A kingdom built with secrets is bound to unravel.

During the month of Amira, the silver moon emerges, and the kingdom of Zyra comes alive with anticipation for its annual ball. Mellana Goodwick, finally at the rightful age of sixteen, receives her first invitation, but when unexpected events take place, immediate regret sets in. Mellana finds herself caught in a strange storm—casting down green lightning and filling the sky with ear-splitting thunder. To make matters worse, the kingdom comes under attack by Prince Lorian, a man removed from the line of succession for murdering his sister, the future queen, and her newborn child.

After escaping the attack with her best friends, Mellana stumbles upon a box left by a woman named Rose. With the power to see glimpses of the future, Rose warns Mellana of hidden powers the kingdom has covered up and Lorian's desire to unleash them all. Rose instructs Mellana to gather the sacred article from each of the seven kingdoms before Lorian and his deadly group can gain access to them. Together, the items unlock a barrier that is meant to stay shut.

In Secrets of a Rose, Mellana will discover remarkable abilities that stir around her and some that even rise within. In order to keep what she loves, she must embark on a race against the person who dares to threaten it all.

Available Now

The Rose and the Claw by Nancy O'Toole

A woman on a mission...

Rose Gardner never thought she'd leave the small town of West Ridge. But when her husband dies at war, she must return his arms to his place of birth to set his spirit to rest. After traveling into enemy territory, Rose falls into a trap. Held captive in an enchanted manor, she finds herself face to face with a beast who is equally horrifying and kind. Will she manage to complete her quest or be pulled in by the secrets of the manor?

A man haunted by his past...

Trapped within his own home and in the body of a hideous beast, Kris never wanted to share his prison with another. As much as Rose may draw him in with her beauty and stubborn strength, he knows she must escape before the next full moon. After all, he remembers all too well what happened to the previous caretaker.

The dead won't let him forget the blood on his hands.

Available Now

www.ingramcontent.com/pod-product-compliance
Lightning Source LLC
Chambersburg PA
CBHW061045310726

48969CB00004B/1086